George
Golding

Stewardess

Stewardess

Robert Serling

ST. MARTIN'S
MAREK

Library of Congress Cataloging in Publication Data

Serling, Robert J.
Stewardess.

"A St. Martin's/Marek Book"

I. Title.
PS3569.E7S7   813'.54   81-21487
ISBN 0-312-76193-7   AACR2

Design by Manuela Paul

10 9 8 7 6 5 4 3 2 1

First Edition

To the following real-life Danni Hendrickses
(but without her faults),
this book is gratefully and
affectionately dedicated:

Winnie Gilbert, Eastern
Clancie Melton, American
Vicki Dokos, Western

Author's acknowledgments:

My heartfelt gratitude to Eastern Airlines for giving me the privilege of attending a flight attendant training class—from start through graduation—as part of the research for this novel. I am especially grateful to Bob Christian, vice president of public relations; training director Darlene Perkins and instructor Marla Talton, and to my fellow students in Class 80-01 for making these four and a half weeks the most rewarding experience of my life.

To Dick Marek, a tough but fair editor, my thanks for his patience, skill and judgment.

To my wife Priscilla, a former stewardess herself, I am beholden for her understanding support and advice.

Grateful appreciation also goes to my agent, Aaron Priest, for his faith in this project and enormous help in getting it off the ground.

Finally, to my many friends in the airline industry, my assurances that the characters portrayed herein are entirely fictitious and that Trans-National also is the product of my imagination.

Robert J. Serling   *Tucson, Arizona*

Stewardess

PART ONE
(1955)

Chapter 1

The anguished clash of metal against metal caused Fred Jordan to look up from his file of stewardess applications.

Curious, he got out of his chair and walked to the window that overlooked the traffic circle in front of Washington National Airport's main terminal. From his second-floor vantage point, he examined the scene below, shaking his head in sympathy and detached disdain at the obvious carelessness that had caused the accident.

A Mercury had rear-ended a tiny red Volkswagen and the two drivers were out of their cars, squaring off like fighters who had just heard the bell. No, not quite, Jordan decided. If it was a confrontation, the Volkswagen driver was at a decided disadvantage—she was trying to talk and press a handkerchief to her bleeding face simultaneously. For that matter, the man in the Mercury didn't seem very belligerent; the sight of blood had unnerved him and he was offering his own handkerchief, which she rejected with an angry shake of her head.

Typically female, Jordan decided. Now she was shaking her head at an airport policeman who had arrived on the scene. Telling him she wasn't badly hurt, Jordan supposed. But the policeman was insistent—he had taken her arm and was steering her toward the terminal even as she gestured toward the Volkswagen, the hood

3

of its rear engine sprung open like the upper jaw of an alligator. Jordan could imagine the unheard dialogue.

"But my car . . . I can't leave it there."

"Another officer will park it for you. Don't worry. We have to get you to first aid."

Jordan decided that the little drama was over and returned to his desk. His decision was confirmed by a secretary poking her head in from an outer office. "The applicants are here," she announced.

Jordan, a small, wiry man in his thirties, wearing rimless glasses that gave his pleasant face a sternly professorial air, opened the first of a pile of application folders. "Send in Julia Granger," he said.

The secretary frowned. "I don't remember her. Did you interview her before?"

"About two months ago. Good kid but her teeth were lousy. I told her to get 'em capped. They all here?"

"Her teeth? I didn't look in her mouth."

"Not her teeth, damnit. The six applicants scheduled for a second screening."

"There are only five girls out there." The secretary's body count was delivered in a tone of perverse satisfaction—overage and overweight, she compensated for her secret desire to be a stewardess with her secret delight every time an applicant failed to show up.

"Who's AWOL?" Jordan asked. Unlike the secretary, he considered every no-show a personal affront.

"I wouldn't know. You've got the list."

"Well," Jordan grumbled, "I'll find out soon enough. Send in Granger."

Julia Granger entered, and Jordan noted with satisfaction the simple but chic dark blue suit she was wearing. Obviously, she was used to good clothes.

She was a tall girl with cropped, honey-colored hair, an aquiline nose whose tiny pinched nostrils somehow achieved a shortening effect, and a stunning torso mounted on a pair of long, slim legs. Leg shape was the first attribute Jordan looked for. His gaze shifted to her attractive face, now dominated by a smile that came uncomfortably close to artificiality.

4

Capped, Jordan thought. *Good for her*. "Have a seat, Miss Granger. I see you've had those teeth capped—as I suggested."

Miss Granger nodded, her mouth still set in a welded smile.

"When did you get the work done?"

Her smile disappeared. "Yetherday," she mumbled.

Jordan laughed. "Yesterday? No wonder you can't talk straight. Why didn't you call us and delay the interview for a few days?"

"Only appointment I could get with my dentist. I didn't want to take a ch . . . afraid I might not get another one."

"Relax, Julia. Talk slowly, and I think that lisp will go away by itself."

It did, as he put her through the usual litany. Why did she want to be a stewardess? (Approximately ninety-nine percent of the applicants gave identical answers—they loved people, loved to travel, and hated the rut of a nine-to-five job.) How big a family did she come from? (Theoretically, girls from large families were better at defending themselves.) Where was she raised? (Another theory held that small-town girls were more dedicated in training because they hated to go home and admit failure.)

Jordan made up his mind quickly. Her answers conformed to the "right" responses that a psychologist had provided the airline, but Jordan preferred to rely on his own instincts. As the lisp smoothed out, her answers came quickly; articulate without being glib, sincere without any indication she was delivering replies manufactured for the occasion. An above-average prospect, Jordan decided.

"You'll be hearing from us again," was the only encouragement he gave her, but his smile told the tall girl she had made a good impression. A far better one, it transpired, than the impression made by the next four applicants, all of whom he rejected. One had committed the cardinal sin of wearing slacks, the second had not only failed to take off the poundage suggested at her first interview but had gained eleven more pounds, and the others seemed more interested in job benefits than in the job itself.

But he wasn't unhappy about today's result: one hire and four rejections. Trans-National Airlines monitored individual interviewers, checking every casualty against the name of the interviewer who had recommended acceptance. A high failure rate could lead to a particular interviewer's own termination. Jordan's failure rate was one of the lowest in the airline, something of which he was especially proud. He had been told that TNA's Training Center in Miami regarded a Fred Jordan selection as almost certain to make it through graduation.

An impulse made him reexamine the sixth folder, which belonged to the no-show candidate. *Diane Victoria Hendricks.* He had already glanced through her application and noted that Mitzi Resnick, an ex-TNA stewardess grounded by marriage and assigned to Personnel, had been the one who screened her initially and recommended a second interview.

This kid's a winner. If she doesn't make one hell of a stewardess I should be interviewing ship cleaners, Mitzie had written on the report form.

Well, Jordan mused, not even Mitzie's enthusiasm for Miss Hendricks could do much good—failing to show up for an interview was an unpardonable transgression. Rules, after all, were rules . . .

"Fred, that sixth applicant is here."

"Did you ask her why the hell she's late?" He didn't wait for the secretary to reply; his annoyance gushed out in a petulant flood. "No damned excuse whatsoever for tardiness in a stewardess applicant. If she's late for an interview, she'll be late for a flight. I've got half a mind to tell her to go home."

"I think you should see her." The secretary didn't wait for him to respond but made the decision for him. "Miss Hendricks, Mr. Jordan will see you now."

Jordan rose as the applicant entered. One of her eyes was swollen shut and already so discolored she seemed to have applied blacklamp to it. Her upper lip was puffed, and there was a Band-aid bridging her nose.

"Jesus," he said, "you were in that accident in front of the terminal."

She nodded, smiling painfully. Fred Jordan felt a stab of guilt. "Look, Miss Hendricks, you're in no shape for an interview. Why don't we reschedule you? Let's say about two weeks from—"

"No." Firmly polite.

"I've been in a couple of accidents myself. They can raise hell emotionally as well as physically."

"I appreciate your concern, Mr. Jordan, but I'm fine. I've been to the airport doctor and he patched me up—although I apologize for my appearance. Including this run in my stocking."

She leaned down to trace the run with a forefinger. Jordan mentally graded her A on her limbs. "I can assure you we won't hold it against you if we postpone our talk," he said. "I really think it's best for you."

Miss Hendricks shook her black hair; the motion achieved grace as well as positiveness. "I'd rather do it today, Mr. Jordan. I've waited a long time for this and I hope to be a stewardess a lot longer than this black eye will last."

Jordan shrugged and leaned back in his chair, fingers cupped under his chin. She wore her hair in bangs, the sides and back sweeping down to the shoulder line. Naturally soft, she was one of that fortunate minority who didn't require the lacquer of a holding spray. Her eyes (at least the one he could see clearly) were a deep brown, set above cheekbones just high enough to hint of some Indian heritage. About five-six or five-seven, Jordan guessed, without referring to her application. The severe cut of her tan suit failed to hide the swell of firm breasts; Jordan found himself thinking that she looked a hell of a lot better bruised than most applicants did unblemished.

"As you wish. Tell me why you'd like to fly with us. Or any other airline."

She seemed to take a deep breath without actually inhaling. "I suppose I could give you the conventional reasons. Love people and travel and hate the confinement of a routine job. I guess most girls tell you that."

Jordan grinned. "About ninety-nine of every hundred."

"You don't hire ninety-nine of a hundred."

"No, we don't. Liking people, wanting to travel, getting away from an office environment—that's all very fine, but it doesn't mean they add up to a good stewardess. I take it your motivation goes a bit deeper."

She said simply, "I like airplanes."

"So do a lot of other people. Including ten-year-old boys."

"Not just any airplanes. Big ones. Carrying people. People who look up to a stewardess. Who rely on her. Whose whole trip depends on the way she does her job. I . . . I've felt that way ever since I was a little girl, when my father took me on a flight from Washington to Chicago. I think I was only seven or eight at the time. All I did was gawk at the stewardess. I remember envying her uniform."

Jordan was incredulous. "You mean you've wanted to be a stewardess since you were eight?"

"Just about."

He opened her folder. "Let's see, you're twenty-three now—almost twenty-four. You seem to have waited quite a few years before applying."

She nodded, unperturbed at the inconsistency. "I'm afraid my parents frowned on the whole idea. Dad insisted that I go to college first and at least try the profession he wanted for me."

"Which was?"

"Teaching. He's a college professor. My mother was a teacher, too. So I tried it—and don't particularly like it."

"What were their objections to your going with an airline?"

"My mother thought it was degrading. My father thought it was too dangerous. I thought they were both full of prune juice, but I'm their only child and I felt I owed them some obligation. So I've been teaching for two years and I finally made them live up to their end of the agreement—if I didn't like it, I could apply to the airlines."

The fact that she was an only child didn't bother Jordan—it was one of those psychological yardsticks he considered over-emphasized. He offered her a cigarette, which she accepted, and that pleased him. He had seen a lot of girls coyly refuse as if the spurning proved their virtue.

"Why did you pick Trans-National?" he asked.

"Size."

8

"Size? You mean because we're the nation's fifth-largest carrier?"

"Big enough to offer some variety in trips. Small enough so I won't get lost in the shuffle, like I might at United, American or Eastern."

Jordan found himself liking the brevity of her answers. He was conscious that even as he examined her, she was studying him. It came close to making him uncomfortable, the marksman suddenly turned into the target.

He glanced down at her application. "You're a third-grade teacher in a private Catholic school, according to this. A very fine profession, teaching. Why do you want to leave it?"

"I suppose because I'm teaching under duress—my family's duress. It isn't the children. I love the children. The trouble is that I've always regarded teaching as temporary, something I was required to do before I became a stewardess. Like taking a required course in college."

"And what college did you attend?" The information already was in the folder but Jordan preferred to judge candidates by the way they answered in person. He had some girls whose nervousness was exposed by their not remembering what they had written down in their applications.

"Antioch, in Ohio."

"Antioch, eh?" he goaded her. "Pretty liberal institution, from what I've heard. About three degrees to the right of socialism."

"It's not socialistic. It *is* too liberal in its permissiveness. In giving too much responsibility to kids who aren't mature enough to handle it."

"You might say the same thing," Jordan suggested softly, "about being a stewardess. We put one hell of a lot of responsibility into the hands of some very immature kids—kids who've just turned twenty, in some cases."

She smiled. "I don't quite buy your analogy, Mr. Jordan. Immature when they start, I'll concede. But isn't one of the purposes of training to get the back of their ears dry?"

He was right, Jordan thought—the interrogator had become the interrogated. This gal was something. "You apparently have a

9

rather idealistic view of the stewardess's profession, Diane."

"I don't think so. I know there are pros and cons."

"Such as?"

"Such as passengers who are unreasonable creeps, who have to be treated as if I enjoyed it. I know I'll meet a cross-section of the male gender from would-be wolves to grouchy businessmen, from spoiled brats to nice youngsters who regard an airplane trip as a wonderful adventure. I know for every three hours of free time there'll be an hour in which I'll be working my butt off, maybe wondering why I ever wanted to be part of the airline business."

Beautiful, Jordan said to himself. *She knows what she's getting into.* "In other words, you don't have any illusions about this being a romantic, glamourous job?"

The one good eyebrow rose. "Oh, I didn't say that. Not having any illusions doesn't mean I'm putting the job down as un-glamourous or unromantic."

Somehow, Jordan felt disappointed. Hearing that answer was like hearing a discordant note played by a skilled musician.

"If you're accepted," he said sternly, "you might as well make up your mind that there is very little glamour. Your disillusion-ment will start from the first day of training and *if* you graduate"—he sucked on the word *if*—"you'll find that the process is very likely to continue. At least it does for many girls. I'm not saying there are few very favorable aspects to the job—I wouldn't be interviewing candidates if I thought that way. But I *am* pointing out that anyone who expects glamour is exactly the type who'll lose her motivation in a hurry. Now I don't mind admitting I've been very impressed with you, Diane. But when you say in one breath that you realize all the pitfalls, and in the next that you still think flying will be romantic and glamourous—well, your inconsistency bothers me."

Diane Hendricks managed another smile. "I see your point, Mr. Jordan, but I deny the inconsistency. I suspect my definition of glamour and romance is somewhat different from yours."

"Oh? Different in what respect?"

She paused before replying, carefully marshalling her words.

"A job is what you make it. No, I don't think being a stewardess is the epitome of fun, the ultimate in romance. I shudder to imagine some of the rules and regulations I'll have to live with—I'm quite sure a lot of them will seem asinine. I know I'm going to resent unreasonable and unruly passengers, including the inevitable boozed-up lechers.

"What excites me about the job, Mr. Jordan, is what I can make of it *despite* all the drawbacks. The chance of making some frightened passenger feel reassured. The opportunity of turning what could be a bad flight into a good one, with just a little extra effort. The realization that I'm part of an exciting, challenging industry. There aren't many professions like that, Mr. Jordan, not for women at least. And if all this comes under the heading of glamour and romanticism, so be it."

Fred Jordan swallowed, resisting his impulse to tell Diane Hendricks that she had been accepted for training right then and there. He cleared his throat as if it were a way to dilute the impact of what she had said.

"That was very well put," he managed. "Your, uh, motivation is commendable. Can you tell me anything that might give you pause about going with us?" He held up his hand before she could answer. "I'm not trying to talk you out of any commitment, believe me. But I'm going to emphasize something I've been telling every applicant lately. This industry is on the threshold of a new era. It may seem premature to be discussing jet travel in nineteen fifty-five, but it's inevitable. Trans-National expects to be operating jets by nineteen fifty-nine—by next fall, we'll be signing with either Boeing or Douglas for jet equipment."

He paused, his face stern. "The jets will carry well over one hundred passengers. They'll be at least double the size of our DC-sevens. That kind of capacity will mean much harder work, with less time in which to perform such work, and when that happens much of the fun will go out of flying. Does the prospect of having a drastically altered working environment give you any reasons for not wanting to be a stewardess?"

"Mr. Jordan," she said simply, "outside of a fatal crash, I can't think of a damned thing."

Jordan stood, holding out his hand. "Thank you for coming, Diane—I appreciate it even more considering what happened to you. You'll hear from us shortly"—he couldn't resist a grin—"one way or another."

She tossed him a faint smile, then closed the door behind her. Jordan sat down, opening her folder once more. In a firm hand he scribbled a notation on the rating sheet and put the folder back in his briefcase.

The most highly motivated candidate I have ever interviewed, he had written. *Recommended without qualification.*

The most highly motivated candidate he had ever interviewed felt drained—battered from the accident and discouraged despite her conviction that Jordan had liked her. She was, she told herself ruefully, introspective to a point where the gray shades of self-analysis could darken suddenly into the blackness of self-criticism and insecurity. It was typical of her that five minutes after the interview had ended, she could remember virtually nothing positive about it. Yet she recalled vividly that she had said "damned" and wondered whether Mr. Jordan's ominous pen had jotted down something like *Profanity a definite minus* on the yellow-ruled scratchpaper at which she had kept trying to peek. After all, hadn't he ended the interview just after she'd said it?

If that weren't bad enough, she was conscious of the way she had looked, with her discolored eye and spattered jacket. Certainly not the image of the perfect stewardess candidate, she decided. The pessimistic mood lasted all the way out to Potomac, Maryland, where the taxi she had been forced to take from the airport dropped her off in front of her parents' red-brick Georgian home.

It was a house quite literally built by a book. John Hendricks had been a professor trying to drill a semblance of appreciation for Shakespeare, Milton, and Galsworthy into the generally unappreciative minds of college students, but then he had begun writing novels, and one—*The Gangster*—had stayed on the *New York Times* bestseller list for twenty-five weeks.

So she had grown up in the affluent Potomac area. She also had grown up far closer to her father than to her mother; much of John Hendricks' own personality and beliefs had gone into the daughter he worshipped as much as the son he originally would have preferred, the boy he would have named Daniel after his own father. The nickname he had bestowed on her from childhood, Danni, at first bothered her because she knew its derivation, but gradually she accepted it for what it became: a nickname of affection, not regret.

When she arrived home, her mother's smile of greeting quickly dissolved into a look of horror.

"My God, Danni, what happened to you?"

"Accident, but I'm fine. Just a little bruised. Is Dad home?"

"He's in the library. Danni, I'll call Dr. Hall . . ."

Danni wasn't listening. She already was en route to the library where she briefed her father on the accident and told him about the interview. "I think I did pretty well," she told him. "I'll tell Sister Celeste she'd better start looking for a replacement right after Easter vacation."

"Do you expect to hear from the airline that soon?" John Hendricks asked. "Easter vacation's over next Monday. You sound very confident."

Danni's enthusiasm took a sudden dip as she again remembered her profanity. "Hopeful, not confident," she confessed. "All Mr. Jordan said was that I'd hear 'shortly'—whether that's a few weeks or a few months, I wish I knew."

"Well," her father grinned, "I'm sure you'll be accepted. I doubt whether they get many applicants with your qualifications."

Danni was both amused and touched. "Only a few hundred," she said. "Including some who don't have my drawbacks."

He was indignant. "Drawbacks? What drawbacks?"

"Such as my propensity for freezing if I'm called on in class. I've had that little habit ever since I can remember. Put me on a one-to-one basis, like my interview today, and I'm fine. But in a room full of people, ask me a question and I'm ready to crawl into the nearest hole. That bothers me, Dad. It could wash me out of training, and if that happens . . ."

The suddenly glistening of her eyes did not escape John Hendricks, who looked rather as if sensing for the first time the extent of her desire.

"You really want this badly, don't you?"

"Very, very much."

"Then I hope with all my heart you get it. What the hell, maybe after a few years you'll decide to go back into teaching."

Something clicked in Danni's brain, like tumblers in a lock. She gave him a curious glance. "My leaving teaching isn't all that's bothering you, is it?"

He shook his head. "No, it's not. I'll be worried about you. Every time you fly."

"And no wonder," Bea Hendricks added. "I've heard all about those stewardess-chasing pilots and all those passengers trying to pick you up. And God knows what kind of girls you'd be living with; what kind of bad influence—"

"Bea, shut up," Hendricks said in a tone milder than his words. "She's my"—he corrected himself—"*our* daughter and I think we've taught her right from wrong. I'm just not convinced that commercial aviation is the safest way to get from one place to another."

"But you fly—a lot."

"Not as much as you will. The law of averages is what worries me."

"Your law of averages caught up with me today," she reminded him. "Pilots say the most dangerous part of their day is the drive to the airport. I think I just proved it."

He grinned and kissed her, a wordless surrender to her inevitable optimism.

A month passed without Danni's hearing from TNA. Then she came home from school one day and found Bea waiting for her, a letter in hand.

"Oh, my God, Mom! Is it from Trans-National?"

Her mother nodded, wearing the stricken look of a woman whose son has just received his draft board notice.

"Why didn't you call me at school?" Danni demanded as she grabbed the envelope.

Bea swapped martyrdom for indignity. "I knew you wouldn't

let me open the letter and I didn't want you to leave your class and rush right home and . . ."

Danni wasn't listening. She had ripped open the envelope. Then she sat down heavily and began to read. Her eyes had absorbed only the first line under the salutation when she jumped up, hugging her mother. "I'm in! I'm in! They took me!"

Bea asked the obvious and anguished question. "When?"

"Let's see . . . June sixth. That gives me a whole month to get ready."

"That's not very long," Bea mourned.

"For God's sake, Mom, I could get ready for my own wedding in a month."

Her mother sniffled. "I only wish it *were* your wedding, instead of this crazy stewardess . . ." she groped for a word that would convey her unhappiness . . . "profession."

But Danni was already climbing above Cloud Nine, oblivious to Bea's pain. As soon as John Hendricks arrived home, Danni rushed him into his study, pushed him into the swivel chair behind his desk, and handed him the already well-worn letter. She didn't say anything and didn't have to—when her father asked, "They accept you?" all she did was nod, her eyes brimming. He began reading.

Dear Miss Hendricks:

This letter is to advise you of your acceptance as a Stewardess Trainee in the June 6, 1955 class.

Please make the necessary arrangements to report to the Everglades Inn, 700 Deer Run Rd., Miami, Florida, on the day before your class begins. Room reservations will be made for your arrival. If at any time prior to your class date unforeseen events make it necessary for you to change your plans, notify us immediately and we will attempt to make alternate arrangements.

Transportation via Trans-National will be furnished you from Washington, D.C. to Miami. Please present this letter at the ticket counter at the airport at least one hour prior to your departure.

We have found from past experience that you will need at least $300 for incidental expenses during training.

It is suggested that you call the TNA reservations number in Washington the day before you leave, advise them that you are a Stewardess Trainee en route to the commencement of class, and ascertain at that time which flight would be best for you in terms of available space. Should you have any difficulty en route, making it impossible to arrive on schedule, please contact the undersigned as soon as is practical (we cannot accept collect calls).

On behalf of Trans-National Airlines, please accept my congratulations on the launching of what we hope will be a successful and satisfactory career.

Sincerely,
Edward P. Perkins
Director, Training Center
Trans-National Airlines, Inc.

John Hendricks looked up. "Come here, baby," he said softly, and Danni pounced into his lap, conscious that she had not done this for a long time.

"I'm proud of you, honey," he whispered.

Tears filled her eyes. "If I make it, will you come down to Miami and pin on my wings?"

He hugged her. "You're goddamned right I will!" he promised.

Chapter 2

"Reservation for Miss Diane Hendricks," she told the desk clerk.

He was a slim young man with floor-mop hair, an under-nourished mustache, and a built-in leer.

"Trainee?" She nodded. He dug her reservation card out of a file box, reached under the counter, and brought forth a manila envelope and a looseleaf book the size of the Manhattan telephone directory.

"These are from your Training Department," he told her. "Just sign this receipt slip and I'll have someone help you with your luggage."

Danni looked around. "Where are the elevators?" she asked.

"Elevators? Trainees don't stay here. This is the main building for regular guests." He made her feel like a Negro trying to get into a restricted Southern hotel. "You're across the roadway, in that two-story dormitory." Her forlorn look was a gap into which he lunged.

"I get off at six, if you'd like to go somewhere for a drink. Tell you all about the better spots in Miami."

The gap closed in a tone that was more like a slammed door. "No thanks. I think I'll start studying right away." She hefted the notebook, not only impressed but scared. The thick, stiff cover carried the words, "Stewardess Training—Property of Trans-

National Airlines." Danni had the uncomfortable feeling that the last five words also applied to her.

Her room, 210, was on the second floor of the dormitory—a long building with a row of rooms on each side of the corridor. Done in pink stucco like the main hotel, it still gave her the impression of an army barracks. The room itself was bright and cheerful enough, no worse than most of the motel rooms she had stayed in. The twin beds at least were generously sized, and the bathroom, while badly in need of repainting, was clean. Danni turned on the hot-water tap and got an almost immediate satisfactory response—she had no way of knowing that for the next five weeks, she and the rest of the class were to learn that the water supply between 5:00 A.M. and 9:00 A.M. apparently was pumped in from the Arctic Ocean.

The manila envelope accompanying the manual contained a brief letter from Edward Perkins, Training Center Director; the concluding paragraph read:

> Please report to Room 400 of the Training Center at 0800 Monday, where you will meet your instructor and be briefed on the curriculum, including all regulations pertinent to your training period. There also will be a test on city codes.

City codes? Danni opened the heavy manual and quickly located the contents page, which informed her that "Codes" could be found on pages 1.16–1.17. An inspection of those pages plunged her into panic—there were eighty-nine cities listed with the letter designations for their airports. Some were obvious, like DCA for Washington National Airport, BOS for Boston, and CLE for Cleveland. But others defied logic, such as BDL for Hartford, Connecticut; GSO for Greensboro/High Point/Winston-Salem, North Carolina; and SDF for Louisville, Kentucky. She was too much of a neophyte to realize that often the letters were derived from the names of the airports and not the cities—BDL, for example, was Bradley Field, and SDF stood for Standiford Field.

If illogic weren't bad enough, the very length of the code list was frightening. Danni abandoned any idea of wandering around the dorm looking for classmates. She unpacked swiftly, donned a pair of shorts and a halter, and propped herself against a pillow on one of the beds, the manual in her lap opened to the codes.

Perversely, her mind was too busy to concentrate. She could not help remembering the four-hour flight to Miami that day, and her kaleidoscope of emotions that ran from delicious anticipation to fear. She had heard that the failure rate was high, that rules were not only strict but deliberately unreasonable to entice and trap a trainee into violations. So she had expected to be nervous on the trip down, and her jitters were compounded by the senior stewardess working the flight.

She was a sharp-featured, rather faded ash-blonde girl whose thin lips seemed to have zippered any existing smiles inside her mouth. She had looked at Danni's pass on boarding, handing it back with a cynical shake of her head.

"Stewardess trainee?"

"Yes."

"I'd better wish you luck now. You'll need it. Why'd you pick this crummy airline?"

Danni was too startled to reply. When she finally opened her mouth, the stewardess chopped her off. "Go take your seat. I've got other passengers boarding."

Jesus, Danni thought, *if the instructors are anything like her, I've got troubles.* As resentful as she was shaken, she spent considerable time observing how the senior stewardess handled her job—with an effortless efficiency that was also impersonal, unsmiling, and abrupt. A *robot could have done just as well,* Danni thought.

She didn't have much chance to talk to the other stewardess until about a half-hour out of Miami, when the girl unexpectedly flopped down in the seat next to her.

"Boy, I know we need customers, but believe me, it's a pleasure to work a trip with this light a load," she began. "Don't often get a chance to relax. By the way, my name's Betty Webster. I hear you're a trainee." Danni had to settle for a nod as the stewardess, a tiny brunette with brown eyes so glossy they seemed like those in a stuffed teddy bear, rushed on. "Well, it's gonna be tough but don't let it get you down—if a dumb-dumb like me could make it, anybody can. That's what got me through, in fact. Whenever I got discouraged, I kept thinking of all those sad sacks I'd seen on flights and told myself there had to be hope for me."

"Is it really tough?"

Betty hesitated. "Funny, now that I look back, it wasn't as tough as I thought at the time. The rough part is that they throw everything at you so fast. There's so damned much to memorize you wouldn't believe it. Some of us used to cry ourselves to sleep— you'd study for three or four hours, with a test coming up the next day, and you were absolutely positive you hadn't learned a damned thing. I guess a lot of it's absorbed by osmosis or something. Anyway, once you start flying everything seems to fall into place."

"How long have you been flying?"

"Almost a year. I'll probably quit in another year—hot pants is getting impatient."

"Hot pants?"

"My boyfriend, back home. You got a special thing waiting for you?"

Danni laughed. "If you mean a steady guy, no. I'd like to make flying pretty much a career."

Betty looked at her curiously, a glance combining cynical amusement and pity. "Most of us say that when we start. Then we decide marriage is better than five A.M. sign-ins, and good-bye Trans-National. The trouble with the job is not the job but its distractions and temptations. You meet a lot of attractive passengers, and there are some pilots on this airline who could park their shoes under my bed anytime—on a temporary basis, that is. Take my advice and don't fall in love with a captain. Most of 'em are married; their battle cry is that their wives don't understand them. Good Joes, by the way. A lot of fun. But they'd lie like Joseph Goebbels to get a stew into the sack. Take Donna, for example. She's a bear to work with these days, all because of a pilot."

"Donna?"

"Senior stew."

"I thought she seemed a little . . . uh, grouchy."

"She's been dating a married captain. Donna's a pretty savvy gal—been flying for five or six years, but she flipped for this guy and a couple of weeks ago he told her he had reconciled with his wife. I'll give you three-to-one he hadn't broken up with his wife in the first place—it was just a come-on for Donna. So for two weeks, she's been carrying a chip on her shoulder the size of a redwood."

Danni frowned. "It doesn't seem fair to carry her personal problems into an airplane. I couldn't help noticing she wasn't very friendly toward the passengers."

Betty smiled tolerantly. "It isn't that easy, my little idealist. You'll find there'll be times when the urge to belt a passenger is almost irresistible. No matter what they tell you in training, it's congenitally impossible to separate personal problems from your job. How well you can hide the former is a matter of degree, but I never knew any gal who could hide them entirely . . ."

Now, sprawled on the bed, the manual foreboding yet challenging, Danni thought, *I don't care what she said—the day I make a flight miserable for a passenger because my love life stinks, that'll be the day I quit flying. . .*

She became so deeply engrossed in memorization that she did not hear the click of a key in the door. She sensed the presence of the tall newcomer before she saw her.

"My God, are you studying already?" the tall girl said.

Danni closed the manual and hopped off the bed, offering her hand. "When you open that brown envelope, you'll find out we've got a test tomorrow. Hi—I'm Danni Hendricks."

"I'm Julia Granger, and call me Julie."

They inspected one another, a wary appraisal that was an unspoken birth of comradeship. Julie was, Danni decided, a striking girl, exuding a kind of brassy confidence softened by a smile that was totally natural.

"What's this about a test?" Julie asked. "You've got to be kidding. Okay, you can bring in that stuff"—the last was delivered to the bellboy standing in the corridor. "How can they test us if we haven't started training yet?"

"City codes. There are eighty-nine of the damned things."

"That's all? A breeze." Her nonchalance stunned Danni, but Julie grinned. "I've been working for a travel agency," she

21

explained. "They're easy once you get the hang of it. Just memorize the tough ones and the rest are obvious. I'll help you get them down straight after I unpack." She gave the bellboy a dollar, ushered him out of the room, and closed the door. "Where do you want me to put my things?"

"I staked out the dresser on the left—the other's yours. Plenty of room in the closet, thank God. Here, I'll help you."

While getting Julie settled, they talked—backgrounds, boyfriends, jobs, and, most of all, what lay ahead. It was dark when Julie decided her roommate had been adequately initiated into the mysteries of city codes.

"Want me to throw a few at you?" Danni offered.

"Nope. I could pass that test in my sleep. Hungry?"

"Not really. I suppose we should go around to the other rooms and introduce ourselves. We can get something to eat later."

"Frankly, I think I should bypass a meal tonight. They'll probably put us on scales tomorrow, and I've had sixteen farewell dinners in the past three weeks. Let's go find some fellow sufferers."

Apparently the rest of their class was either out to dinner or hadn't arrived yet. They did bump into three girls from the previous class; they were in their last week of training and couldn't resist exhibiting an air of superiority that bordered on condescension.

"Who's your instructor?" one of them wanted to know.

"We don't know yet," Danni said.

"Just pray you don't get Marlene Compton. She's a female Dracula. You wind up in her class, you'll think you've joined the Marines."

"Was she your instructor?" Julie asked.

"No, thank God. We had Laura Talton—an absolute doll. We just love her."

Later that night, Danni and Julie had gone to bed, each locked in the citadel of private misgivings.

"Danni?"

"What?"

Julie sighed. "I'll give you any odds you want we draw Compton as our instructor."

They did.

Walking into Room 400, Danni thought, was like getting off a time machine and discovering she had been transported back to her childhood classroom days. There were the combination chair-desks, with the racks under the seats for book storage. She and Julie started to sit in the middle of the three rows of seats, figuring that would be a nice compromise between being too close to the instructor and too far back. They discovered, however, that name tags had already been attached to the seats, arranged alphabetically, and that they were occupying the last two seats on the right side of the first row.

Danni counted heads—twelve girls including Julie and herself. Of the twelve, only four—herself included—were brunettes. The rest were blondes of varying shades and textures, one of them a statuesque girl whose classic features and willowy frame made Danni feel dowdy. The girl could have jumped right off the cover of *Harper's Bazaar*.

The nervous chatter in the room ended when a rear door opened. To the trainees, it was more like a curtain going up, and the young woman who entered was like a star going on stage. For just a few seconds, Danni was positive this could not be the redoubtable Marlene Compton. The woman who came through the door was petite and vivacious, with a Kewpie-doll face, soft hair cropped into a page boy, and a dazzling smile. Slender in build, she had a magnificent bustline that gave her the appearance of a wine glass mounted on two thin stems. She wore the powder-blue uniform of a TNA stewardess, immaculate, perfectly creased, and as unwrinkled as if it were hanging on a mannequin in a Bergdorf Goodman window. The gold wings just above her left breast gleamed impressively; there could have been a tiny spotlight shining on them.

"Good morning," she called out cheerfully.

The class returned the greeting with mumbled, uncertain enthusiasm—Marlene Compton was, to each novice, an instant challenge. *Nobody* could ever achieve such poised perfection. The instructor wheeled around—it was more of an about-face executed with military precision—and in flowing script wrote on the huge blackboard:

WELCOME CLASS 55-10

MARLENE COMPTON—HEMLOCK 4-0566

She wheeled around again. "That's my name and my home telephone number if you ever have to reach me after class. It's unlisted, so please make a note of it." She stopped and surveyed the twelve solemn, hopeful faces, as twelve assorted pens or pencils scribbled down the phone number. *I hope I never have to use this,* Danni thought.

"Ladies, as you can see from the blackboard, I'm Marlene Compton. The very first thing we can establish is that I'd prefer being called by my first name—'Miss Compton' makes me feel too pedantic. The 'fifty-five-ten' refers to your class number—this is the tenth class of nineteen fifty-five. Now, let's start getting to know each other. Some of you have probably met already, but we're going to be pretty close these next five weeks and I, for one, want to begin associating faces with names—not to mention hearing a little bit about your background. We'll start alphabetically in the first row with"—she peered at the name card—"Kathryn Crum."

Kathryn was a shapely girl, slightly on the plump side, with blonde hair that had just the merest suggestion of a reddish tint.

"Hi. I'm Kathryn Crum and I'm from Phoenix, Arizona. Please call me Katie . . . ."

Danni suspected the instructor was obtaining general impressions rather than listening to details, and she found herself appraising along with Compton. *Kathryn had better watch her weight,* Danni thought, *and her hairstyle isn't very becoming. Good personality, though . . .*

". . . I used to work for Hertz at the Phoenix Airport. And . . . and . . . well, I guess that's all, I suppose."

"Any hobbies?" Marlene asked.

"I love to ski. Every chance I get, I go up to Colorado and ski."

"Fine. Next?"

Mary Beth Davenport, the tallest in the class, was the least physically attractive; however, a prominent nose and a flat chest

24

were offset by soft brown hair, a creamy complexion, and a sweet smile that seemed to magically erase every trace of homeliness.

"I'm from Jacksonville, Florida," she announced. "I've had many jobs—medical secretary, typing manuscripts for an author, and most recently hostess in a large restaurant. I'm a nut on sail boating and I love everything about the water, from swimming to fishing . . ."

Danni judged, *She'll make it without trouble. Intelligent, mature, tough to rattle, I'll bet.*

"I'm Meredith Gaskin and I'm from right here in Miami." This was a slender girl but well-proportioned. Very pretty with long eyelashes resembling miniature awnings and hair so blonde it was almost white. "I'm a—I mean, I *was* a desk clerk at the King's Inn—that's on Deer Run, about a block from the hotel where we are."

"That's where Eastern houses its trainees, isn't it?" Marlene asked.

"Yes. I've seen a lot of girls go through there. That's where I got the notion I could be a stewardess." She stopped but left the impression that the next sentence would have been, "And if an airline could hire some of those babes, I shouldn't have much trouble."

Marlene, who apparently could read minds, frowned. "I'm curious to know why you didn't apply to Eastern."

"I liked the places Trans-National flew to better," Meredith explained with more glibness than logic. "And talking to some of their girls, I gathered their training wasn't as good as ours." She seemed to suck on the word *ours* as if waving it patriotically, like a flag.

Marlene frowned again. "Their training's pretty damned good," she commented, while Danni's own eyes narrowed.

I wonder whether she applied to Eastern and got turned down. And she'll have to do something about that hair—there's enough peroxide in it to light up a coal mine.

Meredith talked briefly about her hobbies, particularly the art of raising goldfish. "You'd be amazed how fascinating goldfish are," she said defensively. "There are hundreds, maybe thousands, of individual species, and some are quite beautiful and *very* valuable . . ." She would have continued but the instructor interrupted.

"To each her own," Marlene said. "Miss Granger?"

"I'm Julie Granger, York, Pennsylvania, and I've been a travel agent. Which expresses my hobby. I like to travel. I guess I just like meeting people . . ."

She seems very poised, my roommate. There's a toughness about her—but she could be a good friend. Maybe my best friend. I hope she makes it. And my God, I'm next . . .

"Diane Hendricks."

She stood up, knowing she was blushing and hating herself for that weakness. "I'm known as Danni and I'm from Potomac, Maryland. I taught third grade in a Catholic school and I don't have any hobbies as such, unless horseback riding can be classed as a hobby. I do love animals, though, although I couldn't quite cuddle up to Meredith's goldfish. That's about it, except to say I'm kind of proud to be with all of you."

She sat down. Miss Compton nodded in the direction of the first girl in the second row while Danni's mind raced backward . . .

Well, I don't think I made a bad impression except for that damned blushing. I hate getting up in front of an audience—I'm like a kid being asked to recite before adults. Now I know how my third-graders felt when I called on them. God, I wish I could make it through the whole five weeks without opening my mouth . . .

". . . but Ah jes' got tyud of that receptionist job although it was kinda fun meetin' all those interestin' people. But Ah do declare, Ah have to agree with Danni. Ah'm glad Ah'm in this heah class with you all." Miss Betty Jo Lynch of Atlanta, Georgia took her seat, bathed in the smiles of her classmates. She had an exceptionally beautiful face, her natural blonde hair done in carefully coiffeured bangs, but below that exquisite face was a figure sculptured along the general lines of a pipe cleaner.

"I can't wait for you to try cabin P.A.'s with that drawl, Betty Jo," Marlene smiled. "Our passengers may need an interpreter." The class laughed dutifully and Miss Lynch beamed as if she had just been paid a compliment.

She might have trouble in class, or am I just being prejudiced against Southern girls? That accent can be deceiving.

The next trainee introduced herself rather tersely as Patricia Martin of Chicago, said she had been secretary to a city councilman, and voiced the opinion that working with passengers should be a lot easier than working with politicians. Martin was an ash blonde, with pretty features marred only by a rather hard mouth, the corners of her lips turned down slightly in a kind of perpetual pout. Somehow she reminded Danni of the senior stewardess on the flight down.

She'll probably pull down the highest grades in class but she won't be more than an average stewardess—she's smart but she's a tough cookie with a potential chip on her shoulder . . .

The stunning blonde Danni and Julie had admired turned out to be Linda Percival of Miami, a swimming instructor at a Miami Beach hotel with a degree in physical education. Her voice was unexpectedly high-pitched and little-girlish, yet voice notwithstanding, she seemed extremely self-assured but with a trace of coyness; the incongruity bothered Danni.

A little hard to figure out, this one. Best looker in class, but I can't decide whether that coyness is phony modesty or a way of trying to cover up basic shyness. Probably the former—when you're that beautiful, you tend to put on an act to show you're not aware of it. Yet she also might realize that looks won't get her through the next five weeks—she could be comparing herself with the rest of us and getting competition jitters for the first time in her life.

A surprise was Joan Pierce of Bangor, Maine—sweet-faced, with dark brown hair somewhat washed-out and untidy, and obviously older than the others. She seemed to sense the curiosity about her in the room.

". . . I used to work for Trans-National as a reservations agent in Boston before I got married and moved to Bangor with my husband. He was killed in an auto accident about a year ago and I decided I'd like to be a stewardess—we had no children. Well . . . so here I am." She started to sit down and changed her mind. "Oh yes—I love fishing and all outdoor sports. I used to do a lot of camping with my . . . a lot of camping. You know, things like that." She took her seat so quickly it came close to being an act of escape.

That one I feel sorry for—she's going to have a tough time unless they give her every benefit of the doubt. I'll help nurse her along but I'm afraid she's over her head—although, golly, maybe I'm over my head, too.

Teresa Shannon was the next trainee to speak and she did it effortlessly. She was a bright-eyed bundle of peppery enthusiasm—about Danni's height with cropped, light-brown hair that gave her a fleeting resemblance to Amelia Earhart.

". . . I'm from Daytona Beach and I'm a registered nurse—I guess you might say I'm going from bedpans to burp bags." She glanced at the instructor to see whether any offense had been taken and was rewarded by a slight smile. "I'm with Danni—I'm just awfully glad to be here and . . . and I wish all of us luck."

For some reason, the class applauded. Even Marlene nodded approval. "I'm curious to know why you decided to leave nursing, Teresa," she asked.

"I wish all of you would call me Terry. Anyway, well, I'm an extrovert and I suppose being with sick people all the time just got me down. It's hard to be cheerful and joke with someone you know is in a lot of pain and might even die. I like to laugh a lot, and you don't do much laughing in a hospital."

"There isn't much laughing in airplanes, either," the instructor warned.

Terry Shannon grinned and her black eyes sparkled. "There will be on *my* airplane."

I wish I had her personality—she's going to make one hell of a stewardess. The only thing she has to worry about is overconfidence—she might be thinking training will be a breeze after nursing school.

". . . Rose Steinmetz, Syracuse, New York," the eleventh trainee was saying. Short, big-busted, with blonde hair that would have been attractive if it were not obviously dyed; Danni saw Compton's eyes narrow. "I was a legal secretary and the job got awfully boring, which is why I'm here. As for hobbies, I imagine I'm the only one here who works with miniatures."

28

"Miniatures?" Marlene wanted to know.

"I make dollhouses, shadow boxes—even little pieces of furniture."

"That's quite a hobby," the instructor said admiringly. But Danni was looking at her sharply.

Very wary, uncertain girl. Jewish and a little nervous about it. Wondering whether the class will accept her and whether she'll get a fair shake from Compton. I know she'll get one from me—she reminds me of Ruth Irving, my best friend in high school.

"My name is Carol Veskos," trainee number twelve addressed the class. "I'm from Newark, New Jersey and I was a social worker—mostly with handicapped children. I'm afraid I don't have any hobbies except reading—it seems like I've been working all my life and never had the time."

Danni looked at her hair, as jet black as her own but not as neatly styled, her wide, sensuous mouth, and her very voluptuous figure—potential weight problem, Danni decided reluctantly. The instructor observed, "Your job sounded very worthwhile and rewarding, Carol. What led you to try the airlines?"

"Because I could see myself getting married to my job and it looked like a rather empty marriage. Satisfying, yes, but also frustrating and depressing. I wanted to do much more for those poor kids than I could ever hope to. I just couldn't see myself as a surrogate mother indefinitely—I felt myself growing old prematurely. I guess I was in the same boat as Terry and her attitude toward nursing."

"Thank you, Carol . . ."

Good, solid kid. Mature. I'll bet personal appearance and grooming will be her biggest worries—she's sexy but she doesn't know what to do with it.

". . . and thank all of you. This is one of the smallest classes I've ever taught, which is both good and bad. It's easier to work with relatively few trainees, but by the same token I'll be riding herd on you much harder than I could with a class of twenty or more. I've already formed some preliminary impressions, from the way you talked and acted while you introduced yourselves. By and large, I liked what I saw and heard. I also saw room for improvement in every one of you."

She paused, letting each girl wonder about that last remark and how it applied to her. "There are twelve trainees in this class. I'd like all of you to stand."

They did, almost in unison.

"Thank you. Now four of you can sit down."

They looked at each other, bewildered.

"Any four. Let's make it . . . Danni, Mary Beth, Linda, and Terry. You girls take your seats."

Mystified, they did.

"How many are still standing?"

"Eight," Julie said, staring at Marlene as if she were crazy.

"Eight of twelve, right?" They nodded. "Well, ladies, that's how many are likely to still be around five weeks from now." She waved them back to their seats. "The failure rate per class on this airline averages almost thirty percent, the highest in the industry. I'm not trying to discourage you—I'm only trying to warn you that it's going to be very, very tough. The most intensive, highly disciplined five weeks of your lives. That I can promise you. What I can also promise you is that it'll be worth it. For the next five weeks, some of you—maybe all of you—are going to hate me. But those who survive will be glad I was a slave driver. The day we pin on your wings, you're going to be telling me how great I was."

Marlene Compton felt the twelve pairs of eyes on her and she smiled—a little nastily, Danni thought nervously. "Now for a few basic rules. First, the passing grade on each test is ninety. If you flunk a test, you'll be given one chance at makeup. If you fail two consecutive tests, termination is automatic. The passing grade for the final exam is eighty-five, but if you flunk there's no makeup test. And if you fail that final, you're out—even if you've gotten a hundred on every preceding test. Is that understood?"

Twelve heads nodded.

"Okay. If you're late for class, you'll be given one warning—or rather a reprimand. If you're late for class twice, you'll be terminated and it won't make a bit of difference if you have an

30

excuse that would melt the heart of a Gestapo agent. I've fired girls the day of graduation.

"Maintaining proper weight is vital. If I have to warn you about excess poundage, shape up fast or you're in deep trouble. If I have to warn you twice, school's out. The same rule applies to personal grooming. Once I tell you what corrective measures to take, you'd damned well better comply and don't waste time.

"On page two, section A of your manual, you'll find the entire list of do's and don'ts. Know them and obey them or it's a one-way ticket home. Now, let's take a ten-minute break for coffee. . ."

Danni didn't leave with the rest. She had the manual open to page 2, section A, and her eyes carried warning signals to her brain.

. . . *trainees are expected to be in their rooms by 11:00 P.M. Monday through Thursday and on Sunday. The curfew for Friday and Saturday nights is 1:00 A.M. Violation of curfew is an automatic termination offense.*

. . . *trainees must wear prescribed makeup, including nail polish, hairdo, and lipstick, to class.*

. . . *dresses and high-heel shoes must be worn to class unless otherwise instructed.*

. . . *the cocktail lounge at the hotel is strictly off limits to trainees. Violation of this restriction is an automatic terminal offense.*

. . . *trainees must . . . trainees shall . . . trainees must not* . . . Danni sighed, closed the manual, and joined Julie and the others in the small lounge adjacent to the elevators.

"I feel like going home right now—before they get a chance to lower the boom," she confessed.

"Everybody must feel that way the first day," Julie said cheerfully. "It can't be as bad as it seems. People dumber than us have gotten through."

Pat Martin said sourly, "That figures—it would take a dummy to put up with all these chicken-shit rules. Well, I'll put up with their crap to get through training and off probation. Then I'll start acting like a first-class citizen again."

Militant little bitch, Danni thought, but aloud she settled for a mild admonition. "Well, we'd better get back. One of the commandments is never be late to a class."

For the next hour, they filled out forms. Insurance. Payroll deductions. And an ominous sheet titled "Acceptance of Employment Conditions."

The undersigned clearly understands and accepts the Company's requirement that upon marriage or attainment of age thirty-five her employment as stewardess will be automatically terminated without prejudice, and that the same mandatory resignation will apply to the Employee upon medical evidence of pregnancy, Danni read.

"I might add, ladies," Marlene said, "that if you decide to get married on the q.t. and the company finds out you're married, your resignation will be accepted *with* prejudice—which means you'll stand no chance of getting a ground job with Trans-National."

Danni grimaced and signed, but not without inner resentment. She had known about the rule but hadn't given it much thought until it was put before her in stark reality, a written sword of Damocles. All of a sudden, the prospect of being thirty-five loomed terrifyingly near, even though it was twelve years away. She wondered whether Marlene herself agreed with the age-marriage restriction; she'd probably defend it, Danni reasoned, simply because an instructor was part of management. Maybe there was some logic behind the rule, too—a married stewardess might have divided interests, loyalties, and priorities, while an older stewardess could lack enthusiasm and motivation.

Yet the resentment still burned. She considered the age limit arbitrary although a bit more liberal than the rule on some carriers, which grounded stewardesses as early as age thirty-two. How could any airline, she asked herself, establish a specific cutoff date as the time when a stewardess can be declared deficient in performance and appearance?

And even as she put down her signature, a kind of professional promissory note, she was thinking, *Maybe some day I'll be able to do something about the damned rule . . . some day, when . . .*

The stern voice of Marlene Compton knifed into her budding fantasy. "And now I'll hand out the test on city codes."

Chapter 3

The second day began badly.

"About the best thing I can say to you is that nobody flunked her physical yesterday," Marlene announced. "I wish I could say the same thing about the code test. Seven of you must retake it. Seven! And seven failures in a class of twelve is not only disappointing, it's disgraceful. When we break for coffee, I'd like to see Meredith, Betty Jo, Linda, Terry, Katie, Rose, and Carol. I'll hand out your test papers for you to look over and then we'll go down to room four-oh-seven and start our grooming."

Danni assumed that the seven names mentioned were the seven who had flunked on the codes, but she still found her hands trembling when Marlene handed her the test, face down. Danni turned over the sheet.

"Thank God, ninety-two," she whispered to Julie. "What'd you get?"

"A hundred," Julie said nonchalantly. "Which ones did you miss?"

"Let's see . . . oh, damnit! Orlando's MCO—I wrote ORL. And I knew I'd miss Wilkes-Barre/Scranton. It's AVP and I put down ASP. My God, Julie, it's four points per question—if I had missed one more I would have flunked."

Julie nodded in an unperturbed way—she seemed unflapp-

able, and Danni envied her to the point of resenting her unquench-
able confidence. She wished she could be that sure of herself.

Room 407 reminded Danni of a chorus-line dressing room.
Makeup counters fronted naked marquee lights circling large
mirrors that filled three of the four walls. She looked curiously at
the woman waiting for them when they arrived, a chic, perfectly
groomed, slender person even taller than Mary Beth Davenport.
Danni guessed her to be in her mid-thirties.

"Ladies," Marlene said, "this is Jackie Chase, vice president of
the Beauville Modeling Agency. For the past two years, Jackie has
helped us impart the basics of grooming and makeup to our
trainees. When she's finished, you won't know yourselves. All
right, Jackie, this is class fifty-five-ten and I'll let you take it from
here."

Jackie's deep-set eyes swept the room, pausing briefly at each
face—a searchlight probing for flaws. "As the saying goes," she
smiled, "nobody's perfect. What we'll try to accomplish today is a
program that brings out each individual's facial strengths while
playing down facial weaknesses—we all have both. Overall, Trans-
National's policy is to achieve the so-called natural look in its
stewardesses. We want you to be smart without being garish,
healthy without what we might call the corn-fed look, attractive
without having it seem that you were all poured from the same
mold.

"This can be done through proper use of makeup coordinated
with other aspects of good grooming—care of health and complexion, for example. I'll teach you the right way to walk and to sit.
Even the right way to light your cigarette. Good makeup and good
grooming can work literal miracles. I'm proof of that—I happen to
be fifty-two years old."

She set to work, and Danni had to marvel at some of the
transformations. For Mary Beth Davenport, Mrs. Chase applied a
shade of combined eye and facial makeup that somehow managed
to draw attention away from the trainee's prominent nose, and she
achieved the same metamorphosis in Carol Veskos; softer, more

34

subtle makeup gave her rather heavy features an aura of sleek delicacy.

There were loud protests from those who were told to get their hair cut, but Marlene silenced the objections. "Long hair can be a bother in an aircraft cabin," she explained, "and it's also unsanitary when you're serving food." The instructor had remained in the background, but she always hovered close enough to assert authority. Danni overheard her telling Meredith to "get rid of that peroxide—we don't want a bunch of Jean Harlows around here." And she heard a more serious conversation when Marlene approached Rose.

"I'm just curious why you found it necessary to dye your hair blonde?" Marlene asked in a gentle tone.

"I thought I'd have a better chance of getting accepted."

"Do you honestly feel more comfortable being a blonde?"

"No, but I feel a little less Jewish." The answer was more blurted than spoken, the words flecked with bitterness, and Danni held her breath.

Marlene put her hand on the girl's shoulder. "Rose, we're far more interested in what kind of stewardess you'll make than we are in where you pray. Let's get rid of that dye job, as fast as you can. Just ask Mrs. Chase the best and quickest way."

"Okay." Her acquiescence was more relief than obedience and Marlene smiled. "By the way, what color *is* your hair?"

"Dark brown."

"It'll look great." The instructor moved on to Danni, now under Mrs. Chase's microscope, nodding as Danni was advised to accentuate her cheekbones, using less facial makeup but more eyeshadow. "Plus cutting your hair," Marlene added dryly. Under Mrs. Chase's skillful, almost effortless ministrations, the job was done swiftly, and Danni had to admire the results she saw in the mirror even as the pangs of uncertainty struck her. There was so much to do, so much to learn, and the fact that physical transformation was part of the learning process increased her nervousness.

". . . earrings are permissible provided they are not more than a half-inch in diameter," Marlene was saying. "You are permitted to wear two gold necklaces but they must be slim. Not more than two rings, and they cannot be ostentatious. Danni's turquoise ring, for example, is far too large but that opal Mary Beth is wearing would be fine. Mostly it's a matter of common sense and good taste—you'll find the majority of supervisors fairly lenient about jewelry, but now and then you'll hit one who's a terror. The best advice is to play it safe—if you're not sure, don't wear it on duty . . ."

Danni blushed when Marlene zeroed in on the turquoise ring—it was her favorite, a gift from her father. To her, a thousand eyes centered on that piece of jewelry, which suddenly became symbolic of the disciplined existence to which she had committed herself. That litany of rules, recited in the instructor's deadly dry voice . . .

". . . now there are exactly two parts of the uniform that can be worn in public on layovers—coats, either winter or rain, and your shoes or boots. Hair scarfs are allowed if they're tied so they're not more than a half-inch wide at the knot . . . ."

She knew, even at this stage of training, that most of the rules made sense. That makeup, for instance, was more than merely for appearance—flying dried out the skin and required a daily application of cleansers and toning lotions.

Danni welcomed the lunch break, when the class fled to the TNA West End cafeteria. The food was dull but plentiful and free. Each girl carried a small I.D. card marked "Trainee," which she showed to the cashier who marked the cost of the meal on a long sheet. To Danni the huge room, antiseptic in decor, quickly became an oasis. It was a place where she and her classmates could share concerns, bolster morale, strengthen backbones.

Pressure came from three directions: the need to accumulate a vast amount of knowledge in a pitifully short time; the uncomfortable bounds of rules and regulations foreign to a healthy, free-minded girl; and fear of failure.

What saved Danni was her natural sympathy for classmates even more jittery than herself. Joan Pierce was one of those—she spent the entire lunch hour that second day eating in virtual silence, smiling weakly at the banter and chatter as if she were eavesdropping instead of participating. Walking back to the class-room, she said suddenly, "I guess I might as well go home before they send me home."

"Oh, for God's sake," Julie snorted, "you're doing better than most of the class—you passed codes and seven flunked. Don't talk foolish."

"That may be the only test I pass. I didn't even have to study—I remembered those codes from my res agent days. It's when I think of what we've got ahead of us that I panic. All that safety stuff and cabin service."

Danni had been thinking precisely the same thing, but she put one arm around Joan's shoulders. "It's a mistake to anticipate. We have to take one thing at a time . . . if we start worrying about next week, we won't get through this one."

"Good advice," Julie said, smiling at Danni. She was well aware that her roommate was worried, but if Danni had the gumption to give Joan a pat on the back, she was going to be fine.

Yet not even Julie was prepared for Marlene Compton's angry reaction to a minor transgression committed by the class beauty, Linda Percival. She arrived at the afternoon grooming session five minutes late.

"I'm sorry," she gasped. "I was in the restroom and—"

The instructor chopped off the rest of the explanation. "You can give me your excuse in private after class. And I hope for your sake it's a good one. If there's one thing I will not tolerate it's tardiness, whether it's five seconds or five minutes. You all might as well get used to the idea that as long as you fly, your lives will be ruled by the clock. Anyone who can't accept this might as well start packing. Now, Jackie, I'll let you go into posture . . ."

Danni sneaked a look at Linda's embarrassed face, feeling sympathy along with a deliciously selfish relief. Walking back to the Everglades Inn after class, she asked Linda what Marlene had said to her.

"She really chewed me out. I tried to explain I had just started my period and I was so nervous about being late I had trouble with the Tampax. Marlene said I used bad judgment."

"Bad judgment?"

"Yeah. She said I should have come to the classroom on time, explained the problem, and she would have excused me."

"Christ," Danni breathed, "if it happens to me I'd rather bleed to death."

Pat Martin, walking behind them, said, "Childish crap."

Danni turned around. "Huh?"

"Just plain crap. They're treating us like children. Compton makes a federal case out of Linda being a little late, and all those stupid rules. Like curfews and bed checks and petty grooming regulations. Does wearing the wrong shade of lipstick really make you a bad stewardess?"

"No," Danni said thoughtfully. "But I suppose they figure if you're careless about little things, you'll be careless about the important ones. All I know is that I'm going to play their game. I just want to graduate—I'll gripe about the rules later."

They spent the rest of the first week on aircraft familiarization, from aeronautical nomenclature to intensive study of the three types of planes TNA was operating—Convair 240, Lockheed Constellation, and Douglas DC-7. Danni had flown frequently, but there was a vast chasm between her former role as a passenger and her exposure to an airliner cabin that would be a working environment.

What she had taken for granted or never noticed as a passenger became intricate technical objects to be conquered, even something as simple as the inside lock on a lavatory door. "You have to know how to open it from the outside," Marlene explained, "just in case someone gets stuck in there. All you do is take the tip of a ballpoint pen and slide the latch this way . . ."

Never again would Danni call an airplane lavatory a toilet. It was the Blue Room, a designation whose derivation apparently stemmed from the airlines' general practice of using a blue color scheme. Ironically, TNA's DC-7 Blue Rooms were a light green.

Previously, Danni had ignored such items as oxygen bottles and fire extinguishers. Now she had to learn how they operated. She had seen stewardesses open a passenger service kit to bring out a deck of playing cards; now she had to become familiar with all the contents of such kits—from aspirin to forms that had to be filled out after every trip. She had blithely assumed that serving a pre-dinner cocktail was a task a monkey could be trained to perform. Now she was initiated into the intricacies of the liquor kits, with color-coded tags that indicated what stock was inside and in what quantity.

She fell in love with the twin-engine Convair, simply because it was smaller and therefore less complex than the big Connies and DC-7s. Yet even the 240 seemed huge when she viewed it as a place in which to work. In an empty cabin its forty seats looked like a hundred forty, and its interior was filled with unfamiliar gadgets that to her inexperienced eyes were nothing but booby traps strategically located so a trainee could trip over one and be blown into dismissal. The switch that opened the airstairs . . . the panel for the cabin lights . . . the PA microphone setup, and the cockpit-cabin communications system—one bell indicating they were ready to take off, two bells meaning the pilots were calling, three bells warning that the seat belt sign had been turned on requiring that all belts be checked, and four bells for an impending emergency. It did little good to hear Marlene keep insisting, "By the time you graduate, you'll be as familiar with this stuff as you are now with a knife or spoon." Just when Danni had become reasonably proficient in the technique of unlocking a Blue Room door, she found herself struggling to overcome the complexities of activating an oxygen bottle. It was like climbing one mountain only to find a higher one in her path.

As she had feared, she could not conquer her old phobia—speaking up before the class. Marlene's technique was to fire unexpected questions at random, not only to test knowledge and attention but also to build poise and self-assurance. Danni dreaded these moments. Facts she knew perfectly well seemed frozen in her mind, unable to find the outlet in her tongue. She could see Marlene's impatience and consoled herself with the knowledge that she was doing well on all the tests.

The tests.

Always there were tests.

Tests on the functions of the Civil Aeronautics Board and the

Civil Aeronautics Administration. On TNA history. On uniform regulations and airline terminology. On location of emergency equipment and the twenty-four-hour clock.

Somehow she passed them all that first week, and so did the rest of 55-10, absorbing into their tired brains material that they parroted back on their test papers . . .

. . . *give the location of the walk-around oxygen bottle on the DC-7 . . . what are the three types of fires and which extinguisher would you use on each . . . translate the following Zulu time units into conventional time: 0355; 1330; 0120; 1943 . . . which government agency is responsible for certification of aircraft and crews . . . what are the names of TNA's president and the senior vice presidents of Marketing, Operations, and Finance . . . define the following terms: aileron, elevators, yoke . . .*

Their bodies as well as their brains were on trial. Every morning, Marlene inspected them with the hypercritical eyes of a Marine D.I., and she nailed Danni once for carelessly applied lipstick and the next morning for "inexcusably sloppy hair."

At the end of the first week, the instructor finished a discourse on the procedures for filling out various forms, from Liquor Inventory to Trip Discrepancy Sheet, and surveyed her battered charges. They stared back through dull eyes, a flicker of hate in a few.

"I think you've taken enough for today," she said in a tone of unexpected sympathy, "so I'll dismiss you early. It's been a rough week—I know that. But I'm not just a little bit proud of you. Each one of you was someone special before you started training, because we accept only one of every forty applicants. Now you're even more special—you've come through the first week with no washouts. Usually we lose one or even two in the first five days, but not fifty-five-ten. But don't get cocky—the next four weeks will be even harder. Next Monday we start meal and cocktail service so study your manuals. I expect you to relax some, so just keep the curfew rules in mind—you never know when I'll pull a bed check."

Danni did more studying than relaxing, although she did join Julie, Pat, Rose, and Joan for dinner Saturday night in a Miami restaurant that was a welcome change from the cafeteria menu. On

Sunday afternoon, Julie suggested a respite from the books.

"Let's take a swim," she said.

Danni, tempted, finally shook her head. "I'll pass. I spent all day yesterday at that damned pool and I'm water-logged. You go ahead—I'm going to lie here and think beautiful thoughts."

"If you're as horny as I am, you'll think erotic thoughts. Or don't you indulge in passionate fantasies?" She asked the question so bluntly and unexpectedly that Danni blushed.

"Oh, I indulge now and then," she laughed, a little self-consciously. "But not lately. I can't get worried about sex when I'm so worried about training. I'm either too tired or I'm thinking about the way I get tongue-tied when Marlene throws a question at me."

Julie gave her a glance that mixed curiosity with affection. "Are you a virgin, Danni?"

The answer came promptly, touched with pride and a trace of defiance. "Yes. Although I'm afraid the guy I'll marry won't believe it."

"Why?"

"It seems a horse threw me a couple of years ago and I started to bleed. The doctor told me I ruptured the . . . the, you know . . ."

"Hymen," Julie finished for her. "You were lucky. I always thought we should lose that symbol of virginity at birth, like circumcising boys. Maybe I should use that horseback-riding alibi on my wedding night. It really happened?"

"It did. So I guess I'm a moral if not a technical virgin."

"Well, my class virgin list still stands at a positive four."

"Four? Only four?" Danni was amused yet surprised at Julie's analysis of 55-10's sexual proclivities.

"Katie, Betty Jo, and Mary Beth—they've already confessed to being virgins, if confessed is the right word. I'm not sure about Carol Veskos or Rose. Joan's been married. Linda told me she slept with a guy she went steady with, and Terry's no innocent. Pat Martin's a probable."

"Probable virgin or probable non-virgin?"

"The latter." Julie chuckled. "Carol and Rose just smiled when I asked them. But Pat—she blew my head off. Said it wasn't any of my goddamned business. Boy, she's got a short fuse."

Danni nodded unhappily. "Short fuse and a chip on her shoulder. One week of training and she's already mad at Marlene, the company, and the whole airline industry."

"She doesn't seem too fond of you either," Julie observed.

Danni had already suspected this, more from vibes than from overt animosity, but hearing her suspicions confirmed disturbed her. She was having enough trouble without incurring a classmate's enmity, and somehow she felt a grudging respect for Pat. A feeling that buried under her belligerence was a kind of stubborn courage and honesty. An admission that sometimes Pat gave voice to views the others discreetly kept to themselves. Danni frowned and decided to change the subject.

"You left one gal off your list, Julie. How about Meredith?"

"The class swinger," Julie ruled. "But someone to be envied— she's the only one with a date this weekend. I can't wait for her to come back with all the juicy details. If the rest of us have to take the veil for five weeks, at least we can enjoy life vicariously. God, I never thought I'd see the day when swimming became a form of sublimation. Come on, roomie—a little dip will do you good."

Danni was firm. "Nope. Matter of fact, I think I'll hit the books for a while longer. We start Convair cabin service tomorrow."

Instead of leaving, Julie plopped on Danni's bed. "There's such a thing as over-study, Danni. And you have less to worry about than some of the others. Nobody's getting higher grades than you on the tests."

"Nobody's getting the dirty looks Marlene gives me when I can't answer a verbal question. I'm scared, Julie. I think I'd die if they washed me out."

"You're too damned conscientious, that's your trouble," Julie decided in a burst of instant analysis. "That's probably what's wrong with your sex life. Too much conscience." She chuckled at Danni's expression, half-intrigued and half-disapproving. "Danni, I'm choosier than I sound, honest. I enjoy sex with men I really like. Men who have the same attitude about it as I do—fun with no strings attached. Does that bother you? Make you think less of me?"

42

"No. It just isn't the way I feel about it. I couldn't go to bed with someone I wouldn't want to marry if . . . something went wrong."

Julie sighed. "Typical hang-up. You're afraid of pregnancy, not sex. Which means you may never enjoy sex because all you'll do is worry about getting knocked up."

"I wouldn't worry if I loved him. That's what it's all about, isn't it?"

"Sure, but what do I do while waiting around for Mr. Right Guy—play with myself?"

Danni blushed—masturbation *had* been an occasional means of relief for her, but she'd die before admitting it to Julie or anyone else. "If you keep busy enough, you don't have time to think about sex," she argued, trying to keep in her voice a conviction she did not quite feel, and Julie sensed it.

"Don't build your own prison, Danni," she said seriously. "I'm not saying you should go out and become Miss Round Heels of nineteen fifty-five. I'm not saying you don't need certain moral standards, codes of ethics, or whatever you want to call it. I have my own standards, half-assed as they are compared to yours. But I want to have fun, too. I'm no pushover for anything in pants, Danni—honest to God, I'm not. I want my knight on the white charger someday, too, just like you. I just don't intend to lock myself behind bars waiting for said knight to show up with a set of keys."

"You seem," Danni said without rancor, "to be describing me as one large, living chastity belt."

"No. I'm describing you as a very fine person who worries so much about possible consequences that she's put herself in a kind of straitjacket. Like training, for example. You do great on written tests and you won't open your yap in class. Why? Because you're so damned scared of giving Marlene a wrong answer that you can't remember the right answer."

"You're right," Danni admitted. "I'm afraid of flunking. Of seeing all my dreams go up in smoke."

"How the hell did you become a teacher with an attitude like that?"

"I guess because children aren't my peers. My judges. I suspect I was a good teacher simply because I felt sympathy for little people with my own weakness. Remember when Marlene gave us that first walk-through on the Convair?"

Julie nodded.

"Well, I kept fantasizing there were people sitting in all those empty seats. A whole cabin full of passengers who trusted me, depended on me. Julie, I just can't flunk out . . ."

Impulsively, Julie hugged her. "You won't, roomie. You want it too badly to screw it up."

"Or maybe just too badly, period," Danni said solemnly. "Go take your swim."

They finished studying and had just turned on the eleven o'clock news when Marlene Compton arrived at the dorm for a surprise Sunday night bedcheck. Mary Beth Davenport, who was in the next room, tapped lightly but distinctly on the door of 210.

"It's Marlene," Mary Beth whispered. "She's checking everyone."

"Fine," Julie said. "Let's invite her in for a Coke."

"You don't understand. Meredith's not back yet."

"Oh shit!"

Danni asked in a low voice. "Can we stall her?"

"Only by knocking her cold before she gets to 212," Julie said. "That goddamned stupid Meredith."

"What'll we do?" Mary Beth asked.

Julie had an inspiration. "Tell her Meredith's in the shower."

"That won't do any good," Danni objected. "If she looks in the shower, she's liable to lower the boom on Mary Beth for lying."

"She'll be here any minute," Mary Beth said. "I don't know what to tell her."

"Tell her the truth," Danni advised.

Julie glared at her roommate. "She can't do that. It'll mean a pink slip for Meredith. She deserves one, but I sure wouldn't want to be the fink responsible. Look, Mary Beth, tell Marlene she went downstairs to make a phone call or get a soft drink. Or you *think* she did. Or maybe . . ." Julie stopped, aware that she was improvising hopelessly. They could hear the footsteps on the worn corridor carpeting and tapping on a nearby door.

Mary Beth peeked outside and groaned. "Too late. She just went into two-fifteen. I'd better get back. Oh, damn that roommate of mine!" She went back to 212, leaving Danni and Julie staring at one another; they felt like a pair of helpless Kansas farmers who had seen a tornado form nearby and were waiting for it to strike. It was Danni who half-croaked, "Come in" at the polite, falsely discreet knock.

"Hi," Marlene greeted them. "You two have a good weekend?"

"Great," Julie said weakly. "Just great."

"Something wrong, Julie? You look a bit pale."

"Uh . . . just tired, I guess."

"Oh?" For a moment the instructor paused. "Well, get a good night's sleep. See you in class tomorrow."

"Right."

The door closed behind Marlene, but Julie jumped up as soon as she heard the knock at 212, opening their own door a crack so they could hear.

"Good evening, Mary Beth."

"Hello, Marlene."

A pause. ("She's looking around the room," Julie deduced unnecessarily.)

"Where's Meredith?"

Another pause. ("Poor Mary Beth," Danni whispered.)

"Uh . . . ah . . . I think she . . . she must be down getting a Coke. Or maybe she's making a phone . . . oh shit!" (Sound of sobbing.)

Marlene's own voice was soft and sympathetic. "That's all right, Mary Beth. That's all right. I understand." ("Understand what?" Julie demanded. "Mary Beth's crying or Meredith's being late?")

They heard the door being closed, then another tapping on another door.

Danni and Julie waited with Mary Beth in the latter's room for

Meredith's return. She showed up at 11:45.

"Hi, guys! Boy, what a weekend! Let me tell you, it was . . ." She stopped, suddenly aware that they were staring at her.

"Marlene made a bed check tonight," Mary Beth said quietly.

Meredith turned pale. She sat down heavily on her bed, one trembling hand on her forehead. "Oh, Christ—what did she say?"

"She didn't say anything. Just asked where you were."

"What did you tell her?"

Mary Beth's voice cracked along with her emotions. "What the hell did you expect me to tell her? That you were out with the president of Trans-National?"

"Jesus, you could have said something. Anything to cover up for me." Tears began to flow.

"I . . . I started to tell her you were downstairs getting a Coke or using the pay phone. But I couldn't get the words out. She would have known I was lying. Damn you, Meredith! Goddamn you anyway! You had plenty of time to fuck the whole bloody weekend without missing curfew. And you expected me to lie for you! I couldn't do it. Meredith—I just couldn't. I'm sorry . . ." Now they were both crying.

Danni was crying, too, and Julie covered up her misery the only way she could. With a wisecrack.

"If Marlene lowers the boom," she said, "you've just had the most expensive orgasm in history."

Meredith arrived for class Monday morning with carefully applied makeup and the darker shade of hair Marlene had ordered. To Danni, however, she was a pitiful sight—dressed to be killed, she thought unhappily. And the execution came swiftly.

Meredith was just starting to take her seat when Marlene called her out of the room. "Bring your manual with you," she added. Marlene returned, accompanied by an instructor Danni had not seen before.

"This is Laura Talton," she announced. "I have to go down to Mr. Perkins' office and Laura will start you off on Convair cabin service."

Laura had had time only to show a film on the 240's galley arrangement when Marlene came back, excused the other instructor, and then faced the silent class.

"I think you should know we've terminated Meredith Gaskin," she said. "I know what it means to lose a classmate and I'm truly sorry—believe it or not, *I* hate to lose a student. But we meant business on that curfew rule and I hope you'll all learn from this unhappy experience."

She paused, conscious of the stares from the class—some shocked, some angry. Her jaw tightened. "Any questions?"

Mary Beth cleared her throat nervously. "I'd like to go back to the hotel with her. I could help her pack . . ."

"No." The refusal was kind but firm. "She's already gone, Mary Beth. You can call her at home tonight if you'd like, although I'd suggest you wait for her to call you."

Danni asked impulsively, "Why? I should think she'd want to talk to somebody."

Marlene shook her head. "That's not the way it works. I've seen this happen too many times—in fact, it happened to my roommate two days before graduation. First there were tears, then pleas for another chance, and then comes stage three—resentment and bitterness. It's then that they shouldn't talk to anyone; they're in a state of shock. Meredith will be fine when the initial pain goes away, which is why I suggested you let her call first. If it'll make you feel any better, I told her to wait a month or so and apply to another airline—that if she's learned her lesson, she can still make a good stewardess."

But even as Marlene launched into a lecture on the Convair galley, Danni was thinking, *I wonder how I'd take it if it happened to me.*

Danni, like quite a few thousand other students before her, found cabin service training the most enjoyable part of the five-week ordeal. They practiced in the realistic atmosphere of cabin mockups with authentic seats and galleys that actually worked. The class itself took turns being passengers and stewardesses.

Danni had no trouble with the liquor service; her father was a social drinker and she already knew how to mix a dry martini and the different brands of various whiskeys. In this respect she was considerably ahead of a neophyte like Betty Jo whose knowledge of alcohol was confined to a vague idea of what went into a mint julep, or a teetotaler like Joan who considered one beer a daring foray into depravity.

Meal service was something else. Danni's lack of dexterity was her chief enemy. She was awkward in the galley and not a little clumsy in the service when she had to concentrate on technique. Marlene kept scolding her: "Smile, Danni! Damnit, smile and be pleasant!"

After three days she could provide a reasonably competent meal service, although she had trouble smiling and serving simultaneously—her mind was locked into a single question: *Am I doing it right?*

The afternoon devoted to practice PA announcements was torture. Danni had decided to deliver her "Welcome aboard" messages in a dignified, modulated tone, a decision denounced by Marlene. "Louder! More authoritative! You're not delivering a funeral eulogy, for God's sake! Listen to how Terry does it."

Terry. Even more than Julie, the epitome of a potentially great stewardess. The perfect alchemy of humor and personality. For a moment, Danni hated her.

On Thursday of the second week, however, Terry flunked a DC-7 familiarization test, then failed the retake. She was on her way home that night, tearfully angry but not any more stunned than her classmates. Pat Martin wanted to draw up a petition in her behalf and present it to both Marlene and Ed Perkins; it was Danni who objected.

"You know damned well she'd be a credit to this airline," Pat argued. "Just because she flunked a couple of tests . . ."

"Marlene laid down the rule on our first day. Two failures on any given test and that's it. They can't make any exceptions, Pat. They didn't for Meredith and they couldn't for Terry."

"There was one hell of a lot of difference between Meredith and Terry," Pat said. "Terry deserved a second chance, simply because she was everything a good stewardess should be. Just a little weak on the technical stuff, but we all should have her personality."

"She didn't know the DC-Seven," Danni said. "In an emergency, personality wouldn't do her much good. You said she was 'just a little weak on the technical stuff'—well, in my book that's just as important as being able to smile."

"Spoken like the true company peon," Pat sneered. "Just follow the rules no matter how arbitrary or unfair. Believe everything the company tells you. Obey orders blindly. For Christ's sake, Danni, you might as well have joined the Marines! They've screwed one of your classmates and you haven't got the guts to stand up and fight for her."

"She doesn't deserve to be fought for," Danni snapped. "She flunked two tests in a row, including the retake."

"So what? We should all have her personality—she's everything a good stewardess should be. She's being kicked out on a technicality—a totally unreasonable, unrealistic technicality that makes absolutely no sense."

"It makes a lot of sense. Whether we like it or not, we're caught in a mold, and that's the only way to train a collection of individualists. Maybe some of us can break the mold later, after we've flown a while, but not now. We need a system designed for beginners, and a system means rules and regulations, no matter how silly and petty they seem. Go make cracks about my joining the Marines, Pat, but that's exactly what we've all done. They're teaching us discipline. Maybe that's a dirty word to you but it's not to me. Discipline means automatic reaction to an emergency and that's why Terry flunked. She couldn't react automatically because she didn't know her stuff."

"And you think you know it? You're a fine one to talk—going into a blue funk every time Marlene asks you a question in class. What will *you* do in an emergency—haul out your test grades?"

Danni flushed with an anger so great that she momentarily choked; it was Julie who came to her defense. "Knock it off, Pat! We're discussing what to do about Terry, not Danni."

"If you're all as mealy-mouthed as Danni, you won't do anything. Let me tell all of you something. Before I went to work for a city councilman, I had jobs with five different corporations.

Big ones. And they were all alike. Cold-blooded, unfeeling, inhuman, and ruthless. Full of gung-ho platitudes and phony slogans, just like this beloved airline of ours. If you don't stand up for your rights, they'll walk all over you."

Danni got her voice back. "Trainees don't have any rights, Pat. That's what you can't get through your skull. We're all on probation, through training and for five months after we fly the line. You're ready to declare war and we haven't even learned how to fight yet. I'm just as sorry about Terry as you are, but I won't sign any petition. It's dumb and it's wrong."

"Neither will I," Julie said, and Pat knew she had lost—every class had a leader and theirs was Julie. But in their room later that night, Julie asked Danni a question the latter was asking herself.

"What I can't figure out, roomie, is how come you can stand up to a rabble-rouser like Pat and then go into that deep freeze in class."

"I wish I knew," Danni said.

The next morning was devoted to a lecture on the handling of problem passengers. As usual Danni listened to what was being said, and as usual she made copious notes. Marlene called on her once: "Can you think of another kind of problem that might arise, Danni?"

She shook her head. Marlene frowned and asked Julie, who wondered about the proper etiquette for responding to "a . . . uh . . . ah . . . a goose."

"A firm glare," Marlene advised amid much laughter. "But keep your real opinion to yourself—unless he tries it a second time."

At the lunch break, Danni put her manual under her seat and rose to start out the door with Julie.

"Danni," Marlene called out. "I'd like to see you in my office."

She paused.

"And bring your manual."

Chapter 4

She tried to convince herself she would not cry or plead, a resolve that deteriorated with each step of the way toward Marlene's small office on the first floor of the center. By the time she arrived there, she was battling an urge to surrender—*Make it mercifully quick, tell me I'm through, and send me home.*

Her heart sank even further when she saw that the office was already occupied by a third person: Ed Perkins, the training director.

He was a heavyset man with red hair, freckles, and dimples that were a pair of miniature crevasses. His appearance was deceptively informal and friendly; in actuality, his toughness was reflected by his nickname: the Smiling Executioner. He rose as Danni and Marlene entered, nodding pleasantly, but with a tightness that seemed to harden the dimples.

"Sit down, Danni," Marlene said. "You know Mr. Perkins." It was a statement, not a question. "Danni, I'm afraid Mr. Perkins and I have just about decided you aren't going to make it."

She paused, obviously judging the effect of her words on the girl. "It isn't your grades—they've been fine. But for two weeks you haven't opened your mouth in class. You've given me the impression that either you're in a perpetual state of fright or you're really not too interested. Am I being unfair?"

The fact that she had at least asked the question unlocked Danni's frozen tongue.

"Not unfair." She hesitated. "But you're wrong—I'm nervous, not scared, and I'm very interested." She took a deep breath, conscious that both Perkins and the instructor would be weighing her every word. "I . . . I guess I've always been something of an introvert. Not because I'm afraid to speak up but because I've been taught not to say anything unless it was something important."

Perkins wore a look that Danni could only interpret as a mixture of cynicism and disbelief. But Marlene's lips curled up in a faint smile.

"True, I haven't asked you to deliver any world-shaking pronouncements. But I do expect all trainees to participate in classroom discussions. To volunteer suggestions or opinions. To demonstrate orally that they've grasped the material and at the same time show me a bit of initiative and presence. You can't go through an airline career writing out answers on a test paper. A good stewardess is a combination of mechanical knowledge and the far more intangible quality of personality. In that latter respect, you've shown serious deficiencies."

Ed Perkins spoke. "Which, I might add, surprises me. Fred Jordan, the man who interviewed you, rated you absolutely tops. Is there anything bothering you, Danni? Any personal problems we should know about?"

She shook her head, grateful for his air of sympathy and grasping at it as a glimmer of encouragement. "I . . . I guess I've always been better talking on a one-to-one basis."

Perkins' eyes narrowed. "There are forty passengers on a two-forty, Danni. Sixty-eight on the Connie and seventy-two on the DC-seven. Do I make my point?" He stood up, stared outside the office's small window, and then wheeled back.

"It's my personal judgment that Fred Jordan was wrong about you." Danni's heart sank. "But he isn't wrong very often, and your grades at least show that you're not over your head scholastically. With Marlene's permission, I'm going to give you one more chance."

Danni nodded dumbly.

"Monday morning, I want you to get up in class and talk for at least fifteen minutes on one topic. If Marlene tells me you did okay, I'll let you stay on. But if she doesn't think your performance adequate, I'll have to terminate you. Do you want to try it?"

"I'll try," Danni said. "What should I talk about?"

The director smiled thinly. "Marlene will give you the subject at oh-eight-hundred—when the class begins."

Monday, 0800.

"Danni," Marlene said in a voice of deadly calm, "you will please tell the class everything you know about Eleanor Roosevelt."

Danni's mind went absolutely blank, and only dimly did she hear Julie groan audibly and the rest of the class gasp. She had spent the weekend desperately theorizing what subject Marlene might choose. Julie had been sure it would be an aeronautical topic, while her other concerned classmates guessed at everything from "My Favorite Vacation" to "Infant Care." Even Pat Martin got into the game, suggesting that an autobiographical sketch would be a logical choice, and Danni prayed it would be something as easy as that.

Eleanor Roosevelt? There had to be a cement-filled bowling ball sitting in the pit of her stomach. Of all the lousy, unreasonable, miserable, impossible . . .

Yet with that surge of anger came an erasure of panic and a resentment so strong that it seemed to free her locked brain and begin shoving words out of her mouth.

"As most of you probably know," she began, "Eleanor Roosevelt became famous as the wife of Franklin Delano Roosevelt, the president of the United States. Yet she won additional fame not merely because she was the wife of a president, but also because she was the most active first lady who ever occupied the White House . . ."

Words became sentences, sentences mushroomed into paragraphs, terror was replaced by confidence. In truth, she possessed only a smattering of knowledge about Eleanor Roosevelt, but with the instincts of a gambler, she guessed that nobody else in that

53

room knew much about Eleanor Roosevelt either.

She sneaked a glance at the wall clock, which told her she had exhausted all the factual data available to her memory in the first four minutes. She sighed, took a deep breath, and fell back to the trenches of pure imagination, discussing Eleanor's unconventional methods of raising children, Eleanor's unspoken desire to go into politics herself and become the nation's first woman president—the latter a gold mine of a topic because it allowed her to speculate for a full ten minutes on what kind of president Eleanor would have made.

"But of course," Danni explained, "this ambition was never realized because she decided that her duty to her husband and his career deserved priority over her own dreams . . ."

She sneaked a glance at the wall clock and discovered she had been talking for nineteen minutes. She took a deep breath.

"And finally, it was none other than Franklin Roosevelt's bitterest political rival, Senator Robert Taft, who once declared that the wrong member of the Roosevelt family got elected. I thank you."

The class burst into applause.

She could not resist it. She turned toward Marlene and bowed deeply, the exaggerated gesture merely another way of thumbing her nose.

The experience changed her.

At first she recognized the obvious symptoms, apparent in her new-found classroom confidence. But gradually she began to realize she had undergone not just an application of psychological cosmetics, but a psychological branding that was permanent and deep.

Along with confidence, she felt the first stirrings of a desire to lead and command, not merely to follow. It was as if an emotional logjam had been dynamited, setting free latent abilities and ambitions. She discovered that her gift of introspection, so personally confining and potentially crippling, had suddenly and magically blossomed into an awareness of her strengths.

It was not conceit or overconfidence that had been born within her; it was the acknowledgement that she was more adept than she had ever imagined—she had seen, and would always remember, the kaleidoscope of expressions that coursed over Marlene's face as she ad-libbed her way through the Eleanor Roosevelt ordeal. It ran from concern to surprise to amusement to awe to pride. Almost as if the instructor's reactions were registering Danni's own inner metamorphosis.

By the end of the third week, she had begun to grasp the logic of the entire training process. Her mind and body were becoming disciplined. In the beginning, memorization was merely a tool for passing the tests. But as she became familiar with the aircraft and their myriad items of cabin equipment, the abstract lessons of the classroom began to take on practicality. Theories merged into facts and imagination was transformed into reality.

The sample oxygen bottles hanging on the classroom wall, once so ominous in their complexity, now were inanimate tools as simple to operate as a screwdriver—she could turn the knobs and valves with practiced swiftness and a casualness she never dreamed possible. She had learned how to lift hot entrée dishes out of a galley oven, using the awkward prongs that had to have been designed by a scientist who hated food. She had learned how to carry trays without spilling a drop, flawlessly spread first-class linen on a seatback tray with one hand while holding the meal tray in the other, and aim the white, icy foam of a fire extinguisher at the base of a roaring blaze.

But still there was more memorization. Like section 6, page 5 of the manual—"EMERGENCY PROCEDURES AND EQUIP-MENT":

Planned Emergency

During a known emergency, the Captain will notify the Senior Stewardess of a possible emergency by:
—two bells for the interphone
—if time is critical, the
   PA system.
The Senior should ask the Captain:

—what type of emergency
—how much time to prepare
—when and who will give bracing
   signal
—any special instructions

The following steps outline your planned-emergency responsibilities:

1. Cabin crew coordination
2. Passenger briefing
3. Passenger relocation if necessary
4. Assignment of bracing positions
5. Briefing of able-bodied passengers
6. Securing of cabin
7. Giving of prearranged bracing signal by
   Captain or Senior
8. Turning off cabin lights
9. Assuming stewardess bracing positions

She memorized those nine steps until she could recite them instinctively—and she had to, because Marlene would fire a question on emergency procedures in the middle of such prosaic instructions as the art of serving coffee.

"*. . . and don't forget, offer magazines before you ask whether they'd like coffee. Danni, what's step three in a planned emergency?*"

"*Uh, passenger relocation if necessary.*"

"*Pretty good, but a second too long. Katie, what's step eight?*"

"*Ah . . . uh . . . let's see . . . you secure the cabin.*"

"*Wrong. That's step six. Eight is cabin lights. Kate, what's your boyfriend's name?*"

"*Joe.*"

"*That's how fast I want you to respond. Now the thing to emphasize in pre-takeoff service is . . . .*"

First aid, from delivering babies to recognizing and treating symptoms of lack of oxygen; from bleeding to burns, headaches to heart attacks. Manuals, films, role-playing—Danni simulated a passenger stricken with a coronary while Julie and Mary Beth applied emergency oxygen.

Emergency evacuations. Selection of able-bodied passengers, ABPs, who would have to be the first ones out of the airplane (via ropes) so they could hold the evac slides steady. "Always look for military people, law enforcement officers, or airline employees," Marlene advised. "And don't pick the men you'd like to marry— you'll need the husky ones, the calm ones, not the handsome faces and the Hickey-Freeman suits. And remember, do your mental picking when they board, if possible, because you might not have time when the emergency strikes. Always remember, in an emergency your own life has the lowest priority of all . . ."

The time would come when Danni would remember such things as hand-held evac slides in the same spirit in which a nuclear scientist would look back on oil lamps. But this was 1955, nearing the end of the piston-engine era, and in her eyes the Constellation/DC-7 slides were the last word in safety equipment; her beloved Convairs had only ropes. She kept insisting to Julie that she'd be happy never to bid anything but Convair trips—and knew she'd never stick to this resolve. Even at this stage of training there was an excitement about a career structured around change— different planes, different cities, different people, different hours. The peripatetic aspects of stewardess life were a major part of her professional ambitions to begin with.

At the start of the fourth week, Marlene sent 55-10 to the offices of the local firm that made TNA uniforms, for the exhilarating purpose of being fitted. Danni was surprised to discover she had dropped six pounds—"All of it in blood, sweat, and tears," she sighed to Julie.

"When Winston Churchill coined the phrase," Julie agreed, "he must have had Marlene Compton in mind."

Yet both were aware that the relationship between instructor and class had begun to alter. Danni sensed it before really experiencing it—the pressure, the volume of instruction, the demand for perfection remained the same. Yet in the stridency, the incessant pounding of repeated facts, there was a new note, one of growing respect for the inmates of 55-10, out of the instructor's knowledge that the training was taking effect, that the class was being molded and forged and hardened. The answers now were coming swiftly, without hesitation; the classroom discussions were livelier with more participation—including that of Danni, who could realize in her own strengthened maturity what was happening. The whole class was more confident, more at ease; the lighter moments and the laughs more frequent . . .

"Yes, Danni?"

"Marlene, I was wondering in an emergency evac if we could direct passengers to the cockpit window ropes."

"Generally speaking, it's a lousy idea."

"Why?"

"Because when everything hits the fan, those windows are gonna be full of pilot butts."

The final weekend before graduation was spent in the air, on familiarization flights. Known as FAMS, they were for observation purposes, giving the trainees a chance to see classroom lessons applied to actual service.

They had been split into two groups, Danni and Julie joining Linda, Rose, and Carol on a Miami–New York round trip Saturday and to Chicago and return Sunday. The New York trip was on a DC-7, only half-full on this warm July day, providing the trainees an opportunity to talk to the stewardesses as well as to watch.

The senior had been flying three years. She was a pleasant-faced girl with merry eyes, and her friendliness was warming. Her willingness to impart information emboldened Danni.

"If you need any help, I'd . . . we'd be glad to do whatever you want," she offered. "Anything simple, that is."

The senior's eyes twinkled. "Let's see—you're on a FAM so you must be going into your fourth week."

"Fifth."

"Fifth? We got FAMS after the third week but I guess they must have changed the curriculum since I went through Devil's Island. Well, if a couple of you guys would like to help pass out the breakfast trays, I think I could use you." Danni and Julie had their hands up before she was halfway through the sentence; they were uncomfortably conscious that they looked like a pair of schoolgirls clamoring to recite.

"Okay, you two can come back to the galley with me. Where are the rest of the trainees?" Linda, Rose, and Carol raised their hands. "You three can help with tray pickups afterward."

Trans-National's DC-7s were equipped with seat-back trays; it was a simple task to first go through the cabin making sure the trays were down, and it was just as simple to place the meal trays on top of them—following prescribed procedures. As Danni worked, she could hear Marlene's voice . . .

"*. . . and when you help them lower their trays, be sure and ask, 'Would you care to have breakfast with us?' or 'How about joining us for breakfast?'. . . Don't forget to serve the passenger in the window seat first so you don't have to lean over anyone who's already eating. . . Make sure the entrée is directly in front of the passenger when you put down the tray . . .*"

She couldn't resist asking the senior about certain deviations from the in-flight service rules 55-10 had been taught were sacrosanct. "Like putting the hot breakfast rolls on the tray with the orange juice instead of serving them separately before you bring the breakfast. And I noticed we didn't offer coffee before takeoff."

"Well, it seems Catering was short about ten rolls this morning, which meant nobody was going to get seconds. If we had served them separately beforehand, people probably would have wanted more. As for the coffee, one of our coffee-makers is on the fritz so I decided we'd better conserve the supply and pour it after the breakfast trays were out. As it turned out, we had just about enough."

"Oh," Danni said.

The senior laughed. "I take it you've seen a few rules broken on this trip."

"A few."

"Don't let it get you down. I felt exactly the same way when I was in training and took my first FAM flight. I saw enough rule-bending to make me wonder why the airline bothered to establish the rules in the first place."

"I can understand why you have to bend rules," Danni said, "but what would happen if there were a supervisor check-riding? Wouldn't she write you up?"

"Maybe, but she'd have to be a real shithead to do it. Look, once you graduate you'll find that service procedures and rules are nothing but generalized standards, aimed at stewardesses who can't really think for themselves. Until you're off six-month probation, it's a good idea to go by the book. But there are going to be times when you find the book can't solve every problem. Like today. There's nothing in the manual that tells you what to do when one coffee-maker doesn't work. So you improvise, as I did. What I really faced is what would make passengers the unhappiest—a shortage of coffee or a thirty-minute delay?"

Danni sighed. "I guess I've got a lot to learn."

The senior nodded, her face sober. "Those six months on probation, by the way, are considered an extension of your training. You can get fired pretty damned fast during that time, just as if you were still in school. But by the same token, nobody expects perfection—they assume you'll make mistakes." She looked at Danni's solemn expression. "What return flight do they have you on?"

"Let's see . . ." Danni pawed through her pocketbook and fished out the passes Marlene had distributed for the weekend. "I'm on five-twelve at five o'—I mean seventeen hundred."

The senior smiled. "Good girl. After a while, you'll forget how you used to tell time. Anyway, I'm glad I let you get the feel of things on this trip—you probably won't have much chance going back. That five-twelve's a Kosher Comet and it's always full. The gals'll be too busy to pay any attention to FAM riders."

"What's a Kosher Comet?" Danni asked.

"Lots of Jewish passengers. They're kind of fun. If they're orthodox Jews, they've ordered kosher meals ahead of time, and you sit around praying that Catering has boarded the right number. Hell hath no fury like someone who's ordered a special meal and doesn't get it—including whose who claim they ordered one and you know damned well they're bluffing."

"What do you do in a case like that?" Danni asked. "When

there aren't enough special meals, or when somebody insists they ordered one and you know they didn't?"

The senior shrugged. "Actually, you don't know for sure and that's the trouble. Chances are the passenger's lying but you can't accuse anyone of that. So you just apologize, you explain that Catering apparently has made a mistake, and you scrounge around for a makeshift meal the passenger can eat. Best thing to do is keep telling him how sorry you are and slip him a couple of free liquor miniatures. It'll usually work. Not always but usually."

The Monday morning after the FAMS weekend was devoted to debriefing, with the trainees discussing what they had seen and learned. Danni listened to the general chorus of approval and then raised her hand.

"I think the FAM trips could be a lot better," she said bluntly.

Marlene's eyebrows lifted. "In what way?"

"Well, going up to New York Saturday, the senior let us help serve. I learned more on that one flight than on the rest of the FAMS combined. I think they'd be more valuable if trainees were allowed to work."

"Possibly, except that we've had up to twenty girls on a FAM trip. You couldn't have twenty or even ten trainees wandering around a cabin without making it look like a Chinese fire drill."

"I wouldn't put twenty on one trip," Danni persisted. "I'd limit it to a couple per flight, maybe even one. And instead of just one or two FAMS, I'd assign a class to as many as possible so each flight would have not more than two trainees helping the regular stewardesses."

"I take it you found the experience of actually working more valuable than just observing."

"Much more," Danni said earnestly. "I . . . I got the feeling of what it's all about. It made what we learned in the classroom come alive."

"I see. Well, it's an interesting suggestion. Now, let's go on to . . ." But the instructor was thinking, *This was the class mute, so unsure of herself she didn't dare open her mouth. My God, how she's grown up . . .*

That afternoon, after the lunch break, Marlene turned 55-10 over to a uniformed pilot whom she introduced as Captain Howard McMasters. Danni decided instantly that he did not resemble Central Casting's image of a Greek-god airline captain. He was almost totally bald, with a pot belly and a florid face. Not a very impressive representative of the pilot profession, she thought.

She was wrong. McMasters was a spell-binder—warm, humorous, and above all instructive. Intermixed with his anecdotes was solid advice on the necessity of keeping the captain informed of cabin problems, yet not bothering him with those a stewardess should be able to solve herself.

"You are going to meet captains you'll want to clobber with a fire extinguisher," he said in a rumbly voice that went with his well-fed frame. "Martinets. Mean, foul-tempered bastards. Pilots with more arms than an octopus. Tightwads—hell, I know one captain who walks through a restaurant picking up the tips customers have left on the tables. But just when you're positive we're all unfeeling, lecherous, arrogant sonofabitches, you'll meet one who'll help you with a heavy bag, pick up a dinner check, or show you pictures of his wife and kids. Pilots are just people, kids. Regardless of our faults, we're still dedicated to getting our airplane from Point A to Point B as safely and efficiently as possible."

They applauded him when he finished. And Danni was thinking he didn't look ugly and fat as he left the room, giving Marlene a discreet but affectionate kiss on the check.

The next day, for the first time in 55-10's history, Marlene was late to class. At 0822 Laura Tilton came in, her face grim.

"Marlene's been detained," she announced in a low voice. "Unless you were watching or listening to the news this morning, you probably don't know we had a crash."

Danni felt a chill. "It was a training flight," Laura continued, "about an hour and a half ago. One of our DC-sevens collided with a Bolivian air cargo plane over the Everglades. There were no survivors. The captain was a close friend of Marlene's. That's all we know about the accident right now. I'm going to ask you to study quietly by yourselves—just review any material you're not sure of. Marlene will be here as soon as she can."

She walked out.

"Marlene must be crying her heart out," Julie guessed.

Pat Martin said, "I'll bet she doesn't show up at all."

"She will," Danni said, without knowing exactly why.

And twelve minutes later, Marlene arrived, facing the silent class with red eyes. For some reason, she fixed her gaze on Danni, as if she had only enough strength to look at one girl in the class.

"I apologize for being late," she smiled slightly, with an effort. "I seem to recall telling you that tardiness is an airline sin of major proportions, so I ask your forgiveness." She stopped, choked up, and for what seemed an eternity stared at the floor. Yet when she finally looked up again and spoke, her voice was steady and calm— so calm that Danni shuddered in realization of the willpower behind it.

"You all know what happened. Unfortunately, tragedy is a part of flying. It may affect one of you someday, maybe all of you. If and when it occurs, I hope you will show more than just courage—that you will maintain your faith in aviation and regard an accident as a temporary step backward while we are taking ten thousand steps forward. I appreciate your forbearance. Let's get back to work."

They were walking on eggs the last two days. The largest and most fragile egg was the final exam, a 100-question marathon that surprisingly turned out to be easier than Danni or anyone else expected, easier, in fact, than all the preceding tests.

"I was expecting a written version of the Spanish Inquisition," Julie marveled. "The damned thing was a snap."

But Danni's interpretation of why a threatened storm had turned into a gentle wind was closer to the truth. "We just didn't realize how much we've learned," she said. She had seen the once-jittery Linda breezing through tests, had watched the change in Joan who was beginning to carry an air of self-assurance no one would have believed possible four weeks ago. Even Betty Jo's drawl

63

seemed to have diminished in direct proportion to her acquired knowledge; it flowed instead of oozed.

Marlene told dire stories of trainees who washed out only hours before the graduation ceremony, but the pressure from her seemed half-hearted. Danni had noticed this as early as the fourth week. Marlene scolded Carol for her makeup and she bawled out Danni for a run in her stocking, but there was a difference—as if she were going through disciplinary motions automatically. It was not a weakening of authority, Danni knew, but an acceptance of 55-10's readiness. Marlene no longer needed her toughness to ensure performance.

Two nights before graduation, she showed up at the dorm ostensibly for a curfew check. Julie heard her knocking on doors and muttered, "This is chicken shit!" But when Marlene arrived at 210, Danni noticed she was carrying a large briefcase.

"The damned thing's getting too heavy," she announced, plopping herself on Danni's bed. "Julie, go get the rest of the class—and tell 'em to bring glasses." She opened the briefcase and pulled out two bottles of white wine, winking at Danni as she unscrewed the top of one. . .

Danni had reserved a room at the Everglades for her parents, who arrived Thursday, the day before graduation. There was a class dinner scheduled that night and Danni had time only for a quick drink with her parents in the Everglades cocktail lounge. Julie came along, a little downcast because her own father, a widower, couldn't get away from the neighborhood market he operated in York. Danni worried that her mother would show her anti-stewardess bias, but her concern was unjustified—Bea Hendricks could charm an IRS agent if she put her mind to it, and sensing Julie's disappointment she went out of her way to be nice.

"Do you know where you'll be based, Danni?" her father asked after the drinks had been served.

"I bid Miami first, Atlanta second, and then Washington, Dad—and so did Julie—but we never know where they'll send us. Probably New York, which nobody wants."

64

"Maybe you and Julie could spend a couple of days with us before you start flying."

"Dad, they ship us out right after graduation."

"Jesus," he grumbled, "they don't waste any goddamned time."

"That's the airline business," Julie said cheerfully. "Danni, we'd better get going—class dinner starts in fifteen minutes."

There was a final class session Friday morning, with graduation scheduled for noon. Marlene, resplendent in the uniform she hadn't worn since the first day of training, greeted them affectionately. The instructor looked tired and her eyes were still bloodshot; Danni was sure she had shed not a few tears since the crash.

"I'm going to read your base assignments first," she began. "Now don't panic or pout if you didn't get what you asked for—remember, when probation is over you can put in for transfers. Right after graduation, I'll hand out passes for the first available flight to your respective bases.

"Katie Crum, Chicago. Mary Beth Davenport, Washington. Julie Granger, Washington. Danni Hendricks, Washington . . ." Julie and Danni hugged each other, then squeezed Mary Beth while Marlene droned on. "Betty Jo Lynch—you're going to be a damned Yankee, Betty Jo. New York. Pat Martin, Miami. Linda Percival, Chicago. Joan Pierce, Chicago. Rose Steinmetz, New York. Carol Veskos, Miami."

She waited for the hubbub to die down—the reaction was what she expected. Frowns and groans, some squeals of delight, some murmurs of disappointment. "Okay, settle down. This is my last chance to talk to you and I want to give you a few words of final advice.

"It's going to be fun, provided you keep your sense of humor. Without a sense of humor, you won't survive. You'll be working around some people with negative attitudes. They'll tell you the airline stinks, the airplanes stink, nobody cares and nothing ever gets done. Hogwash! It just isn't true. You're not going into a perfect world—you'd be a fool to expect that, and I'd be a liar if I told you to expect it. But it's going to be as challenging, happy, exciting, and rewarding as you want to make it. If there's never any challenge, get out.

"You're going into an environment that never stops changing, and the biggest changes will come when the jets start flying in a few years. If you're still around by then, you can help with those changes and be a part of them. I'd say that five percent of our stewardesses don't belong in this business. They're complainers. They drink too much or they're lazy or both. The other ninety-five percent pull their own weight, make their own decisions, and do their jobs. They're the ones who found out it takes a hell of a lot of effort to be negative and very, very little to be positive.

"Inside of a year, some of you in this class will turn out to be bad stewardesses. You'll be calling in sick when you're not sick, because you want to do something else besides fly your trip. In my book, that's tantamount to stealing.

"Remember this: we didn't knock on your door and say, please come be a stewardess for us. It was the other way around. So when you're all dressed up for a date with Mr. Perfect and just as you're leaving the apartment the phone rings and it's Crew Sked telling you to get your ass out to the airport, just remember you were the one who said, please give me this job, I love people and I love travel and I hate a structured life. The sad part is that some of you really like a structured life without realizing it—nine-to-five, Monday through Friday. And after about a year of flying, you'll draw away from people whose whole world is airlines and you'll be drawn to people who do have every weekend off.

"You told us you loved people. Well, TNA is going to give you people. People you never saw before. People who are unreasonable, vicious, whining, complaining, impossible to please, and downright unpleasant. And chances are some of you will discover you don't like people as much as you thought you would. If that happens, quit.

"That's the end of my sermon. Don't forget, when you report to your base, you'll be on reserve, so stay close to the phone—God help you if a crew scheduler can't find you. Any questions? Okay, go back to the hotel and change into uniform. I'll see you at graduation."

*   *   *

It occurred to Danni that the Washington assignment might present parental problems. Her mother and possibly her father were going to insist on her living at home—which was why she had listed Washington as a very lukewarm third pick. She and Julie already had agreed to get an apartment together if they drew the same base, and they knew now that Mary Beth would want to come in.

Her parents, however, surrendered at the sound of the first shot. She broke the news when she met them back at the hotel. "I think that's great," Bea said promptly. "I realize you'll want an apartment by yourselves, but at least we'll get a chance to see you now and then, won't we, John?"

"Probably want to find something near the airport anyway," he said gruffly. "Tell you what, though, Danni—you kids are welcome to stay with us until you locate your own place. Plenty of room."

"We might do that," Danni agreed cautiously. "Of course, we won't know until we get there and see our supervisor—she might have a hotel room already reserved, or maybe a good lead on an apartment." She did not add, because it would require too much explaining, that her reserve status would make staying in Potomac almost impossible—it was too far from National Airport.

Graduation was held in the Board of Directors' room on the seventh floor of TNA's General Offices building—a chamber of enormous proportions and so richly furnished that Danni felt like a street urchin invited into the king's palace. A photographer took individual head shots and then a class picture. It was too bad, Danni thought, that a similar shot wasn't taken the day training started; the contrast would have been startling. These *were* airline stewardesses. Immaculately groomed, with makeup perfectly applied and coiffures unobtrusively sleek, and casually stylish.

The guests were seated first. The front row was reserved for the graduates, who entered in single file while flashbulbs from family cameras popped like huge fireflies. It was the first time Beatrice Hendricks had seen Danni in her uniform, and she experienced the disorienting feeling that she was looking at a stranger. Not even when Danni had graduated from college had she been so impressively distant, so disturbingly mature. This wasn't her daughter;

it was a stunning young woman who looked like Diane Victoria Hendricks but couldn't possibly be the same girl. Not with that erect carriage, that poise and confidence.

"Jesus Christ," John Hendricks muttered. "She's gorgeous."

Marlene Compton took over, apologized for the inability of President Evan Belnap to be present, and introduced Mr. Harmon Gillespie, senior vice president of Marketing and Sales. Gillespie, who looked even handsomer than the photograph 55-10 had seen while memorizing executive names and faces, delivered a few appropriate if prosaic remarks. Danni had the distinct impression he was staring at her through most of his brief speech, and then decided she must be imagining it. Yet when Marlene had introduced them earlier, he had held her hand so long it made her uncomfortable—or had that been her imagination, too?

The wings. Marlene began handing out the wings.

Hers was the fourth name called. "Diane Hendricks, Potomac, Maryland," Marlene said. "Diane's wings will be pinned on by her father, Mr. John Hendricks."

She rose from her front-row seat, dimly conscious of 55-10's applause, her heart pounding and her eyes glistening. *I can't cry*, she kept telling herself. *Dad would kill me if I cried . . .*

She felt his big hands trembling as he fumbled with the unfamiliar clasp. She looked over his bowed head into Marlene's face and incongruously thought that she had never seen the instructor look so beautiful. How could she ever have been so afraid of this kindly, understanding, sympathetic . . . ?

The wings attached, her father looked up, and their eyes locked. She saw in his face an expression of pride she had not seen since she was a little girl. She had no way of knowing he saw the same pride in her own face—the pride of achievement over adversity. The accomplishment of turning fantasy into reality. The awareness of how training had honed and fine-tuned and molded her. She had looked at her classmates and marveled at their transformations; now she was feeling her own transformation, sensing her newly acquired poise without having to spell it out. She was wearing maturity like a dress and knowledge like the underclothes beneath that dress . . .

". . . Congratulations, honey," her father was saying. He

68

kissed her gently on the cheek and she hugged him, fighting back the tears. "I'm glad you came," she whispered. She turned to receive Marlene's congratulations and both fell into a tearful clinch.

"You're going to be a great stew," the instructor choked. "Just keep your damned nose clean and you'll have my job someday."

As she returned to her seat, she happened to glance at Pat Martin. At the class dinner the night before, amid the chatter about visiting parents, Pat had said with studied casualness, "Mine aren't coming—they think my being a stewardess is the stupidest thing I've ever done." Now, she realized, Pat was looking at her and Danni could swear there was envy and sadness in those unblinking eyes . . .

The class bolted back to the hotel to change into dresses for travel and to finish packing. When Danni went to the desk to pay for the previous week's phone calls, the clerk handed her a yellow envelope. "Telegram came in a couple of hours ago."

She tore it open.

CLASS 55-10
% DANNI HENDRICKS
EVERGLADES HOTEL
MIAMI, FLORIDA

MY THOUGHTS ARE WITH ALL OF YOU ON THIS DAY. GOOD LUCK AND GOD BLESS YOU.

TERRY

She had no chance to show it to anyone except Julie and Mary Beth on the flight to Washington, and it was Julie who pronounced Terry Shannon's epitaph.

"Poor kid. If she hadn't been so goddamned overconfident . . ."

Danni said nothing. Her mind was alternating between thoughts of what lay ahead and the memories of training. Curiously, the latter seemed to focus on the one thing she would have preferred to forget:

The way Marlene Compton looked the day that pilot died.

PART
TWO
(1955–1957)

Chapter 5

Danni Hendricks began her airline career suffering from menstrual cramps and a bad case of nerves. Then things got worse.

She was summoned for her first flight only an hour after the three girls had moved into their new home—a furnished two-bedroom apartment vacated the day before by a pair of TNA stewardesses who had just won transfers to Miami.

Unpacking finished, they explored their quarters with more pride of possession than aesthetic appreciation. The living room walls were a bilious green, and both bedrooms were done in what at one time might have been an attractive light blue but had long since faded to a nondescript off-white. The furniture was serviceable, if worn—"That couch must have gone through the Battle of the Bulge," Julie theorized.

The phone had been left connected—an arrangement made possible by the airline's influence with the Chesapeake and Potomac Telephone Company. The unexpected jangle of that phone, not ten minutes after they arrived, startled them. Julie answered.

"Is Ann there?" a male voice asked.

"Ann who?"

"Uh, is this Granite 8-7759?"

Julie checked the number on the dial. "Yes, it is, but there's no Ann here."

"Well, I know I've got the right number. I'm a friend of hers from Baltimore and I've called her here several times."

"Is she a Trans-National stewardess?"

"Yes."

Julie chuckled. "I hate to break the news to you, but she's transferred to Miami. Along with her roommate. We're the new occupants."

He never broke stride. "Well, there, hi! Maybe I could come over tonight and have a drink with you. Ann and me were good friends—very good friends. You're probably lonesome and—"

"Not that lonesome," Julie interrupted. "Look, chum, we're just getting settled, we're tired, and we don't know you from Adam. Some other time." She hung up.

"Who was it?" Mary Beth asked.

"Some friend of the departed, and from the sound of his voice and his general approach, the departed had lousy taste in men. He wanted to come over."

"Maybe you were too hasty," Mary Beth said. "Be kind of nice to have some male company after five weeks in a nunnery."

Julie snorted. "Not that creep. I think I need a drink after that minor league Jack the Ripper—you suppose our predecessors left any booze around?"

Mary Beth shook her head. "I don't think we should. We're on reserve and Crew Sked might call."

"Fat chance," Julie said. "They told us we probably wouldn't be called out for a couple more days. Come on, Danni, let's go check the cupboards."

Danni hesitated. "Mary Beth's right—they *could* call. And I'm wound up so tight I don't think I'd want to stop after one drink."

She must have been clairvoyant. The phone rang again and Danni, closest to it, answered.

"Good afternoon, this is Jim Miller at Crew Sked. Is this Davenport, Hendricks, or Granger?"

"Hendricks," Danni said, her heart pounding.

"Too bad, honey. Should have let Davenport or Granger answer. The reserve who picks up the phone is our pigeon—and we'd like this little pigeon to work six-twenty this afternoon. Be here in forty-five minutes."

"Wait a minute," Danni said frantically, "where's six-twenty going?"

"Look it up in the schedule. 'Bye."

The disconnecting click sounded like a thunderclap. "Oh my gawd!" Danni yelped. "I've got a trip—in less than an hour! Who has the schedule sheet? Where's my makeup kit . . . ?"

Mary Beth fished a copy of the TNA flight-listing sheet out of a cavernous pocketbook and searched for flight 620. Danni shoved various items into her suitcase. "What's it say about six-twenty?" she called out from the bathroom a minute later.

"I'm still trying to find it . . . I swear, there's no such . . . here it is! Washington–Philadelphia–New York—my God, it goes every place!—New York–Syracuse and then back to Washington. You get in about midnight, Danni. It's a real puddle-jumper."

"What's the equipment?"

"Convair. I'll bet you work it alone on the last leg."

"That's all I need on my first trip. Wonder if . . . oh, shit!"

"What's wrong?" Julie asked.

"I started my period. Two days early—wouldn't you know it?"

"You need any Kotex?"

"Got some. I'll throw it into my suitcase."

"You don't have to take a bag," Mary Beth said. "I told you, you get back tonight."

"Remember what that Miami crew scheduler told us? Always take your suitcase. I could get stuck in Syracuse."

The excitement she felt on the occasion of her first trip sign-in was almost eradicated by an onslaught of cramps so stabbing that the crew scheduler noticed her grimace.

"You feel okay? You look like somebody just punched you in the stomach."

Danni would have absorbed twice the pain before admitting she felt ill. "Just a little indigestion. I'll be fine."

She walked into the stewardess lounge adjacent to Crew Schedule, feeling miserably self-conscious even in a room full of powder-blue uniforms exactly like hers; the difference was the crackling newness of hers—she was sure its untouched immaculateness was a sign that fairly shrieked, "It's my first flight!"

The lounge was the antithesis of its well-groomed occupants—an oasis of cheerful disarray in which Danni could find no ashtray that wasn't full, nor a piece of furniture that wouldn't have given a Salvation Army collector pause. There were cigarette burns on both plastic-covered couches, and the various chairs scattered around were all pleading silently for honorable retirement. Her own apartment, Danni thought, was the Taj Mahal by comparison.

The untidy, stale-smoke atmosphere was thickened by strewn newspapers and magazines—Danni picked up a copy of *Time* and noticed it was eighteen months old. Yet for all its decrepit appearance, the lounge had an air of happy anticipation that affected her. Sloppy it may have been, but it was part of her airline environment, instinctively recognizable and instantly acceptable. She felt at home without knowing why, and the friendliness of the lounge inhabitants reinforced that feeling. Several introduced themselves and somewhat to her surprise did not show the patronization she had expected. Most of them were junior enough not to have forgotten their own fears on their first flight; to Danni, they displayed sympathy, not superiority.

"Anybody here named Hendricks?"

"Here," Danni gulped, and turned around to face a tall, red-haired girl with an ingratiating grin.

"I'm Sue Lehman, senior on six-twenty. I hear it's your first trip."

"Very first," Danni confessed. "Name's Danni."

"Scared?"

"A little."

The senior laughed. "By the time it's over, you'll be a veteran—the first one's always the hardest. Don't worry, I'll help you all I can. You're flying with a grizzled vet."

Danni mentally thanked the powers-that-be who had given her an experienced senior. "How long have you been flying?" she asked.

"Two and a half months," said the grizzled vet. "Come on, Danni, let's board—we're at gate eighteen."

How could she ever have imagined that the 240 was a small

76

aircraft? Airplane N-328TN (for some reason, she glanced at the fuselage number as she boarded) looked enormous. When she entered the cabin, the forty empty seats seemed to stretch endlessly. Forty pillboxes, she thought, each about to be occupied by a hostile sharpshooter . . .

The senior's calm, understanding voice splashed over her fears. "Tell you what, Danni, I'll do the paperwork and galley check and you can make preflight inspection. Know what to do?"

The very question thawed her frozen knowledge valves. *Check all oxygen bottles and extinguishers to determine whether fully charged . . . make sure first aid kit is fully supplied . . . check magazine supply . . . inspect lavatory facilities for cleanliness. . . .*

The two pilots came aboard while she was in the midst of preflight, and when she finished, she decided she had better follow prescribed etiquette as taught in the Marlene Compton University of Cabin/Cockpit Relationships (page 31, section B-5 of the training manual).

"I guess I'll introduce myself to the crew," she said.

The senior looked doubtful. "The captain's Penrose Cockrell. He's, uh, a little hard to understand until you get to know him. Maybe you . . ."

"Protocol is protocol," Danni said airily, and went forward to the cockpit.

The copilot, a slender, sandy-haired youngster, shook her hand a bit limply and wished her luck. Captain Cockrell merely turned around, glared, and muttered, "Jesus, another greenhorn. Look, girlie, just forget everything they taught you in that goddamned school and you might stand a fighting chance."

He was a stocky man with thinning hair and a bulbous nose who reminded Danni of W.C. Fields. She glared back at him without saying a word, then decided diplomacy was in order. "Anytime you catch me doing something you think is wrong, I'd appreciate your telling me, Captain."

Cockrell frowned. "That'll take up the whole goddamned trip," he announced. "For the time being, just remember I take my coffee black with sugar and I want it before we leave the gate."

Danni managed to stop gritting her teeth by the time the first passengers climbed the Convair's integral stairs, and she greeted them with the smile ordained by the Marlene Compton University of Welcoming Passengers (page 33, section B-5). With Danni, however, the smile was not artificially applied, like lipstick; it was completely natural, as much a part of her as the uniform she wore. She felt confidence taking over, forgetting her pains and the captain's rudeness in the euphoria of the moment.

Unfortunately, menstrual cramps and rudeness were not all she forgot. The Convair was waddling away from the gate, its two engines grumbling and belching, when she realized she had neglected Captain Penrose Cockrell's edict on coffee.

She confessed her transgression to the senior. "It's too late for Penny's coffee," Sue said. "I'll bring it to him after we're airborne."

"I'm sorry," Danni apologized. "I goofed so I might as well face him myself. Anyway, I can't see him making a federal case out of a cup of coffee."

"You don't know Captain Cockrell. But it's your funeral."

"Should I bring it to him now? We'll be taking off in a couple of minutes."

"Wait until after takeoff."

When they were in the air, Danni entered the cockpit and stuck the paper cup of coffee in front of Cockrell.

"What the hell's this?" he demanded.

"Your coffee, Captain. I apologize for being so late but I got so busy back there . . ."

"I said I wanted coffee before we left the gate. We left the gate fifteen minutes ago. Get the hell out of here and take the coffee with you."

Shaken but angry, she intercepted the copilot's sympathetic glance, started to say something, but caught the almost imperceptible shake of his head.

"I'm sorry, Captain Cockrell. It won't happen again." His voice came back to her as she left the flight deck and closed the door behind her. "You're goddamned right it won't happen again. Not on my airplane!"

After they landed in Philadelphia, Danni poured a fresh cup, stirred in a lump of sugar, and carried it to the cockpit. With an effort, she smiled as she offered it to the frog-faced man in the left seat. He ignored the steaming cup and stared at her.

"What did you say your name was?"

"Hendricks, sir. Danni Hendricks."

"Do you know where we are?"

"Yes, sir. Philadelphia."

"Very good. Now then, Miss Hendricks, by any chance did they happen to teach you the approximate distance between Washington and Philadelphia, when you were in that monument to impractical theory known as stewardess school?"

She knew this foul-dispositioned little creep was toying with her, but she had no choice.

"I'd say about a hundred miles, Captain."

"Well, young lady, that means we're a hundred miles from the gate at which I very politely requested my predeparture coffee. So you can march right out of here again—and take the god-damned coffee with you."

She surrendered. "Yes, sir."

She informed Sue of her clash with Cockrell. The senior smiled tolerantly. "He's a holy terror with new stews, Danni, so don't let it worry you. Just the same, better try again with that coffee before you leave La Guardia."

"Before *I* leave?"

The senior nodded. "I'm afraid six-twenty's a one-woman trip on the next two legs—you'll be alone up to Syracuse and back to Washington. It's easy, Danni. Just beverage service on both legs."

Danni quailed inside. After they reached La Guardia, she saw Cockrell in Operations but avoided him. When he reboarded, she already was in the airplane.

"Do you suppose you could possibly bring me coffee before we leave the gate *this* time?" he asked.

"I won't forget, Captain. Black with sugar."

His answer was an unintelligible grunt. The copilot, boarding after his walk-around inspection, greeted her with a smile.

"Don't let Cockrell get you down," he advised. "He seems like an old bear but he's really more of a pussycat. They say if he likes you, he'll do anything in the world for you."

Danni grinned. "I'd say that might occur by nineteen seventy-five, give or take a year. How is he to fly with?"

"One hell of a teacher. If you can please Penny Cockrell, you can please any captain on this airline. I've learned more in the three trips I've had with him than I did in four weeks of initial training."

Danni sighed. "Well, I hope he gets off my back. By the way, you wouldn't know how much sugar he likes, would you? I'm afraid to ask."

"I'm not sure. One lump, I think. Good luck."

It turned out he was off by several lumps. When Danni brought Cockrell his coffee, her thanks consisted of another outburst.

"For Christ's sake! This goddamned stuff tastes like hot water. What the hell are you trying to do—ration the bloody sugar? Take it back and put in a couple more lumps. Jesus, what do they teach you in stew school? How to drive captains nuts?"

Danni slammed the cockpit door shut. Very deliberately, she got out a fresh paper cup, took a pencil out of her pocketbook, and wrote three words on the bottom of the cup. She filled the cup with coffee, dropped in the sugar, and brought it to the cockpit.

She felt much better, so much so that instead of being nervous about her first PA, she sailed through it with the poise of a veteran. That poise almost deserted her halfway to Syracuse.

The Convair began bucking in the turbulence of a thunderstorm. Danni had always imagined that on such occasions she would be too busy to be afraid and too conscious of her image to show fear. But she felt actual terror when the plane dropped a sickening two thousand feet in a sudden downdraft; her stomach somewhere in the vicinity of her chest, she turned white.

She heard the sounds of retching that seemed to spread through the cabin, and she had to force herself out of the jump seat to offer aid. It took equal willpower to resist fleeing to the cockpit as a kind of haven occupied by two strong males who presumably knew what they were doing. Yet it was not entirely willpower; it was also the knowledge of what she had written on the bottom of the cup.

80

Flight 620 was clear of the storm area and droning peacefully toward the Syracuse airport when Captain Cockrell, his arms weary from wrestling the yoke, finally found time to drain the cold remnants of his coffee.

He did a double-take and turned red.

Go to hell.

"That little bitch!" Cockrell growled, a sound that fell just short of being a chuckle. "That spunky little bitch!"

New stewardesses walked on eggs during the probationary period and Danni was no exception—check-rides were frequent and her immediate supervisor had the reputation of being a woman whose bite was worse than her bark. She was tall with straight, almost stringy brown hair which she wore in bangs. Her name was Harriet Nash, and her outstanding feature was her large, doelike brown eyes; they gave her an aura of deceptive mildness, belying her inner toughness. She was tolerant toward a first mistake, rough when it was repeated, and unforgiving if it happened a third time. Danni loved and feared her in equal proportions, as did her roommates.

They had found themselves compatible for three girls of varying backgrounds, their friendship molded by a common love of airline life and kept alive by a willingness to compromise. Mary Beth's Achilles' heel was cooking—"Jesus, you could burn water," was Julie's verdict—but Mary Beth also was a fastidious and compulsive cleaner who actually enjoyed scrubbing floors. Julie's forte was her culinary skill, a somewhat treacherous asset because she also was a comparison shopper who took twenty minutes to circumnavigate a meat counter. Danni assumed the shopping chores after Julie consumed two hours purchasing eight dollars and twelve cents worth of groceries.

Beatrice Hendricks would have stocked Apartment 203 with enough food, furniture, and linens to operate a twenty-room motel, but Danni spurned this generosity, mostly out of her desire for independence. Their major shortage was in bath towels, a crisis that led to Julie's suggestion that they resort to discreet thefts from layover hotels.

"From now on," she announced firmly, "anyone who comes back from an overnight trip without a bath towel doesn't get in."

Danni voiced her sanctimonious opposition. "That's stealing, Julie. Wait 'til our next paychecks and we'll buy some new towels."

"The rent comes out of our next paychecks along with deductions for our uniforms, medical insurance, and life insurance. We won't have enough left over to buy a washcloth."

"But . . ."

"But nothing. The older stews told me everyone takes a towel now and then. Besides, if you weren't so stiff-necked about accepting things from your mother, we wouldn't be in this bind."

When Mary Beth sided with Julie, Danni gave in—in principle. She could never bring herself to steal anything.

All three dated—Danni sporadically and Julie frequently—but it was Mary Beth who fell in love. With a whipcord-slender flight engineer named Jack Nowalski, who had the face of a choirboy and a manner of diffident shyness that generated irresistible maternal instincts in Mary Beth. For his part, he saw something in the tall, comparatively homely stewardess. Her quiet sense of humor, the calmness that she wore like a lumpy, formless coat over latent sexuality—these appealed to him in a way he did not quite understand until he discovered he was in love with her, too. By the time she discovered that his shyness was conquerable and he found out that her discreet poise could be shattered by intense passion, it was too late for both of them. They became engaged two months after they met on a flight, although Mary Beth firmly refused to get married until she had flown at least a year—"And maybe longer, so we can save up some money."

"Which is fine with me," Danni told Julie later. "It gives us some time to plan a nice wedding gift when we have some dough ourselves."

"She'll probably get married in between paychecks, just when we're broke," Julie predicted. "Which gives me an idea—we'll give her the greatest gift in the history of commercial aviation and it won't cost us a cent."

"You going from stealing towels to robbing banks?"

Julie grinned. "I figure if from now on each of us takes just one or two little items off every flight we work, by the time Mary Beth and Jack get married we'll have enough loot to furnish their apartment. A glass here, a few forks and spoons there—maybe even a blanket now and then. And plenty of liquor miniatures . . . boy, she'll flip!"

"So will Harriet Nash if we're caught," Danni warned.

"We won't get caught if we don't get greedy. One item at a time, never more than two. In a year, Mary Beth and Jack can start their own airline. Don't look so worried, Danni. Everybody takes stuff off airplanes and we're doing it for a good cause."

"It's still stealing," Danni objected, but in so mild a tone that Julie knew she was hooked on the idea, too.

They had to consider an eventual replacement for their departing roommate. Except for briefly exciting encounters in various operations offices, they had lost contact with their 55-10 classmates and had no way of knowing who might want to transfer to Washington when probation was over.

"Betty Jo Lynch, maybe," Danni suggested. "She almost cried when she got New York."

"I'm not sure I could put up with that little dingbat," Julie laughed. "I wonder if she'll ever live down that gyro story."

Danni began laughing, too. The airplane grapevine had swiftly spread the tale of Miss Lynch's *faux-pas* aboard a Constellation that had been delayed leaving the gate. Betty Jo had gone into the cockpit to inquire about the cause.

"It's the damned gyro," the captain explained. He pointed to one of several hundred bewildering instruments on the cockpit panel. "I can't get the damned thing to erect."

Betty Jo thanked him, returned to the cabin, and picked up the PA mike.

"Ladies and gentlemen," she drawled. "The captain advises me he is waiting for an erection after which we'll be on our way. Thank y'all."

When Danni heard the story, she could not help wishing it had been the redoubtable Captain Penrose Cockrell whom Betty Jo had embarrassed. She had flown with him several times since their clash on 620, and they treated each other with the cold formality of two enemy soldiers exchanging salutes during an armed truce.

Three days before her probationary period ended, Danni drew another Cockrell trip, a late-night Washington-Columbus flight with a layover in the Ohio city and the return trip early the next morning. The load was light; Danni was the only stewardess. A half-hour out of Columbus she found most of the passengers asleep, so she parked in an aisle seat of the last row to sneak an illegal cigarette.

Feeling a little guilty, she took only a few drags before grinding it into the ashtray. She began browsing through an *Esquire* a passenger had left in the seatback but soon dozed off, only to be awakened by a heavy hand pressing on her shoulder. Startled, she opened her eyes and saw the ugly, reptilian face of the captain.

"Nobody sleeps on a Penrose Cockrell trip!"

By the time she had sprung from the seat, his fireplug figure was striding down the aisle toward the flight deck. She could do nothing but stare helplessly after him, sickeningly conscious that of all the captains to catch her asleep on duty—an offense calling for at least suspension—it had to be that bastard Cockrell. And she'd be lucky to draw a suspension, for she still was on probation, and if the captain reported her, she would almost certainly be fired.

The crew didn't get to the Columbus hotel until close to midnight, but Danni was too upset to sleep. She put on the simple dress she had packed for the layover and went to the hotel newstand looking for something to read. Listlessly examining a row of paperbacks, she felt someone tap her shoulder. She jumped and turned around to confront Penrose Cockrell, still in uniform.

"Come have a cup of coffee with me," he said.

Danni started to refuse, then changed her mind. She had, she decided, nothing to lose. "I think I will," she said in a low voice. "It'll give me a chance to tell you to your face I think you're a mean, miserable, contemptible, foul-mouthed, totally unreasonable, arrogant son of a bitch."

He laughed, and it mysteriously transformed his almost gargoylian features into a kind of wistful ugliness, as though the very act of smiling had produced cracks through which she could glimpse a human being. He took her arm with surprising gentleness and steered her toward the hotels' all-night coffee shop. "I hear everyone calls you Danni—I got tagged with Penny. . ."

For three hours they talked. Danni about her family, her dream of becoming a stewardess, her love of the airlines business. He talked about combat flying in World War II—he had been a B-25 pilot—and she sensed his pride and his commitment.

She warmed to his affection for his family. "I married a TNA stew—she's even prettier than you. Got a ten-year-old boy who looks just like me, the poor little bastard, and a seven-year-old daughter who looks just like her mother. Thank God, or I'd have to marry her off to an orangutan . . ."

At two they decided to have ham and eggs, and around two-thirty, Danni mustered up the courage to ask the question uppermost in her mind. "Why are you such a monster on an airplane? You're really such a nice guy."

"It is the Penrose Cockrell baptism of fire," he explained. "If a stew can put up with the shit I toss at her, I figure she's worth having as a friend. Actually, I decided you were okay on that first day—when you wrote 'Go to hell' at the bottom of that cup."

Danni laughed. "I wish you had told me I passed the test that soon—you would have saved me a lot of grief."

"My kind of grief is healthy. Keeps you on your toes. But you're a damned good stew, Danni."

"How would you know? The only time you've seen me is when I brought you coffee or a crew meal—and I'm afraid I didn't serve you very graciously."

His eyes twinkled. "Every time you've had a check-ride, I've talked to the supervisor doing the check. Except for the fact that nobody mentioned your chief failing, they were goddamned good reports."

Danni was surprised at his interest, grateful for what he had said. "What's my chief failing, then?"

"You still get my coffee either too sweet or not sweet enough." He laughed. "We'd better get some sleep. Sign-in's at eight."

She went to bed feeling happier than she had for a long time, convinced she had made a friend. But in her fatigue and euphoria, she forgot to leave a wake-up call. When the phone finally rang, it was not the switchboard operator but Captain Cockrell.

"Where the hell are you?" he demanded without preamble. "We leave in twenty minutes."

She looked at her wristwatch in panicky disbelief. It was 8:40! "Oh my God!" she howled. "I forgot to leave a wake-up—I'll be there as fast as I can." But even as she said it she knew she was dead, and Cockrell confirmed it.

"I can't delay a flight for a stupid stew," he said in his old voice. "If you're not here in twenty minutes, we're leaving without you—we'll pull someone off six forty-eight to work your trip."

She tried, but twenty minutes might as well have been two. Even though she dressed in less than five, didn't bother with makeup, and caught a taxi immediately, she still didn't get to the airport until almost 9:30. Her flight had departed on time, and she couldn't blame Cockrell. Nor could she blame him for not calling her before he left the hotel—the pilots often took their own cabs to the airport without waiting for the stewardesses.

She sat in Columbus Operations until 1:00 P.M., when an eastbound flight came through from St. Louis with space for one stewardess dead-heading back to Washington and certain dismissal. Glumly, she remembered what Marlene had said over and over again during training. "... *believe me, missing a trip is THE cardinal sin on this or any other airline.*" She had absolutely no alibi. Her flying career was over.

By the time her flight had snorted up to its assigned gate at National, she was resigned to her fate. With face white but jaw set, she walked into Operations and confronted one of the three crew schedulers on duty.

"I'm Danni Hendricks," she said in a voice that was close to cracking. "I overslept and missed my trip this morning—six twenty-seven out of Columbus."

The crew scheduler looked up from the pilot roster he had been studying. "Hendricks? Oh, yeah, we know all about it. Captain Cockrell told us what happened. Hotel switchboard was out and he forgot to wake you like he promised. Guess you can go home. Call you if we need you."

She didn't move. For some reason she could never explain, she swallowed hard and said, "Captain Cockrell was just protecting me. I missed the trip because I forgot to leave a wake-up call."

The scheduler had a funny smile on his face.

"Let's see, Hendricks . . . your supervisor's Harriet Nash, isn't it?"

She nodded.

"Well, all I know is that Penny Cockrell walked in here today and told me and the other crew schedulers that if we informed Harriet Nash you missed a trip, he'd personally kick our asses all the way to the West Coast. His version's already gone into your supervisor's office, and if you wanna tell her Cockrell's a liar, you go right ahead."

She tried to say a simple "Thanks," but the one word clogged in her throat. She turned away quickly, so the scheduler could not see the tears that trickled uninvited from her eyes.

"I just want you to know I didn't buy that crap from Penny Cockrell about why you missed that trip the other day," Harriet Nash said.

Danni flushed but remained quiet—she couldn't talk anyway, not with her heart in her mouth.

"I have to let you get away with it because I can't accuse a four-striper of being the biggest liar since Ananias. But from now on, you take an alarm clock along with you on layovers—I wouldn't depend on a hotel wake-up call if Alexander Graham Bell were running the switchboard."

"Yes, ma'am." Danni had been calling the supervisor Harriet for almost six months, but she figured the occasion warranted total subservience.

"Good. Now, then, your check-rides have been all excellent." She began sifting through several sheets. "Appearance above average . . . good eye contact with passengers . . . a little slow on meal service once or twice but that'll come with practice. Your PA's have been improving steadily . . . your attitude is excellent. . . ." She put the check reports back in a folder and smiled genially. "You're off probation, Danni. Any personal problems?"

Danni was startled. "No. I'm . . . I'm curious to know why you asked."

"Well, your roommate Julie was in earlier today. We got to talking about you and she worries about you at times—says you hardly ever date."

That damned Julie, Danni thought. Aloud, she said defensively, "I don't see any point in going out with a guy just for the sake of going out. I guess I'm looking for a Greek god who can carry on an intelligent conversation."

"Your standards are commendable if impractical," Harriet commented dryly. "Unfortunately, or maybe fortunately, that eliminates about seventy percent of our pilots."

"From which category?" Danni asked. The supervisor laughed.

"That's all, Danni. Fly a straight and narrow path—and don't forget that alarm clock."

She didn't forget, nor could she put out of her mind what Harriet had said about her dating. She was feeling the same kind of pressure Julie had applied that day during training. She knew part of her reason for abstinence lay in her Catholic upbringing, but an even stronger motivation was a nonreligious philosophy that banned casual intimacies. As she had told Julie, she did not want to go to bed with a man for whom she felt nothing. She had known schoolgirl crushes, but with her gift for introspection she always recognized them as such. And so far she had never been in love. She didn't even want to be at this point—a conviction reinforced by Julie herself. For Julie did fall in love, with a married captain named Mark Thornton.

It had started innocently enough—a few drinks and a fun dinner during a layover. Julie came back from that trip raving about Thornton—"An absolute doll," she gushed.

"Is he married?" Danni, like all stewardesses, had been thoroughly briefed on that handful of lordly captains who tried to hide or disguise their marital status.

"Yes, but they don't get along too well. Mark says they've been discussing a separation." The alarm bells began ringing in Danni's brain but she kept her cynicism to herself—Julie was too wise, she decided, to get hurt by an obvious philanderer. Unfortunately, not even Julie had the insight to ward off skilled seduction; she went to bed with Thornton on their next flight together and was hopelessly infatuated. As far as possible, she bid trips coinciding with his own scheduling, and the affair lasted about a month—at which point Thornton tired of her and in tones of self-righteous sacrifice informed her that "my wife and I have decided to reconcile—for the sake of the children," he added solemnly.

"He lied to me," Julie sobbed to Danni after the break-up. "He never had any intention of splitting up with his wife. He just wanted to get me into the sack, that no-good sonofabitch!"

Danni hugged her, mixed a stiff drink, and calmed her down into a reasonable restoration of her old wisecracking self. But the pain in her eyes lasted longer than Danni had thought possible. For a while she stopped dating, and when her social life resumed, she displayed a nasty cynicism toward even the most well-meaning, decent men. And there were a few nights when Danni heard her sobbing softly, the façade of carefree noninvolvement cracked open.

She announced firmly to Danni, "I'll never date another pilot again. They're all a bunch of cheating bastards."

"No, they're not, Julie. You'd find the same percentage of unfaithful, lying creeps in any profession or any office. Pilots just get more chance to stray. You had the bad luck to get involved with a heel like Thornton, but you know yourself there are some awfully nice guys around this airline. Like Penny Cockrell, for example."

Julie nodded, a gesture of agreement diluted by a sudden stab of painful memory. "Christ, Mark was good in bed, Danni. All I could think of was spending the rest of my life with someone like that."

"And you will, Julie. Someone who's just as exciting and with some decency to go along with the sex appeal. Come on, honey"—Julie had started to cry—"forget the louse. I only wish there were some way to get even with him."

Only a week later she found herself flying a trip with Captain

Thornton, and she confessed, if only to herself, that she could understand why Julie had gone overboard. He was tall and slim, with black wavy hair carelessly tousled, his light blue eyes carrying a glint of boyish mischievousness and his demeanor so friendly and helpful that Danni momentarily wondered whether he could be as bad as Julie now thought. Only the memory of Julie's unhappiness snapped her back to reality, and instinctively she began plotting revenge. Unwittingly, Thornton played right into her hands.

Her campaign of deviousness was aided by the fact that he did not know she was Julie Granger's roommate. It so happened that she flew several times with him over the next few weeks, and each time he had the same copilot—a dimpled, prematurely bald youngster named Dave Mulvaney who was obviously smitten with Danni. With inherent skill she toyed with both of them—a hint that fell short of an outright promise, a discreet come-on toward each without the other's knowing. The less-experienced Mulvaney was a pushover; she was far more careful with Thornton, waiting for him to make his inevitable move.

It came on their last trip of the month together, a Constellation flight to Miami with a one-night layover. En route, Thornton came back to the galley on a pretext of getting coffee.

"Didn't want to bother you," he explained. "You girls have enough to do without catering to us prima donnas up front."

"I wish all captains were that thoughtful," Danni said softly. "You're quite a guy, Mark." She looked into his eyes, invitation glittering in hers.

"Any plans for when we get in, Danni?"

"No. I'm . . . uh, available." There was enough hidden meaning in those words to seduce a Trappist monk.

He said eagerly, "How about just the two of us getting together?"

"You mean for dinner? Dave's already said something about us going to a Mexican restaurant."

Thornton smiled. "Yeah, he talked to me about it. The flight engineer's got a sister in Miami so he won't go. And frankly, the prospect of sharing you with my copilot leaves me cold. He's been along every time we've gone out."

90

He's hooked, Danni thought. "Well, I kind of agree with you, but I'd hate to hurt his feelings, Mark. He's a nice kid." Thornton's face fell and to Danni it was a trap door dropping. "Tell you what— why don't I have a bite to eat with Dave and a quiet drink with you later?"

"Now that's an excellent idea," he said happily. "Around nine, in the cocktail lounge?"

Danni pursed her lips thoughtfully. "No, Dave might see us."

She looked at him provocatively. "I could come down to your room, if you'd leave an extra key for me in my box—in an envelope, of course."

"All you have to do is knock on the door of eight twenty-three," Thornton said, puzzled. "Why the extra key?"

She lowered her eyes demurely, turning away as if too embarrassed to face him. "I don't like knocking on a captain's door in the middle of the night. You never know who might be in the corridor. I'd rather let myself in, quietly and discreetly, if you know what I mean."

He knew—she could almost hear him panting. "The key will be in your box an hour after we check in, Danni."

Mulvaney was just as easy. She informed him that Captain Thornton had other plans and they could be by themselves. After dinner, she gave him a look that would have melted asbestos. "How about buying me a drink at the hotel, Dave?"

He agreed so quickly she almost felt sorry for him, but her regret was tempered by the knowledge that Dave Mulvaney was married, too. They returned to the hotel and went into the cocktail lounge. After Danni finished her drink, she glanced at her wristwatch. It was 8:53.

"You're married, aren't you, Dave?"

Mulvaney's conscience wrestled with his libido and lost. "Well, technically speaking, I am. But I'm having a little trouble at home . . . my marriage . . . you see, my wife . . ."

She put him out of his misery. "Unhappily married, is that it?"

He nodded vigorously, his bald head bobbing as if tied to a puppeteer's strings. "*Very* unhappily," he murmured gratefully.

"That's all I wanted to know," she said. "I don't believe in playing games." She fished in her pocketbook and brought out a room key, making sure it was 823 and not 511. "Here's the key to my room. I don't want anyone to see us going up in the elevator together. I'll wait here for five minutes and then go up and join you."

"I'll be waiting," he gulped, and departed.

"Bingo," Danni said aloud. Within the next five minutes she was in a taxi heading for Marlene Compton's apartment, where she had already promised to have a drink. She would have given a month's pay to witness the confrontation between Captain Thornton and First Officer Mulvaney.

The story spread around the airline with the speed of a laser beam. Most of the stewardess corps considered Danni a heroine; quite a few pilots labeled her a female Benedict Arnold. The very mention of her name, however casual, invariably brought out, "Hendricks—isn't she the stew who lowered the boom on Mark Thornton?"

More importantly, what had admittedly created more notoriety than fame was exactly what Julie needed to snap her out of her doldrums—she laughed until the tears came when Danni told her what she had done. Their friendship, already deep, was hardened into an unspoken bond.

Chapter 6

She may not have dated her passengers but she liked them and pampered them, rapidly winning a reputation for the way she worked her trips.

"I wish I could film her on one of her flights," a check-riding supervisor told Harriet Nash. "We could show it to training classes and they'd learn more from her than the damned manual."

The introvert of 55-10 had become a master of quick decisions, carried out by the force of her new personality. She really loved her job and it showed; the more challenging the crisis, the better she seemed to respond. She earned one commendation for her handling of a Jewish Anti-Defamation Society charter from Washington to Miami—it was a mid-afternoon flight and the caterer by mistake boarded sixty-five ham sandwiches as the meal snack. She talked a rabbi into explaining the situation on the PA, announced that all the drinks were on the house (they would have been anyway, but most of the inexperienced passengers didn't know that), and was so profusely apologetic that Trans-National received twenty complimentary letters and not one complaint.

Yet she was no paragon of aeronautical virtue—like all good stewardesses, the more she relaxed on the job, the more she winked at a few rules. On one flight a passenger was so taken by Danni's efficiency and friendliness, he surreptitiously snapped a picture of her in the galley and sent a print to the airline along with a letter of fulsome praise.

Both the letter and the snapshot came to Nash's attention and she called Danni in, handing her the letter. Danni read it and handed it back.

"Nice of him," she said. "Was that all you wanted to see me about?"

"No. Take a look at this snapshot."

Danni complied and turned red.

"Excellent photography," Harriet commented. "You can even see the smoke curling up from that highly illegal cigarette. And you're standing there with your damned shoes off. You're grounded for one week without pay."

She had just gotten off that brief suspension when she found herself assigned as senior on flight 275, a Constellation trip to Chicago. The captain was Bob Jackman, a slim, pleasant-mannered veteran who was one of Danni's favorite pilots. A widower with two teenaged girls, Jackman was too mature and solemn for the tastes of younger stewardesses, but Danni liked him for his unfailing politeness and easy efficiency.

He greeted her warmly as she was signing in; Danni noticed that when he smiled, it had the effect of erasing years. Jackman's eyes were fenced in by the crow's feet so typical of veteran airmen, giving them a perpetual squint as if they were always looking into a bright sun. The smile turned the lines into merry crinkles.

"Thunderstorms around Gary," he told her. "Supposed to be severe along with tornado warnings, but not until early evening. We should be on the ground before the front moves in. I think you can plan on a normal meal service."

She was grateful—he was one of those captains who made a point of briefing stewardesses before takeoff. "Thanks, Bob. I'll bring you a Coke right after we're in the air."

His jaw dropped. "How did you remember that? We've had only two trips together."

"Easy. I keep a little black book. Every time I fly, I put down crew beverage preferences. I keep an alphabetical list, and when I see who's up front, I just open my book to refresh my memory. I started after my first trip with Cockrell—in self-defense. See you on board."

All but five seats were filled, and Danni was handicapped by the inexperience of the two junior stewardesses, both only two weeks out of the Miami hatchery. Remembering her own rookie days—which now seemed ten years ago instead of only ten months—she tried not only to overlook their fumbling eagerness but also to compensate for it, thus tripling her own workload. She had to take over in the galley from the girl she originally had assigned there, and then rushed to the other's aid during liquor service. Danni was so busy that she had time for only a hasty glimpse of a woman sitting in 12A; tall, homely, and heavyset, she seemed vaguely familiar, but Danni was too busy to dwell on where she had seen her before.

The general confusion made meal service later than she planned, and she had just delivered the final tray when Jackman summoned her to the cockpit. She closed the flight deck door behind her, automatically reaching for a precious cigarette—the cockpit was a sanctuary for stewardess smokers. "You guys want your dinners now?" she asked. "The passengers are all fed."

Jackman turned around, the eye crinkles appearing more pronounced, tiny ridges instead of thin lines. "That damned front's moved in faster than anyone expected," he said. "I think we can climb above the worst of it but we may get kicked around a little. You say everyone's been fed?"

"Everyone but you three."

"Well, better tell your girls to strap themselves in, and that includes you. I'll give you no more than ten minutes for whatever chores you can finish. Don't bother serving seconds on coffee, or have you already started?"

"Negative, unless my partners have done it on their own. Which I doubt."

"Just as well. Radar shows us in the clear so far, but I've got a hunch we may take a beating. I'll turn on the seat belt sign and you'd better start checking the customers."

Danni nodded, unperturbed. She took a final drag on the cigarette and snuffed it out in the flight engineer's ashtray. "So long, you guys. I'll rely heavily on your heroics."

She didn't get the ten-minute grace period Jackman had promised. What she got was about ninety seconds—just enough time for the three stewardesses to check passenger seat belts and for the two juniors to strap themselves into the aft jump seats. Danni, walking back toward the forward jump seat, had just passed the galley area when the cabin floor seemed to cave in under her. The Connie, caught in the clutches of a massive downdraft, plunged straight down with the sickening swiftness of a runaway elevator. Danni was thrown to her knees and was still crawling toward her jump seat when the big Lockheed bucked, shuddered violently, and then suddenly rolled over on its back.

Curiously she felt no fear, even though she mumbled a prayer of contrition. Only dimly did she hear the screams of passengers, as if she were listening to a cacaphony of fear echoing a mile away.

There were more sounds. The metallic crash of galley equipment tearing loose. Meal trays bouncing off walls and ceilings. Carry-on baggage from overhead racks tumbling out with the haphazard inevitability of a rockslide.

Danni, the only one not strapped down, was saved by the freakiest chance. When the Connie rolled, Danni was thrown against the jump seat and clung to the sturdy harness just long enough to keep from being hurled head-first against the ceiling. For a few seconds she hung there precariously, and then the plane, like a playful giant porpoise, rolled back onto its belly. The loose objects began flying again but with less force and projectory; Jackman had regained control and the recovery roll was far more gentle.

Danni climbed painfully to her feet, sure that every inch of her body had been bruised, but one look at the shambles in front of her erased all thoughts of her own possible injuries. The sounds of hysteria filled her ears—sobbing, incoherent cursing, retching, and the continuing screams of one woman passenger who hadn't realized the plane had been righted. Danny went straight to her first, taking her hands and squeezing hard. "Now calm down. Just calm down. I want you to listen to something. Listen, now . . . Listen . . ."

The woman's screaming diminished to a whisper.

"Hear those engines? All four of those beautiful engines are still running and that's what's important. We're going to be all right. We're safe. Now promise me you'll be quiet and I'll get back to you as soon as I find out whether anyone's injured and needs medical aid. Are you okay?"

The woman nodded. "I think so," she muttered. "I'm too scared to know if I'm hurt."

Danni patted her head. "We're all scared, including me. But the worst is over." She started up the aisle again but stopped when she felt a hand on her elbow. It was the woman in 12A, the one who had looked so vaguely familiar.

"Is there anything I can do to help you?" she asked. Danni, looking at the passenger's pale face, felt a surge of gratitude. "No, ma'am. Everything's going to be fine. You just sit there and relax."

"What happened, Danni?" The second stewardess, a lump on her forehead, had come up to them.

"Damned if I know. I'll check up front as soon as I get a chance. Where's your pal?"

"Still back in the jumpseat. I don't think she's hurt but she hasn't moved since we rolled."

"I'll take a look. Meanwhile, get out the first aid kit. See if anyone needs immediate help. I'll be with you as fast as I can."

It was quickly apparent that only a psychiatrist could help the other stewardess. Danni found her staring straight ahead, in an almost catatonic state. Poor kid, Danni thought. They'd probably never be able to get her on an airplane again. And maybe most of these passengers, too. Gotta do something about that. She sighed and made for the forward section, picking her way carefully through the debris, assuring those who called out to her that she would be right back. Finally, she reached the PA mike.

"Ladies and gentlemen, may I have your attention? I know you've all been through quite an experience but Captain Jackman has things under control. I don't know what happened but I'm sure he'll be able to explain in a few moments. He's one of the finest pilots on the line and you can be absolutely confident he'll get us down safely. I realize this place is a mess—it looks a little like my

97

apartment, as a matter of fact"—her weak attempt at humor produced a few nervous smiles if not laughter—"but first things first. The most important thing is to take care of anyone who's injured. Norma's already making an initial check and I'll join her shortly. Meanwhile, let me see if I can get the captain to talk to us."

She hung up the mike and was just about to enter the cockpit when the first officer emerged.

"Jesus Christ," he blurted. "It'll take 'em a year to clean up this airplane." He turned to Danni. "Bob wants to know if you're okay and is anyone seriously hurt?"

"I'm fine. We've already started checking for injuries; I'll report back to him as soon as we finish. What the hell happened?"

"We aren't sure, but Jackman thinks we hit the top of a tornado funnel—a freak high-altitude twister that didn't show up on radar. We're lucky the wings stayed on."

"I think I'll write Lockheed a fan letter when we get back. Are we going into Chicago or is Bob going to put down somewhere else?"

"All the controls are normal and so are the engines. We've already advised Chicago Approach Control we're declaring an emergency and they've cleared us for a straight-in approach. We should be on the ground in less than thirty minutes."

Danni surveyed the cabin and sighed. "No time to pick up this mess. Tell Bob a PA from the cockpit would do these people a lot of good. And just to play it safe, if he agrees, it might be a good idea to have a couple of ambulances meet us."

"Sure thing. Other stews okay?"

"Norma's doing fine. Phyllis is somewhere in outer space— she hasn't moved from the jump seat since we rolled."

She made one final PA just before they landed, thanking the passengers for their courage and concluding: "Captain Jackman has asked me to add his thanks for your cooperation. He also advises that medical personnel will meet our flight, first to provide any necessary further treatment and second to check every individual to make sure there are no injuries of which you may not be aware. I promise you, the delay will be as short as possible. Also, we'll have agents on hand to take down every name and address, because this airline is going to have quite a dry-cleaning bill! Thank you, and God bless all of you."

The click of the mike disconnect was audible throughout the quiet cabin. A passenger started to applaud, and spontaneously the clapping spread until it became an ovation. After they landed, the passengers insisted on shaking Danni's hand—including the woman in 12A.

"I just want you to know I intend to write your president a letter," she said. "I happen to know Mr. Belnap personally and I'm going to tell him you're a credit to your profession."

"Thank you," Danni said. As the passenger turned away, Danni added, "Ma'am, have we met before? You look awfully familiar."

The woman smiled. "We've never met, but you may have heard of me. I'm Eleanor Roosevelt."

Among those congratulating Danni on her flight 275 performance was Penny Cockrell. He was so intensely proud of her that he even bragged to other pilots about their friendship.

One of them was a tall captain named Anthony Buchanan, who had never flown with Danni but expressed a desire to meet her.

"She's the best goddamned stew on the line," Cockrell proclaimed. "First chance I get, I'll introduce you."

Penny happened to be one of the few pilots who could stand Captain Anthony Buchanan. Actually, they had almost nothing in common except their profession, but the little pilot sensed that Buchanan was lonely and he sympathized.

Outwardly, Tony Buchanan was rather cold and austere, a martinet on the flight deck detested by copilots who flew with him. They resented his affectations, such as his habit of wearing black leather gloves on winter flights, even though TNA's cockpits were adequately heated. And his faintly tinged British accent, somewhere between the supercilious tones of a Harvard professor and the lilting resonance of a Jamaican native.

No one knew that Captain Buchanan, if he had cared to turn an awesome portfolio of blue-chip stocks into ready cash, could have bought enough shares of Trans-National stock to acquire control of the airline itself. He was divorced and lived in a surprisingly simple apartment near the airport. His only concession to ostentatiousness was the Bentley he drove. Parked amid Fords, Chevrolets, and Plymouths in front of the red brick shoebox that was his apartment building, the Bentley was an orchid in a row of nondescript weeds.

Buchanan certainly didn't dress like the wealthy man he was; he looked neat and fastidious, almost immaculately groomed right down to manicured fingernails that somehow escaped effeminacy. But his clothes invariably looked slightly threadbare, like those of a once-opulent dowager whose expensive wardrobe had seen better days. This could not be said of his uniforms. No one in Operations had ever seen him report for duty without razor-creased trousers, his brass buttons and wings always polished. Even the gold braid on his captain's cap looked richer than anyone else's.

"If you turned out all the lights in this damned place," a crew scheduler once remarked, "you could find Buchanan in the dark just by the gleam from his uniform hardware."

He was a loner, dignified and polite in a detached sort of way, rebuffing overtures of friendship simply by ignoring them. He often acted like a bored, disdainful adult thrust in among unruly children, and nowhere was this more apparent than in his relationships with stewardesses. His aloofness awed the younger ones, and the veterans regarded him as something of a colorless fish. In the comradely world of flight crews, all but the newest stewardesses called pilots by their first names or even nicknames; but with him it was always "Captain Buchanan," never "Anthony" nor, God forbid, "Tony." He never requested such formality; it came naturally.

How he became friendly with a pilot who was his antithesis in so many ways was something neither Cockrell nor Buchanan could explain. Even the word "friendly" was stretching the truth a bit; Penny actually liked Buchanan, whereas Buchanan merely tolerated Cockrell. He considered him bawdy and vulgar yet respected

100

his cockpit professionalism, quietly envied his rapport and popularity with other crew members, and was secretly if intermittently
grateful that Cockrell had somehow seen the loneliness under the
icy reserve.

They were first drawn together on a layover in New York when
Cockrell, who hated to eat alone, asked Buchanan out to dinner.
Buchanan accepted more out of boredom than anything else.
Before the evening was over, he discovered that Penrose Cockrell
was more than an airplane jockey. He was a vociferous reader,
especially of Antoine de Saint-Exupéry, from whose works he
quoted profusely. This intellectual depth so surprised Buchanan
that over the next few months he found himself confiding in
Cockrell to an extent he never dreamed possible.

Penny learned about the source of his wealth—Buchanan's
father had made a fortune in oil leases before succumbing to a heart
attack and leaving his wife and only child not only with the well-
invested money from those enterprises but with thousands of acres
of valuable timberland as well. The widow, as financially astute as
her late husband, pyramided the holdings into additional millions.

"She's nothing but a coupon-clipper these days," Buchanan
told Cockrell. "She could teach an investment course to a Wall
Street broker. I don't bother with anything but flying airplanes—
she does all my investing as well as her own."

"Why the hell did you become an airline pilot?" Penny asked.

"Well, I flew B-seventeens in World War II and found I was
pretty good. Mother wanted to set me up in my own business but I
couldn't find anything that really interested me. Not the way flying
did."

"From the way you describe her, she could have bought you a
whole damned airline and let you run it."

Buchanan permitted himself one of his rare smiles. "We
Buchanans are fiercely, if foolishly, independent. She actually
suggested something along those lines when I told her I wanted to
make flying a profession. If I hadn't put my foot down, I think she
might have tried to buy TWA away from Howard Hughes."

Cockrell had heard Buchanan was divorced about a year
before he joined TNA. He was curious about this phase of the

man's life, but Buchanan never volunteered details and Penny did not press him. He did learn that Buchanan had a son and a daughter from that marriage and gathered that he missed them deeply. It was only too apparent to Cockrell that separation from the children he loved was the source of his loneliness and, to a great extent, his coldness. Penny got the idea that Buchanan was basically unhappy but too proud to admit it, and too bruised from his broken marriage to seek another woman. It was this reasoning that led him to suggest an introduction to Danni.

Danni had been flying for nearly a year when they finally met. She thought it was by chance; actually, she was working a trip with Cockrell who tipped off Buchanan that she was on his flight.

"You just gotta meet her," Penny insisted. "You're taking out seventy-eight Tuesday, right?"

"Affirmative. Sign-in at fourteen-hundred."

"Perfect. We get in at thirteen-thirty. Just make sure you're in Operations and I'll introduce you."

Thus it was that Anthony Buchanan, airline pilot and divorced father of two, was presented to Diane Victoria Hendricks and was vastly impressed. By her eyes, merry yet with a kind of alert directness that seemed to probe as well as see. By her warm and genuine smile. By her voice, modulated and devoid of coyness. By her figure and her grace.

He was aware that she was studying him, forming an impression as instantaneous as an image captured by a camera lens. She was intrigued by his gray eyes, instinctively perceiving their sadness. By his handshake, a welcome compromise between the limp-rag feel of some men and the viselike squeeze of the super-masculine types. By his patrician features, which softened when he smiled. By his whipcord build, slender but strong.

"Miss Hendricks," he acknowledged in a tone of faintly mocking formality.

"Captain Buchanan," she responded simply.

They stared at each other, oblivious to Cockrell's presence. It was Buchanan who broke the silence. "I've been anxious to meet the young lady of double fame—the heroine of flight two-seventy-five and the demolisher of Mr. Thornton."

"Did you come to bury me or to praise me?" Danni asked.

"Praise, by all means," he smiled. "And frankly, Miss Hendricks, I find it not only surprising but refreshing that your question indicates a nodding acquaintance with Shakespeare."

"It shouldn't be surprising," Danni said sweetly. "You pilots are so interested in bodies, you don't take the time to investigate brains."

Buchanan had the grace to blush. "Your criticism is justified," he apologized. "I, for one, am . . . uh . . . interested in both, with brains enjoying a possibly higher priority." Encouraged by her quick smile, he continued. "That's why I hoped to meet you one of these days and why I'm glad I bumped into Cockrell here today."

Danni felt a little flustered without knowing why. "It's been a pleasure," she murmured. "I hope I'll have a chance to fly with you one of these days." She turned to go.

"Ah . . . I'd . . . I'd . . . would you care to have dinner with me later this week? I get back around noon tomorrow. I . . . uh . . . I have no plans for tomorrow night. Unless you have other commitments, of course. Or perhaps you have to fly . . . ?" He was embarrassingly aware that the words had tumbled out in a disjointed, schoolboy flurry.

His lack of confidence and loss of poise touched her. "I'm free tomorrow night," Danni said. She took one of her stewardess calling cards from her wallet—furnished by the airline, they discreetly omitted a home telephone number—and wrote the apartment address and phone number on the back. "Is seven too early? I have a trip the next day and I'd like to get in before midnight."

The pleased look on the face of Captain Buchanan fell just short of achieving an outright grin. "Suppose we make it six-thirty, then. Do you have a choice of restaurants? A favorite place, for example?"

"Man's choice," Danni said. She started to tell him she was not overly fond of French cooking but decided this might be unfair—he looked like the type who would know every French maître d' in Washington. She said good-bye to Cockrell, nodded pleasantly to Buchanan, and went off to check the stewardess mailboxes.

"A damned fine young woman," Buchanan said. "I'm most grateful for that introduction, Cockrell."

Penny just grunted. He was thinking, *My God, I hope I did the right thing. All of a sudden, there's something about this guy that bugs me . . .*

As she expected, he was punctual. Also as she expected, he took her to a French restaurant on Pennsylvania Avenue, where the food was overpriced and, to Danni's taste, overseasoned. And finally, as she expected, the maître d' inundated her with Gallic obsequiousness.

"I wonder if he'd go to the bathroom for me," she murmured.

"I beg your pardon?" Buchanan asked.

"Nothing. Just a little joke." She had the uncomfortable notion that he had no sense of humor.

They engaged in wary small talk at the start of the evening and progressed to serious discussions on topics ranging from the advantages (and disadvantages) of private schools to the current state of American literature.

"With the exception of Fitzgerald, Wolfe, and—in a rather crude sense, Hemingway—there hasn't been an American novelist of stature since Henry James," he proclaimed. "Wouldn't you agree?"

"No, I wouldn't," she said firmly. "That's absolute nonsense and you know it. What would you call Sinclair Lewis?"

"A caricaturist of some skill, but not a novelist. As *Babbitt* proved."

"You wouldn't call *Arrowsmith* a novel? Or *Main Street? Dodsworth?*"

"Of the three, I've only read *Arrowsmith*. And I'll agree, it could be classed as half-caricature, half-novel. Certainly not in the same league as Fitzgerald."

"Fitzgerald was the most overrated writer in American literature. I'll admit I admire Wolfe but he could be awfully dull."

"How can you say that? Good God, have you read him?"

"Yes, which is why I'm a better judge than you are about Lewis. You've admitted you never read *Main Street* or *Dodsworth* and those were two of his greatest . . ."

They talked and argued about books until the maître d' gently reminded them it was closing time.

"Closing time?" Buchanan said, surprised. "You're a bit early tonight."

"It's after eleven, Captain Buchanan. I'm terribly sorry—you and the young lady seem to be enjoying yourselves."

Buchanan glanced at Danni as if to seek confirmation of Henri's observation. Again, there was a kind of sadness in those gray eyes, a pleading that made her warm to this outwardly confident, even stuffy man. She didn't want the evening to end, but she stood up.

"I've got that trip tomorrow," she said. "I think we'd better be on our way."

On the way home, Danni curled up in the luxurious soft leather of the Bentley's front seat and studied Buchanan's lean, rather stern profile as he talked. About himself, mostly. His unhappy marriage. His two children—the boy, Geoffrey, was now fourteen and his daughter Leslie was sixteen. Danni was pleased that he did not attempt to portray his ex-wife as a witch. "A splendid person, actually," he conceded. "We simply were badly matched."

"Different backgrounds?"

Buchanan frowned. "No, our backgrounds were quite similar. There were . . . uh . . . other factors." He changed the subject. "Tell me about you. Your family."

Danni told him about her father's teaching career and his unexpected literary windfalls. Buchanan sighed in relief. This not only explained her interest in books and authors but cleansed her of the "She's beneath me" stigma that had marched uninvited into his brain.

"I'd like to meet your parents," he said.

Danni was properly cagey. "I think we should know—get to

105

know each other better before I bring you home—God, that sounds like step five in a book on courtship etiquette."

"I'd like very much to know you better," he smiled. "I can't remember when I've had a more enjoyable evening. Or a more stimulating one."

She chuckled. "You sure you haven't mistaken irritation for stimulation? I was giving you a pretty rough time."

"Deservedly so. There are occasions when I suspect I'm a pompous ass. My upbringing, no doubt. As I believe I told you, my father died when I was quite young, and being raised as an only child by just a mother—well, I suppose that leads to a somewhat lopsided personality."

"I gather you're very fond of your mother."

He did not comment on her observation right away but seemed to be wading through a morass of memories. Danni saw his finely chiseled jaw tighten. "She's strong. Also domineering. Bigoted in some respects. Rather snobbish, I'm afraid."

Danni felt a sudden chill. "Such as feeling that dating stewardesses is beneath you?"

He said, far too quickly for her to really believe him, "Oh, that would depend on the stewardess. She couldn't help but like *you*."

"I'll bet." The tone was so sarcastic that Buchanan pulled back. "I think I may have given you an unfair picture of her," he said. "She's really warm-hearted and generous. If she likes someone, there isn't anything she wouldn't do." When Danni said nothing, he shifted to an attempt at light-hearted banter. "After all, I'm her son, and if *I* like you, that's half the battle."

He was trying so hard that she softened. "Come to think of it, she sounds a little like my own mother—if yours looks up her nose at stews, mine looks down hers at pilots."

Before they reached the apartment, Buchanan asked her for another date and she accepted. Whistling, he parked in front of her building and started to open the door. She pulled at his arm. "You don't have to see me to my apartment."

"I really don't mind. I . . ."

"Anthony, I want you to kiss me good-night but I'll be damned if I'll smooch in a lighted corridor with my snoopy roommates flapping their ears for sounds of passion. I had a wonderful time. I'll see you Sunday night."

He kissed her; his lips felt cold and stiff. For a moment she felt let down, but as she broke off the kiss and pulled slightly away, she saw he was trembling.

The courtship, like the man, had its ponderous side. There was an Old World quality about Anthony Buchanan, a tendency to put his Special Woman on a pedestal, while making sure the pedestal provided her with no height advantage.

Her roommates were at opposite poles in their opinion of Danni's "boyfriend"—a phrase that would have sickened him if he had heard it. Mary Beth regarded him with awe; Julie thought him a self-important bore. Still, as Danni gradually melted the captain's reserve, Julie was sharp enough to grasp the subtle changes in his personality. It helped that he genuinely liked her; she knew he saw her own fondness for Danni, her reciprocal loyalty.

But even as Julie's attitude softened, she questioned Danni's growing emotional commitment.

"I keep thinking he's just not your type," she said one night when Danni was dressing for a dinner date.

"I'm not sure there's really any such thing as a 'type,'" Danni answered. "If a girl starts limiting herself to one particular kind of guy, she's putting herself in a straitjacket. Tony's got his faults, but he has virtues, too. 'Type' implies you're looking for perfection."

"No, I'm not. A beer-drinking slob with a vocabulary of all four-letter words is one type. A long-haired intellectual is another. Your Captain Buchanan is a type—rich, a bit snooty, a little superficial, and decidedly pompous, although I'll admit he seems to be improving. Incidentally, when did you muster up the courage to call him Tony?"

"Since our third date. He told me nobody's called him Tony since he was a little boy."

"Score one for your side. Somehow I got the impression he never was a little boy."

Danni buttoned her blouse. "There's a lot of little boy in him.

107

I think that's one of the things that attracts me to him."

"On a scale of one to ten, how would you rate him in bed?"

Danni laughed without humor. "I was waiting for that question. I haven't slept with him. In one sense I want to, and in another I'm afraid to."

Julie scoffed. "Afraid? Christ, you're what the poor sap needs. I'll bet he's crawling with inhibitions."

Danni smiled. "So am I. Julie, I'm congenitally incapable of taking the initiative. I'll admit he puzzles me. Judging from his displays of passion so far, he may get around to suggesting sex in approximately five years. I keep wondering if there's something wrong with me. But then I'll rationalize that maybe he's waiting for the same thing I am. Marriage."

Julie frowned. Her improved opinion of Buchanan had not progressed to the extent that she wanted Danni to marry him. "Danni, so help me, he's the kind of man I'd want to try out first before any marriage bit. Maybe he isn't the cold fish I suspect, but you'd better make sure."

"That's foolish," Danni said, but with a lack of conviction that made Julie laugh.

"Come on, Danni, admit it. Look at the other side of the coin. Suppose a good roll in the hay is all he needs to loosen up and be human. With someone he's nuts about—and I'll say that for him, he's hooked on you. Ever ask him why he got divorced?"

"Well, we talked about it a little. It doesn't seem to be his favorite topic. I gather they just weren't compatible. She probably enjoyed sex and he didn't give her enough of it."

Julie said positively, "If that's true I wish you'd do some research before you take a dive into that marriage pool. The water may be a little shallow." Danni said nothing, and Julie sighed. "Where are you two going tonight?"

"To that French restaurant where we had our first date."

"Perfect. Shock the hell out of him. Tell him you'd like to go away with him next weekend. It's time he lost a few of his repressions and it's also time you lost your virginity. Even if you have to take the initiative."

Danni shook her head. "If I took the initiative with Anthony Buchanan," she said slowly, "I'm afraid I'd lose him."

They were halfway through dinner when Captain Buchanan took the initiative. A bit haltingly, with not a little embarrassment, but definitely the initiative.

"Let's see," he began, "you have next weekend off?"

"Yep. Don't have to fly until Monday."

He toyed with the stem of his wine glass, cleared his throat nervously, and then looked into her brown eyes with the intensity of a searchlight. "Uh, what would you say to the two of us going off somewhere? Cape Cod, perhaps. Or New York. We could see a play or two and I know some fabulous restaurants."

He actually was blushing, and Danni felt a surge of affection so great that her response was blurted.

"Separate rooms, Tony?"

His jaw tightened and for one sickening moment she thought it was a gesture of anger. But his answer was so soft, it was almost a tone of reluctance.

"I . . . uh . . . I was rather hoping we . . . ah . . . could share a room."

He misinterpreted her silence for disapproval. "Naturally, separate rooms if you prefer," he said hastily. "I apologize for even suggesting it, Danni. Please forgive me."

She reached across the table and took his hand. "There's nothing to forgive. But there is a question I have to ask."

"Ask it."

"Do you love me?"

"Very much. I thought you knew."

"I suspected it. But you haven't exactly been demonstrating deep passion."

His gray eyes seemed to cloud—whether from anger or hurt she could not tell. But his voice was calm and his big hand enveloped hers, the long, tapering fingers exuding a kind of gentle yet intense pressure. "I am not a very demonstrative person, Danni, as you well know. But my lack of 'deep passion,' as you put it, does not reflect how I feel about you. I consider you the most desirable woman I've ever known. If I've failed to convey this to you, it is simply because I put respect ahead of desire. And I do respect you."

She could not help asking a woman's inevitable if hackneyed question. "How much respect will you have if I tell you not to get separate rooms?"

"Then I shall have to ask you what you asked me. Do you love me?"

"Yes."

"Then I will show you a different kind of respect. That which a man has for the woman he loves, and who loves him."

She had the feeling she was sticking her arm into a whirling propeller, and when she finally spoke, it was almost a whisper.

"You'd better know right now, Tony. I'm a virgin. But I do love you." She took a deep breath. "Separate rooms would be an awful waste of money."

Before their weekend, she bought what she had never dreamed of wearing outside the sanctity of marriage—a gossamer-thin black nightgown, so blatantly wicked that she did not dare show it to Julie. Nor did she confide in her roommate about the trip to New York—none of Julie's business, she lied defiantly to herself while tucking away in a corner of her mind the guilt she felt. Both her roommates were flying that weekend; she decided she *probably* would tell Julie later, and possibly Mary Beth, but only if everything went well. Except that she was terribly uncertain about what really constituted "went well." She worried about her inexperience. Would she have to fake orgasms? Would Tony prove to be an inadequate lover? Or worse, would he be guilty of that cruelest of male syndromes—the boredom, indifference, and cooled ardor that so often follows conquest? It was a risk that ranked only slightly lower than unwanted pregnancy, and she wondered why she feared the former more than the latter.

Twice she came close to calling him to cancel the trip, and twice she resisted the temptation. And she knew why. She wanted to sleep with him. She wanted to give her body to a man she loved, and her doubts, her nervousness, were overwhelmed by delicious anticipation. It was almost frightening to admit that from the moment she agreed to a liaison, she began to feel a warmth in her loins that generated sexual fantasies.

They flew to New York early Saturday morning, spent the day sightseeing and shopping, and went to *Teahouse of the August Moon* that night—"I thought a light comedy might be preferable to *Cat On a Hot Tin Roof,*" Buchanan explained solemnly. After a late dinner at Sardi's, where Danni gaped like a schoolgirl at the celebrities she saw, they returned to their hotel and went up the elevator holding hands—the light contact of flesh somehow becoming a kind of preliminary caress.

When Danni emerged from the bathroom in the black nightgown, Buchanan could only gasp in admiration. It barely hid her proud, firm young breasts. She was conscious of his stare, conscious that her nipples already were swollen, conscious that her legs felt weak as if the growing heat invading her entire torso had somehow weakened the bones.

"My God, you're magnificent," he breathed. Her throat was constricted and she was trembling, but when he kissed her the doubts and fears were swept away. She opened her mouth and their tongues touched and the heat within her turned into fire.

She was so anxious to please him that her inhibitions melted as she discovered not only a man's body but her own. A woman's body that wanted to both give and receive, to satiate his satisfaction even as it craved its own. Her eroticism was instinctive, fed by the mysterious alchemy of her feelings toward the man; she was surprised at his fumbling technique, and as if by impulse she became the teacher—encouraging, correcting, and manipulating without bruising his ego. Anthony Buchanan, for the first time in his life, finally discovered real sexual fulfillment—a residue of affection left over in the wake of satisfied desire.

Yet she was as grateful as he. What Buchanan lacked in finesse he more than compensated for in stamina. The teacher became a subservient pupil, as insatiable as her lover. She lost count of orgasms, as the waves of sensual gratification blotted out all but the trip-hammer intensity within her.

* * *

111

"Getting hungry?"

"No. Anyway, I think I'm too weak to eat." She propped up the pillow behind her and examined Buchanan. He wore the complacent look of a man who knows he has satisfied a woman. Danni giggled.

"Something strike you as amusing? I know I need a shave but . . ."

"I was just thinking. Only about a few days ago, I figured you were a rat fink."

"A what?"

"Rat fink. Know what a rat fink is?"

"The connotation is apparently derogatory, but the exact definition escapes me."

"A rat fink is the kind of guy who unhooks a girl's bra and then kisses her on the cheek."

Anthony Buchanan blinked uncertainly, not sure whether he had just been insulted or complimented. "I take it I've graduated from the rat fink category." He hesitated, his smile turning into a slight frown. "For that matter, you've changed categories yourself."

"Oh? From what to what?"

"I considered you a very prim and proper young lady. Now I find you're a wanton little witch."

The frown had disappeared, but not from Danni's mind. "If you have any regrets about all this, Tony, speak up now."

He took her hands and kissed them gently. "I love you. I have no regrets whatsoever. I'd be very proud if you thought about spending the rest of our lives together."

Something in his voice was out of synchronization with the words. Danni moved away. "Please tell me what's bothering you."

"Nothing's bothering me. I told you. I'd be very . . ."

"The hell it's not. What you said had no relationship to the tone of your voice. You said 'I love you' like you were reading back an ATC clearance."

Buchanan took a deep breath. "You've given me happiness I didn't know existed. But please remember the kind of life I've had. My sex life was one my mother built and then condescended to equip with a cellmate of her own choosing—something I didn't

112

realize until the marriage fell apart. Then you came along, and I had never known anyone like you. Your passion. Your—" he was groping now—"your frankness and, uh, zest."

"I think I'm beginning to understand," Danni said quietly. "Too passionate, perhaps?"

Buchanan looked miserable, as if the sharpness of her intuition had stabbed him. "The extent of your skills surprised me. So did the extent of your . . . uh . . . desire. No, let me finish"— her eyes were shooting sparks of anger—"please believe me, I'm not being critical. If anything, I'm displaying the symptoms of a jealous, lovesick adolescent. I simply do not want to imagine that you could give any other man what you've given me, and yet I know that's not only foolish but unfair."

"Also inaccurate," Danni snapped. "I told you I was a virgin. I've also explained, as delicately as possible, why I didn't bleed the . . . the first time. What happened last night was as big a surprise to me as it was to you. And if you're complaining about my enthusiastic responses, for Christ's sake, Tony, I love you!"

She started to cry. Buchanan put his arms around her, murmuring endearments that were also apologies. When the sobs ceased, he put his hands on her breasts and felt the nipples swell. He touched her moistness and her slim hips began to writhe with a life of their own.

"I love you, you goddamned stupid bastard! Jesus God in Heaven, do it to me!"

He plunged into her, his hips pounding into her, and only dimly did he hear her cries of climax. Even as he shook violently with the exquisite impact of his own orgasm, thoughts strayed into his mind . . .

. . . *She's wonderful . . . I never dreamed she could be so passionate . . . I've never dreamed a woman could get that hot . . . I do love her . . . I'm so proud I was her first . . . but God, those groans—even screams . . . she said she was a virgin and if I love her I have to believe her . . . but those sheets . . . not a stain on them . . . and I hardly hurt her . . . she was tight but not that tight . . . she might have lied, but if she did it was for my sake . . . that's what's important—that she loves me . . . even if she did lie. . . .*

. . . he was still moving inside her and she screamed as another orgasm convulsed her without her even knowing she had screamed.

There was one more thing she did not know. That every sound, every incoherent word, every sweaty motion, was being registered in a brain in which lay the dormant seeds of schizophrenia.

Chapter 7

She introduced him to her parents. Bea Hendricks, after two hours of exposure to his impeccable manners, cultured voice, and easy deference began mentally computing the logistics of a large wedding.

Danni expected that. What did surprise her was John Hendricks' rapport with Buchanan. They progressed from a kind of polite wariness to mutual admiration.

Anthony left without her—he had a trip the next day and Danni had decided to spend the night with her parents. She actually enjoyed seeing him depart, filled as she was with the delicious anticipation of asking, "Well, how did you like him?" for she knew their answers in advance.

"Very nice," her mother said. "*Very* nice."

Her father gave more cautious approval. "He's quite a guy. Frankly, I liked him very much. Seems a bit old for you, quite conservative. But then, you've always been more mature than your years." He searched his daughter's face, noting the half-smile and the brightness in her eyes. "I take it this is getting serious."

"Afraid so."

Bea had a sudden, happy thought. "You'll have to quit flying, won't you?"

Danni tried to keep irritation out of her voice. "Not right away. Tony knows I want to keep flying for a while and he understands why. After we're married, I'll stay with the airline, as an instructor or supervisor. I need about a year's more experience in line flying before they'd consider me."

Hendricks' eyes shot up. "Sounds to me like he's already proposed."

"Discussed, Dad. Not proposed. To tell you the truth, I think he's more anxious to get married than I am."

"Captain Buchanan, welcome home!"

"Good to see you again, Helena. This is Miss Hendricks— Danni, Helena has been our housekeeper for many years. Where's Mother, Helena?"

"Waiting for you in the library."

Danni was able to get only a fleeting impression of the interior as Tony took her arm and steered her toward a pair of closed French doors at the left of the foyer. The exterior had already depressed her—the house was right out of a gothic novel, a mausoleum-like structure whose well-manicured lawn could not offset its musty aura. Yet inside she had to admit the decor was brighter and more cheerful than she expected; the walls were a pleasant light pastel and the furniture tasteful and unostentatious.

But for the life of her she would be unable to remember the library into which she was ushered. The momentary glimpse she got of dark pine paneling and hundreds of books was erased by the presence of Ethel Buchanan, who rose from a red leather easy chair as they entered and graciously extended her hand.

"Miss Hendricks, it's a pleasure to meet such a good friend of Anthony's."

Danni felt tongue-tied, a commoner who has just been introduced to royalty. She managed to murmur, "The pleasure is mine, Mrs. Buchanan," and digested her first sight of Tony's mother. Danni was prepared for a woman whose physical mien would jibe with a domineering personality. But Mrs. Buchanan was small, barely five feet tall, with dainty, almost fluttery hands and a reedy body that on a younger person would have been skinny. Facially, Tony Buchanan was a blown-up replica of his mother— he had her thin strong lips, patrician nose, and gray eyes.

"I have your Bristol Cream all ready for you, Anthony," she said, as he leaned down to kiss her cheek. She handed him a glass.

"And you, Miss Hendricks? What would you like?"

"Sherry would be fine," Danni said, although she had a sudden, insatiable craving for a straight scotch.

"I'm glad to find a young lady who appreciates sherry," Mrs. Buchanan said, filling another glass. "Well, shall we all sit down and be comfortable? I know we have much to talk about." She motioned Danni into one of four red leather chairs; Danni sat down as if it were wired for an electric shock.

"I understand you're a stewardess, Miss Hendricks."

"I am," Danni replied, a sliver of coldness edging into her voice. Buchanan cleared his throat.

"I think you should know, Mother, that Danni and I are . . . uh . . . considering marriage. Strongly considering it. That's why I wanted you to meet her and, I'm sure, get to like her."

Ethel Buchanan looked at her son and then at Danni, the sardonic expression she had tossed at Buchanan altering to one the girl could not exactly identify. Hostility, perhaps? Or was there a flicker of sympathy in that steady gaze?

"You're a grown man, Anthony. You make your own decisions, with or without my approval. I feel, however, that it's a mother's privilege and even duty to ask a few pertinent questions. For example, when you say 'considering marriage,' it does indicate a certain mutual reluctance to actually go through with it."

"Not reluctance," Buchanan said. "It's just that our marriage plans are uncertain as to time. Danni wants to continue flying and, as you know, she would have to resign upon marriage."

"I see. Miss Hendricks, may I—"

"Please, call me Danni."

"I think that under the circumstances 'Miss Hendricks' would be not only preferable but far less hypocritical. I know nothing about you, other than the rather astonishing fact that my forty-two-year-old son here has suddenly announced he is infatuated with one of his little stewardesses and expects me to accept her into the family."

Buchanan flushed. "That's totally unfair! This isn't infatuation. We love each other."

Mrs. Buchanan smiled; Danni felt she was watching the

117

mouth of a cobra hinge open. "What you're saying is that you've been sleeping together and would like to rationalize your tawdry relationship into what you insist is love."

"Goddamnit, Mother—!"

"Temper, Anthony." She turned back to Danni, the reptilian smile still on her face. "I don't mean to be cruel, my dear. I'm even willing to give you the benefit of the doubt by asking you some basic questions—those I'd ask of any young woman seeking to become my daughter-in-law. For example, tell me about your family. What does your father do?"

For one glorious second, Danni was on the verge of telling her to stuff all questions. Then she caught sight of the misery clouding Tony's face and reached deep into her reserves of self-control.

"My father is a college professor and an author. He has written several successful novels. We have a four-bedroom home in Potomac, Maryland. It has inside plumbing. The house cost approximately fifty-five thousand dollars and my father has no difficulty meeting mortgage payments because his annual income runs about forty thousand a year. I'm a college graduate, I taught school before I became a stewardess, and I'm very proud of my present profession. Incidentally, I'm a Catholic and hope our children will be raised in that faith."

To Danni's amazement, Ethel Buchanan laughed. "Very good, Miss Hendricks. She has spunk, Anthony, I'll say that much for her. And I'm sure your family are fine people, although they showed questionable judgment in allowing their daughter to squander her education by becoming a stewardess."

Danni started to retort but felt Buchanan's hand on her shoulder. His own voice was shaky. "Danni and I are going to get married, Mother, with or without your blessing."

Her voice grew cold. "Is that your final word?"

"It is."

She turned to Danni, suddenly smiling again. "Well then, Danni, I suppose I should give you both my blessing and ask forgiveness—at my age, one's prejudices become rather ingrained. Please let me fill your glass again and we'll drink a toast to your future happiness."

118

I don't believe it, Danni thought. *Nobody could do a one-eighty that fast. She's plotting something. Probably figures she has plenty of time to break us up.*

Weddings, Danni realized, were as catching as measles. When Mary Beth got married, the heady enticement of gowns and gifts, bridesmaids and bliss, was enough in itself to make her waver.

Among Mary Beth's presents was the one from Danni and Julie—a complete set of Trans-National stainless steel flatware serving eight, two TNA blankets, three TNA pillows, thirty-eight liquor miniatures, ten cocktail glasses with the TNA logo, and hundreds of cocktail napkins. They held their breaths when Mary Beth displayed the contents—Harriet Nash was at the reception—but she said nothing.

Buchanan was present—for Danni's sake, Mary Beth had invited him—and his gift was a sterling silver tea service that must have cost a fortune. Danni complimented him on his taste, although she thought privately that for a couple like Mary Beth and Jack, it was woefully impractical.

His gesture touched her, however. It was typical of his sometimes painful efforts to please her. To become part of the one thing he knew she loved as much as she did him—her airline world.

She was aware he always avoided off-duty contact with that world. He was a man who regarded a cockpit as a business office; he was an airborne executive who kept his work and his relationship with his peers entirely separate from his personal life.

She realized this was not so much aloofness as it was a brand of shyness; he had a real fear that unwinding would make him appear ridiculous, like a dignified collie clumsily trying to play with unruly puppies. Danni appreciated the extent to which he agreed to socialize with her friends, double-dating on occasions although she knew he preferred to be just with her.

Eventually, he even began to enjoy himself. One night they played charades at a party; Buchanan drew the title of a play, *Desire Under the Elms*, which he acted out with frantic gestures.

"Three words," he began, making the sign of a curtain.

"Play," someone called out.

He held up one finger.

"First word," Danni said.

Buchanan nodded, his face a study in misery. By the time he finished his portrayal of desire, his interpretation coming close to that of a woman in labor, he had the audience in hysterics and his allotted three minutes were up. But Danni was proud of him, and even prouder when a pilot told her, "He's a different person since he met you."

Later that night, Buchanan said the same thing. "For the first time in my life, I feel alive thanks to you. I find myself actually liking people instead of merely tolerating them. And you know, I think your friends like me." He spoke in wonder, giving her a glimpse of his private tortures and self-imposed loneliness.

He asked her to bid his trips so they could be together on layovers; this was a source of tension. Other stewardesses welcomed layovers as a chance to get some privacy away from roommates—and, occasionally, wives. But Danni recoiled from this convenient freedom. To her it still smacked of cheapness, their weekend in New York notwithstanding. She treasured their intimacy, but on layovers it was almost like flaunting it.

Inevitably, she had to compromise. She bid at least one trip a month to coincide with his own flight schedule, her love for him rationalizing away the clash with her morality. In this way, she managed to keep them both reasonably satisfied physically, although he rightly argued that it was a poor substitute for marriage. She finally accepted Buchanan's offer of an engagement ring and agreed that they would be married in about a year.

The ring, when he gave it to her, seemed a few centimeters smaller than an electric light bulb. She showed it to Julie, who insisted on having it unofficially appraised by a young jeweler she was dating. He whistled when he saw it. "Offhand, I'd say it cost about two grand more than that new Caddie I've got parked outside," he said.

Danni nodded, a little sadly. It was too gaudy for her own taste, and it didn't mesh with his conservatism—it was almost as if he had changed personality again.

* * *

She could not pinpoint when the almost imperceptible altering of their relationship began. Little things, mostly, cropped up, things she wrote off as the natural product of their unnatural situation—a man in love with a woman who was not ready to commit herself to marriage. An increasing irritability on his part, taking the form of abruptness or even indifference at times, as if his mind was a thousand miles away. A gradual increase in the number of times he complained or even balked about going out with others.

Once she told him she had invited Julie along to dinner.

"No, damnit!" he said sharply. "I'd prefer that we had dinner alone, just the two of us. Frankly, Danni, I'm beginning to find Julie rather boring. She thinks of nothing but sex."

She was so shocked and hurt she didn't even feel like fighting back. Yet the next night he came to the apartment with a bouquet of flowers for Julie and insisted on her accompanying them to dinner.

"Making amends for the stupid things I said yesterday," he explained to Danni later. "I don't know what's wrong with me these days. I get into these fits of depression and take it out on you, your friends, and everyone else—including fellow crew members. I wouldn't win any flight-deck popularity contest, I'm afraid."

She found out herself how true that last remark was. In Operations one day, she ran into Carol Veskos, who had recently transferred to Washington.

"You flying Saturday?" Danni asked. "If not, maybe you could have dinner with Tony and me."

"No, thanks," Carol said. "Look, Danni, I think the world of you but keep that boyfriend of yours out of sight."

Danni was stunned at her vehemence. "What on earth is wrong?"

"I'll tell you what's wrong. I drew a trip with your Captain Buchanan last week. I asked him whether we could expect any en-route turbulence, so I could plan meal service accordingly. He yelled at me. Said if I was stupid enough to serve in rough weather, I didn't deserve to be a stewardess. Then . . ." Her voice choked, blocked by her anger.

"Then what, Carol?" Danni pressed.

121

"Then on the return trip he accused me of sleeping with his flight engineer the night before. He . . . he said there was no use denying it because he could tell from the way I walked that we had had sex. I told him it wasn't true but even if I had, it was none of his damned business. I'm sorry, Danni, I don't ever want to speak to the bastard again."

Danni wrestled with her inclination to question Tony about the incident. She finally decided not to, telling herself unconvincingly that Penny Cockrell would pull that kind of stuff on stews and get away with it. Yet, she thought, Buchanan was no Cockrell. Tony was standoffish with crews but she had never known him to be mean or unreasonable. Something was wrong . . .

A few days later, Buchanan matter-of-factly mentioned that he had been forced to report a stewardess named Priscilla Mitchell for insubordination.

"What did she do?" Danni asked.

He answered easily, as if the matter were of no real concern. "She made some disparaging remarks about me in public."

"What kind of remarks?"

"Nothing important. I simply felt she should show more discretion and I told Harriet Nash about it. I did say to Harriet that I merely wanted the girl reprimanded, not punished. I didn't want to be vindictive about it."

Danni wondered whether the remarks had concerned her, but Buchanan would discuss the matter no further. The next day, she happened to draw a trip with Priscilla and asked her why Buchanan had reported her. The girl looked at Danni as if she were crazy.

"You're asking me? How the hell would I know? I haven't flown with him for two months and all of a sudden Harriet calls me in and asks what I said to make Captain Buchanan mad. I told her I didn't know what either she or Buchanan was talking about, that I hadn't said word one to him since our last trip together, which happened to be last April. Harriet said to forget it. If you know what's bugging your guy, Danni, I wish you'd tell me."

This time, she did ask him. And got an explanation that made her wish she hadn't asked.

"She said she'd hate to marry an airline captain, because he'd be away from his family too much."

Danni couldn't believe it. "You reported she was insubordinate for *that?*"

"I considered it a totally uncalled-for remark."

"Did she say it to you?"

"She might as well have said it to me. She was talking to another stewardess and I wasn't five feet away." He seemed puzzled by the incredulous look on her face. "Danni, she might have been talking about *us*. In fact, I think she was."

She shook her head. "I think you should apologize to her."

"I'll be damned if I will. I don't go around apologizing to brainless females who make insinuating remarks about me . . . about us."

A little afraid, she tried to reason with him. "You're reading too much into a harmless remark. Priscilla couldn't have meant anything personal."

He calmed down, but sullenly. "Well, if you feel that way, I'll give her the benefit of the doubt. But I don't intend to apologize. I'll simply forget the whole thing ever happened."

"Nothing *did* happen, Tony. Will you tell me what's bothering you? It just isn't like you to be so unreasonable. So oversensitive."

"Nothing's bothering me and I'm not oversensitive," he barked. "I don't want to discuss this asinine episode further."

His moods became more mercurial and unpredictable: she attributed this to his growing impatience for their marriage. Almost against her will, she decided that the cure was to give him the sex marriage would bring, and for a while it seemed to work. He became his old self—thoughtful, attentive, and physically exciting. Yet even here there was a cloud. At times, he became so rough and demanding that she cried out in pain.

One night, she asked him about his first marriage—a subject both had avoided.

"Valerie was a very fine person," he said. "Excellent mother to our children."

Danni smiled to herself. "That's a stock answer to every ex-wife question. I . . . I guess I'm indulging in some feminine curiosity about her as a woman."

"Woman?"

"Well, damnit, I mean—how was she in bed?"

Buchanan stared at her, as if she had marched into a conjugal bedroom to stare at an act of copulation. When he finally answered, each word was coated with venom. "She was a frigid bitch. Making love to her was like coupling with a corpse."

Danni took his hands in hers. "I'm sorry, Tony. I didn't mean to pry. It's just that knowing what went wrong in the first marriage helps to make the second one better. I don't want to make the same mistakes she did."

He smiled thinly. "Frigidity is definitely not one of your handicaps."

Her curiosity was still unsatisfied. "Did Valerie get along with your mother?"

The smile evaporated. "Famously. After all, Valerie was her choice more than mine—the right family background, beauty, wealth, all the necessary trappings. She's still friendly with my mother, incidentally. And not just because of the children. Mother really likes her. When divorce became inevitable, it was Mother who decided Geoffrey and Leslie belonged with Val. I'm afraid I didn't have much say in the matter."

"Did you ask for the divorce?"

"She did. The usual grounds. Incompatibility. Cruelty."

Danni kissed him on the cheek. "I can't imagine you being cruel. I hate such a legalistic term."

His mouth was set in a grim line. "It wasn't so legalistic in this case. She asked for a divorce after I raped her one night."

A long time from now, she would remember that conversation as her first real insight into the demons that lurked within the façade he had erected. That her insight took so long to achieve was understandable; she loved him, and she twisted every aberration of his into a rational consequence of their delayed marriage. She even blamed herself for his increasingly black moods; when he shifted back into the old Buchanan charm, with his cavalierish attentions and almost heavy-handed generosity, she felt this confirmed her assumption of blame.

124

But as his reason decayed, the demons sought an outlet, and their target was his fellow pilots. The word went swiftly around that Buchanan was acting strangely, the evidence coming from copilots who flew with him. The first one to voice suspicion was Willie Baxter, a thoroughly competent and unflappable first officer who was already performing pre-engine-start chores before a trip to Chicago when Buchanan entered the cockpit, nodded perfunctorily as he sat in the left seat, and opened his "brain bag"—the fat briefcase containing aircraft manuals and Jeppesen airway maps.

He did not, however, take out any manual or map. He pawed through the brain bag's contents and came up with a Bible. Buchanan had marked some passage with a bookmark; he opened at that page and began reading aloud.

"The Lord is my shepherd; I shall not want. In verdant pastures he gives me repose; beside restful waters he leads me . . ."

Baxter kept staring at the patrician profile of the captain, the thin lips undulating with the words, the gray eyes searching the tiny print.

". . . though I walk in the dark valley, I fear no evil; for you are at my side with your rod and your staff that give me courage."

Buchanan closed the Bible and put it back in his brain bag. "Beautiful thing, the Twenty-third Psalm," he said pleasantly. "I believe what I've read to you is a Catholic version—I seem to recall memorizing something slightly different. I'm using a Catholic Bible because that's Danni's faith, as you probably know. Well, I wonder what's keeping our esteemed flight engineer?"

"He's doing the walk-around," Baxter said in a strained voice. He was not a little shaken but decided to be casually light-hearted. "When did you start including the Bible as part of the checklist?"

"I'm convinced," Buchanan said, "that the Scriptures should be *required* reading for all pilots before a flight. It would serve to remind us that we are fragile beings in fragile machines, entirely in God's hands. Frankly, Baxter, I intend to do more of this from now on. I'd even be willing to wager that our passengers would enjoy the comfort and reassurance of a few words from the good book. I could read a passage or two over the PA."

"I don't think they need *that* kind of reassurance."

"A little exposure to God's word would do all of us some good," Buchanan said. "Particularly pilots—it might take their minds off those little harlots in the cabin."

Baxter said nothing further on the subject, but when they returned from Chicago the next day, he encountered Penny Cockrell in Operations and told him about the incident.

"Christ, Willie, there's no law against being religious. I'll admit it sounds screwy but Buchanan's not the only pilot around with a few idiosyncracies. How about Jimmy Stanton? Some pilot picked up Stanton's brain bag by mistake, and when he opened it up later to get a Connie manual, he found about two hundred porno pictures inside. Is reading the Bible aloud any worse than being a dirty old man?"

"If I want to fly with a captain who's sane, I prefer the dirty old man. Damnit, Penny, you weren't there when Buchanan pulled out that Bible. I tell you, the guy was weird."

"Yeah," Cockrell said. "Look, Willie, maybe you'd better keep this to yourself—at least for the time being. Buchanan could be crucified if it gets around. I'll keep my ears open."

Baxter snorted. "I know one thing—I'm not bidding any trip from now on that takes me within a mile of Anthony Buchanan."

But the word did get around, not because Willie Baxter talked, but because Captain Buchanan persisted in proselytizing the Bible every time he flew. Eventually, Danni saw for herself.

She was working a Buchanan trip. Just before they left the gate, she opened the cockpit door, intending to ask whether anyone wanted coffee. Both the flight engineer and the copilot were staring transfixed at Buchanan, whose head was bowed; the flight engineer, sensing Danni's presence rather than hearing her come in, turned to look at her, his eyes wide, and put a finger to his lips. Buchanan's deep, resonant voice filled the cockpit . . .

". . . and Lord, grant us a safe flight, for we commit our bodies and minds and souls to Thy everlasting mercy. Protect this captain and his fellow airmen from the transgressions of the weak and depraved. We ask Thee in the name of Thy son, Jesus Christ. Amen."

Danni closed the door, slipped into the Blue Room, and threw up.

126

"What makes you think I need help?"

Harriet Nash's eyes managed to convey both sympathy and sternness.

"Because you've gotten yourself involved with a psychopath."

Danni, too startled to get angry, shivered in fear and tried to hide it by blustering, "I don't know what you're talking about."

"I find that hard to believe. Danni, there are at this moment, sitting on the desk of Chris Canastele, our chief base pilot, exactly fifteen requests from crew members asking that they not be assigned to any trip commanded by Anthony Buchanan. Ten are from first officers and the rest from flight engineers. In my own desk are similar requests from stewardesses. For your information, at two o'clock this afternoon Buchanan appeared before Captain Canastele and was asked to explain his erratic cockpit behavior. You may not realize it, but a lot of people around here are fond of you—including myself and also the chief pilot. Which is why Chris made a point of briefing me on what happened at that meeting. He asked Buchanan to undergo a psychiatric examination and grounded him pending the results of that examination."

Harriet drummed a pencil on the edge of her desk; it had the effect of a kettle drum in the silence of the supervisor's office. Flustered and frightened, Danni had the crazy idea the pencil was keeping in rhythm with her heart.

"I'd like to know what you mean by 'erratic cockpit behavior,'" she finally managed to ask.

"Reading aloud from the Bible as part of the predeparture checklist. Lecturing cockpit and cabin crews on the evils of sex, infidelity, and alcohol. Accusing them of fornicating, intoxication, and general disregard of the Ten Commandments. Making life miserable for everyone who flies with him."

Danni said weakly, "I don't see why a deeply religious man should . . ."

"Bullshit, Danni. You're supposed to be marrying the guy one of these days. Has he ever given you any indication that he's deeply religious?"

Religion, Danni realized, was something they seldom discussed. "No, but—"

127

"A sudden conversion to religious fanaticism wouldn't be enough to have Chris call him in. But Danni, here's a responsible captain who becomes an overnight evangelist. More, he's become a petty, bigoted tyrant making wild accusations of totally imaginary sins—good God, don't you have to question his mental stability?"

Danni said nothing, but her face was an outward reflection of the tortures boiling within her. She had kept her fears to herself with one exception—Julie knew something was wrong, and not merely through the rumors and whispers concerning Buchanan that had raced through the airline. Two weeks before, Danni had come home from a date and when Julie casually asked her, "Have fun?" Danni had begun to cry.

"There's something wrong with him," she had sobbed. "He isn't the same person."

"So I hear. The grapevine has it he's gone off his rocker. Danni, get the hell out of this mess before it's too late."

"I can't. He needs me."

He needs me. That, in her eyes, was the tragic truth that bound her to a loyalty she otherwise would have questioned. She had come to dread sex with him—of late, he had taken her with an almost desperate brutality, and then, sensing the hurt of a violated woman, he had begged forgiveness. The gradual destruction of what had once been tender intimacy was something she could not confess to anyone, not even Julie. But to Danni, this was far more painful than the unexplainable insanities he had displayed in the cockpit. She could almost rationalize the latter, just as she had always rationalized his moodiness and temper flare-ups as something that was partially her fault. Now Harriet Nash had demolished the last vestige of rationalization and she was left facing the real truth: she was in love with a madman. Only dimly, as if in a bad dream, did she hear Harriet's final words . . . "It isn't just that he's become a potential menace to his passengers and crew—he could be a menace to you."

And she knew this, too, was true.

When Anthony called her late that afternoon, she was unprepared for the casualness in his voice. He sounded cheerful, certainly unconcerned, and merely asked whether it would be convenient for him to drop over. When he arrived, he kissed her affectionately and brought up the day's events off-handedly.

"Oh, by the way, had a nice chat with Chris Canastele this afternoon."

She was not quite sure what to say and settled for, "Anything special?"

"Not really. Remember I told you I've been a bit testy of late—taking my moods out on crew members and so forth. Well, I had a frank talk with Chris about the whole matter. Told me what with our delayed wedding plans and all that, I simply wasn't much fun to fly with these days and probably the best thing was to take a little time off. Damned if Chris didn't agree. Said I needed a rest and that I deserved one. So we decided I'd take a few weeks' vacation. I was delighted to see him so reasonable. It'll be great for us. We don't have to worry about our off-duty days coinciding—when you're not flying, I won't be either."

She found herself half-believing him. She was too honest, however, to drop the matter entirely. "I was worried Canastele might have called you in about this Bible business."

He laughed. "Well, I'll be damned! Did you hear those ridiculous stories?"

"Just rumors," Danni said.

"I'll put those rumors to rest right now. I *have* been reading the Bible lately. After all, I'm marrying a Catholic, right? And I've been taking the good book with me on trips. Some passages affect me deeply, so deeply that I want to share them with others. Well, occasionally I've read those passages aloud to my crew and I'm afraid a few of those flying heathens took offense. They even spread the word that I was praying before every flight. Did you ever hear anything so asinine? I swear, this airline runs more on cheap gossip than on fuel. Even Chris brought it up today. I assure you that when I got through giving him the facts, he understood my motives completely. I even read him a few of the passages that impressed me so much. Believe me, he was fascinated. Absolutely fascinated. I was actually surprised, although I shouldn't have been—I believe he's Greek Orthodox, and, of course, that's a branch of the

Catholic church. So naturally he was impressed with my selections." He paused and grinned at her. "Now what bothers me, Danni, is that my fellow pilots would misinterpret my motives to the point of spreading rumors. I want you to know I minced no words in discussing this with our chief pilot. I told Chris I try to run a democratic cockpit even while exercising the prerogatives of command, but that I deeply resented any crew member of mine casting aspersions on a man's motives, his religious beliefs, or his sincerity. I made it very clear to Chris that I voluntarily fought in World War II against just that sort of religious prejudice. Not that I think my airline brethren are Nazis—I made that very clear to Chris—but that I considered their tactics against me disturbingly similar to what motivated Hitler. And I think I opened his eyes. He seemed deeply moved when I made that comparison. But when he tried to change the subject, I refused to let him forget my great disappointment that the very men I fly with, men I've taught, men I've commanded and trained to be better airline pilots, that these ingrates would actually spread libelous canards . . ."

He rambled on in this vein for another few minutes, until Danni was ready to scream. Julie's return saved her own sanity, for as soon as she entered Buchanan got up to leave.

"Let's run up to Philadelphia tomorrow," he said to Danni as he stood in the doorway. "I haven't seen Mother for ages and there are some personal papers I'd like to bring back with me."

She agreed, fearing that a refusal might lead to an argument. But when he closed the door behind him and she heard his footsteps fade, she collapsed, sobbing, in Julie's arms.

Never in her life had she dreaded anything as much as she did the drive to Philadelphia. She even called Harriet Nash and asked whether she could work a trip that day.

"I'd like to oblige," Harriet said, "but you've already flown your maximum hours this month and I can't afford the overtime—Miami's been raising hell about crew expenses. Any particular reason for the request?"

Danni, on the verge of divulging her fears, decided against it.

130

"No. I just felt like flying, I guess."

Tony was in a good mood when he picked her up, and she began to feel a little easier. But his mood evaporated when Danni told him she could not spend the night at his mother's house.

"Why not?" he demanded.

"I promised Julie I'd work her trip tomorrow," she lied. "It's her father's birthday and she wants to go up to York."

He sulked all the way to Philadelphia. When they arrived at the Buchanan home, he was sickeningly attentive to his mother and so viciously indifferent to Danni that even Ethel Buchanan was surprised.

Danni talked listlessly to her while Tony went upstairs to retrieve the papers he wanted. He searched in vain through the files he kept in his room, then remembered that some of his papers had been moved to an antique secretary. He found what he was looking for, records of previous stock transactions, and was about to close the drawer when his eyes fell on a large, sealed envelope. It was the printed words in the upper left-hand corner that caught his attention . . .

Lakeside Hospital.

Only dimly did he recall the place and the time he had spent there. And the reason—his mother and the doctors had explained that he was highly emotional, exceptionally brilliant, and they wanted some psychological testing to determine the future course of his education. Now something drove him to open the envelope.

Inside was a single sheet of paper, signed at the bottom by three consulting physicians. His eyes gravitated to the final paragraph above their signatures.

"*. . . with schizophrenic symptoms which, while currently in a remissive state, indicate an unfavorable prognosis if subject is exposed to prolonged stress of an emotional nature.*"

And the demons in his sick mind burst their remaining bonds.

"Come on, Danni, we have to get back to Washington."

Ethel Buchanan pouted. "Anthony, you just got here."

"I know, but I only came up for those stock records and *Danni* has a trip tomorrow." The emphasis he gave to her name was not lost on Danni—it was a one-word accusation, but she did not protest. She wanted to get out of that house. When she bid a polite farewell to Mrs. Buchanan, she had the feeling she would never see her again.

They rode in silence all the way to U.S. 1's four-lane highway. The car's powerful acceleration pressed Danni back into her seat and she caught a glimpse of the speedometer edging to the right like the winding altimeter on a climbing airplane.

She saw 60, 65, 70, 75, 80 . . .

Danni shut her eyes.

Mary, Mother of Jesus, please have a cop stop us. Please. I'll get out of this damned car and never see him again . . .

He spoke softly, the incongruity of his calmness swelling her terror.

"Y'know, Danni, if I moved this wheel a few inches to the left, we'd cross that median strip and we'd hit that oncoming truck head-on. There wouldn't be any pain. It would be all over in a split second. Like an aircraft hitting a mountain."

Where she found the courage not to scream she would never know. She could feel the sweat on her face and tightly clenched fists, yet her body seemed to be encased in a block of ice.

Eighty-five, 90 . . .

I'm going to die. I'm going to die.

He nudged the wheel to the left, and in a blur she saw the median strip edge closer. She shut her eyes and then felt the car swerve slightly to the right.

He's toying with me. He's gone mad. Please, God, make him stop . . .

He had the accelerator down to the floorboard but only dimly could she hear the roar of the engine. Out of a throat constricted with fright, she somehow achieved words that did not quaver.

"Tony, they're awfully tough on speeders on this road."

As she spoke, she forced herself to open her eyes and look at him. His eyes, she thought numbly, were like those of a shark. Absolutely expressionless. Yet she had temporarily caged the demons, for he slowed down. Obviously he did not want the police to stop him. She could get away if that happened . . .

They were silent for the rest of the trip. Sullen, brooding silence on his part. A terrified, numbed silence on hers. Buchanan spoke his first words when they were on the outskirts of Washington.

"Will Julie be home? I'd like to make love."

She was startled. Trying hard not to shatter the precarious fragility of what sanity remained, she said carefully, "It would be nice, but Julie is home. I'm pretty beat, anyway."

"You've been tired before and you never turned me down."

She had the feeling she was walking next to a precipice and that the wrong response would push her over the edge. Or him. She knew his next suggestion would be to go to his apartment; she also knew he would have to drag her there by force. Her fear had been joined by a revulsion that shocked her, as if she were about to be violated by a total stranger, and as she realized this, she hated herself for turning against him. *I should reason with him*, she thought. *Be gentle and understanding* . . .

But she could not. Her overwhelming desire was to get out of his sight and out of his life. To wake up from what had to be a nightmare. She spoke, conscious that her voice was high-pitched, and she fought to keep it from quavering.

"Why don't you take me home first and we'll see if Julie's back. She might be out on a date."

"We could go to my place," he said.

She decided on a delaying tactic. "Okay," she said with as much feigned enthusiasm as she could muster. "But first, let's stop at my apartment so I can freshen up."

It was impossible to fool him. She saw his lean jaw tighten. "Do you or don't you want to make love?" The tone was deadly in its softness.

Her answer came out of a deep well of courage. "Not tonight."

"Well, damnit, I do!" He swung the Bentley down a side street and turned right at the next intersection.

"Where are you going?"

"To a motel."

She surrendered, huddled against the car door until he found

133

what he was looking for. The VACANCY sign read like an obscene word. He got out of the car, taking the ignition keys with him. He walked around to her side and opened the door, grabbing her arm.

"Better stay with me while I register."

"Tony, please. I—"

"Shut up!"

His grip was not tight enough to hurt, but there was pain nevertheless, humiliation and fear. She wanted to cry out while he scribbled something on a registration slip, but now fear had been replaced by a drugged, torpid kind of hopeless resignation. Wordlessly, she accompanied Buchanan to the room. For the rest of her life she would be unable to remember a single detail of its interior—the color of the walls, the furnishings, or anything else. What she never forgot was the sight of the stranger in that room and what he did to her.

"Get undressed," he ordered, and as she obeyed he disrobed himself, standing naked in front of her. He grabbed her by the hair and forced her to her knees.

"Suck me."

"For God's sake—"

"Suck me, you goddamned whoring cunt. You stinking bitch. You disgusting, depraved little slut—you taught me all about it, didn't you? Told me it was nothing to be ashamed of if two people loved each other. So go right ahead. Suck it until I come right into your filthy mouth. You do it, or so help me God, I'll kill you!"

She complied, but as her mouth touched him, a wave of nausea overcame her. She pulled back and vomited, the retching sounds intermingling with her sobs. He yanked her to her feet, and still gripping her hair, he punched her twice—first in the mouth and then in the left eye. She fell back on the bed and groaned as he fell on top of her.

He did not just enter her; he rammed her, a pile-driver of mixed lust and hate, until he exploded and pulled away, both anger and passion spent. He mumbled something, so incoherently that she did not know what he had said, but she could not have replied anyway. Her throat was constricted and she could still taste the vomit in her mouth.

134

Danni did not know how long they lay there. She wanted to cry but no tears came. Her body hurt, but even more painful was the humiliation, and the knowledge that he no longer loved her. Numbly, she wondered whether she could still love him. Right now she hated him, but she also felt pity, without understanding what was wrong with him, and in that pity she allowed the vestiges of love to remain alive. She turned her head slightly, fearful that she would find him looking at her, and she did not want to see his face. She would never forget how he had looked when he was inside her, his contorted features twisted into a mask of madness.

But now his back was to her and he apparently was asleep. She had to get out of that room but she was afraid to move. When she finally heard him breathing evenly, she decided to risk it. Painfully and slowly, she eased out of the bed and began to dress, knowing that if he even stirred she would bolt out the door half-nude.

She would never know whether he was really asleep, but at least he made no move to stop her. He was lying on his stomach, face pressed into the soiled pillow. As she closed the door, the last thing she heard was the sound of sobbing.

With instinctive wisdom, Julie asked no questions until she had cleaned Danni up, given her a drink, and insisted on calling Dr. Lerch, Trans-National's medical consultant for the Washington base.

All this accomplished, Julie refilled the scotch glass and folded her arms over her knees, looking at Danni lying on the couch. "Was it Tony?"

Danni nodded.

"He go off his rocker?"

"Yes," Danni whispered.

"You've got to tell Harriet. If you don't, I will."

Danni, totally defeated, nodded again. "You call her."

"Sure thing. Let me get some more ice for that lip and eye."

Waiting for Dr. Lerch to arrive, Danni provided the details, in a monotone so low Julie could hardly hear her. By the time Lerch came, Julie had gotten her undressed and into bed. The doctor's examination was mercifully quick.

"I'd like to take an X-ray of that jaw," he said. "I don't think anything's broken, but let's make sure. Julie, you bring her to my airport office at nine A.M. tomorrow. Meanwhile, keep applying those ice packs and I'll leave a sedative—no more scotch, by the way. She's passed the point where alcohol will do her any good. Have you notified Harriet Nash yet?"

"I was just about to when you arrived."

"Better let me do it. Obviously, she can't fly for a while. From what you told me on the phone, I'd also better call Chris Canastele. Buchanan's dangerous. Can I use your phone?"

"The person I should really see is Tony," Danni muttered. "He's the one who needs help, not me. I'm the only one who can help him."

"You're nuttier than he is," Julie said. "After what he did to you?"

"You don't understand. You just don't. Neither of you. I heard him crying when I left that damned room. He was crying, Julie. And I loved him."

She was in Lerch's office the next day when Penny Cockrell came in, his homely face wearing an unfamiliar expression of sympathy. Somehow, Danni knew.

"Where's Tony?"

Cockrell grimaced. "He's dead, Danni. Christ, I'm sorry."

Dully, she heard herself asking, "How did he die?" She already knew the answer . . .

. . . *He killed himself. That's what must have happened. But why? Why? He knew I loved him. Why did he turn on me? Why did he turn on himself? He raped me because he hated me, but why did he hate me, all of a sudden? What did I do wrong? What did I do to him to make him hate me so? He called me a slut. I never should have gone to bed with him. I should have waited until we were married. Yes, that's why he did it. He didn't respect me any more. I should have married him long ago and this never would have happened. It's my fault . . . God forgive me, it was all my fault . . .*

136

". . . shot himself in a motel room," Cockrell was saying in a choked voice. "I don't think you have to know anything else."

"Yes I do, Penny. I have to know."

"He must have kept the gun in his car. He called me just before he did it—told me what . . . what was going to happen. I called the police but by the time they got there, it was over."

Danni said, dry-eyed but dully, "Did . . . did he say . . . leave a note or something?"

"No." Cockrell's answer came so fast that Danni was sure he was lying.

"He did, but you don't want to show it to me."

Penny nodded, his own eyes full of pain. "There were two notes, Danni. One to his mother and the other to you. The police have them."

"Did you see them? What did they say?"

His answer mercifully circumnavigated the truth. "He was a sick, tortured man. The guy who wrote those notes wasn't Anthony Buchanan."

In accordance with Buchanan's own request, the funeral was held three days later at Arlington National Cemetery, with full military honors for a former major in the United States Army Air Forces.

Danni almost did not attend. The day after Tony's death, she had called Tony's mother to offer condolences: there was only cold hostility in the older woman's voice.

"So nice of you to call, Miss Hendricks," Ethel said icily.

And hung up.

Danni called her right back. "Look, Mrs. Buchanan, Tony and I were engaged to be married and I'd like to be at the funeral with you. We were the two people in this world he loved the most, except for his children."

"That's exactly why I don't want you there. His children will be present, along with Anthony's wife. It would be not only embarrassing but indecent for you to be there."

"I think I have a right to be there. I was . . . ."

"You haven't any more right than a common whore. Anthony

would be alive today if it weren't for you. I've been in contact with the police. They read me his . . . his last note. Addressed to me, his mother. Not to you. You meant nothing to him. It made him feel guilty that he even imagined he loved you. His conscience killed him, that much I can tell you. And if you have any semblance of decency left in your debauched, greedy brain, you'll pay your respects by staying away!"

This time, it was Danni who hung up. Later, she told both Julie and Harriet Nash what Mrs. Buchanan had said. "Maybe she's right," she added. "The man they're burying isn't the one I would have married. I don't know what was in that suicide note and I guess I never want to know, but whatever it said Tony didn't write it."

The supervisor eyed her shrewdly. "I tend to agree with you. But if you don't go, it's a victory for her."

"Not much of a victory," Danni said, "but something. I'll risk it. I can't be with the immediate family at the graveside, of course. But I hate to go there practically alone. He didn't have many friends at TNA, just Penny Cockrell, maybe. Would you two go with me? So Tony will have at least somebody from the airline saying good-bye?"

"Julie will be there," Harriet promised. "I've already given her trip tomorrow to a reserve. And me too—don't worry, Danni. We won't let you down."

John and Bea Hendricks wanted to come but Danni talked them out of it. "It seems cruel to say it," she told them, "but except for Julie, Harriet Nash, and maybe one or two pilots, there won't be anyone else there from Trans-National. I think I can take that, well, humiliation, if you aren't there to witness it. But Julie and I will come over right after the ceremony—Harriet, too, if it's all right with you."

"Bring anyone," her father said.

Danni drove to Arlington with Julie, Harriet, and Penny Cockrell. They arrived fifteen minutes before the services and approached the gravesite. Then Danni stopped in her tracks.

All she could see was uniforms. Airline uniforms. The powder blue of the stewardesses. The dark-blue serge of the pilots. She guessed there must be 200 crew members there! At least some of

138

her sadness was washed away in a flood of gratitude and pride. The ranks have closed, she thought. How and why Tony had died was not as important as this last tribute to Captain Anthony Buchanan. It did not quite occur to her until later that it was also a tribute to her.

"My God," she said to Harriet Nash, her voice choked. "The whole base came."

"Damned near," the supervisor agreed cheerfully. "Where's Mrs. Buchanan?"

Danni located her under a small awning by the graveside, where several chairs had been placed for the immediate family. A boy sat at one side, a girl at the other, obviously Anthony's children. The hurt returned—Tony and she had planned to fly to the West Coast so she could meet them. The attractive, pale-faced woman sitting next to the girl must be Valerie Buchanan, Danni realized. What was she thinking? Did she know about Danni? Did the children know? And what did any of them know that hadn't been filtered through the poisoned tongue of Ethel Buchanan? It was at this very moment that, as if by telepathy, Mrs. Buchanan turned around and saw Danni. A shadow of hate passed over the old woman's face, a look that went beyond the girl toward the solid phalanx of uniforms that already had begun to form in back of Danni.

The services went by in a blur, Danni oblivious to what was being said at the grave. She closed her eyes when the casket was lowered and ached with bitterness when the flag that had been draped over it was carefully and deftly folded—and handed to Valerie Buchanan. She watched clear-eyed as three volleys were fired over the grave and sobbed at the sweet, sad notes of "Taps." She looked up, startled, at the sound of an approaching airplane, the roar of its twin engines becoming louder as it passed overhead. It banked steeply, nose down, and thundered toward them again at a lower altitude, so low that Danni could see a familiar blue streak under the fuselage windows and the letters TNA on the tail. A cockpit window was open and a small wreath was tossed out. It fell only a few feet to the right of the grave, and the plane rocked its wings gently in final salute.

"Bob Jackman's flying it," Harriet murmured. "Chris arranged the fly-by. They figured Tony would have liked it. They had to get special permission but old man Belnap pulled some strings."

Danni could only nod. She scarcely heard the murmurs of condolence and affection from the pilots and stewardesses as the crowd dispersed. Then she felt a hand on her shoulder and looked into the face of Valerie Buchanan.

"You must be Danni?"

"Yes."

Valerie took her hand and pressed it quickly. "Thank you for coming. Anthony wrote me about you some time ago. He loved you very much, no matter what his mother says. I wish I could have gotten to know you."

"So do I," Danni said softly.

The ex-wife's eyes were clear. "He was a deeply troubled man. I think you gave him the only taste of happiness in his whole life. God bless you."

She turned and walked rapidly away before Danni could reply, toward Ethel Buchanan, whose face was contorted with rage.

"Come on, Danni," Julie said. "Let's go home."

PART THREE

(1957–1965)

Chapter 8

The wounds were deep. She bore not just scars but gouges that bled whenever a sight or sound reminded her of him.

She saw a pilot in Atlanta one day; he was tall with graying temples. Tony's image flashed instantly to her brain, as if she had just seen a ghost.

When she noticed a pair of newlyweds on a plane holding hands, Danni remembered their own electric contact of entwining fingers and the slight pressure that was unspoken affection.

Seeing Julie kiss a date good-night was enough to start thoughts that became scenes past. That first weekend in New York . . .

And sleep brought no escape, not when Danni's nights were filled with confused dreams. Some were terrifying playbacks of the ride and the brutality of the motel room. Some were bittersweet, in which Tony appeared so alive and well and loving that his death seemed to be the fantasy and the dream a reality. She awoke from the nightmares on the verge of screaming, but this was no less painful than the cruelty of awakening from the dreams that had brought false illusions.

It was Anthony Buchanan's dual personality that made her adjustment to his death so difficult. Her friends kept telling her how lucky she was that the tragedy occurred before they were married. This was true, she conceded bitterly, except that its logic collided head-on with her memories of a man who was incredibly kind and intensely if awkwardly affectionate. The conflict in her own mind was nearly as traumatic as the struggle that had destroyed Tony. She could have forgotten either Anthony Buchanan eventually, but it was unbearably hard to forget both.

She mailed the engagement ring to Ethel Buchanan, along with a note: "I thought you should have this. Sincerely, Diane Hendricks." The gesture gave her a moment of perverse satisfaction—it was something Mrs. Buchanan would not have expected of her. But she cried as she closed the lid of the ring box for the last time, and Julie was the one who finally mailed the package.

Julie was never quite sure how to handle her roommate's grief. Do you remind her of Mr. Hyde, or console her with sympathy toward Dr. Jekyll? There was futility in either approach, and Julie came to realize that part of Danni grieved for the man she loved and for what might have been, while part of her felt guilt for what had happened.

Julie went out to dinner one night with a Dr. Tom Bradbury, a bearded, pipe-smoking young psychiatrist she had met on a flight. It was at Danni's insistence that Julie was going out at all—she had refused to leave Danni alone since the funeral, other than the times she was flying.

"I'll be fine," Danni assured her. "There's no point in your taking the veil just because I don't feel like going out."

"Well," Julie said doubtfully, "I won't be out late. And you can have a drink with us before we leave. You'll like him, Danni—for a shrink he seems absolutely normal."

Danni smiled. "That why you're dating him? Figure he'll give me a free analysis?"

"Won't hurt you to talk to him. He might have something helpful to tell you. I told him all about . . . about Tony."

He did have something to tell her. He was obviously uneasy when he met her, but eventually Danni came to the point.

"Julie told me you're a psychiatrist. I . . . I was wondering whether schizophrenia is curable."

"At present, no. I'm afraid we know precious little about this particular mental disease. I take it your, uh, friend was schizophrenic?"

"So I was told."

"Well, the prevailing theory is that the condition stems from some kind of chemical imbalance. There are certain drugs that may or may not provide some measure of control or remission, but they're purely experimental, and thus far any improvement seems to be temporary."

Danni's voice was controlled, but low and grim. "What sets off an attack? What triggers . . . violent behavior?"

Bradbury took several puffs on his pipe. "Any number of things. Emotional stress, mostly."

"Such as stress applied by someone else? Someone he was close to?"

The psychiatrist looked at her. "Look, there's no point in feeling guilty. I don't know a damned thing about your friend clinically speaking, but schizophrenia is no overnight mental disturbance. The roots go very deep and they grow over a long period of time. Your own relationship with him was probably a stimulant to remission, not a triggering force. Except for you, it's very possible he would have cracked even before he did."

"That," Danni said, "I find hard to believe." She hesitated, unwilling to share too much with a stranger. "There was a suicide note," she went on. "I never found out what was in it, but I've been led to believe"—her voice cracked slightly and tears came to her eyes—"to believe it was not very favorable to me."

"Figures. In the suicidal mode that's so often part of the schizophrenic pattern, the disturbed person turns violently against the one he loves most. Now . . . oh, here's Julie. Come see me if I can help you in any way. Talking it out with another person—a trained person, I might add—may be the best medicine in the world."

She never did call Dr. Bradbury. In her grief-filled mind, what he had said merely reinforced her guilt. Their sexual relationship, the delay she had imposed on marriage—they had to be the triggering device and no psychiatrist could talk her out of it. She felt stained, not from Tony but from herself.

She had taken some time off after the funeral, largely to recover from her bruises. The external healing, however, was mere makeup hiding the internal damage—she could not stand being alone, yet she did not want to be with anyone except Julie. She moped around her parents' home for several days, resenting her mother's false cheerfulness and enduring her father's awkward attempts at solace. When she finally was able to resume flying, it was with a sense of relief, but she quickly discovered that work was no panacea.

She had not lost her competence, but the challenge and motivation were gone. Thanks to her gift of introspection, she could wryly remember telling herself that she would never let personal troubles affect her job—*The day I make a flight miserable for a passenger because of my own problems, that'll be the day I quit flying.*

She was too professional to inflict her misery on her passengers; she merely avoided them as much as possible, requesting the galley assignment or assuming noncontact duties automatically when she flew as senior stewardess. But in her retreat to mechanical chores, she began to chafe at their dullness.

More in desperation than in hope, she formally applied for a supervisor's job. Harriet Nash bluntly told her she had little chance.

"You're not ready yet," she said. "I'll put your application through but don't hold your breath. First, there are no openings right now, and second, you need more experience."

"I've been flying for two years, Harriet."

"I flew for seven before I made supervisor. I know you're going through a rough time, but be patient."

In her mood of defeatism and self-doubt, her ambition was passive and confined, a kind of restlessness she did not quite recognize. Management seemed more like an enemy than a goal; it was people like Marlene Compton and Harriet Nash, but it also was the remote, almost faceless executives in Miami who issued decisions and judgments without understanding how things really were. It was martinet supervisors like Martha Devins, who drew Danni on a check-ride one day.

Danni had heard of her reputation for nit-picking and was

rather surprised at her friendliness. Toward the end of the trip, Martha invited Danni to sit down with her in the DC-7 rear lounge and offered her a cigarette. Danni took it without thinking, smoked and chatted for a few minutes, and then left for her prelanding duties. The next day, she was called into Harriet's office.

"Martha Devins wrote you up," Harriet said bluntly.

"For what?"

"For smoking on duty."

"That bitch!" Danni spat. "She offered me a cigarette and like a trusting damned fool, I took it."

Harriet nodded, her eyes twinkling. "Yep, she trapped you. Which is why I'm letting you off with a reprimand. Just watch it from now on, Danni—I don't have any control over supervisors from other bases. Frankly, Martha's check-riding techniques make me sick, but that's the way she operates."

Danni was still seething. "That's the way too many supervisors operate. Where do we get 'em—out of the Gestapo?"

It was in this mood that she went to a union meeting for the first time, half-convinced that unionism was the road to reform. She sat through three hours of futile bickering, antimanagement tirades, petty griping, and empty threats. The union, Danni decided, was no better than management and not nearly as cohesive. Only a handful of stewardesses were present, and several, Danni realized, were the perennial malcontents and loud-mouths—like Pat Martin had been, she thought. Yet Pat had brains. She was running for the union presidency and Danni knew she'd probably vote for her, more out of loyalty to a former classmate than any real conviction that she could do much good. Airline stewardess unions were traditionally weak; the membership was too fluid and impermanent.

So Danni went back to routine, existing rather than living. She refused to date, and Julie's efforts to draw her out of the reclusive shell she had erected were useless. One night, Captain Jackman called and invited her to dinner.

"Got too many things to do," Julie heard her say.

"Who is it?" Julie whispered.

Danni cupped her hand over the phone. "Bob Jackman. He

147

wants me to have dinner with him."

"Accept, for God's sake!"

Danni ignored her. "I'm sorry, Bob. To tell the truth, I just don't feel like going out."

Julie grimaced. Danni listened to Jackman with an expression of impatience on her face, then finally cut him off.

"I said no, and I mean it. No offense, Bob, but I'd be awfully poor company and there's no use in discussing it any further. Thank you for asking me."

She hung up, so abruptly that Julie jumped.

"Why'd you turn him down?" she asked. "In such a way, I might add, that he'll never ask you again."

"So what?"

"Call him back."

"I will not. I just told him—"

"Call him back. I'm tired of seeing you sit around this apartment feeling sorry for yourself. Using me like a cripple leaning on a goddamned crutch. I know you miss Tony but he's dead, and damnit, you've got your own life to lead. Maybe Bob Jackman isn't your Captain Buchanan, but he's a decent, understanding guy you can talk to and that's what you need."

Danni started to argue but stopped; her roommate's face was a portrait of sympathetic determination. "Okay, I'll call him," Danni said.

She went out with Captain Jackman that night, but it didn't help—all Danni did was emerge from her prison long enough to give the pilot a glimpse of the cell to which she had sentenced herself. Throughout dinner, he tried to keep the conversation light. She talked rarely and only picked at her food.

During after-dinner coffee, he made one last try. "I know it hasn't been much of an evening, but I hope it's done you some good to get out again." He laughed. "In fact, I'd like to have dinner with you again soon. I think I'm a reasonably nice guy."

"I contaminate nice guys," Danni said.

In the end, it was Harriet Nash who saved her. She called Danni in exactly three months after Buchanan's death.

"How would you like to transfer to Miami, as an instructor?"

Danni was too surprised to give an immediate answer. "Gosh, Harriet, I just don't know. I'm pleased, of course, but I suppose there are some arguments against it."

"Such as?"

"Well, for one thing I'm not ready to quit flying yet and . . ."

"Bull. You're just going through the motions on every trip and you know it. Anything else?"

"I wouldn't want to leave Julie."

"Julie can transfer to Miami. She's senior enough to bid any base she wants. Maybe not right away but in a few weeks at the most. You need a change of scenery, and I don't mean exchanging this base for a few palm trees. I mean work scenery. New responsibility and challenge. You've earned a promotion—up to three months ago, you were the best stewardess I've ever seen. And what happened to you in those three months wasn't your fault. I would have transferred you long ago but the instructor vacancy just opened up. Isn't this what you've always wanted?"

Danni hesitated before replying. "I guess I've still been hoping I could make supervisor—working under you right here."

"That thought also occurred to me. I decided against it, and you might as well know why. You're too confused emotionally to become part of management."

"Instructors are part of management."

"They're pretty much on the fringe. You'll make a hell of a supervisor some day, but as I told you three months ago, not quite yet. Instructor, yes. You could teach a gorilla to be a stewardess. You need a little more experience in handling airline people—I mean semi-peer groups like students—before you're ready to become a real part of management. Are you angry? Hurt?"

Danni knew better than to lie. "Disappointed, I suppose. I figured I was ready to move upward. I even had a few ideas on some things I'd do differently if I were in a job like yours."

The supervisor's eyebrows shot up. "Oh? And just where have I gone wrong?"

"Not you," Danni said hurriedly. "But for starters, I'd never try entrapment on a check-ride—like Martha Devins pulled on me. She's a classic example of supervisors who look for minor violations and petty deviations from procedures, almost as if they're deliberately going out of their way to find fault instead of judging performance. There's no such thing as a stew who can work a perfect trip, Harriet. Why give top priority to making passengers happy if you know a check-ride is just a game of trivial fault-finding?"

"Martha's not the typical supervisor, thank God. Look, young lady, even a good-natured, overly lenient schmuck like me can see a reason for what seems to you petty and unimportant. The same reason you'll be teaching rules and regulations in class. Some people need a boot in the ass now and then, just to cure terminal carelessness. How about the girls who really need that occasional kick? With some of them, cheating on minor rules means that eventually they'll graduate to cheating on major ones. That's the first lesson in basic airline management philosophy, and you need some basic training. I think you'll get it as an instructor. As a supervisor, I'm afraid you'd over-identify with your girls. Am I wrong?"

Danni frowned. "No. I figure I'd do fine if I supervised the way you do. You know how to combine discipline with compassion."

Harriet smiled. "I was a lot like you when I first became a supervisor. But I wasn't a very good one, not for a year or so. Not until I learned that very fragile margin that separates natural sympathy for a fellow woman from responsibility to the company. You won't learn that flying the line, but you will as an instructor. You game?"

"I'm game," Danni sighed.

Yet pleased though she was at the promotion, there was a nagging disappointment, for which she scolded herself. There was a time when she would have regarded an instructorship as a true achievement—she had no reason to feel let down. Still, she knew it was a mere foot in the door, not a full-scale entrance into the world of management. And this, so she reasoned, explained her stab of disappointment.

150

But she failed to grasp the real import of her reasoning. Without knowing it, without even suspecting it, she had begun to harden.

Ed Perkins followed the prescribed ritual for welcoming new instructors—he took Danni into the office of Harmon Gillespie, senior vice president of Marketing and Sales.

"Just to pay your respects," Perkins explained. "He insists on meeting the 'faculty,' so to speak—Gillespie keeps a pretty good check on the training department. The stewardesses are responsible to the Marketing division, as you know only too damned well."

Danni nodded. "We heard some talk that we might be transferred into Operations. Anything ever come of it?"

Perkins chuckled. "I've been hearing that rumor for the past four years. You can expect ten inches of snow in Miami before Gillespie would let it happen. He doesn't get along too well with our esteemed senior vice president of Operations."

"Frank Ladell?"

"That's the boy. There's a real power struggle going on. They'd both like to succeed the old man when he retires. Gillespie's supposed to have the inside track, but you never know. Personally, I don't think Belnap will ever quit. He's the die-with-his-boots-on type. Ever meet him?"

"I had him on a flight once. Nice, but gruff."

Perkins chuckled. "Gruff's the right word. He has a very short fuse and a very long memory for anyone who crosses him. For that matter, so does Gillespie. The difference is that he's smooth. Belnap's an old-fashioned cutlass. Gillespie's a rapier."

They were walking from the Training Department to the seven-story general offices building, and Danni could sense that Perkins was nervous. She remembered how afraid of him she had been that day she was almost terminated. Now she felt superior to the man who was her immediate boss. He obviously dreaded the ordeal of visiting the senior vice president of Marketing; she looked forward to it with a total lack of fear. The scar tissue from Tony's death had become a kind of armor; nothing could be as bad as what she had gone through, and no one could frighten her, not even an Evan Belnap or a Harmon Gillespie. . . .

"Welcome to Miami, Miss Hendricks," Gillespie said.

He was, Danni decided, just as handsome as he had been when she had seen him at graduation. The graying temples had taken on a slightly more silverish tinge, but the effect was added dignity, not age. He was tall, though not as tall as Tony, and somewhat heavier, a man in his mid-forties with penetrating blue eyes. There was a slight flabbiness around his pink, well-shaved jowls, but this was the only discordant note in his features, from his curly dark hair past a Barrymore nose down to a wide, sensuous mouth parted in just enough of a dignified smile to display the teeth of a Pepsodent ad. His voice was deep and carefully modulated.

"It's a pleasure to meet you in person," he was saying. "Harriet Nash recommended you most highly and I seem to remember a number of complimentary passenger letters carrying your name."

"We've met before, Mr. Gillespie," Danni said with a slight smile. "You spoke at our graduation."

He recovered smoothly. "Damn, I thought you looked familiar. Please forgive me—I speak at so many graduations, I forget both names and faces. But I do remember you now. You were the prettiest girl in your class—let's see, that was almost two years ago, wasn't it?"

"A little over two years, so no apology is necessary."

They stared at each other, long enough to make Perkins feel uncomfortable. The training director coughed. "I've got a meeting in ten minutes, so I'll take Danni back with me and let her get acclimated—she starts her first class Monday."

Gillespie glanced at him. "Why don't you go ahead, Ed. I'll chat with her a few minutes and then send her along."

Perkins left, tossing Danni a look that was either reproach or warning—she could not tell which and didn't care.

Gillespie offered her a cigarette, which she took, conscious of his eyes on her as he lit it. "I assume you've heard we've ordered fifteen Boeing seven-oh-sevens, with an option for ten more," he said.

152

"Yes, sir. I can't wait—it almost makes me wish I hadn't quit line flying. Working a jet trip will really be something."

"You can always go back to the line; there'll be plenty of time for you to fly the jets. But right now, our first priority has to be training for them." He paused, his eyes still on her. "We'll be putting into service one hundred eleven passenger airplanes, and that means new standards of in-flight service. We'll be almost doubling speed, which means we'll have to serve twice as many people in half the time we now allow. We have to increase efficiency without sacrificing graciousness and courtesy. A very large order—as far as customer service is concerned, easily the biggest challenge this industry has ever faced. That's why training is so important. Why . . ."

He stopped and looked over Danni's shoulder at someone who had just entered unannounced. "Well, well. We have company."

Danni turned around, startled to see the towering figure of Trans-National president Evan Belnap. She had only glimpsed him briefly before—she had been working the galley—but now, at close range, he was far more imposing. His stern, lined face could have been carved out of hardened lava, and his white hair, crew-cut to a bristle, gave him the appearance of a Prussian officer. Danni knew he was in his sixties, but except for a slight stoop in his shoulders and a discernible pot belly, he did not look that old. When he spoke, it was with a gravely rumble as if the words were being propelled from an enormous cavern.

"Didn't know you had anyone with you, Harmon. Sorry to interrupt but I've just been talking to Bill Allen at Boeing. I told him I didn't give a damn what Pan Am is doing; I still want twenty-two seats in first class. That'll leave us with eighty-nine in coach, and if we're off base, the bulkhead's adjustable. That still okay with your department?"

"That was our original seven-oh-seven configuration and I see no reason for changing. Evan, I'd like you to meet Miss Hendricks. She's just been promoted to stewardess instructor. I've been briefing her on how our new bird will affect in-flight service."

Danni rose politely and put out her hand, which he took with the surprising gentleness of so many big men. "Very pleased to meet you, Mr. Belnap."

He examined her. "Hendricks. Why the hell is that name so familiar?"

"You were on my airplane a couple of months ago, Mr. Belnap. But I'm sure you wouldn't remember me."

"Damnation, I remember you from somewhere. Remember that name, anyway."

"The Eleanor Roosevelt letter, Evan," Gillespie said. "Danni was senior on that flight."

The thin, tight lips creased in a smile. "That's where I heard your name, young lady. Damned fine job!" He turned back to Gillespie. "Did you write her a letter, as I told you?"

He hadn't, but Danni said quickly, "He did, Mr. Belnap—it's one of my proudest possessions." She stole a glance at the senior vice president and was pleased to see his look of relief. Belnap himself grunted.

"Come down to see me after you get through here," he rumbled to the vice president. "Got a few things I wanna talk over."

"I'll be right down," Gillespie promised. He waited until the president had left, then turned back to Danni. "I didn't send you any letter—why did you think you had to lie for me?"

"It wasn't a lie, not really. You did send me a copy of Mrs. Roosevelt's letter—or you sent it to Harriet and she gave it to me."

Gillespie shook his head, whether in bewilderment or gratitude she could not tell. "I should have written a separate note to you, as Belnap suggested. I'm a bit remiss in such protocol. But I can tell you face to face, you did one hell of a job." He picked up some papers on his desk and she recognized it as a sign of dismissal.

"Thank you very much, Mr. Gillespie," she said simply. But as she turned to go, his voice stopped her.

"My door's always open to you, Danni. Anytime. Please remember that."

"I will," she replied.

And realized that she meant it.

During the two years Danni had flown, there had been almost 100 percent turnover in the instructors' cadre—most of her colleagues, she discovered, weren't much more experienced than she in classroom training. At first, she regretted this; she knew she would have benefited from the counsel and guidance of someone like Marlene Compton. But Marlene had gotten married a month before Danni transferred to Miami and had moved from the area. So Danni, the oldest chronologically, found herself leading the others instead of following them.

As a teacher, she tried to model herself after Marlene—with a little bit of Harriet Nash tossed in. She was tough but fair, and she related the problems of her trainees to those she had experienced herself. But she quickly discovered the truth of Harriet's warning not to over-identify with students. She learned how to close her eyes to tears, turn deaf ears to sobs, and differentiate between a phony alibi and a legitimate excuse.

She probably would have been easier on her trainees if Julie had been there, but Julie's transfer to Miami was delayed indefinitely when her father became ill.

"York's less than a two-hour drive from Washington," she explained to Danni in a phone call. "Until Dad's better, I'd rather be able to get home in a hurry. I'm sorry, Danni—as soon as I can, I'll apply for the transfer."

Certainly Julie would have tried to talk Danni out of an action that sent shock waves through the Training Department and up to the desk of Harmon Gillespie. It involved curfew violations, a subject on which Danni had mixed feelings. She hated to make surprise curfew checks—they made her feel like a cheap detective gathering evidence in a divorce case. But she also hated the lying that curfew transgressors pulled on all instructors.

It was in the third week of the second class Danni taught, 57-04, that a trainee named Angela Van Buren went out on a date and failed to return by curfew. Danni had picked that night for a check, and when she reached Angela's room, the AWOL girl's roommate resorted to a time-tested evasive strategy—she turned on the shower and shut the bathroom door.

"Evening, Sue—where's Angela?"

"She's in the shower."

Danni was well aware of the tactic, but Sue Warner was one

of the best trainees in the class and she decided to take her word. She nodded, left, and was just walking out of the dorm when Angela burst in, out of breath. Her jaw dropped as she spotted Danni, but she never got a chance to say anything.

"Tell your roommate we met," Danni said, and walked away.

The next day, she informed Perkins she wanted both girls terminated.

"I'll gladly lower the boom on Van Buren," Perkins agreed, "but for Christ's sake, Danni, the other kid was just trying to protect her."

"She lied to protect her. That makes her just as guilty as if she had violated curfew herself."

"Danni, I can't do it. I know I'm called the Smiling Executioner around here, but even I couldn't be that cruel. Jesus, this isn't West Point with a goddamned honor code."

"It might as well be. If you have rules, you can't make exceptions."

"Warner didn't break a rule—her roommate did."

"Sue tried to cover it up. She's equally to blame."

"Well," Perkins said doggedly, "I'm supposed to back up our instructors but damned if I think this is fair. Sorry, Danni, but I'm gonna pass the buck to Gillespie."

"Do that," Danni said tartly.

He did. Gillespie ordered him to fire both trainees.

Once it was done, however, Danni had second thoughts. She was not sorry about Angela, but Sue Warner's tearful pleas for a second chance had disturbed her. They started a mental film projector whirring through her mind—of Terry and Meredith and Danni's own close brush with ruthless dismissal. Of hated martinets like Martha Devins and mavericks like Julie who made a daring game of flaunting rules. Even thinking about Julie was a needle pricking her conscience—she knew Julie would have tried to talk her out of axing Sue.

Memories were an insidious poison, Danni told herself. Like those she had of Tony—fortifying the guilt she had built out of her sexual aggressiveness, her delaying marriage. She could do nothing about these memories, she was convinced—they had been applied with a branding iron. But hadn't she doomed Sue Warner? Destroyed her ambitious dreams with impersonal efficiency and maybe inflicting the same permanent scars that Danni carried—all because the girl had displayed the priceless quality of loyalty? What, Danni asked herself, was she turning into? Sue could have been Danni Hendricks . . .

Facing class 57-04 after the termination, she could feel the trainees' resentment—an unspoken, sullen fog of both hatred and fear. That same night, she sat down at her battered Remington portable and hammered out a memo to Ed Perkins, with a copy to Harmon Gillespie. Two days later, she and Perkins were called to the vice president's office.

"I can't believe you wrote this," Gillespie said, fingering the memo. "From an instructor who's just given us a pretty good imitation of Captain Bligh, I now get a recommendation that curfews should be abolished."

Danni flushed. "I think I was wrong in Sue Warner's case. It's too late to make amends, but she was a classic example of someone victimized by a rule that's basically unnecessary."

"Curfews," Gillespie said, "were instituted as a means of teaching self-discipline."

Ed Perkins bobbed his head. "You're taking the Warner business too hard. I know I fought you on it, but damned if I don't think you were right."

Only because Gillespie sided with me, Danni thought. Aloud she said, "I think the issue goes beyond what I did to that girl. We're teaching trainees to accept responsibility, and at the same time we treat them like irresponsible juveniles. We don't need curfews to instill discipline."

"I disagree," Perkins said blandly. "Most of 'em *are* irresponsible juveniles. Take away those curfew rules and you'd have ninety percent of every class so bleary-eyed they couldn't learn the alphabet."

"They're already bleary-eyed," Danni retorted, "from trying to cram the equivalent of five months' learning into five weeks. Training pressures in themselves are a form of discipline, and adding curfews on top of them is unnecessary discipline."

157

Gillespie had been following the exchange with the concentration of a man watching a tennis game. "We're not alone in imposing curfews," he said. "Virtually every airline has them."

"That's no excuse for perpetuating an anachronism."

Gillespie chuckled. "Well put. But there's still a danger that if you're wrong, we could wind up with some serious disciplinary problems."

"Then try it for just two or three classes. See whether there *is* a breakdown. If trainees can't handle a more lenient policy with some maturity, put the curfews back in."

Perkins frowned, evidently sensing Gillespie's ambivalence.

"Won't do any harm to try," he said diplomatically.

"Then we'll do it," Gillespie declared.

Danni had a curious reaction to this relatively minor victory. It began as relief from a guilty conscience—she couldn't help Sue anymore, but there wouldn't be any future curfew terminations, either. And she also felt the exhilaration of achievement—she had forged a change in company policy and demonstrated to a power like Harmon Gillespie that she was capable of independent thinking. There were other things she could try, like the Familiarization Flight plan she had proposed to Marlene during training—letting trainees actually work on FAM trips instead of just observing. Perkins, she had heard, vetoed it as too complex.

She waited until the next three classes had graduated; the trainees showed no inclination to stray off the curfewless reservation. Armed with this success, she renewed her FAM flight suggestion in the form of another memo to Perkins, copy to Gillespie. The training director demurred.

"I'll admit your idea has merit," he allowed, "but it's still impractical."

"Why?"

"You want to put no more than two students on each FAM trip. It might work with a small class but you had twenty-three girls in fifty-seven-eight. You can't handle that number in a single weekend. It would involve sending 'em out on at least ten different flights."

"So what's the problem? We dispatch forty trips a day out of

Miami. Loads are light on Saturdays and up to mid-afternoon Sundays—we'd have no trouble getting space."

He shook his head. "Well, maybe, but even if we did it this way, I still can't buy running FAMS on two weekends during training instead of one."

"One at the end of the second week, the other the final weekend before graduation," Danni said. "What's wrong with it?"

"You're not giving them enough time off. They work hard enough as it is without making 'em fly that last weekend."

"Trade-off," Danni said.

"Huh?"

"No curfews in exchange for the second FAM weekend. Remember, they'll be working those trips. They'll be getting experience no classroom lecture can match. Come on, Ed, let's try it for a while. The curfew elimination worked, didn't it?"

"So far," Perkins said grudgingly. "Well, you've already given Gillespie a peek at this plan so we might as well sound him out."

The senior vice president of Marketing had already bought it. As soon as they walked into his office, Gillespie announced his immediate blessing.

"An excellent suggestion," he beamed. "I think it'll improve training considerably. You know, I've heard Eastern's doing the same thing—I wish we had thought of it sooner . . ."

Somewhere she had read that the way to get ahead in any company was to put one's name on as much interoffice correspondence as possible. She kept her old Remington busy with various suggestions and projects—from proposed changes in the current training curriculum to a tentative layout for future 707 training. The latter was a twelve-page outline which she composed after obtaining and thoroughly studying the Boeing cabin configuration TNA had ordered—and this memo she sent not only to Perkins and Gillespie but to Belnap himself. She knew it smacked of self-serving, but she didn't really care. Maybe her personal life was a mess, but she was going to make sure her professional one was at best satisfying, and at worst an effective time-consuming distraction.

She would have socialized more with her fellow instructors but they had their own commitments—two were engaged, one married, and the fourth was going to college at night. Danni had frequent offers for dates, but the prospect of even the most casual relationship with a man was a chilling turn-off. She still felt soiled, afraid. Yet she also realized that a different reason was beginning to fuel her reluctance—a growing, gnawing feeling of cynicism about men. It was vague, like a dull toothache; she could neither define nor admit it, but she knew it was there. She could sense it in her attitude toward Perkins and Gillespie. The former was competent enough, but so insecure he was afraid to gamble on the new or untried. The latter was obviously able, even brilliant in some respects, yet even to Danni's inexperienced eyes, he was a man infatuated with self-importance.

Toward Perkins she felt superiority; toward Gillespie, equality, and she wondered at her temerity—two years of line flying and a few months of instructing, and here she was telling herself, *They're no better than I* . . .

But it's true, she thought. I'm just as capable. All I need is more experience and a couple of breaks . . .

One-half of her mind began to forget the past represented by Anthony Buchanan. And the other half was fragmented into conflicting emotions—along with the guilt, a terrible, longing loneliness; a reservoir of deep pity for a man who was so tortured and doomed; a festering resentment, not merely for the hurt he had inflicted and the fact that he had died, but for events forcing her life into a course she had never intended.

For of one thing she was sure. Her job had become her lover, and to her new lover she was totally committed.

Chapter 9

On an impulse one day, she called Pat Martin.

Danni had written her a short note of congratulations after her election as union president, without getting any acknowledgement. Later she had seen her once in the cafeteria and talked briefly and vaguely about "getting together one of these nights."

"Yes, we should do that some time," Pat had said, equally noncommittal.

But in actually inviting her to dinner, Danni's motive was only partially social. Gillespie had sent her a typewritten note complimenting her on the 707 training outline and adding a P.S. in his spiky, almost feminine handwriting. *I'll be talking with you further about this.*

Now, she decided, it was time to sound out the union on her ideas for manning the jets. She remembered only too well the friction that had existed between them during training, and that Pat didn't even like her. Yet that was a long time ago, and she felt she could talk frankly with her. After all, neither was far removed from line flying and they still had much in common. Pat might even welcome an honest and open discussion with a member of management—she must still be feeling her way as the new union president.

Danni's first mistake was to announce, as soon as they were seated in the restaurant, "You're my guest, Pat, or rather the company's. This is all on expense account so splurge." She meant it to put Pat at ease, for the restaurant Danni had chosen was fairly expensive, but Martin's reaction was a sardonic smile.

"You're really trying to impress me, aren't you?" she said. "I always thought you'd wind up as one of those management finks."

Danni tried to pass it off. "On the totem pole of management, I'm located about three inches off the ground."

They did talk about their training days, but even this subject produced acrimony. "They should spend three weeks on safety and one week on cabin service instead of the other way around," Pat said.

"Be practical, Pat. We serve fifty million meals for every emergency. Safety training's more than adequate—it'll have to be tougher when we start flying jets, sure, but you can't expect the company to devote seventy-five percent of training time to situations the average stew won't encounter if she flies for ten years."

"That's exactly what I do expect. Plus a few other things."

"Such as?"

"Such as paying trainees. Such as reducing the probationary period to one month instead of six. Such as—"

"Hold it. You know damned well it's impossible to judge performance in a month."

"You could if training were improved."

"Balderdash. Why don't you admit the real reason—a one-month probation would mean you wouldn't have to wait six months to acquire new union members."

"I see nothing wrong in that. Six months' probation is just a blank check for management to fire anyone who doesn't fit into their mold. Six months is what the cold-blooded bastards need to brainwash every naive kid who puts on a pair of wings. You're a perfect example."

"Me?"

"Yes, you. After six months, you were so pro-management it made me sick. Sucking up to supervisors like Harriet Nash. And from what I hear, you haven't changed a bit."

"Exactly what have you heard?" Danni asked.

"That you're Harmon Gillespie's fair-haired girl. That he

thinks you're the greatest thing to hit the airline industry since jets."

"You make it sound like a crime. The trouble with you, Pat, is that you're so blindly anti-company you're suspicious of anyone who doesn't wear a union label. Just take off those blinders for a minute and you'll see that I'm no enemy. I could even do you some good."

"Oh? How?"

"Who the hell do you think got Gillespie to drop those stupid curfews?"

"According to gossip," Martin conceded, "it was Danni Hendricks."

"You're damned right it was. And I'm not finished. I hope to have something to say about seven-oh-seven training. Maybe even crew complement. Damnit, Pat, I want to work with you, not against you. I know management can be unreasonable at times. But it's not a collection of villains. I've gotten to know quite a few officers—they're intelligent and fair-minded. Take Gillespie—he may be a smooth-talking sonofabitch but he's good at his job and he'll listen to reason."

"According to equally foul-mouthed gossip," Pat said in a tone that was more matter-of-fact than critical, "you've been sleeping with him."

Danni's anger came out in the form of a blush, and she was miserably conscious that to Pat it could be a visible manifestation of guilt, not resentment.

"That would be nobody's damned business, but for your information, I haven't," Danni snapped.

The smile on Martin's face showed exactly how she had interpreted that blush. "Be that as it may," she said easily, "and assuming you're climbing the corporate ladder purely on merit, I still wouldn't want to work with you."

"Why not?"

"Because ambition can be smelled like a dog in heat. Maybe you haven't spread your legs for Harmon Gillespie, but if you have to, you will."

Later that night, just before she fell asleep, she thought of what Pat Martin had said. The bitch had been wrong, of course.

Ambitious, yes. That much was true. But prostituting her body? Not the daughter of John Hendricks. Not the Danni Tony Buchanan had loved. Not the girl she knew herself to be. Not in a million years. Except . . .

Except I'm already soiled and unworthy . . . Would it be so bad? Getting ahead is all I've got to look forward to . . . it's my life now, without Tony . . .

She finally dozed off, and for the first time in months, she dreamed not of a dead airline captain but of someone else. It was a deliciously sensuous, wicked dream.

It was of Harmon Gillespie.

Almost a year after Danni had become an instructor, Julie Granger's father died of cancer. Julie requested a transfer to Miami and moved into Danni's apartment two weeks later.

Their reunion was joyous, yet somehow a little strained—like that of sisters whose separation had made them strangers.

They talked through most of the first night. About Julie's father and about Tony. About the latest gossip from the Washington base—Harriet Nash, for example, was going steady with a lawyer and might get married soon. And about Julie's flight escapades.

". . . so the guy gets on with this bull fiddle; the damned thing looked two feet shorter than the Washington Monument. He puts it on the seat next to him and I tell him, 'Sir, our manifest shows we've got a full plane and somebody's going to want that seat—if that happens, we'll have to put the fiddle in the baggage compartment.' He says, 'Let 'em sit somewhere else—the agent let me board with it.' I was trying to stay cool so I very politely informed him it was company policy to sell him a seat if he insisted on filling it with personal property. He says to me, 'You can stick that company policy up your ass.' And that did it. I said, 'Sir, if you can do the same thing with that damned fiddle, we've got the whole thing solved.' Well, naturally he wrote the company a nasty letter and Harriet grounded me for a week."

Danni laughed. "You should have gotten a medal, not a week off."

"That's what I told Harriet. Actually, she agreed with me but it seems that prick Gillespie saw the letter and ordered her to suspend me."

"Harmon's not a bad guy," Danni said. "He's been damned good to me."

Julie's eyes narrowed. "It's 'Harmon' now? You two have something going?"

"Good God, no. Around here, you get in the habit of calling even senior vice presidents by their first name."

"From what I've heard," Julie said, "Gillespie wouldn't go to the john without an ulterior motive. If he's nice to you, there has to be a reason."

Danni bristled. "His reason is simple. He thinks I'm doing a good job." Her voice took on a defiant tone. "He's taking me to Seattle next week. And lower your eyebrows—it's strictly business."

"Business? What kind of business?"

"To see the seven-oh-seven mockups. He has to decide on galley equipment, cabin configurations, evac slides—you know, all that kind of stuff. He wants someone with line experience as a kind of consultant. Technical advisor, I guess you'd call it."

"Pardon my suspicious nature," Julie snorted, "but this airline has approximately five hundred stews with more line experience than you have. Did he pick your name out of a hat?"

Danni's tone was testy. "No, he didn't. Ed Perkins has had me doing a lot of work getting ready for seven-oh-seven training and I seem to have become the resident expert."

Julie poured the last contents of a wine bottle into a stemmed glass and studied her friend. "I assume you know Gillespie's married."

"Of course I know it. What's that got to do with it?"

"Nothing, I hope. But it sounds . . . well, fishy. A junior instructor telling a senior vice president what to put into one of our oversized blowtorches?"

"'Fishy'? I've already told you there's nothing between

165

Gillespie and me. I haven't slept with him and I have no intention of doing so."

"I'm not accusing you of anything. It's Gillespie who bothers me. He's bedded more than one stew on this airline, including a couple who made supervisor in a disgustingly short space of time between assignation and promotion. He's got a lousy reputation. You could get hurt."

Danni couldn't resist it. "How—by getting promoted?"

"No. By falling in love with the creep. And you're just the type who would. How many times have you told me you wouldn't want to sleep with a guy unless you loved him?"

Danni didn't answer. She was thinking, *I guess I have changed, because I don't feel that way anymore.*

On the flight to Seattle, Harmon Gillespie was the model of proper, circumspect executive decorum, treating her with detached politeness.

Small matter, she mused. She was going to do a job for the airline, not a job on one of its vice presidents, and what pleased her most was the rapport between them, for all his mild aloofness. He read, napped, and did a little work, but there was plenty of time for talk on the long flight, Danni indulging in the twin luxuries of a first-class pass and the chance to observe the stewardesses. She noticed that Gillespie kept glancing at his watch through the meal service.

"Are you timing them?" she asked.

He nodded. "I often do. I'm trying to get some ideas on cutting down wasted motion. Now these girls have all the time in the world for their service, but that wouldn't be true on shorter segments and it certainly won't be true for even long-haul trips when the jets start operating. It's not my idea, by the way—Dick Ensign at Western tried time-motion studies a few years ago. He held stop-watches on his girls and he wound up cutting more than twenty minutes of serving time between Los Angeles and San Francisco."

166

Danni was fascinated. "On a ninety-minute leg? I don't see how he did it."

"Basically, what he did was to save a few seconds for every operation. For example, Western saved seven minutes by opening two-thirds of the champagne bottles before the flight left the gate. It's things like this I want you to look for when we see our new birds. Boeing will be showing us several types of galleys. Look for models that offer the most convenience, the fastest serving time. Tell me honestly what you think of galley locations—I'd rather relocate a coat rack if the space could be better utilized for galley efficiency. See what I mean?"

"Yes," Danni said. And she was thinking, *Julie had this guy pegged wrong—he wants me to work.*

"I don't mind telling you I was one of those who insisted on the seven-oh-seven," Gillespie was saying with an air of pride. "Take United—Pat Patterson will be up the well-known creek because he went for the DC-eight. Douglas will be a year behind Boeing in putting that airplane into service, and for that year United will be trying to compete transcontinentally with DC-sevens against TWA's and American's seven-oh-sevens. And my God, if Evan Belnap had had his way, we'd even be trailing United."

Danni asked, puzzled, "You mean Mr. Belnap didn't want us to have any jets?"

"Exactly. His idea was to order Lockheed Electras as a kind of interim plane—they're propjets. 'Why the hell should we buy the *Queen Mary* to sail across Lake Michigan?' he said. A very short-sighted attitude, I'm afraid."

Danni said nothing; he seemed to sense her shock at a high-ranking officer's expressing such criticism of the company president. "Don't get me wrong," he said, "Evan Belnap is one of the great men of this industry. But he's getting old. He looks back, not ahead! And you can't take this company into the jet age with a mind that's still back with the pistons."

She was silent. Gillespie patted her hand; the slight physical contact caused her to look at him. Into eyes that were shrewd and cold. "If I've embarrassed you, I'm sorry," he said. "I have the utmost respect and affection for Belnap. However, I don't think any

167

of us should follow a man blindly, forgiving all his faults and mistakes. Perhaps I shouldn't have even mentioned it."

"Well," Danni hedged, "I guess we should change the subject. I'm just a working stiff—I don't have to choose sides."

"Nor should you. I merely brought it up because you're a very intelligent girl, one with a great future in this airline. I want us to be friends, and as my friend you have a right to know my thoughts and opinions." He laughed with a practiced nonchalance whose hypocrisy did not escape her.

"It's between the two of us," she assured him, and hated her own hypocrisy for saying it. She had the feeling she should have defended Belnap, but she was also uncomfortably aware of an unexpected excitement—that of being involved. She could almost feel the strands of ordained conduct being strained and weakened. . .

All her life, she would remember the time she spent at Boeing with a mixture of emotions. Awe at what she saw. Pride in being a part of an industry capable of creating the huge jetliner. Satisfaction in what she had accomplished and gratitude to Gillespie for giving her the assignment.

The Boeing official assigned to them was William Gordon, a young products engineer specializing in aircraft interiors. A slender, short man with rimless glasses and an always-present pipe, he had a professorial air softened by an easy, quick smile. Danni liked him immediately. He was willing to share his knowledge, not flaunt it.

"I want to hear your ideas, not just sell you Boeing's," he told them at their first meeting.

She had fantasized about producing suggestions, criticism, and advice in such a voluminous flow that both Gillespie and Gordon would be in awe. But her daydream foundered on the rocks of realism—she discovered that Boeing generally knew what it was doing. Yet still she was able to contribute. She managed, for example, to convince Gillespie that the galley equipment he preferred because of its low cost actually would not work out.

168

"It's not only impractical but dangerous," she told him. "Look at all the sharp edges—any stewardess working in a hurry is liable to cut herself if she grabs the wrong way. And it's too flimsy. Now that other model we looked at . . ."

On the second day, while Gillespie was lunching with Boeing executives, Gordon took Danni to the Renton facility where the 707 assembly line had been established. There she had her first view of an actual fuselage. Stripped of seats and other interior fittings, it seemed to her like an unending tunnel. She saw the massive wing spars, as thick as bridge girders; the skeleton frame with its powerfully built cross-beams, rings, and stringers; the enormous tail, measuring almost forty feet from the top of the vertical fin to the ground—the height of a four-story building.

"It's almost too big," she marveled.

Gordon grinned. "I'll tell you a little story. Back in 1932, we rolled out the first Boeing two forty-seven. A revolutionary plane—two engines, all-metal construction, carried twelve passengers. One of our engineers looked at it and said, 'They'll never build a bigger airplane!' Don't ever underestimate technology. Some day you'll be flying around in a transport twice the size of this one. Although"—he looked at the giant plane with pride—"for the time being, this one's big enough. Well, you've seen all the mockups and now the real airplane. What's our reaction?"

"The coffee-makers are too small," Danni said with total seriousness.

"A five-million-dollar, one-hundred-twenty-ton jet that can fly coast to coast in less than six hours, and all you can say is that the coffee-makers are too small?"

She laughed. "I know that sounds petty. But I'm a stewardess, Bill. And a stewardess couldn't care less how much a seven-oh-seven costs. She does care about things like coffee-makers. And safety equipment—like those stew jumpseats on the mockups. I noticed they had no shoulder harnesses, just waist belts."

"Shoulder harnesses are available, but optional. You'd have to take that up with your boss. Anything else on your mind?"

"I'm not sold on the location of the CO_2 bottles. They'd be hard to reach and . . ."

They talked on in this manner on the way back to the Seattle complex, and when they ran out of conversation, Gordon turned on the car radio. He was fiddling with the dial to get some music when the voice of a news announcer froze his fingers.

". . . there's no word on a fatality count thus far, but it's apparent there has been a heavy loss of life. Trans-National officials say there were forty-eight passengers and a crew of five aboard the DC-seven when it crashed while trying to land in a heavy fog at New York's Idlewild Airport. An airline spokesman says, and we quote, 'There are some survivors but it looks bad.' From Washington, a Senate committee has . . ."

Gordon flicked off the radio and glanced at Danni. She was pale and staring straight ahead. The Boeing official patted her shoulder. "Damn, I'm sorry, Danni. Every crash is an industrywide black eye no matter who's involved or what happened. But I know it's worse for the airline whose bird went down."

She nodded. "All I can think about is the crew. Who was flying the trip. Who was working the cabin. And was it anyone I know."

"Probably not. TNA's a pretty damned big airline."

Danni's eyes brimmed. "Somebody knew the crew. That's what hurts."

Gillespie was waiting for them in Gordon's office, a somber look on his face.

"We dropped one," he said without preamble. "A DC-seven at Idlewild—I've just been talking to Belnap."

"We heard it on the radio," Danni said. "No details, just that it crashed landing in a fog. Did you hear anything else—what flight it was? Any word on the crew?"

"Miami–New York, with an intermediate stop in Atlanta. Evan says the pilot apparently tried to abort at the last minute but hooked a wing and they cartwheeled. The pilots survived."

Something in his voice chilled Danni. "The stewardesses?" she asked.

He shook his head. "All three were killed." He hesitated, and

170

the chill turned into an icy cold. "Two of them were in your class, Danni. Betty Jo Lynch and Rose Steinmetz. I'm sorry."

She was too numb to cry, yet penetrating the numbness was a throb of relief—for one horrifying second she thought Julie had been on that plane. But the silent prayer of thanks was replaced by a surge of pain and grief. Funny little Betty Jo with her thick accent and gift for innocent malaprops. Rose, with her quiet sense of humor. . .

Danni began to tremble. Gordon steered her toward a chair, almost forcefully pushing her into it. "Can I get you some water?"

"I think I could use a real drink."

"So could I," Gillespie said.

"I'll be right back," Gordon said. "I know where there's a bottle stashed away."

Even as he left, Danni's tears began to flow. She didn't want to cry and she didn't mean to cry, but her mind was filled with images. Of crumpling metal and crackling flames with black, oily, choking smoke, feeding ravenously from ruptured fuel tanks. The false security of an aircraft cabin transformed in the blink of an eye into a nightmare of panic and death. Betty Jo and Rose . . .

Bitterness intruded on her grief. Resentment that the familiar, symmetrical beauty of an airliner could have betrayed them. That it could prove so vulnerable as to make their training a mockery. She wondered whether they had had any chance to get out, and she prayed the end had been swift and merciful . . .

". . . Here, Danni. Bourbon was all I could find." Gordon had poured a generous slug into a paper cup and was handing it to her. She sipped it gratefully. The Boeing engineer handed Gillespie a second cup; the vice president gulped the contents in one swallow.

"We'll have to go back tomorrow morning," Gillespie said. "Northwest has an eight A.M. flight to Chicago. Bill, suppose you can drive us back to the hotel? I'd like Danni to get some rest and then take her out for a quiet dinner."

"I'll be fine," Danni protested half-heartedly. "We've still got work to do here and . . ."

"As a matter of fact, we're about finished. When we get home, you can write up your comments, we'll go over them, and I'll phone Boeing on what we'll be needing. That okay with you, Bill?"

"Fine with me," Gordon said. "I'll go get my car and see you out front."

At the hotel, Gillespie suggested they meet in the lobby in two hours. She welcomed the chance to be alone for a little while. By now, logic had begun to override anger.

She thought back to what Marlene had taught them. Crash survival depended on many factors, and good training was merely one. There also had to be luck—luck in the way the impact force was distributed, luck in the speed at which fire and smoke spread, luck in the way the passengers reacted to danger. Marlene had told them of one crash in which twenty persons had died because they froze in panic, perishing even though almost five minutes elapsed before flames enveloped the cabin.

She thought of what she had seen that very day. The brute strength of the 707 airframe, built with the sinews of a battleship. The turbine engine, many times more powerful than the biggest piston yet with hundreds of fewer parts to go wrong. The size of the fuselage, one hundred forty-five feet long and a third wider than any piston-engine airliner ever built.

Accidents, she knew, were the mistakes of aviation. Yet for every mistake, there had been ten thousand miracles—the 707 itself was a 240,000-pound miracle made possible by the lessons learned from mistakes. Yes, she decided, that was the only fair way to look at it. Except . . .

Betty Jo and Rose.

The bitterness returned, uninvited but insidious. The teachings of her church, supposedly a bulwark against sorrow, seemed as empty and useless as they had been when Tony died. Betty Jo and Rose, too, had had deep faith. Once more, she could not reconcile her Catholicism with the unjustness of tragedy. She did not blame the church; she merely admitted that her own faith was not deep enough—it was an armor against adversity too thin to do her much good.

Danni stretched out on the bed and had almost dozed off when someone knocked on the door. She opened it to see a bellhop carrying a bucket of ice enclosing a bottle of wine.

"Mr. Gillespie sent it up," he said.

Nice of him, Danni thought. A rubber band around the bottle held a note, which she unfolded.

Danni—thought this might help you relax. See you at dinner.

Harmon

Trying to make Brownie points, she decided. But maybe that wasn't fair—he was just being thoughtful and kind. Like Tony, before he got sick. Damnit, why did she have to think of Tony? Even the wine itself reminded her of him—he had loved good wine and had taught her how to judge bouquet and body. Poor Tony . . .

She got a glass from the bathroom, filled it to the brim, and lay on the bed, her back against the headboard pillows, sipping. And thinking . . .

About her dead classmates, their young lives over. Betty Jo probably died a virgin. If I had been she, Danni mused, regret would have been my last thought. No, probably not . . . I would have been too frightened to think about anything except not wanting to die. Still, when it happens to me at least I'll know what it felt like to have a man inside me. Someone I loved—that made it even better. Why the hell am I thinking this way?. . .

She knew why. She damn well knew why. The stiff slug of bourbon in Gordon's office, the wine she was drinking, the deaths of two friends that made her want to live for the moment . . . she could feel tantalizing warmth, as if the wine had flowed down to her limbs. For the first time in a long, long time, desire consumed her . . .

She tried to recoil. The obvious target was Harmon Gillespie, and it was foolish to want him. Not just foolish—stupid. A married man, a rumored philanderer, a ruthless seeker of power. And if it happened, how could she explain it to Julie? How could she justify it? And not just to Julie—to herself . . .

Easy, Danni. What are you getting into? Sure you want sex. Tony taught you how much you wanted it. Nothing abnormal

173

about it . . . nothing to be ashamed of. But not with someone like Harmon Gillespie. That's not what you've been taught . . . I couldn't face my parents or Julie or anyone else. Be patient. Wait for the right guy . . . Wait a minute—what right guy? Miss Round Heels herself, that's me. So damned oversexed I drove Tony right over the brink. There may never be another Tony. At least with Harmon, I'd be going to bed with him for practical reasons. Sure it's partly physical, but logical, too. Scold all you want, Julie, but you told me about two stews who got promoted because they went to bed with him. That's where I'd be different—I'm good, damnit. I'm smart and capable and determined . . . I wouldn't be using sex to get what I don't deserve. All I need is a chance to show what I can do and the hell with everybody else. If screwing a vice president gets me that chance . . . Especially the hell with you, Julie—a fat lot of good it did Betty Jo and Rose to be decent and moral . . . oh for Christ's sake, what am I saying? It's just that there's nothing ahead for me except the goddamned job . . . I have to think of myself . . . my own future. And sleeping with Harmon wouldn't be so bad . . . I'll bet he's good . . . damned good. And I need someone . . . oh Christ, I do need it . . .

Now she was touching herself, first gently, then frantically, trying to find in sexual release a way to turn back. But when the climax came, it was a mere throbbing—and miserably she thought of the pleasure Tony had given her. She felt disgust and disappointment, but also defeat.

She took a quick bath, donned the one good dress she had brought a low-cut black chiffon—and went down to the lobby to begin the seduction of Harmon Gillespie.

She had invited him into her room for an after-dinner nightcap—"There's still quite a bit left of that wine you sent me," she said.

His hesitation seemed practiced; in trying to hide alacrity, he emphasized it. "Well, just for a few minutes. I know you're tired." The eagerness in his eyes gave him away.

They indulged in small talk while sipping the still-chilled

wine. As he had during dinner, Gillespie tried to avoid mentioning the crash, but deliberately she steered him into it by mentioning Betty Jo and Rose. She reminisced about their training days, recalling them with warmth and a kind of sad humor. Gillespie thought how courageously resilient she was, never suspecting she was skillfully erecting an image of a vulnerable, decent woman who would want him purely as an antidote to sorrow.

"I guess I'd better send you on your way," she finally said in a regretful tone. "It's getting late."

He rose reluctantly, putting out his hand, but when she took it, her responding pressure surprised and excited him.

"It was a lovely evening," Danni murmured. "I'm grateful for every moment of it."

She kissed him, lightly at first in a gesture of gentle gratitude, but she did not draw away, and as his lips pressed slightly harder, she opened her mouth and probed for his tongue.

"Don't go," she breathed. "I don't want to be alone tonight."

"Jesus," said Harmon Gillespie, reaching for the zipper on the back of her dress.

She was disappointed.

Not because of him but because of herself. When he entered her, she felt nothing, his hard maleness producing the incongruous illusion that her body was still empty. Memories of Tony swept through her mind momentarily, but she forced them out through sheer willpower, and, realizing she was never going to climax, she faked passion with convincing moans and cries. Gillespie decided she was wonderful: Danni decided she was a better actress than she thought.

"You're very good," she told him later.

"So are you. The word 'good' seems inadequate. You're wonderful."

She sat up and reached for her cigarettes on the nightstand. "Want one?"

"No thanks. Tell me, what is there about post-sex that gives a woman an overwhelming desire to smoke?"

"Damned if I know. Maybe it provides a chance to ponder what's just happened."

"And what did just happen, Danni?"

She took a deep drag before answering. "Well, it was very nice. For both of us. Which, in a way, worries me."

"That's a cause for worry?"

"I just don't want you to assume it's going to happen again. Not with any frequency, and maybe never again. I know you're married. I also know we made love because the timing was exactly right. I was lonely and scared and hurting and I'm damned grateful to you. Given the right circumstances, it could happen again. But don't expect any promises."

She had composed those lines while he still was pounding away at her, and he proceeded to follow her script perfectly.

"I don't regard this as a cheap, one-night stand," he said. "I understand your motives and respect them. I hope you won't misinterpret my motives, either—I'm not infatuated with you but I'm tremendously fond of you."

"Vice versa. We'll let it stand right there, Harmon. No serious involvement. Just a two-person mutual admiration society, and if we both want to get together again, so be it. Okay?"

"Eminently okay. Danni, you're amazing. So honest. So straightforward. There isn't anything in the world I wouldn't do for you. If you ever need anything, just ask."

Into her mind swam the image of a hooked fish. Accompanied by the sudden and disturbing recollection of what Pat Martin had said.

. . . *Maybe you haven't spread your legs for Harmon Gillespie, but if you have to, you will.*

Chapter 10

Her consuming need for professional recognition soon paled the shame, shoving it into a tiny corner of her conscience. The self-deception was effortless mostly because of Gillespie. She didn't have to ask for favors—he volunteered them, giving her new projects and fresh responsibilities that challenged her abilities and kept her blessedly busy.

She spent hours composing her 707 report, particularly her crew-complement recommendations, for she knew they contradicted Gillespie's own plans for staffing the big jets. Coming back from Seattle, he had told her that TNA would operate Boeing trips with four stewardesses.

"I don't think four girls are enough," she had argued. "The workload would be unacceptable to anyone but an octopus."

"I think you're exaggerating the difficulties," he had replied. "But if you want to, put your ideas on staffing into your reports and I assure you we'll give them every reasonable consideration."

She suspected that "reasonable consideration" meant polite rejection, but she went ahead anyway and now was taking one last look at what she had written.

I further recommend that a minimum cabin crew of five be assigned to 707 schedules, said complement to be raised to six if advance bookings indicate a load factor of ninety percent or more.

The above staffing would involve two stewardesses in first class and three (or four) serving the coach section. The five-girl quota, however, is predicated on a Company decision to equip our 707 aircraft with a double-galley configuration—a forward galley for first class and a mid-cabin or aft galley serving the coach area. I strongly urge that the Company opt for double galleys as a means of achieving maximum efficiency along with the continuation of our traditionally gracious service.

Aside from the service aspects, however, the crew complement decision must take into account the additional and vital factor of safety. It must be emphasized that the 707 will be carrying more than 110 passengers. In any kind of situation involving an emergency evacuation, we must assume the possibility of at least some cabin crew incapacitation. There are eight emergency exits on the 707—four A or primary exits with slides and four overwing window exits. It is absolutely essential to have an adequate number of stewardesses to handle the evacuation flow. . .

She was proud of the report—a bit stilted, she figured, but thorough and objective. Now all she had to do was wait for the powers-that-be to make up their collective mind, a process that apparently was fueled by molasses. Three weeks went by with no reaction from anyone except Ed Perkins; the training director told her he liked her ideas but cautioned her against expecting too much.

"I'm not expecting anything but a little logic," she responded. "Four girls can't do the job—it's as simple as that."

"Not as simple as you think. There's one hell of a difference in operating costs between four stews and five. And God knows what the jets will do to our training budget—even with four girls, we'll need five hundred bodies a week just for seven-oh-seven trips. What's killing us is the damned turnover rate. It's still well over forty percent annually, and all we're doing now is hiring replacements. Which reminds me, Fred Jordan's in town—said he'd like to say hello to you."

"Fred Jordan? I haven't seen him since the day he hired me. Is he around the building?"

"He's using Bobbie Tripp's office while she's on vacation. Doing some Miami interviews for a couple of days."

Danni went to Tripp's office, where she found the door closed. She knocked tentatively; Jordan's voice came back. "It's not locked."

She entered. Jordan was not alone. Across the desk from him sat a handsome black girl—very poised, Danni decided instantly. Aloud, she said, "Just wanted to say hi, Fred—didn't mean to interrupt anything."

He rose, smiling broadly. "I'm just about finished." He turned to the black girl. "Thank you for coming in, Hester. We'll be in touch with you." As soon as she left, Jordan shook his head in a gesture of frustration.

"Stewardess applicant?"

"Yeah. Meets every qualification but one."

Danni nodded her understanding. "Too bad. I take it hiring Negroes is still *verboten*."

"Unfortunately, yes," Jordan said grimly. "I'd like to have a buck for every rejection I've had to make on racial grounds. That kid I just interviewed, for example. College graduate, good personality, and you saw the way she looked—hell, I've hired too many white turkeys compared to her. But enough of my troubles. How about lunch? I want to hear all about you . . ."

"Sure," Danni said. But her mind wasn't on lunch. She was mentally composing another memo.

She never got a chance to write it, for the next day Gillespie invited her to attend a meeting on stewardess-recruiting requirements, based on acquisition of the new 707 fleet.

Perkins was present, plus several lesser officials from Marketing and Sales, the chief stewardess supervisor in Miami—a comely, self-assured girl named Trudy Simon—and the senior vice president of Operations, Frank Ladell.

"What's he here for?" Danni whispered to Perkins. "Operations hasn't anything to do with cabin crews."

"Belnap's idea. He told both Gillespie and Ladell he wanted

someone from Operations to sit in on any Marketing meeting involving the seven-oh-seven and vice versa. There was an interoffice directive on it."

Danni examined Ladell with some distaste. He had a long, thin face, a receding hairline, and narrow eyes. His stern mouth was unsmiling, and the overall effect, accentuated by a large nose and high cheekbones, was that of a bad-tempered Indian. She also was aware that Ladell was scrutinizing her with an air of suspicion.

The grapevine had firmly established the fact that Gillespie and Ladell were enemies—even now, Danni noticed, neither man tried very hard to hide his dislike; they seemed to exchange glares instead of glances. Without looking at Ladell, she could feel his squinting eyes on her, and she wondered, uncomfortably if illogically, whether he knew about Gillespie and her.

". . . and, of course," Gillespie was saying in his mellifluous voice, "I assume you've all read Danni's memo on the seven-oh-seven. I want to take this opportunity to thank her, and to compliment her, on that excellent presentation." He smiled slightly in her direction and she nodded acknowledgement, even though she could smell what was coming.

"Overall," he continued, "I would say her recommendations have considerable merit. For example, we've decided to install two galleys." He glanced at her again, as if expecting her to bow in gratitude. "However, it has become increasingly apparent that the price tag on these airplanes is being revised upward to an alarming extent. It costs a lot of money, for example, for such items as an extra galley. I'm afraid we're going to have to cut corners, and it seems to me the logical place to start is the size of the cabin crew. Danni, here, has recommended a minimum of five stewardesses. Any of you care to comment?"

The sonofabitch, Danni thought. *He's already made up his mind and he wants us to rubber-stamp.* But she said nothing, waiting for someone else to speak. It was Perkins who began.

"Assuming we can't afford five stewardesses, what minimum do you have in mind?"

"I think we could get along with four," Gillespie replied, and as his eyes collided with Danni's frown, he added, "at least

180

temporarily. Until we can judge the effects on in-flight service."

Ladell put one long leg over the other and stared at his fellow vice president. "I fail to see what the shooting's about. You're doing it ass-backward, Harmon. Go with five and reduce it to four after we get some operating experience. The important thing is to get jet service off to the best possible start, even if it means overstaffing for a while."

"That makes sense," Trudy Simon said, but she caught the narrowing of Gillespie's eyes. "If we can afford the fifth girl."

"Not only can we not afford it," Gillespie snapped, "but it's highly improbable we could recruit in sufficient numbers to fulfill that kind of crew complement. What you all seem to be forgetting is that our jet fleet will require at least seventy-five stewardesses daily, with four girls per flight. And that's why I called this meeting. I think it's time we considered lowering our eligibility standards."

There was silence. Perkins was the first to relocate his voice. "That sounds pretty drastic. I realize recruiting's a headache, but aren't we pushing the panic button? We'll be phasing out Connies and DC-sevens simultaneously with seven-oh-seven deliveries. We're modernizing the fleet, not expanding it."

"Don't count on early phase-outs," Ladell said glumly, as if he hated to agree with Gillespie. "If just half the old man's route expansion plans go through, we'll be lucky to retire a fifth of our pistons over the next five years."

Perkins slumped back in his chair. "In that case," he said weakly, "I guess we do have a problem."

"Exactly," Gillespie said. "Which is why lowering our hiring standards just a trifle might—"

"Just a minute," Danni interrupted.

"Yes, Danni?"

She took a deep breath and fired. "As a former line stewardess and an instructor as well, I'd have to object to any lowering of standards. Not when you have a golden opportunity to solve what everyone admits is the main problem—turnover. All you have to do is abolish the major factor in turnover: mandatory retirement."

Perkins and Gillespie frowned at her, but the look Frank

Ladell gave her was one of surprised, grudging respect.

"I think you're out of order," Gillespie said. "Our rules concerning stewardess termination were implemented after careful study and for very good reasons. I think I'd prefer training new girls, even those perhaps not as highly qualified as they've been in the past, to retaining stewardesses who are too old to fly or faced with the divided loyalties inherent in any marriage-versus-job situation. I believe, Danni, we can consider the matter closed."

Danni's jaw tightened. "I'm sorry you feel that way, because you're speaking from an untenable position."

Gillespie exploded. "Untenable? What the devil's untenable about wanting to keep our stewardesses fresh in attitude as well as appearance? Is it untenable to demand that our girls give their jobs the highest priority?"

She was conscious that every eye in the room was on her, that her face was flushed, and that she was juggling with dynamite, challenging a senior vice president on a battleground even the stewardess union had avoided. But she had the bit in her teeth, she refused to back away, and her voice was firm.

"Both those premises are based on false assumptions. First, you're wrongly assuming that a stewardess loses pride in her personal appearance after she's thirty-five. Second, there is absolutely no evidence or data to back up a supposition that a married stewardess would have divided loyalties."

"I don't need evidence or data," Gillespie snorted. "All I need is common sense."

"Common sense is not synonymous with arbitrary judgment. And that's all the retire-at-thirty-five rule is—arbitrary. The same goes for quit-when-you-marry. Both arbitrary, because they're based on nothing more than, well, I'll use the word again: on nothing more than untenable theory."

This time his voice was coated with anger. "You're indicting not just Trans-National but virtually the entire airline industry. There are few carriers that don't have our termination policies. As a matter of fact, we're more lenient than most: American requires resignation at thirty-two."

"All that means," Danni said mildly, "is that we're three years

182

less arbitrary than American. And just because the industry follows a practice doesn't mean it's right." There was a nervous laugh somewhere in the back of the room—Danni thought it was Trudy Simon—and the sound gave her new momentum, like a cheer spurring on an athlete. "You mentioned common sense. Look, we're all agreed we should do something about turnover. But if you insist on mentioning common sense, isn't it common sense to eliminate its biggest cause?"

"I don't deny there's logic in your argument," Gillespie said. "But even if our policies aren't entirely wise or even just, they should be subject to evolution, not revolution. Because these policies are the whole industry's, no single airline can really modify them effectively. It's something all airlines should agree on." He glanced at Ladell, seeking an ally. "Don't you agree, Frank?"

"Yes and no," Ladell said. "In theory, the young lady makes a lot of sense—we *could* solve turnover fast if we changed our rules." Danni threw him a smile that was erased quickly by his next words. "On the other hand, I'd hate to have us be the airline that opens a can of worms for the rest of the industry. The minute you offer these bleeding-heart liberals a helping hand, they reach for the whole arm. Next thing you know, we'll be told we have to hire niggers."

The room was silent. Danni looked around. Gillespie wore a small smile. Perkins was studying his shoetops as if his correct reply were written on the leather like a crib note. Trudy stared at Danni in what might have been an unspoken plea to stay quiet.

Danni didn't. "Which might be something to consider seriously, as an alternative to lowering standards," she said, her voice still mild.

Surprisingly, Gillespie laughed. "Well, I'm certainly opposed to race prejudice as such, but we have to be practical. Remember, a fair-sized proportion of our route structure is in the South, and there'd be considerable resentment toward Negro stewardesses. Anyway, we've had applications from these people for as long as I can remember, and we've always found reasons for rejecting them."

"Such as?" Danni asked.

"Such as not being able to meet our stringent requirements."

"What requirements wouldn't they be able to meet?"

Trudy Simons sucked in her breath at Danni's audacity.

"Uh, physical for the most part. Hairdo, body proportions— they all have broad hips, for example. And let's face the truth. I'm not prejudiced against Negroes, but I doubt whether a colored girl could make it through training, simply on the basis of . . . well . . . intelligence."

She could not believe a man of his intelligence could have made such a remark. She thought of the girl in Fred Jordan's office and she felt a twinge of self-disgust that she had bedded this bigot. Disbelief and anger fed adrenalin to her tongue.

"Tell me, Mr. Gillespie," she said quietly, "are you really sorry Booth shot Lincoln?"

Her audacity seemed to freeze the room. There was dead silence, shattered finally by Gillespie's icy voice. "I would suggest that in the future, Miss Hendricks, you confine your remarks to whatever issue is being discussed instead of making smart-aleck cracks about your superiors. I consider the subject closed and would appreciate your doing likewise."

She had not only defied but insulted a senior vice president in front of his staff and another senior vice president. She wasn't afraid of being fired, but she half-expected to be sent back to the line for insubordination.

"There aren't any suggestion boxes in aircraft cabins," Danni sighed to Julie after recounting the scene in Gillespie's office.

Her roommate looked puzzled. "What do you mean?"

"I mean, if I'm demoted from instructor, I might as well forget writing another memo. No more ideas for reforms, policy changes, or anything else—nobody's going to listen to a plain, ordinary stewardess."

"Well, I like that! This plain, ordinary stewardess doesn't regard herself as a nonentity."

"I didn't mean it that way, Julie. It's just that . . . that, well, losing my instructor's status means I won't be part of management anymore. And management doesn't really listen to ideas from the rank and file. It isn't that I'd mind going back to flying—in some ways I'd be a lot happier. But Julie, there's so much more I could do in management. You can change minds and influence decisions, because they at least listen."

"All from the exalted position of instructor?" Julie asked with more sarcasm than she meant.

Danni's eyes were shining but her face was sober. "I don't intend to stay on as instructor forever. There are other jobs. Maybe Ed Perkins' assistant. Maybe even Trudy Simon's job, eventually."

"I'm not sure ambition becomes you," Julie said, not unkindly.

Yet Danni was stung. "And what's wrong with being ambitious? What do I have to look forward to except my career? Fly until I'm thirty-five and then take a job in reservations?"

"For starters, you can stop feeling sorry for yourself, go out, and meet some men. Meeting new people is one of the underrated fringe benefits of being a plain, ordinary stewardess. You sound like you're willing to marry Trans-National and raise a lot of little memos."

Danni laughed. She was honest enough to admit that Julie's barb amounted to a bull's-eye. "I want to get ahead in the company, Julie. I know I can if I get a few breaks. And that's all I want. A chance not just to make good but to do some good. I don't ever want to fall in love again. I don't ever want to be hurt again. Maybe you think ambition in a woman is abnormal, but so help me it's the only way I can live with myself."

Their eyes met. It was Julie who broke the uncomfortable silence.

"You've changed," she said simply.

Danni nodded. "For the worse?"

"Maybe. Too early to tell. But you're harder. And I'll have to admit, if you insist on being Scarlett O'Hara with a pair of wings, I can't blame you. That doesn't mean I think you're right, though. Your ambition is just a form of running away. It's almost a kind of punishment you've inflicted on yourself—changing into a person you don't really want to be. I'd buy that reasoning if you actually had something to feel guilty about, but you don't."

"Matter of opinion," Danni said softly. "Anyway, I've had fun. I've enjoyed writing my little memos and seeing some of them actually bear fruit."

Julie grinned. "Okay. Go after old man Belnap's job if you want and more power to you. I only hope for your sake that Gillespie doesn't lower the boom." She giggled. "Asking him if he's sorry Booth shot Lincoln. For Christ's sake, you're lucky he didn't can you on the spot."

"Do you think I should apologize to him?"

"Hell, no! I'd rather see you go to bed with the bastard than admit you were out of line!"

Danni said slowly, "Going to bed with him would be one way of apologizing without saying I was wrong."

Julie grabbed her by the shoulders and squeezed so hard she winced. "Don't you ever give me that kind of crap again! You're no whore!"

"Don't worry," Danni said, "I wouldn't sleep with him." But she turned her face away.

Harmon Gillespie not only didn't demote her, he gave no indication he bore a grudge. In fact he went out of his way to demonstrate otherwise.

A week after the turbulent recruitment meeting, he called a conference with Perkins and all the instructors to review the 707 training program and announce that the first jet delivery would take place in less than two months.

"The target date for inauguration of seven-oh-seven service is January tenth, which means starting off the year nineteen-fifty-nine with the hardest job this airline has ever faced. We'll have to start training all present stewardesses now to have crews ready in time for the jet schedules. Ed, what's your estimate for seven-oh-seven qualification?"

"I think we can train 'em in two weeks."

Gillespie frowned. "Two weeks? That seems exhorbitant."

Perkins glanced unhappily at Danni—she was the one who

186

had mapped out the 707 training program. She interpreted his look as a plea for support. "I'm the one who suggested two weeks," she said. "One week on service familiarization and procedures, and the second week on safety."

"Why do they need a full week on safety?" Gillespie demanded. "One day would be sufficient."

Danni shook her head. She was still unafraid to fight him. "It's an entirely different and far more complicated evacuation system," she said in a voice that quavered just a trifle. "Not to mention familiarization with oxygen masks, stuff we've never had on pistons."

"Two weeks is out of the question," the senior vice president decreed. "I'm afraid you instructors will have to stick to a one-week schedule." He tossed Danni a no-hard-feelings smile of sufficient wattage to encourage her to lag behind when the meeting ended and the room emptied.

"I seem to be your hairy shirt," she told him.

"On the contrary, I admire your spunk. I never take offense at a subordinate who argues with me, just so long as he accepts my final decision in good spirit."

She smiled wickedly. "Oh, I will. I was worried you'd give us only three days—I'll settle for one week, gladly."

Gillespie laughed. "You little devil—that two-week timetable was strictly for bargaining purposes, wasn't it?"

"It was. But I didn't tell Ed that."

He looked at her admiringly. "You're smart. Too damned smart to be just an instructor."

She knew her heart was pounding and scolded herself for knowing why. In the infinitesimal split-second in which she absorbed what Gillespie had said, she could hear Julie's voice . . . *It's almost a kind of punishment you've inflicted on yourself— changing into a person you don't really want to be . . .* Yet she was powerless to stop the surge of triumph she felt; it was as if Harmon Gillespie were once again mouthing a script she had written, reciting words she had fantasized.

"It's true that teaching stewardess classes isn't much of a challenge anymore," she said.

"I can understand that. Of course, Ed thinks you're the best instructor he has. He'd raise holy hell if I took you off his staff, and with the jets coming up, good training is absolutely essential. On the other hand . . . well, what *would* you like to do?"

She tried not to blurt an answer, even though she had one on the tip of her tongue. "I've been working on this plan," she began. "It hasn't quite jelled in my own mind, so let's call it a skeleton of an idea. Basically, I'd like to assign a kind of supervisor to every jet trip—an extra crew member who'd oversee the entire service operation. He'd be a member of management, that's essential. He'd literally be representing management on the airplane. He'd handle special requests from passengers, like making reservations for return flights or arranging for rental cars. He'd handle any unusual problems that might come up. He'd . . ."

"You keep saying 'he,'" Gillespie said. "Are you suggesting we hire male cabin attendants?"

"No, I'm not. My IFS would—"

"Your what?"

"In-flight supervisors. That's what I'd call them. They wouldn't be serving meals or cocktails. They'd be sort of airborne maître 'ds, keeping the service flow efficient, answering questions. For that matter, the IFS could be a woman as well as a man."

Gillespie looked at her sharply. "Is this all your idea?"

"It is."

"I've heard rumors American and Continental are planning to use supervisory personnel on their jets. You didn't by any chance pick up those reports and appropriate them as your own?"

"I didn't! But the fact that American and Continental are considering it merely supports the plan's validity."

Gillespie smiled. "When I heard about those two carriers, I gave some thought to our adopting a similar arrangement, but it amounts to nothing more than adding an extra crew member, and it's just too expensive."

"Look," she said. "Go beyond immediate operating costs and consider the long-range benefits. It's nothing but management training, the kind you couldn't buy without setting up an expensive training program for promising young executives. What better experience could you give them than working directly with on-line problems and situations? I'll bet you've got some youngsters right in your own Marketing division who could learn one hell of a lot about the airline business if you got them away from their desks and put them in airplanes."

Gillespie nodded thoughtfully. "I think," he said pontifically, "you might have something with this IFS scheme of yours. Obviously, it needs a great amount of detailed refinement, and I'd like to work with you on that. Are you teaching at all this weekend?"

"No, my current class has Saturday and Sunday off."

"Good. I'm going up to New York Saturday morning for a meeting with a couple of uniform suppliers. I'll arrange for you to get a C-one pass and you can come up Saturday afternoon. We can have a quiet dinner that night and discuss this IFS business further. How does that sound?"

She did not answer immediately. "As a matter of fact," he added quickly, "it might be a good idea for you to take a mid-morning flight—I'd like you to meet these suppliers. I believe it would make a lot of sense if you served on our uniform selection committee. I haven't announced it yet, but I want completely new stewardess uniforms by late spring."

"I thought Trudy Simon was on the committee," Danni said suspiciously.

"She is—and will be again. But Trudy's the only woman on the committee, and she's been telling me for years we need more female input. She'll be delighted to have some company."

His attitude irked her—it was out of character for the great senior vice president of Marketing. A *damned adolescent afraid a girl is going to turn him down*, she thought. "Maybe Trudy should go up with me," she said innocently.

"Not necessary," Gillespie said. "She's, uh, already met the people we'll be seeing."

Thoughts of Seattle raced through her. A quick memory of the emptiness she had felt, her phony responses, her careful manipulation of an atmosphere in which the seduced believed he was the seducer. And now she was considering going to bed with him

189

again—a conceited, malicious bigot.

But also one who held her professional future in the palm of his hand. Direct involvement with the uniform committee—real management responsibility, that's what he was promising. . .

"Where do you want me to meet you?" Danni asked.

Gillespie introduced her to a pair of top officials from two uniform suppliers. She liked one of them, a bubbly, fireplug of a man named Aaron Malinchek who showed them some impressive preliminary designs. The other manufacturer gave her the feeling his tongue was coated with oil that greased every word he uttered; she disliked Jerome Eaton on sight, and every subsequent minute intensified her impression.

What bothered her even more was Gillespie's attitude toward them. He was brusque and indifferent, almost rude, to Malinchek, while he treated Eaton with a respect Danni thought was undeserved. Eaton's product presentation was so cursory she got the idea he didn't really care whether he won a TNA contract.

Eaton was polite enough to her, but it was a politeness redolent of insincerity and patronization. Danni tried to be objective, not an easy task when objectivity collided with her opinion of the burly, heavily joweled owner of Eaton Uniform Creations. She could feel his piggish eyes sneaking looks at her bustline, his fat lips set in a perpetual smirk. But later, when Gillespie took her back to the Plaza Hotel for predinner cocktails, the vice president airily dismissed her unfavorable verdict.

"Jerry's not a bad guy," he assured her. "What you have to remember is price. That'll be the deciding factor, assuming, of course, that the products are about equal."

"But they aren't equal," Danni protested. "Malinchek showed us style, along with practicality and originality. That simple beige number with the blaze orange scarf, for example—God, Harmon, it was smart, bright, cheerful . . ."

"And expensive. We're spending company money. Always have to keep that in mind. However, I assure you I'll give every consideration to the Malinchek line."

190

He had gotten her a room at the Plaza, but with misgivings and renewed guilt she slept in his suite that night—as he had expected and as she had resigned herself to do. She was simply afraid to take a chance on alienating him; as cheap as it made her feel, she was able to rationalize it as the only course she could take. So she turned off her conscience again and opened her body to him, mouthing the required litany of passion being fulfilled.

She awoke in the middle of the night, craving a cigarette. She had finished her last pack earlier, so she crawled out of the luxurious bed, careful not to disturb Gillespie, and tiptoed to the closet where he had hung his coat. She found an open pack in a side pocket, and as she removed it, the coat slipped from its hanger and fell to the floor.

Danni picked it up and was about to rehang it when she noticed that an open envelope had fallen from an inside pocket. Before she replaced it in the coat she spotted the letterhead.

Eaton Uniform Creations.

She could not explain why, but she stared at the envelope for a few seconds, and then, after looking in the direction of her sleeping companion, she turned on the closet light and removed the contents.

It was a check, made out to Gillespie Aviation Consultants, Inc., for ten thousand dollars. And it was signed by Jerome Eaton.

She put the check back in the envelope and restored it to the pocket from which it had fallen. She went into the suite's living room, lit a cigarette, and sat in the dark, smoking. And thinking.

One week later, Harmon Gillespie announced that a contract for a new stewardess uniform had been awarded to Eaton Uniform Creations.

Chapter 11

Pat Martin raised hell about the IFS plan, so loudly that Danni, as its author, was summoned to a meeting in Belnap's office to discuss the union's objections.

"What you're actually proposing is to put a company spy on every jet flight," Pat said.

"Totally untrue," Gillespie said, so calmly that Danni had a momentary notion that he actually might have such a devious motive.

"Bullshit," Pat said. "Why don't you go whole hog and assign a supervisor to all trips? Just to make sure there's a management fink looking over every stew's shoulder seven days a week."

Gillespie laughed. "I only wish we could afford such a luxury. We might get rid of a few deadbeats that way. But that's beside the point. I categorically deny we have any intention of using these IFS as a means of, uh, checking up on the girls. Naturally, they'd be free to report any major deviations from company rules and procedures."

"Ahah!" Pat declared. "In other words, regular supervisors under a different name."

Evan Belnap's gravelly voice cut in. "Danni, inasmuch as you thought up this whole idea, I'd like to hear your feelings."

"I understand Pat's fears," she said, "but I want her to know I had no intention of turning the IFS into a disciplinary weapon, and neither did Mr. Gillespie."

"And next time you can tell me there's really an Easter bunny—"

"Let me finish, damn you!" Danni snapped, and Belnap's bushy eyebrows lifted in surprise. "The sensible thing to do is spell out an in-flight supervisor's responsibilities so we won't be giving any of them a chance to become little Hitlers. They'd have every right to report a stew for something major—discourtesy or blatant goofing off for example. The same right any passenger would have. But we shouldn't have them nit-picking about runs in stockings, or how they pour a cup of coffee."

"It still sounds like a blank check for harrassment," Pat Martin said.

"I'd like to think it's a blank check for cooperation," Danni replied, trying to keep her voice steady. "There might be some resentment at first, but if we pick the right people for IFS, I believe the girls eventually will be glad they're on the airplane. It means a lighter workload, for one thing. The stewardesses can concentrate on service."

"Makes sense to me," Belnap growled. "Well, Pat, feel better about it?"

"Not in the slightest. Unfortunately, there's nothing I can do to prevent you from going ahead, but you can be damned certain I'll be riding herd on these IFS, just in case any of 'em gets the idea he can exceed his authority."

"Fair enough," Belnap said affably.

"But I won't forget this little end run you're pulling," the union president continued. "Just wait for the next contract negotiations—Danni here will wish she had never thought up this stupid idea and you gentlemen will wish you had never heard of Danni. I bid you all a good morning."

She left, the unknown import of her words hanging in the air like the frozen contrail of a jet.

"Now what the hell did she mean by that crack?" Belnap demanded.

"Just an empty bluff, Evan," Gillespie said. "She loves to make threats she knows she can't carry out. Standard operating procedure for every union official."

"Don't underestimate her," Danni warned, and noticed that Belnap was nodding in agreement.

"Goddamned Lucretia Borgia," he said. "She's got something cookin' in that evil little mind of hers and I don't like it one bit. Harmon, get the hell out of here—I wanna talk to Danni a couple of minutes."

Gillespie looked hurt but complied. Belnap rose and walked with him toward the door, whispering something, while Danni had a chance to look around the huge presidential office for the first time. It was a third larger than Gillespie's, and while his contained models of airliners in TNA colors, Belnap's was filled with ship models.

She recognized a frigate, a couple of Spanish galleons, an English man-of-war circa 1600, and a magnificent replica of Nelson's flagship, Victory. She was examining the Victory when she sensed Belnap peering over her shoulder and looked up to see a pleased expression on his lined face.

"Beautiful, isn't she?" he said with simple pride. "I don't suppose you're interested in old ships, by any chance?"

"As a matter of fact," she told him, "I'm very interested. My father is a devoted fan of Captain Horatio Hornblower and he got me to read every book in the Hornblower series." She smiled. "I think C. S. Forester ranks right up there with Shakespeare."

"A goddamned hack compared to Forester!" Belnap bellowed. "By God, let me show you these models . . ."

For the next fifteen minutes Danni inspected the tiny ships, detailed right down to the rigging and brass cannons. She spent more time at the Victory than any of the others.

"My father would give up the last five years of his life to own this," she confided.

"My favorite, too," the president said happily. "Picked it up in a London antique shop before the war. I could have bought a DC-three for what it cost me, but it's worth every penny and more."

"It must be," Danni agreed. "I saw the real Victory once. This is incredibly accurate."

"By God, I saw the old ship, too. When were you over there?"

"About six or seven years ago, with my parents. Dad insisted on heading for Portsmouth the day after we arrived. Said I had to see her because it would make Hornblower come alive. And it did, Mr. Belnap. The minute I went aboard, I was back in the seventeen-hundreds with Hornblower and Lieutenant Bush and coxswain Brown . . ."

"I know what you mean," Belnap said, beaming. "Those were the days! Wooden ships and iron men. Now when you're called a buccaneer, you're a corporate killer." He sighed. "So much for nostalgia—let's talk."

She sat in the black leather chair that faced his desk. Belnap lit a cigar and peered at her through the pungent smoke. "Two things," he began. "First, if you can, find out what Pat Martin meant about getting even with us when contract talks start next month."

"I'll try," she promised, "but my contacts with line stewardesses aren't exactly numerous."

"You room with one," Belnap said, and she was a little surprised at this bit of knowledge. Gillespie may have briefed him, of course.

"I'll talk to her," Danni said. "I'm not sure how much she could find out or whether she'd be willing to tell me. She's no gung-ho union member, Mr. Belnap, but she knows I'm management and she may not think it's ethical to be a, well, a kind of informant."

"I'm not asking her to play Mata Hari. I just want some inkling of what that goddamned bitch is gonna throw at us. Just see what you can do."

"I'll try," Danni repeated.

"Good. Second thing I'd like to discuss with you is a new job. Gillespie says you're teaching a class. When does it graduate?"

"In two weeks." Her heart was pounding again.

"It'll be your last stewardess class, at least for a while. I want you to start off this IFS program."

Startled, she said, "I'm not sure what you mean by starting it off."

"Set up a training program for these IFS of yours. And while you're at it, train yourself. I'd like you to work a few trips as an in-flight supervisor—I guess you'd be the first one. Get your own feet wet and you'll find out whether these IFS are worth a damn. Agreed?"

She resisted an impulse to hug him. "Agreed. And grateful, Mr. Belnap. To you and Mr. Gillespie both—I assume he's approved this. It's his department and . . ."

"He okayed it," Belnap said. "Frankly, it was his suggestion that you train IFS, but it was mine to have you become one yourself. Harmon didn't think much of that idea. Told me you'd regard it as a demotion, that you might as well be going back to the line."

"But that's not true. The main purpose is management training. I don't consider that a demotion."

"Neither do I, and that settles it." He stood up, the sunlight from the window in back of the desk silhouetting his bulky frame. "Come see me anytime. And don't forget to talk to—what's her name?—Julie."

She had qualms about asking Julie, a free-spoken soul who had never tried to hide her dislike of Pat Martin. This, plus the fact that she roomed with Danni, might make suspect any questions Julie asked. Julie was a rather indifferent union member, and of late she had been confiding to Danni that she might like to try for a supervisor's job.

"That would be great," Danni said in what she hoped was a tone of enthusiasm. Privately, she had her doubts. She loved Julie, but she questioned whether she had the self-discipline to govern others. Like a man who climbs a mountain just because it's there, Julie broke rules just because they were there. She got away with about ninety-nine percent of her transgressions for the simple reason that she was one of the best stewardesses on the line, and it was a rare supervisor who was willing to nail her on fine print. But to Danni, Julie was setting a pattern of defiance.

Once Danni had asked her, "How the hell could you discipline a stew for breaking a rule you've ignored yourself a hundred times?"

"Oh, I could do it," Julie said airily. "I've sinned so often myself, it would be easier for me to spot a sinner."

196

"Would you crack down on a girl caught taking a drink on an airplane?"

"I suppose so. It would depend on the circumstances."

"What circumstances? The rule is specific—it's an automatic termination offense."

"Oh, come on, Danni. Some people can take a nip and they might as well be sipping coffee. Me, for instance."

"Yeah," Danni said slowly. "I've seen you sneaking a belt or two in the galley. I never thought of reporting you but you're damned lucky no supervisor ever caught you."

"No supervisor ever will. I'm too careful."

"Another stew might catch you."

"Maybe. Life's full of chances, isn't it?"

Danni had given up; living dangerously was Julie's *modus operandi*, and to reform her would have involved changing her carefree attitude. She *was* drinking a lot, though, Danni thought . . . all she needed was a few martinis and she'd be asking Pat Martin herself, "What's all this crap you're plotting against the company?" No, Danni decided, she couldn't follow Belnap's request.

As it turned out, she didn't have to. Julie came home from a union meeting infuriated.

"You'll never guess what Martin's pulling," she announced. "She's gonna tell the company that if any stew becomes supervisor and then decides to go back on the line, she'll lose her seniority."

"All of it?" Danni asked.

"Seniority would be suspended for as long as she held supervisor. It's a crummy deal. Suppose I flew for five years, then worked supervisor for three. If I wanted to fly again, I'd lose all three years—I'd go back to the line with only five years' seniority."

It was a crummy deal, Danni thought. But also a clever move on Pat's part. The majority of supervisors eventually found the job palling and returned to line flying with no loss of seniority. If Pat got away with this, the company would have a devil of a time finding qualified supervisors . . .

". . . it's dirty pool for someone like me," Julie was complaining. "Damned if I want to make supervisor now—I'd be cutting my own throat."

"I'll talk to Gillespie about it," Danni said. "I'm quite sure the company won't let her get away with it."

"I don't regard it as a major union demand," Harmon Gillespie said, unconcerned.

"Don't you see what she's doing?" Danni asked. "She's just getting back at us for the IFS program."

"I fail to see any connection."

"She'll make a connection, damnit. No stewardess who takes any kind of management position will be able to fly again unless she accepts lower seniority, less pay, and lousy trips. If you let her put this little stink bomb into the next contract, it'll come back to haunt you."

His voice was mocking. "You seem to assume that stewardesses will become IFS. I doubt whether that will happen very often, except in your own case, of course. And I don't mind telling you I consider Belnap's plans for you a decided mistake. It flaunts the very concept of the IFS program—that of training young executives."

"You mean male employees. No women allowed?"

"There are plenty of management jobs for women. Instructor. Supervisor. We have a number of female management personnel in Reservations. To be perfectly candid, though, I have no intention of turning this airline into an all-girl orchestra, not even for you. I've told you that you have a great future with this company, but not if you let Evan Belnap do your planning. He's nothing but a pirate and pirates are an anachronism."

Pirate, she thought. *Synonymous with buccaneer.*

". . . while I'm not yet in a position to oppose him," he was saying, "the fact remains that he's not going to be around forever. I once told you it wasn't necessary to choose up sides. But I might suggest you decide whose advice you should take. You don't belong in the air. You belong right here on the ground, working for me and with me."

For a moment she felt she was weakening. Then she remembered the old man with his ships and the gruffness that was so obviously thin tinplate over vulnerable, old-fashioned trust. *Careful, though. Don't antagonize Gillespie. You're in no position to challenge him. Not yet . . .*

"I'll think about it," she said. "Meanwhile, I take it you're going to let Pat get away with it?"

"Let's say I'll use it as a bargaining weapon. Something to offer her when she comes in with far worse demands. After all, it affects relatively few people."

She allowed herself the chancy luxury of a glare. "Those relatively few you seem so indifferent toward are the backbone of In-Flight Service. You're not only callous but short-sighted."

"And you're too damned impertinent! Kindly remember who I am, young lady."

"I keep remembering who you *were*. Not the same guy who told me not too long ago you welcomed an employee with spunk enough to argue with you."

"And I also told you the argument stops when I've made my decision."

"Your decisions usually are made before anyone argues with you, and then it's too late."

"All right, then tell me why I'm being callous and short-sighted. I'm perfectly willing to listen."

"Harmon, you hear. You don't really listen. But I'll try to tell you. You're callous and short-sighted because you're stabbing every supervisor right in the back. Only the veterans like Harriet Nash can't go back to flying. Most supervisors are young enough to get bored eventually with all the paperwork and the nine-to-five bit. If you let Pat Martin put in that new seniority rule, we'll lose most of the young ones and we won't get any decent applicants for replacement. Who would want the damned job?"

"Plenty of girls. Those who'd trade a little seniority for a taste of authority."

"And that's the kind of person you'd want for supervisor? A potential martinet like that goddamned Martha Devins in Atlanta? I can't believe you're that stupid."

His suddenly florid face told her she had gone too far, but she no longer cared.

"Watch your tongue!" he warned sharply. "This is a senior vice president you're talking to, and don't you ever forget it. Along with how you got this far in the company."

Now the look on *her* face told him he had gone too far. Her voice was halfway between a sob and a snarl. "You sonofabitch! I can't ever forget it. But only a lousy heel would remind me of it."

He knew he had lost her for good, and only the memory of their affair kept him from firing her on the spot. That and the knowledge that he could never explain it to Evan Belnap. And she *was* smart, capable of making him look good. He tried to retreat gracefully. "Danni, I'm sorry I said that. I know I've helped you for . . . uh . . . various reasons. Including respect for your ability. Don't be a fool. Stick with me. You won't be disappointed."

"I'm already disappointed," she said bitterly. "In myself."

She walked out, leaving that last remark trailing behind her like an enigmatic scent to be analyzed and interpreted.

Harmon Gillespie, being no fool, did analyze and interpret it. He reached the instinctive conclusion that somehow Danni's ambition was now a potential menace to his own.

In the ensuing weeks Danni not only laid out an IFS training program but also designed uniforms for the men: blue blazers with tiny gold wings embroidered over the chest pockets, like those of Royal Air Force pilots, and dark gray slacks. For the women she used the same blazer with a more feminine cut, plus a simple gray skirt.

When she presented the training program to Gillespie, he objected to the inclusion of safety procedures in the curriculum.

"Absolutely unnecessary," he told her sharply. "I warned you about trying to sneak a fifth crew member aboard via this program and I won't stand for it."

"I'm not trying to sneak anything in," she said. "They should at least know the basics of an emergency evacuation. Is that too much to ask?"

200

"It is. They're on board to serve the public. Period."

She was tempted to take the matter up with Belnap but decided against it. The old man seemed preoccupied these days. On the few occasions when she saw him, his face wore an expression of concern, a frown that seemed to have been creased into his heavy features. He had too much on his mind, Danni reasoned, to be bothered with her own relatively petty problems. And compared to his, they *were* petty. The enormous commitment for the 707 fleet had coincided with seven consecutive quarters of operating deficits. Danni had heard rumors that the Board of Directors was on Belnap's back—which, she thought glumly, should please Gillespie.

She did send Belnap a note outlining Pat Martin's proposal to abolish supervisors' seniority, but she received no acknowledgement. She assumed Gillespie had convinced Belnap it was worth nothing more than expendable bargaining ammunition.

Gillespie. She had grown to hate the very sight of him. She did not really regret the road she had taken in the name of ambition, but she was not proud of choosing this man as her vehicle. The way he kept bad-mouthing Belnap. And that mysterious check—she could never get that out of her mind.

At least she had gotten her foot in the executive door and never mind how she had opened it; once inside, she had accomplished a lot through ability and initiative. Could she have done it any other way? By becoming active in the union, perhaps? She wouldn't have been a Pat Martin, whose belligerence made compromise seem like surrender. Pat's tactics merely caused the company to react with equally blind militance toward the union. And this was inevitable, Danni knew, because Pat Martin had become the union.

Once when Danni asked Julie about Pat's qualities as a union leader, surprisingly Julie had defended her.

"Pat's not so bad," she said. "Oh, I know she's tough and unreasonable at times, but she gets things done and she works like a demon. That's more than you can say for ninety percent of us, and that's why she's president."

Which, Danni understood, was precisely the trouble. Anyone

201

with ambition, perseverance, and a need for power could mold a union in her own image. Staff it with sycophants, as Pat had, and run it like a miniature dictatorship. There were times when Danni saw a little of herself in Pat Martin.

Just before jet service started, Pat put across a change in the union's bylaws. "Any member who says or does anything detrimental to the union shall be expelled by a majority vote of the Executive Committee," it read. Since Pat herself headed the rubber-stamp committee, she became virtually the sole judge of what constituted deeds or words detrimental to the union—and by her own interpretation, this included criticism of union officers. Julie was furious and lobbied against it, but the new bylaw passed by a two-to-one majority.

"Why don't you run against her in the next election?" Danni asked. "If there's one stew on the whole airline with the popularity and reputation to beat her, it's you."

"No, thanks. Being president of the union is damned near a full-time job. I like my days off. I work hard when I fly. I do a good job for my passengers, but when a trip's over I wanna have fun. The only kind of person capable of running Pat Martin out of office is someone like yourself."

Which was true, Danni realized. Except she had put her chips on management's table.

"I'd have to go back on the line," she said, "and that's impossible. All I can hope is that most of the girls eventually will realize that Pat isn't a good president. I've met a few union officials on other airlines. They're solid, reasonable people. They win good contracts without resorting to trumped-up hysteria. They can see enough of management's side to accept compromise."

"Utopia," Julie agreed. "Except that management's as bad as the union. I wouldn't want to negotiate the time of day with your boy Gillespie."

"True," Danni acknowledged, and Julie's eyebrows lifted.

"I take it he's no longer your boy."

Danni avoided an answer by changing the subject. "You know what I'd really like? To be on the other side of the bargaining table from Pat. That's what's wrong. The stews aren't getting any more support from management than they're getting from her. Which is why they turn to her."

Even as she spoke, an idea, a dream, began gestating in her mind.

She had not realized how much she had missed flying until she boarded Trans-National's inaugural 707 flight, Miami–Los Angeles, as the airline's first in-flight supervisor. Nothing she had ever experienced before could match the thrill of flying in the graceful, powerful 707.

Takeoffs. Accelerations so slow at first that 240,000 pounds of aluminum, plastic, cloth, rubber, and fuel seemed glued to the runway. Then the exhilarating sensation of increasing speed as the turbines screamed defiance of gravity and the moment when the nose wheel lifted off the ground and the racing wind caught the airfoil of the wings like a giant hand pushing the plane up.

Climb and cruise. The jets simply accentuated and heightened what had always intrigued her about flight. The magnificent moment when the giant bird broke through dark overcast into a world of bright sunlight, skimming effortlessly above cottony clouds, mocking the prosaic earth that lay unseen beneath the great wings. The incredible knowledge that this 120-ton monster was covering almost ten miles every minute, and doing it so quietly and smoothly that it seemed to be suspended in the sky.

Letdown and landing. A return to earth with a controlled steadiness that made one think the jetliner was riding an enormous railroad track toward the ground. The slight protesting squeal of tires at touchdown. The awesome decelerating power of the thrust reversers, like another giant hand pushing against the nose instead of under the wings.

To Danni, flight was adventure without real danger, sense-quickening without concern, excitement without fear. She noticed that the jets were already attracting new kinds of passengers—more women and children, for example—an indication of a not-so-far-away future when half the passengers on any given flight would be flying for nonbusiness reasons.

She encountered some resentment from stewardesses at first—Pat Martin's "company spy" propaganda had infected the ranks. But gradually she overcame such antagonism by paying more attention to the passengers than to the stewardesses. She never interfered with the girls except to help with service when needed or when asked. And the value of the IFS concept was driven home by the very number of first-time fliers—by mid-1960, the airlines were boarding some 70,000 passengers daily who had never flown commercially before. Much of Danni's in-flight time was spent allaying fears, answering questions about unfamiliar noises and sensations, and imparting information about jets in general.

Admittedly, she felt more like a kind of supernumerary stewardess than a representative of management, but this was true only for her, not for the male IFS she trained—she *had* been a stewardess and it was hard to break some of the old habits, including her rapport with pilots.

One was Captain Granville Stennis, who had flown with Danni several times out of Washington. He was a close friend of Penny Cockrell and was a great deal like him. Danni was standing by the intercom on a Miami–Chicago trip when Stennis called and demanded coffee. Danni, who had established a rule that IFS were not to serve the cockpit, was brusquer than she intended.

"Damnit, Granny, the girls have just started breakfast service. If you want coffee, tell the flight engineer to come back and get it."

The flight engineer did, under duress. A few minutes later, the voice of Captain Stennis boomed through the cabin.

"Ladies and gentlemen, this is your captain. Two pieces of good news. First, we're going to arrive in Chicago ten minutes ahead of schedule. Second, you're indeed fortunate to have as your in-flight supervisor Miss Danni Hendricks, who happens to make the best cup of hot chocolate in the entire airline industry. Why, I've actually known passengers to change their travel plans just to get on an airplane where Miss Hendricks is serving hot chocolate. I urge you to ask her for some—you won't regret it."

Seventy-eight cups of hot chocolate later, Danni came up to the cockpit. "You win, you sonofabitch," she told Stennis. "Next time I'll bring you your damned coffee myself."

Such rediscovered camaraderie was not enough to make her want to keep flying indefinitely. For one thing, she found herself being occasionally critical of the other stewardesses, particularly the younger ones, although she kept her opinions of their perfunctory attitude to herself. She was surprised and disturbed on a trip with Julie, when Danni noticed her sneaking a drink in the galley. She felt they were good enough friends for her to bring the subject up after the flight ended, but Julie merely laughed.

"I knew you saw me. Wondered whether you'd mention it. Look, Danni, did I do my job? Did I show any effects from those little nips?"

"That's not the point. Why did you have to take a drink? For God's sake, you're beginning to act like an alcoholic. It wouldn't have hurt you to wait until we landed. I don't mind a little booze myself after a tough day."

"You've never seen me drunk, Danni, and you won't. If liquor ever interferes with the way I perform on an airplane, nobody'll have to tell me to quit."

This was true, Danni knew—Julie had the liquor capacity of a thirsty camel. The drinking on duty seemed to manifest an irresistible urge to flaunt authority. She worried about Julie's someday getting caught, but she decided this was her roommate's problem—she had enough of her own, mostly centering around Gillespie. She had resumed her output of memos, suggestions for improving service, which Gillespie rejected or ignored. He began to oppose her in mean and petty ways. On an Easter weekend flight, which she was working as an IFS, she called Reservations beforehand to determine whether there would be a number of children aboard. "At least nine so far," Reservations informed her.

So Danni brought aboard a number of hard-boiled eggs which she and Julie had dyed the night before. She and the stewardess hid the eggs throughout the cabin, and after the flight took off, they staged an egg hunt for the kids—the finder of the most eggs receiving a stuffed bunny and the parents a free bottle of wine.

This extracurricular entertainment was brought to Gillespie's attention via the flight's liquor control report, listing the donated wine. He sent Danni a note.

"I appreciate the goodwill aspects of your little gesture, but please realize that if every in-flight supervisor and/or stewardess took it upon his own initiative to give away such items, we'd rapidly go broke. I do not want this to happen again."

Danni gritted her teeth and did it again, anyway, awarding the wine to winners of such contests as guessing the gross takeoff weight of the airplane or the combined ages of the stewardesses. Gillespie didn't know she was trying the games until passengers began writing in, praising the gimmick. This time he summoned Danni to his office, tossing her a pile of complimentary letters.

"I thought I told you to quit handing out free wine."

"You did. And I stopped."

"Then kindly explain these letters. And while you're at it, you might explain why the wine didn't appear on the liquor dispensing sheets."

"I paid for the wine myself."

He stared at her, speechless; she had mouse-trapped him.

Danni, who had rapidly sifted through the letters, said sweetly, "I gather from these, people like the games."

"That's entirely beside the point. It's not your job to institute in-flight service policies. You had no right to experiment without advance approval."

"If I had asked for advance approval, there wouldn't have been any contests. What happened to the other suggestions I've been making?"

"They were rejected as impractically expensive, or unworthy of comment."

"Are these contests impractically expensive or unworthy of comment?"

She was needling him deliberately, goading him toward an explosion, but he kept his temper. "I don't deny this contest idea of yours has merit—passenger reaction has been excellent. The point is that you should have checked with me first. I would have let you try it—and paid for the wine, incidentally."

She knew she had won the skirmish but sensed it was no time to push him further. "I'm glad, Harmon. With your permission, I'd like to suggest to all IFS that they try out these games. Or maybe it would be better if you made it official, with a directive."

"I'll do just that. And congratulations." He obviously had decided to be magnanimous. "The wine you bought—put it on your expense account and I'll okay it."

"Thank you," she said, "but that won't be necessary. Consider it my contribution to Marketing."

Evan Belnap was a passenger on Danni's next IFS trip, occupying his usual first-class seat. They had been airborne for thirty minutes before she had a chance to squat briefly beside him.

"Am I eligible for your game?" he asked with a twinkle. "I know the answer."

She laughed. "Company policy, Mr. Belnap—no employees can participate."

The senior stewardess, Karen Jellicoe, was standing in the aisle. "Sorry to bother you, Danni—hi again, Mr. Belnap—Danni, could I see you for a minute?"

"Sure." She motioned the senior toward the galley.

"Take a look at twenty-three D if you get a chance," Karen said. "Kid with jeans, long hair, and a pockmarked face. Brown paper bag in his lap—probably doesn't know we serve lunch."

"Adonis with acne?" Danni joked.

"That's not what I mean. Look at his eyes. They're . . . kind of wild. Keeps staring around the cabin; he gives me the creeps."

"He making any trouble? Bothering the other passengers?"

"No, except that every time I walk past him, he laughs in this funny way. It's a nervous laugh, almost a giggle. A real weirdo."

Danni sighed. Since the advent of the jets, they seemed to be getting an increasing share of kooks—sometimes youngsters obviously on drugs.

Uppermost in her mind was the threat of hijacking, already an industry problem. Yet Danni knew that hippies were not hijacking types; what worried her about the boy in 23D was the possibility of mental derangement.

"I'll keep an eye on him," she promised Karen. "If you see him pull anything abnormal, we'll tell Captain Sullivan. And you'd better warn the other girls, too."

The advice came too late. A stewardess had stopped by 23D to take the occupant's cocktail order. He asked for a bourbon and ginger ale, politely enough yet in a curious monotone. Then he held out the paper bag he had been clutching in his lap.

"Have a chocolate-chip cookie," he offered. "My mom made them for me—they're awfully good."

The stewardess hesitated—his eyes disturbed her. But Shelly Douglas was a girl with an insatiable sweet tooth. The boy took a cookie out of the bag and began nibbling on it.

"Come on," he coaxed. "You've never tasted homemade cookies like these."

"Well, just one." He gave her two.

"There are four more left—why don't you take them up to the pilots? I've had my fill and they'd just get stale."

The cookies tasted delicious. She took the bag, thanked him, and marched toward the cockpit. As she passed the forward galley, Danni stopped her. "What's in the bag, Shelly?"

"Homemade cookies. One of the passengers gave them to me and said the pilots might like some. They're awfully good. Want one? I've got four in here."

Danni's love of sweets was satisfied by an occasional ice cream cone, and she shook her head. As Shelly resumed her trip to the flight deck, an alarm bell sounded in Danni's brain.

"I don't think we should be giving the crew anything that didn't come from our own galley," she said. "That paper bag—did twenty-three D give it to you?"

"Sure. But how did you know? Why shouldn't . . . ?"

"Take it back to him. Tell him the pilots didn't want any."

"Aw, Danni, I was hoping I could make points with Captain Sullivan."

Danni laughed. "Get rid of those cookies and forget about your sex life."

Grumbling about the injustice of it all, Shelly headed back toward the coach section, devouring another cookie. When she reached 23D, she handed the bag to the young man.

"I'm sorry, but the pilots said they weren't hungry—guess

you'll have to eat the rest of them yourself." She was dimly conscious that her voice was slurring. She could not explain that, or the onslaught of light-headedness. Funny, but the whole cabin seemed to be inside a floating white cloud. The youth was saying something to her but she couldn't hear him . . .

Danni was in first class telling a couple about the wonders of Disneyland when Karen tapped her on the shoulder. "Better come aft with me."

"Something wrong?"

"Doreen says Shelly's drunk."

"Drunk? How the hell . . . ?"

"She's trying to open the rear exit—says she needs air."

"That's a plug door—she can't open it when we're pressurized."

"I know that. But Doreen says the passengers are starting to get nervous—she's got one woman almost in hysterics."

They raced to the rear of the plane and pulled Shelly Douglas away from the door, Danni slamming her fist down on Shelly's hands to break the grip she had on the handle.

Danni propelled her toward the aft jump seat. "You stay put for the rest of the trip," she ordered in a low voice. "Make one move out of that seat and so help me I'll use a fire extinguisher on your skull. Doreen," she said, addressing the other stewardess, "you stay with her."

"But what about meal service? I just got started with the trays."

"Shit," Danni muttered. "Shelly, promise to stay in that seat?"

The girl looked at her through glazed eyes. Danni slapped Shelly on the left cheek, hard, the clap of the palm on flesh sounding throughout the stilled cabin.

"Did you have anything to drink?"

The stewardess opened her mouth like a fish out of water. No words came out but she managed to shake her head.

"C . . . c . . . cookies," she mumbled.

"Cookies? You ate some of those cookies you were taking to the cockpit?"

A slight nod.

"That sonofabitch!" Danni growled. "Doreen, go ahead with your service. Anybody asks you what's wrong, tell 'em Shelly's sick. I'm going up to the cockpit."

She was halfway down the aisle when she was stopped by a woman's muffled scream. The woman pointed in front of her. The passenger in 23D had left his seat and was walking just behind Karen. In his left hand was the bag of cookies; in his right was a wicked, open switchblade knife, its point touching the girl's back. They were heading toward the cockpit; Danni, five yards behind, could hear his monotonous voice.

". . . those flyboys think they're too good for the cookies, huh? You just get me into that cockpit and I'll make 'em eat them. Come on, move it!"

Danni was in the first-class aisle as they reached the flight-deck door. As they passed Belnap he rose halfway out of his seat, but Danni shook her head and motioned him to sit down. His eyes were wide but she had no time to explain. Her own gaze went to the left overhead bin, just above the first two seats in first class.

To the red CO_2 fire extinguisher attached to the bin bulkhead.

Swiftly, noiselessly, she lifted the holding brackets and removed the extinguisher. She raised the horn nozzle 90 degrees with her left hand, held the trigger handle with her right, and walked on until she was standing only five feet from the passenger and the helpless senior stewardess, who was in the process of inserting her cockpit key. The youth was behind her, the blade still pressed against her back.

"Hey, buster," Danni said quietly.

He turned around, startled.

"Duck, Karen!" Danni yelled, and pressed the trigger.

The hissing stream of angry white foam hit the passenger squarely in the face. He screamed and clawed at his eyes, both the knife and the bag dropping to the floor. Danni gave him another blast in his half-covered face and then swung the extinguisher at his arm, knocking him to one side.

"Open the door!" Danni told Karen. She complied and Danni, holding the extinguisher like a gun on the writhing youth, shouted for the flight engineer. He came running from the cockpit.

210

"Jesus, what the hell . . . ?"

Belnap was out of his seat by now and had grabbed the passenger, shoving him into the seat next to his. "Tell Sully to get his ass back here," he ordered. "I'll sit on this bastard until he comes."

"Sure, but I'd better get some cold water and paper towels— I'll have to wash out his eyes."

The boy was in such pain there was no fight left in him, and when Captain Sullivan arrived, Belnap had tied his hands in back of him with a seatbelt extension.

"Where the hell are we?" the president growled to Sullivan.

"About a hundred miles east of Dallas."

"Good. Land there and turn this prick over to the police. I want the sonofabitch off this airplane and I'm not gonna wait 'til we get to L.A."

Danni had picked up the paper bag, with three cookies still inside. She handed it to Sullivan. "If we're going to make an unscheduled landing, I think we'd better get Shelly to a hospital. And give the police what's in this bag. I'll give you odds those cookies are full of some drug."

Not until long after they had left Dallas did she have a chance to talk to Belnap. One stewardess short, she had helped with the interrupted meal service, and they were almost at Los Angeles when she slipped wearily into the seat beside him.

"That was one hell of a job," he said. "I won't forget it."

There was no false modesty in Danni Hendricks. She warmed to his praise, basking in the double knowledge that it was totally sincere and that it also was deserved—she *had* performed well. But with the feeling of self-satisfaction came the unpleasant intrusion of another feeling—guilt.

". . . I *won't forget it*," Belnap had said. Implied reward. Advancement purely on merit. Achievement solely on ability. Not the path she had trod with Harmon Gillespie. *I was too impatient,* she decided. *Well, it's over and done with. From now on, I'm on my own . . .*

". . . I hope they throw the book at that bastard," Belnap was saying.

She sighed. "I wonder what was in the cookies?"

"LSD, probably. Enough to give a hippo hallucinations. Christ, I'm proud of you. He was crazy enough to knife the crew. Or worse—they could have tasted one of those cookies."

"All in a day's work," Danni said. "But maybe now you know why I said we needed five stews on the jets. I hope you'll tell Gillespie what happened."

"I'll tell him more than that," Belnap said.

Danni smiled to herself.

Chapter 12

"You're out of your mind," the senior vice president of Marketing said to Evan Belnap.

"Why?"

"She's had only five years with the company, that's why. She's never even been a supervisor and you want to make her chief supervisor. She's not only unqualified and too inexperienced, but we'd be knifing Trudy Simon in the back."

"Balls, Harmon. Trudy's been after us for months to transfer her to Marketing, and you told me yourself you'd like to do it as soon as we could get someone to replace her."

"There are other replacements far more qualified. Harriet Nash in Washington, for example. Martha Devins from Atlanta— she'd be perfect."

"She'd be a disaster and you know it. The stews hate her guts."

"Pure gossip," Gillespie protested. "She's very efficient."

"Oh for Christ's sake, Harmon! She's management's version of Pat Martin and that ain't no gossip. She's in your department, but for my dough you oughta think about canning her, not promoting her."

The advice went over Gillespie's head. "Well, then, how about Nash?"

"I called her before I decided on Danni. She said she wouldn't work in Miami if we tripled her salary. She's getting married to some Washington lawyer."

"I have to tell you," Gillespie said, "I rather resent *your* deciding. The system chief supervisor reports to me. You tell me I should fire Devins because she's my responsibility. Well, by the same token I should say who replaces Trudy."

"What have you got against Danni?" Belnap asked.

Gillespie didn't like the narrowing of the presidential eyes. "Nothing in particular. A bit too ambitious for her own good. Too young. Too . . . uh . . . pushy."

"Shit, man, she's come up with more original ideas in the last year than the rest of your pencil-pushers combined. And since when has ambition been a crime?"

"I'll concede," Gillespie said, "she's demonstrated considerable initiative. However, I've also found her rather impertinent. And very radical in some of her views. Abolishing our stewardess retirement rules. Hiring Negro girls. You may be letting the fox into the chicken coop, Evan."

"I'll chance it. The kid deserves some reward for what she did on four-fifteen that day."

"Why not a nice cash bonus. A raise?"

"Nope. My mind's made up. She's just too damned capable to keep buried in some half-assed job, like flying jet trips. Besides"— the old man smiled benignly—"I've got a hunch you're worried about letting her into *your* chicken coop."

She sat in Belnap's office that same day, dressed in a simple brown skirt with a V-neck white blouse that accentuated her soft dark hair. Belnap stared at her in sheer admiration.

"I'll take the job," she said. "But I want you to know my methods won't necessarily be Trudy's. Or Mr. Gillespie's either. I expect to step on a few toes, raise a few hackles, and get a few people mad at me, maybe including yourself."

"I'm not particularly interested in your methods. I'm interested in your goals."

"The best stewardesses in the industry. Girls who are proud of their jobs and their company."

"I'll buy that."

214

She took a deep breath. "You may have to buy more than that. If you want stewardesses who produce, Trans-National may have to do some producing itself."

The old man grinned. "Sounds like you're spoiling for a scrap. What's on your mind? The age limit? The marriage rule? Hiring black girls?" She flushed and Belnap chuckled. "Yeah, I heard all about that little bombshell you tossed at the recruitment meeting."

She set her jaw. "I won't lie to you. We have to consider changing policies that are not only wrong but stupid because in the long run, they'll hurt the airline. They're already hurting us."

"I'm not saying you're wrong. But is that how you see your job—as being some kind of crusader? If that's the case, you're getting off on the wrong foot. Your responsibility is to ride herd on twenty-eight hundred stewardesses. Personnel policies are in somebody else's ballpark. I want your views on those policies. I want your opinion. But I don't want our system chief supervisor to be nothing but a reformer who's so busy fighting for the underdog that she can't find time for her primary responsibility."

She took it all calmly. "Mind if I smoke, Mr. Belnap?"

"Hell, no. Mind if I light up a cigar?"

They inspected each other through the smoke, a pair of pit bulls circling warily. It was Danni who spoke first.

"I'd like to tell you exactly how I see this job. It's a chance to do something about motivation. That's the magic word. Motivation. Every stew graduates ready to eat fire. Six months later, she's forgotten her manuals because she's too busy memorizing her union contract. She worries more about injustices to herself than what makes a passenger happy. In other words, she's lost her motivation.

"But Mr. Belnap, it's not all their fault. Part of it's management's fault. The company lets them down. Through too many petty rules and regulations. Too many nit-picking check-rides—a check-ride should be positive and constructive, not punitive. I want to get rid of every line supervisor who turns a check-ride into a fault-finding expedition."

She stopped, a time-out to judge the effect of what she had said on Belnap. He merely nodded. "Go on."

215

"The thing is, there are too many instances where nobody bothers to find out *why* a stewardess did something wrong. Too many reprimands going into a girl's file without adequate investigation. And is it really important to insist on a certain shade of lipstick when another shade would do just fine? That's one of the rules I call petty. These . . . these . . ."

"Chicken-shit rules," Belnap finished helpfully. "I kind of wish we were taping this so Gillespie could hear it."

The very mention of the vice president's name brought her up short. "I'm sorry. I guess I should be firing these salvos in his direction, not yours. Except that . . ." Her voice trailed off.

"Except that he doesn't listen. The trouble is, stewardesses are part of Marketing and you're going to have to sell Gillespie on your ideas. I'll support you when I think you're right but I can't promise anything."

"I don't expect you to. All I ask is that the company support the stewardesses. Not me—the stewardesses. Because if the stews can't be loyal to the company, they'll give their loyalty to the union. That's the source of Pat's strength."

Evan Belnap rose wearily and walked over to the model of the *Victory*. "Why," he asked softly, "do I have the feeling that behind all these noble generalities you've just expounded, you have a specific plan?"

"I do."

"Want to share it with me?"

"No, sir. First I'm going to make you the best damned system chief supervisor in TNA's history."

She called a meeting in Miami of all base supervisors a week after her appointment was announced. In that week, she formulated the blueprints for her new regime and then went through hell trying to get them past Gillespie. She deliberately recommended more than she expected to get, hoping that her more excessive reforms would provide a kind of bargaining buffer zone. Indeed, Gillespie rejected every one. But in getting him to concentrate his anger on the more radical proposals, she trapped him into accepting the basic changes she wanted more than anything else. And it was these particular reforms that the base supervisors heard with disbelieving ears.

Before the meeting began, Danni was acutely aware of one problem—natural resentment on the part of at least a few supervisors toward a new superior younger than any woman in the room. It wasn't true of those like Harriet Nash, who had been among the handful of those who telephoned or wrote their congratulations. But when Danni called the meeting to order on that warm Monday afternoon in April 1961, she could feel the chill of animosity on the part of about half the thirty supervisors present.

And even Harriet Nash looked askance at Pat Martin, whom Danni had personally invited. She explained why in her opening remarks.

"I asked Pat to be here for a specific reason," she began. "I want to reduce the number of minor-league grievances that have been piling up to the point of ridiculousness. Every grievance is time-consuming and too often unnecessary, and sometimes it's as much the company's fault as the union's or the individual stewardess's. If we're going to cut down the number of petty grievances, we have to reduce pettiness itself—management and union alike. If this new broom sweeps clean in any one area, it'll be to eliminate as much as possible the bickering that goes on between the union and management.

"To show management's good faith, I want to announce a brand-new policy. From now on, no major detrimental report stemming from a check-ride, a passenger complaint, or a captain's write-up will be allowed to go into an individual's personnel file until I have reviewed the case through a personal or designated investigation. To put is as simply as I can, a stewardess will be considered innocent until *proven* guilty."

She was conscious of murmurs throughout the room, but she could not tell whether they were rounds of approval, anger, or surprise.

"The second reform, if you want to call it that, involves check-rides. In the folders handed to you as you entered, you'll find a new check-ride form. Generally speaking, it puts increased emphasis on

217

what admittedly may be intangibles. Attitude. Rapport with passengers. Personality, including that very simple attribute of smiling even when it hurts. The form does not do away with personal appearance as an item to be judged, but I think we've overemphasized this area in the past. I'm going to take a jaundiced view of supervisory reports that harp on minor sins—a run in a stocking, a hairdo that isn't quite regulation. I know some of you have measured hair length with a ruler, and that is the kind of petty nonsense I want stopped."

There were more murmurs and Danni caught a pained expression on the face of Martha Devins.

"Finally, I'm not suggesting that we lower any standards. I merely want all of you to demonstrate some common sense in judging a girl's appearance. The new bottom line is performance on the job—it's as simple as that. All I'm trying to achieve is a better relationship between stewardesses and their supervisors. I'm asking not for coddling, but for more understanding. I firmly believe this will convince the union that management, as represented by the supervisory staff, is willing to meet it halfway in achieving a better working climate." She paused, breathing rapidly. "Okay, that's my little sermon. The floor is now open to the congregation."

Martha Devins rose, her voice angry. "I can't believe Mr. Gillespie approved all this," she said. "It's nothing but kow-towing to the union. You aren't going to achieve anything but anarchy."

"Mr. Gillespie approved this new policy yesterday morning," Danni said softly. "If you can't live with it, you can always go back to the line."

Barbara Rogers, a trim, no-nonsense supervisor from Chicago whom Danni had always respected, raised her hand. "Danni, there's no reference in this folder to weight checks. Can we assume minimum weight standards still apply?"

"Absolutely. There's no excuse for a stewardess to look like a blimp. But here again, use a little common sense along with the weight charts. A few extra pounds on some girls means nothing, while on others excess weight looks terrible. Exercise judgment and

I'll back you up. You're dealing with individuals and no set of rules will fit every individual."

There was a flurry of additional discussion, mostly favorable and friendly, much to Danni's relief. Then Pat Martin spoke.

"Are a few comments from the union in order?" she inquired. Her tone was pleasant.

"Feel free, Pat. That's why I invited you."

"As far as the union's concerned, all you've provided is platitudes. I haven't heard one word about management's correcting the multitude of injustices that the company has foisted on my members for years. There has been absolutely no mention of unresolved major issues like—"

Danni's voice cracked like a bullwhip. "Hold it, Pat! You weren't invited here to hold contract negotiations. Ladies, thank you for coming. I'll be happy to talk to you individually if you have further questions."

"Just a minute," Pat shouted. "I haven't finished yet."

"You've finished as far as this meeting is concerned," Danni said. "The meeting is adjourned."

The union president was still shouting as the supervisors filed out. Danni, still standing at the podium, was talking to Harriet Nash when Pat grabbed her arm.

"Don't you *dare* ignore me," she yelled. "You know damned well what issues I wanted discussed."

Danni's retort was filtered through gritted teeth. "You wouldn't recognize management compromise if it walked up and bit you."

"Compromise hell! Cheap handouts. Crumbs instead of bread."

"Then go negotiate with a baker. I asked you here as a gesture of friendship. I figured you'd realize we're on the same team and can work together. You thanked me by trying to turn the meeting into a union gripe session. Now you can get the hell out of here before I really lose my temper."

"Thanks for nothing," Pat snarled. She wheeled around and stomped out.

"I hate her guts," Danni whispered.

Harriet Nash nodded gravely. "With justification. But she's also someone to fear."

She had something else to fear—the deterioration of her relationship with Julie Granger.

When Danni told her of the promotion, Julie had joked, "My God, how can I stand living with a big shot?"

But Danni, more than her roommate, knew there was truth in the remark. Much of their friendship was based on a mutual sharing of experiences; each was the other's receptacle for frustrations, concerns, and crises, more often than not job-related. This had been true even when Danni was an instructor—management, yes, but in a fringe area never intruding on their closeness.

Now she was Management proper, part of a chain of command that reached down to Julie herself. There suddenly was a barrier between them, constructed partially out of Danni's direct authority but also out of her inability to confide the daily events flowing from that same authority. She knew Julie was an incurable gossip, an ebullient, well-meaning one, but a gossip nevertheless, and Danni came home at night with a stock answer to Julie's cheerful, "What's new at the office?"

"Nothing much. The usual junk."

Inevitably, Julie retaliated by withdrawing from Danni's professional world. The schism was widened further by the disparity in their social life. Julie dated frequently and enjoyed talking about it; Danni worked a fifteen-hour day and had nothing to talk about. They began to bore each other.

But more than anything else, Danni dreaded the possibility that she might have to adjudicate disciplinary action against her best friend. She kept telling herself that she could be toughly impartial, but the thought made her tremble.

Julie's drinking bothered Danni more than anything else—it was a keg of dynamite waiting to explode. She held her liquor too well to be classed as an alcoholic—at least Danni hoped that was the case. But she could turn into one if that habit of sneaking drinks on airplanes were any indication. If anyone reported her, Danni would have to fire her. So she finally confronted Julie on the issue.

"I want you to promise me you'll never take another drink on duty," she said firmly.

"Okay, I promise," Julie said unconvincingly.

"I mean it, Julie. If you keep it up and you're caught, I can't protect you. And don't even ask me to."

Julie started to make a wisecrack, but she stopped when she saw tears begin to glisten in Danni's eyes. "You're serious, aren't you?"

"Damned serious. Don't make me lower the boom on someone I love. And I do love you. You're the best friend I've ever had."

Julie hugged her. "If you ever had to can me, I'd understand. I'd never hold it against you."

Danni grabbed her roommate's shoulders, squeezing so hard that Julie winced. "Damnit, listen to me! I don't care whether you'd understand! I just don't want to be put on that kind of spot! From now on, you walk the straight and narrow or you'll lose more than a job. You'll lose me as a friend. I'd hate you as much as I'd hate myself."

Now it was Julie who had tears in her eyes. "You know me. You know I can't resist trying to get away with something. I'm a maverick trying to buck a system. But I'm also one hell of a stew. To me, that's more important than a few rules. I've always felt that way and I don't know if I can change."

"I don't want you to change. I can face up to disciplining you for something that's not a major offense. But drinking on the job is something else. It's automatic dismissal and not even Belnap could save you. That's all I want you to promise me, Julie. Don't ever take another drink on an airplane. Do I have your word?"

"You do," Julie said solemnly.

"Fine," Danni said, "but there's one more thing—how about knocking off this two-bit larceny habit of yours?"

"If you're referring to my bringing home those liquor miniatures," Julie said nonchalantly, "I've seen you mix a few drinks with 'em yourself."

"I don't deny it. But believe me, Julie, Gillespie's starting to make waves about stealing stuff off airplanes. If he tells me to crack down, I'll have to get tough."

"I'll be careful."

"Careful's not good enough. Quit it! You make enough to buy your own booze without stooping to petty thievery."

"Oh, come on—you've swiped a few bottles yourself. I remember Mary Beth's wedding. . ."

"That was a gag and it was a long time ago. Things have changed—including the airline's financial health. Those miniatures cost money we can't afford to waste just because a few of you free souls can't resist temptation."

"Well," Julie said with a casualness Danni resented, "I'll try, but nobody's gonna reform me overnight—me and a lot of other girls."

"You'd better and so had the rest of them," Danni said with a grimace that made Julie frown.

Gillespie called a Marketing staff meeting on employee thefts not too long after Danni's conversation with Julie. For several weeks he had been hounding Danni with constant criticism and petty interference; she began worrying about whether he was looking for an excuse to fire her or making life so miserable she'd be forced to resign. And during the session on theft, he kept looking directly at her as if she were personally responsible for the problem, and as if he knew all about Julie.

"It may surprise you—no, shock you," he declared sternly, "that thefts by stewardesses alone cost this company more than a quarter of a million dollars last year. This unforgiveable state of affairs can be blamed almost entirely on the weak-livered leniency demonstrated by supervisory personnel—from top to bottom."

Danni flushed but said nothing.

"Now, I don't intend to rob my own department's budget of that sum without doing something drastic. From now on, any stewardess caught stealing anything from an airplane will be terminated instantly. And when I say anything, I mean exactly that. Even a plastic cocktail stirrer or a paper napkin. I don't give a damn whether she's a ten-year veteran with a perfect record—if she's caught stealing, I want her fired!"

He turned his gaze away from Danni toward a man sitting in the back of the room, and her eyes followed Gillespie's as he continued, "There will be an announcement in the employee newspaper next week concerning this policy. That's why I asked Ray Daley, our new vice president of Public Relations, to be present today. Ray's department puts out the newspaper."

All heads swiveled toward Daley, whose appearance intrigued Danni. He was a tall, slim, sport-jacketed man with thick silver hair that belied his youthful, cherubic face. Prematurely gray, she decided instantly, for she was intrigued by his boyish features—he smiled his acknowledgement of Gillespie's introduction and she had never seen a warmer, friendlier smile. Yet under his smooth, rosy complexion was a hint of stubborn strength . . . a subtle suggestion that the innocent face was a mask hiding a lode of steel.

"Getting back to the new policy," Gillespie was saying. "I expect all of you to enforce it to the letter. Danni, I sense from the expression on your face that you seem to be in disagreement."

"Not disagreement, Harmon. I merely think we should let a little time go by before putting automatic termination into effect. Stewardesses have—"

"The rule means precisely what it says. If you're caught stealing you're fired." His voice rose. "There will be no mollycoddling of thieves, Danni. Get that through your head!"

She kept her own voice steady but it took on an undertone of barely suppressed anger. "Please let me finish. I simply ask you to consider an airline fact of life—stews have been taking stuff off airplanes since the dawn of time. You can't reform twenty-eight hundred girls overnight. I've stolen and so has every stew I know, including a few of our best supervisors if you want to know the truth. If you put that rule into effect, you're liable to nail some of our finest stewardesses who aren't guilty of anything except the inability to shake a bad habit in twenty-four hours."

"I see. And just how do you propose to stop this inexcusable stealing—by slapping them gently on the wrist?"

"No. All I'm asking is that we make it a two-step enforcement process—automatic two- to four-week suspension for the first violation, and automatic dismissal if she's caught a second time."

Gillespie shook his head. "If that's not mollycoddling, I don't know what is. So what if we lose a few of our better girls? It'll make the others realize we mean business. What's more important, saving the tender feelings of a handful of stews or saving this company at least two hundred fifty thousand dollars a year?"

"I'd hate to put a price tag on the ability, loyalty, and experience of your so-called handful," Danni said with obvious bitterness, and she was thinking of girls like Julie when she said it. "Anyway, you're comparing apples and oranges. I'm not saying the money we lost in thefts isn't important. But I do think a more gradual policy implementation will achieve the same results without risking another kind of loss—skilled personnel."

"Thank you for your views," Gillespie said. "I'm afraid, however, that your suggested leniency offers more a demonstration of weakness on management's part than a show of determination. I'm sorry, but the policy will go into effect next Monday—the newspaper comes out this Friday. Ray, I'd appreciate it very much if you make sure the announcement is placed on page one. And Danni, I think it would be a good idea if you also made mention of it in a special stewardess bulletin."

Danni glared. "I fail to see the necessity of calling this meeting in the first place. Am I the only one in this room who thinks you're overreacting? Isn't there going to be any discussion or are we expected to rubber-stamp the whole damned thing?"

The senior vice president flushed. "The policy is being put into effect in all departments, not just In-Flight. I didn't call this meeting to discuss anything. I called it to announce a high-level policy decision, agreed upon by the company's senior officers. However, if you insist, I'll ask whether anyone else would like to comment."

No one spoke. Gillespie smiled. "Good. I think that concludes—"

"Just a minute, Harmon."

Gillespie was unable to keep annoyance off his face. The

224

interruption had come from Ray Daley.

He winked at Danni. "I've held back a temptation to comment on what Miss Hendricks said because In-Flight isn't my bailiwick. But inasmuch as nobody in the department except her seems willing to open his yap, I guess I'd better. Unless, Harmon, you think I'm out of order."

Gillespie frowned. "Ray, I'm sure we'd all like to hear your, ah, appraisal of the situation."

"Thanks," Daley said. "If you ever put this can of worms you're about to open up for a vote, I'm afraid I'd have to side with the young lady. That gradual implementation she recommended— damn if it doesn't make sense. Four weeks' suspension is pretty drastic in itself. I kinda figure it would be an effective deterrent even without your version of capital punishment."

He smiled benignly at Gillespie, but once again Danni sensed there was resolve beneath the smile, a façade of innocence that somehow conveyed a warning. She felt surprise and gratitude that he had interfered and she thought, *I've found a friend.*

"You were present at the executive staff meeting when the overall policy was discussed," Gillespie reminded him. "You didn't bring up any objections then."

"Nope," Daley agreed blandly, "but I'm the new boy on the block and at the time I didn't have the benefit of Miss Hendricks' logical mind."

Gillespie waved this aside. "I repeat, for the benefit of Miss Hendricks and for you, too, Ray, that I'll fire anyone caught stealing and I don't care if she's Orville Wright's great-grandaughter! That's all I have to say this morning. I appreciate your coming."

Danni lagged behind for a few seconds, hoping to thank Daley for his support, but he was conversing earnestly with Gillespie off in a corner. She would have given a month's pay to hear what they were saying—the senior vice president's face was still red and he didn't appear too happy. Danni shrugged and went back to her office, smouldering.

She was still thinking about Gillespie when she went to lunch at the cafeteria, eating alone because it was late.

"Mind if I join you?"

She looked up into the face of Ray Daley, a visage so at odds with the dignified silver hair and lean frame that it seemed to have been grafted into somebody else's body.

"Sure," Danni said, pleased. "You're lunching even later than I."

He removed a grilled ham sandwich and a glass of iced tea from his tray and sat down. "Much later. I usually try to beat the mob in here before noon, but I was too busy trying to knock some sense into our boy."

"Our boy?"

"Lord Harmon, whose brain appears to be a medical miracle since it's apparently located between his legs."

He munched away cheerfully on his sandwich. "Lousy food, but that's par for the course in an airline caf. Actually, it's better than what I used to force down at my old company."

Danni put down her fork, having failed to locate the tuna in her tuna fish salad. "Did you get anywhere with him?"

"Christ, no. Getting someone like Harmon Gillespie to change his mind is like mining coal with a dull nail file. Funny thing, though. I can't make up my mind whether he rates you as a boon to aviation or a rabble-rousing Communist. He was praising you one minute and cursing you the next." He paused, suddenly serious. "He's afraid of you. I wonder why."

"If you're right, maybe it's because he knows Mr. Belnap likes me."

Daley's ice-blue eyes twinkled. "Possible, but not probable. That would mean he's afraid of the old man, not you. And he's not afraid of Belnap; if anything, Belnap's afraid of him. Well, not afraid but worried. Gillespie's a smooth operator, and I've seen a lot of smooth operators after twenty years. I knew him before I came to Trans-National. He's a corporate killer, with ambition oozing out of every pore. But he's so damned slick he can knife you without your even knowing you've been stabbed—until you see your blood dripping on the carpet. I wouldn't be surprised if he gets Belnap's job one of these days—he's just waiting for the right time, like when a couple of the older directors loyal to Evan have to retire."

Danni was fascinated. "What about Frank Ladell?" she asked, remembering what she had heard about the senior vice president of Operations and his ambitions to beat Gillespie to Belnap's job.

"Strictly a long shot. Good operations man, but nuts-and-bolts types usually don't make good airline presidents. They have no financial background and they couldn't sell kosher hot dogs at an Israeli ballgame. Frank's only chance is to force a stalemate when Belnap and Gillespie finally collide at a board meeting. If they knock each other out, Ladell might sneak in as a compromise choice."

Danni grimaced. "You sound as if it's all . . . inevitable. Did you know all this before you came here?"

"More or less. There aren't many secrets in the airline business."

"Then why did you leave your old airline? Would you want to work for a creep like Gillespie, knowing he'd probably become president?"

"Nope."

"Then why? I should think—"

"Let me finish. I came over to Trans-National because I've admired Evan Belnap for as long as I've been in the industry. He's a giant, right up there with the C. R. Smiths and Pattersons and Woolmans and Rickenbackers and Trippes and Bob Sixes." Daley looked into Danni's brown eyes and he was no longer smiling. "I came because Evan Belnap told me he needed help to keep that prick Gillespie's hands off his airline. I'm not sure what the hell kind of help I can give him, but you can bet I'm gonna try."

"You could lose. Or rather Mr. Belnap could. Then where would you be?"

The boyish smile was back. "False modesty makes me throw up. If Gillespie or Ladell takes over, I'll kiss 'em good-bye and go with another carrier—it isn't arrogance to say I can take my choice. I've got five offers in my hip pocket right now. Anyway, stop worrying—it'll ruin your complexion."

"I'm not worrying about you," Danni said. "It's Mr. Belnap who concerns me. And I'm thinking about myself, too. I'd quit if Gillespie were running TNA."

"Somehow I doubt that. Evan told me about you. Said you love challenge, and you're not afraid to fight. In some ways, we're alike. I probably like fighting too much—at least that's what my ex-wife used to say. She even hated to fly—scared her to death. So she divorced both me and the airline business and I've lived happily alone ever since." He paused. "We had one boy and he stayed with his mother, thank God. I miss him but he's better off. She remarried and the kid loves his stepfather—a nice, sane CPA who thinks God invented trout fishing. Me, I always rooted for the fish."

A sudden silence hung between them, broken by a question propelled out of Danni's mixed anger and hope. "Am I correct in assuming you got nowhere with Gillespie on this theft business?"

"Stone wall. Sorry, but it's not the issue on which to make our stand at Thermopylae. Gillespie's right—the stealing has to stop. I agree with you there are better ways to stop it, but Harmon's sold even Belnap on the drastic course."

Danni said glumly, "I wonder which one of my girls will be the first sucker to get caught?"

Exactly nine days later, she found out.

It was Julie Granger.

It was a "ghost rider" who nailed Julie—a check stewardess from a different base, riding incognito supposedly as a paying passenger.

Sometimes a ghost rider was easy to spot, but not this one. Julie's flight was crowded, and the check stewardess was new to her and boarded with a regular ticket instead of the usual pass. Julie also was fooled by her appearance; she was wearing a cheap, low-cut dress that fairly shrieked "hooker."

She was almost the last one to deplane and saw Julie sneak two liquor miniatures into her pocketbook. When Julie walked into Operations, the ghost rider was waiting for her and ordered her to open the pocketbook.

With deliberate maliciousness, Gillespie gave the firing task to Danni.

"I know it'll be tough," he said, "but I warned you there would be no exceptions."

"Haven't you got the guts to fire her yourself?" Danni raged. "It'll tear me apart and you know it!"

"*Miss* Hendricks, I have the guts to fire her or anyone else including you. My courage isn't at question here. It's *your* courage. You're the chief supervisor, damnit, so act like one!"

"I'll go to Belnap. So help me, I'll go to him and he'll—"

"He'll do absolutely nothing. I've already discussed the Granger case with him. He backs me up completely."

"But my own roommate. My best friend—"

"Airlines aren't run on sentiment. That goes with the territory. This is a test of your own managerial ability. A company policy has been set and the fact that you don't agree with the policy has no bearing on your responsibility to carry it out. Incidentally, the union won't intercede, either—I've already talked to Pat Martin. In other words, you'll either fire Granger or you'll leave with her."

Every ounce of decency, every iota of self-respect within her told her to defy him. Into her seething mind sprang the vision of that check from Jerome Eaton. For a moment she thought of running to Belnap anyway and then realized she had no real proof that Gillespie, too, was a crook—taking graft from a supplier. It would be Harmon's word against hers. With that realization came a surge of anger against Julie for putting her into this spot. Her resolve to fight for her roommate suddenly turned flat as she instinctively transferred resentment toward Gillespie into resentment toward Julie. That damned, stupid Julie. . .

Danni dreaded the confrontation and deliberately staged it in her office rather than in the apartment—it was more impersonal and official that way, as if Julie were facing not her best friend but her superior.

With effort, Danni kept her voice cold. "Gillespie's ordered me to fire you. I don't seem to have much choice."

Julie's eyes were bloodshot; she obviously had been crying and her own voice was listless, defeated. Yet she still managed a weak

229

grin. "Is it kosher to ask whether you put up a fight?"

"I did. Not that you deserved one—I warned you and you let me down."

"For that, I'm truly sorry, believe me." She started to cry, and Danni fought the urge to hug and comfort her, anger suddenly washed away in a tide of sympathy. She held back, sympathy blocked by resignation, but her voice softened.

"Why, Julie? Why did you do it?"

The crying ceased and Julie looked right into her eyes. "I swear I don't really know. Every rule's a challenge, every no-no a temptation. I've been that way all my life."

"When you took the liquor, didn't you remember our talk?"

"I remembered." She smiled sadly. "I guess I was overconfident."

"Overconfident?"

"That I wouldn't get caught," Julie hesitated, her eyes lowering. "Also, I suppose, that somehow you'd bail me out if I were."

The coldness was back in Danni's tone. "Well, now you know. I can't. I almost wish they had nailed you for drinking on duty—it would have been easier on both of us. To fire you for a couple of fifty-cent miniatures—my God!"

"I take it I *am* fired."

"I'm afraid so."

"How about letting me resign? Then theft wouldn't be on my record."

Danni stared at her without seeing her. Why hadn't she herself thought of that before? It was a way to punish with a minimum of scars. An effective deterrent, but less cruel.

"Wait outside a minute," she told Julie. She'd call Gillespie . . . surely he'd buy resignation instead of outright dismissal, particularly for veteran stewardesses.

He didn't.

"I told you to fire her and I'm fed up with your soft-hearted procrastinating," he declared. "That's my final word so don't come back to me with any more of this weak-kneed pleading. And by the way, don't bother running to Belnap. He feels just as I do."

230

She slammed down the phone, fought back her own tears, and summoned Julie, who looked at her through eyes filled with mixed hope and fear.

"Gillespie wouldn't buy it," Danni said sullenly. She looked so miserable that now it was Julie who resisted the impulse to comfort.

"Well, I guess that's it," she said without rancor. "I just want you to know I'll never hold it against you. Knowing you has been the best thing that ever happened to me on this airline, so let's part friends."

"What will you do, Julie?"

"Go back to York for now. Think things over. Probably try for a job with some nonscheduled airline that doesn't ask too many questions. I'll say good-bye now—I'd like to be out of the apartment by the time you get home tonight. Always did hate good-byes. Love you, Danni."

She was out of the office before Danni could say anything. When she finally did, it was to herself.

It's my fault, too. I should have thought of that resignation-out myself. If I had suggested it at a staff meeting, Ray would have backed me up. Belnap, too, if I could have gotten to him before Gillespie did. Now it's too late . . .

She picked up the personnel file labeled "Julia Granger" and with a metal clip attached the yellow piece of paper that already had typed on it:

Terminated for theft.

Under it, she signed her name and title.

Chapter 13

"In Julie's case," Pat Martin was saying, "she did something so stupid I couldn't defend her. She was aware of the new policy and she ignored it. I'd look pretty damned silly defending an outright thief."

"Drop the holier-than-thou crap," Danni snorted. "You've stolen, too."

"Not after that policy was announced. I had no legal grounds for protesting her dismissal."

"Try entrapment. That ghost rider was a plant—and one of Martha Devins' check stews, incidentally."

"You haven't objected to ghost riders before."

"Only because there are certain times when an incognito supervisor is valuable—during a final probation check-ride, for instance."

"Or stopping a stew from stealing. Is that all you called me in for?"

"I just wanted to know why you didn't put up a fight for Julie. You would have for any other girl."

"I don't tilt at windmills," Pat said. "They nailed Julie but good. If anyone should have fought for her, it was you. But you didn't, did you?"

"The hell I didn't. Gillespie said—" She choked off what she was about to say; Pat was the last person who should know about

232

that ultimatum. "Never mind what he said. I did the best I could."

"Well, I don't mind telling you I'm going to bring up entrapment at the next contract talks. Maybe Julie died for a good cause. Anything else on your mind?"

"Nothing that's printable. It's like you once said—thanks for nothing."

But when the union leader had left, Danni castigated herself for even talking to her—*A cop-out for my conscience*, she thought bitterly. *I should have gone to Belnap anyway. Can't figure out why he backed up that creep. Maybe Daley was right—the old man's getting to be afraid of Gillespie. But that doesn't excuse what I did. Nothing* can.

The senior vice president of Marketing and Sales looked around the long rectangular table in the Board Room where the executives had gathered for the regular Friday morning meeting.

"I am very happy to report," he proclaimed, "that our crackdown on stewardess thefts has reduced pilferage by seventy-eight percent since we instituted our get-tough policy. I know some of you questioned the drastic measures I recommended, but it seems obvious they've succeeded."

Ray Daley, sitting at one end of the conference table, leaned back in the stiff-backed leather chair. "It also seems obvious we've been throwing out the baby along with the bath water," he said.

Harmon Gillespie flushed. "And what exactly is that supposed to mean?"

"It means we've lost a number of fine stewardesses unnecessarily. And for my dough, your seventy-eight percent theft reduction doesn't mean a goddamned thing. If you had followed Danni's advice, we probably would have ended up with around a seventy-five percent reduction and still have had the services of some very loyal and capable employees."

"I'd like to point out to the vice president of Public Relations that the anti-theft measures had Evan Belnap's full approval." Gillespie, his skin tomato-colored, turned to the president. "Isn't that right, Evan?"

Belnap nodded, but his forehead was furrowed. "What was Danni's advice?" Belnap asked Daley.

"She wanted to slap a few wrists," Gillespie snapped, "and I told her—"

Belnap held up a hand. "Just a goddamned minute. What was Danni's plan, Ray?"

"A stiff suspension for a first offense, termination if the stewardess was caught again. Her argument made sense. She said swiping stuff off airplanes has been a way of life for stews since the airlines hired their first girl, and that we couldn't expect 'em to break the habit overnight. Harmon, she warned you that this get-tough policy of yours was going to cost us some of our best people. The older girls were the worst offenders simply because the habit was more ingrained."

"And that," Gillespie said, "is precisely why my policy's worked. The fact that we've had to fire a few veterans is an effective deterrent for the younger ones."

"You would have achieved the same deterrent with a few suspensions," Daley said in a voice so deceptively soft it was like silk wrapped around barbed wire.

Gillespie looked around the room for support.

"How about you, Garland?" he asked the senior vice president of Maintenance and Engineering. "Theft was a major problem in your department, too—and you told me just the other day it was pretty much under control."

Garland Massorelli was a ham-fisted, barrel-chested man with steel-gray hair who could still lick ninety-five percent of his mechanics. He had been a mechanic himself thirty years ago, and he always felt out of place in this plush Board Room, like a Cockney invited to Buckingham Palace. He worshipped Evan Belnap with the same intensity that he disliked Harmon Gillespie.

"It worked," he grumbled in a deep voice. "But I didn't have to fire anybody to make it work. I just passed the word to the union that the first sonofabitch caught stealing a tool would find three times the cost of that tool deducted from his next paycheck. And I didn't get any static from the union, either."

"That's not what you implied!" Gillespie protested. "I asked

234

you whether the new policy was working and you said—"

"You asked if I had a theft problem anymore and I told you no. You didn't ask me why. You seem to have a conveniently short memory, Harmon. When you first proposed this anti-theft strategy of yours, I told you I wasn't gonna fire any twenty-five-year mechanic for swiping a twenty-five-cent item from the shops!"

Ray Daley chuckled. "Are good stewardesses more expendable than good mechanics?"

"You're damned right they are!" Gillespie retorted—and then wished he hadn't said it.

Evan Belnap's face clouded over. "How many stews have you fired?" he asked.

"Seven—no, eight. We terminated another girl just yester-day."

"Of the eight, were they all senior girls?"

"I have no idea. Seniority was not considered a mitigating factor so I didn't ask. That's what you agreed to, Evan. You gave me carte blanche to—"

"Shit, I know what I gave you. But I'm beginning to think I was nuts. From now on, I want the personnel records of every kid you decide to can *before* you can 'em. I'm afraid to ask which ones we've already let go."

"I can assure you," Gillespie said, "that we have not lost any stewardess who might remotely be considered indispensable."

"Indispensable," Daley said, "is not synonymous with valu-able. Or loyal. Nobody's indispensable, including me or you. I agree that seniority *per se* shouldn't be considered a mitigating factor. But damned if I can say that about qualities like competence and loyalty. Qualities that a kid like Julie Granger had. She was one of your victims."

Belnap's head snapped up. "Julie Granger? I know her—one of our best girls. Wait a minute. Isn't she Danni's roommate?"

"Was," Daley said. "She was terminated around the time you went to Arizona, Evan. That's probably why you didn't hear about it—that little dismissal was all over the airline."

"You fired Granger?" Belnap asked Gillespie.

"No, I didn't. Danni fired her." Gillespie wore a look of noble

235

self-justification but Daley saw something else. Just a hint, a subtle, almost imperceptible sliver of evasion.

"That," the president sighed, "is hard to believe."

"It's the truth."

Belnap sighed again. "Well, I think we've spent enough time on the subject. We're on the verge of ordering twenty-five seven-twenty-sevens, we're phasing out the Connie fleet, so let's get on with it . . ."

A few years ago the old man wouldn't have dropped the subject, Daley thought. *Wonder why Danni didn't go to him about Granger? I know she fired the girl, but there had to be a reason. Gillespie, probably. I'll give odds he made her do it, and if Belnap knew that . . . but what the hell, a few years ago Gillespie couldn't have talked him into this situation in the first place. Belnap would have insisted on knowing the names of the stews being fired, so he could give some clemency. He let Gillespie off a hook today because he feels guilty. He never should have given Gillespie a blank check and he knows it. That's what worries him. He's starting to give in . . .*

". . . before leaving the subject of stewardesses," Gillespie was saying, "I have just learned something I feel should be brought to the attention of the executive committee . . ."

Ed Perkins called Danni with the news, his voice blending excitement with concern.

"I just learned American's hired six black girls," he told her. "I think the flag's going up and we'd better be getting ready to salute."

"Well," Danni said, "I'd rather salute than push a panic button. Does Gillespie know?"

"That's how I heard. He wants me to go out and find a black trainee. Repeat, *a* black trainee. One who looks like Lena Horne, has Pearl Bailey's personality, and holds the political convictions of Aunt Jemima."

Danni snorted. "In other words, a token who'll make Gillespie an overnight liberal. It won't wash, Ed. The color line's been broken, and I don't mean just American. At least two other carriers have been sued for racial discrimination and they aren't even bothering to fight it out in court. Hiring one black girl is like trying to bail out the *Titanic* with a pail."

"You know that and I know that, but Gillespie wasn't kidding. He really did tell me to get one who looks like Lena Horne. And he says she has to be picked in time to start with sixty-three-oh-two, two weeks from now."

"Any prospects?"

"Five, if you can call them prospects. Believe me, none of them looks like Lena Horne. Danni, so help me, if these kids were white I'd have to turn 'em down."

"I know what you mean," Danni said. "I've got an idea. Let me call you back."

"Make it before lunch. After lunch I'm committing hari-kari."

Danni called Harriet Nash in Washington, filling her in on the situation. "You told me once you have a file of qualified black girls who've come to you personally and asked about their chances."

"I do, but it isn't exactly an active file. I have to assume most of them gave up hope and got jobs elsewhere. Damnit, I had to tell them the truth—that we weren't hiring black stewardesses."

"Can you at least try to get in touch with some of the better prospects? I'll authorize CR-ones so they can fly down here for interviews."

"Frankly," said Harriet Nash, "I hope they tell us to go to hell. It's what Gillespie deserves."

They didn't, though. Three days later, Danni sat in on Ed Perkins' interviews with two girls Harriet had talked into flying to Miami.

The first was Hope Fairchild, a lithe young woman with an Afro hairdo and skin so lightly complexioned she might have passed for Caucasian. But Danni was not pleased by the interview. She sensed a belligerence Hope did not try to hide. When Perkins asked her why she wanted to be a stewardess, she almost spit out the answer.

"To prove that a black girl can make it," she said.

"That's an understandable reason," Ed said weakly, and Danni grimaced.

The second girl was Valerie Jackson. Very dark, tiny, with a dazzling smile and the personality of a puppy. Danni liked her, and she also liked what she said. "I've always wanted to be a stewardess, ever since I was a little girl. Never thought I'd have a chance, being black. Believe me, Mr. Perkins, if I'm accepted and make it through training, you'll never regret it."

"Mind if I ask Valerie something?" Danni said.

"Sure, go right ahead."

"I'm just curious to know whether you're trying to prove you can make it as a person, or to prove that someone who's black can make it."

The girl nodded. "In other words, you'd like to know whether I regard myself as a kind of symbol, not just an individual who happens to be black."

"You put it well," Danni said.

"Okay. I don't care whether I'm Trans-National's first black stewardess or its fiftieth. I just want to fly. Does that answer your question?"

"Perfectly," Danni said, smiling. "I've got one more. Do you feel in any way that you're a special kind of applicant—to put it as bluntly as possible, that you'd be our token black?"

"No, ma'am, I don't," the black girl said gently. "I figure if I do a good job, there'll never be need again to hire a token black. You'll take us on merit, just like you would anyone else."

Danni and Perkins exchanged glances. "If you'll just wait outside with Miss Fairchild," Perkins said, "we'll call you in again in a few minutes."

She left, tossing a nervous smile at them as she went out the door. Perkins sighed. "Not much on looks, but I sure as hell liked her attitude."

"So did I. Ed, it's your decision but I'd grab that Jackson kid. Hope Fairchild is nothing but trouble waiting for a place to happen."

"She's damned good-looking, Danni. Know who she reminded me of?"

"Yeah. But you're picking a stewardess, Ed, not Lena Horne's double. Hope's problem is simple. She knows we need a token black and she resents it. I can't say that I blame her, but her attitude is strictly chip-on-the-shoulder, and I'll bet she'll carry that chip all the way through training and right onto our airplanes—*if* she graduates."

"That worries me, too. How the hell can we flunk a black girl? She'll scream prejudice all the way to Washington. Trouble is, Fairchild will also scream prejudice if we don't hire her. I'd rather have the Jackson girl but I'm afraid not to hire the other one."

"Take both," Danni said.

"Both? Gillespie said one black."

"He'll take two," Danni said positively. "And I know just the guy who'll convince him."

"The guy" was Ray Daley, who listened good-naturedly, then gave her a nod that conveyed as much doubt as agreement. "I'll give it a try," he said, "but I seem to be *persona non grata* with Gillespie these days. It's a good idea to hire both girls, but Harmon's already sold the executive committee on taking just one. Come to think of it, I was the only one in the room who said we should hire more than one."

"How about Mr. Belnap? He'd—"

"If Belnap had his way, we wouldn't be hiring one unless we were forced to. The old man has some old-fashioned prejudices. No, I've got to go through Gillespie."

"We don't have much time," she said. "We told both applicants to go have lunch and come back at two for the verdict."

"That means I gotta hit him right away." Daley frowned. "It's a long shot, but I'll try it. I'll call you at your office in about fifteen minutes."

He phoned Gillespie. "Harmon, I just got a call from Tommy Sandifer—you know, the *Herald's* aviation editor. He heard a rumor we were hiring a black stew."

"So what's the problem? We are."

"He pointed out a few things I hadn't thought of. That we'll be accused of hiring a token black. And that if she doesn't make it through training, she'll claim prejudice and we're back to square one. He said if we hired two, we'd have a better chance of graduating our token. And we've got two of 'em standing in the wings."

"We've already agreed on one," Gillespie said testily.

"I know that, but Sandifer thinks one will look pretty silly compared to American's six blacks. And he hinted the *Herald* might be running an editorial that could harp on that point. Look, the original release you okayed quotes Belnap on the hiring decision. I'd like to add a quote from you—something to the effect that TNA could have taken on one black girl as a token, but that you don't regard any stewardess trainee as a token of anything except Trans-National's determination not to discriminate. That both applicants were highly qualified and were therefore accepted, as will future applicants of any color, race, or creed."

"You'll quote *me* on that and not Belnap?"

"Absolutely. You'll sound like the most progressive senior vice president of Marketing in the whole damned industry."

"Well," Gillespie said, mollified, "I guess it's all right, then. But I hope we don't have to hire any more for a while."

Daley smiled. "Thanks, Harmon. Call Ed Perkins and tell him what you've decided."

Danni's instincts about Hope Fairchild were correct. She was intelligent and sharp, and she won her wings legitimately, but Danni kept getting disturbing feedbacks from 63-02's instructor that Hope's pugnacious attitude was set in concrete. Standing one hundred eighty degrees in the other direction was Valerie Jackson, who was well-liked even in a predominantly Southern class.

The difference between the two girls was brought home to Danni the day she pinned on their wings at graduation. When Danni murmured, "Congratulations, Hope, you should be very proud," the girl said coldly, "Proud of what? You had to let me graduate."

Valerie's reaction to the ceremony was to nearly suffocate both Danni and her instructor with hugs. But while the fruit punch was being served, Danni drew Valerie off to one side.

"Is there anything we can do to knock that chip off Hope's shoulder?" she asked. "Be honest, please. Maybe you know how to approach her or can tell us how. With that attitude of hers, she won't be worth a damn on an airplane, and she's going to be hurting more people than herself—like you, for instance, and all other blacks."

Valerie sighed. "I've already talked to her, many times, all through training. The truth is, Hope doesn't really want to be a stewardess and has absolutely no intention of staying with TNA any longer than she has to. If she flies the line for a month, I'll be surprised."

"It costs us about ten thousand dollars to train one girl," Danni said. "If she didn't want to fly, why the hell did she apply in the first place?"

Valerie shrugged. "I asked her that, too. She wouldn't tell me but she didn't have to. I already knew the answer."

Danni thought back to the day the two girls were hired. "When we interviewed her, she said she wanted to prove a black could make it. Damnit, she's proved it—so why all the bitterness, the I-don't-give-a-damn attitude?"

"Because she *doesn't* give a damn. I see myself as a stewardess. Hope sees herself as just a token black. I think I got through training on my own merits. Hope figures you *had* to graduate her. But she believes blacks will always be a tiny handful of in-house niggers. And *that's* why I expect her to quit the first time she gets any static from either a passenger or a fellow crew member."

Hope Fairchild lasted long enough to report in for one flight. The captain was an unreconstructed Southerner. When he boarded the plane and saw Hope, he immediately deplaned, went into Operations, and announced that his aircraft would not leave the gate until "that fire hazard is removed."

"What fire hazard?" the dispatcher asked.

"That nigger with the Afro haircut. Anyone who wears her hair like that is a fire hazard and I ain't movin' that ship one inch until she's off."

To placate him, they called in a reserve stew to take Hope's place; her supervisor immediately notified Danni. But by the time

Danni got to Operations, it was too late—Hope had quit.

Danni's efforts to contact the girl failed. She did demand an investigation of the captain's conduct and had the dubious satisfaction of seeing him grounded—for two weeks—on Frank Ladell's orders.

She derived even greater satisfaction from a personal encounter with the pilot a month later. He was in Operations signing in for a trip and Danni happened to be coming out of a line supervisor's office. She walked up behind him, tapped his arm, and when he turned, slapped his face.

"What the hell do you think you're doing?"

"That was for Hope Fairchild."

"Who the . . . ?"

"She was the black girl you booted off your plane and out of the airline business. You're a despicable bigot, and if you ever pull that stunt again on one of my girls, I'll haul your butt right into Belnap's office!"

"Now just a goddamned minute—"

"I wouldn't listen to you for two seconds. Get it through your thick skull that stew wings are all the same color even if the skins aren't. In another few years you're going to be up to your ass in black stews, so you might as well get used to the idea."

His red flush of anger had flowed over the mark where her open palm had struck his face. Both the slap and Danni's voice had been loud enough to be heard throughout the big Operations room. Danni was conscious of stares, uncomfortable silence, and in a few cases giggles from stewardesses.

"By the time you lousy female do-gooders finish," he shouted, "I'll probably have some nigger bastard sitting in my cockpit telling me he's an airline pilot."

"It'll be worse than that," Danni said. "One of these days you'll have some female sitting in your cockpit telling you *she's* an airline pilot! And it'll be all the better if she's black!"

Soon after the incident in Operations, Danni received a note:

242

I just wanted you to know how much I appreciated the stand you took in behalf of Hope Fairchild. I have always felt that despite our differences, due largely to our divergent if inevitable loyalties, we do have common goals. I would like very much to discuss with you a number of problems for which we might find mutually acceptable solutions.

Sincerely,
Pat Martin

She showed the note to Daley. "It's the first indication she's willing to stop acting like a female Jimmy Hoffa."

"Maybe."

"Are you being cynical or merely cautious?"

"A little of both, I guess." Daley lit one of his well-worn briars. "She seems to mean well. But I have a very low tolerance for loud-mouths like Martin. They can be all sweetness and loving when you agree with them. The first time you disagree, they turn in the olive branch for a gun."

"I still think I should talk to her," Danni said. "If she's willing to be reasonable, it sure would improve the atmosphere around here."

Daley laid the pipe in a large ashtray. "If you're guilty of overoptimism, maybe I'm guilty of over-pessimism. However, remember that brother Gillespie believes firmly in guilt by association. If you start playing footsies with the president of that union and he hears about it, your shapely little derrière will be in the well-known sling. and I wouldn't put it past sister Martin to make sure he did hear about it, particularly if she decides you can't do her any good. Matter of fact, this little *billet doux* of hers might simply be a trap."

"Why?"

"Why should she come to you for—" he looked at the note again—"for finding 'mutually acceptable solutions'? You're no vice president. Your authority is confined to a few thousand stewardesses and you report directly to Gillespie. If she wants to solve problems, she should take them up with Harmon, not you. Unless she thinks you have more influence with Gillespie than I think you do."

"I think you're wrong," Danni said firmly. "I'd at least like to find out how sincere she is." She did not have the courage to tell Daley what she was really thinking. That if she could talk Pat Martin into a less bellicose attitude, it would be quite a feather in her cap . . .

Pat did visit Danni's office, and her sincerity was hard to question—particularly after she opened the discussion on the frankest note possible.

"I don't really like you," she said. "I think you're too ambitious. You've sold your soul to management. But I'll concede you're honest, you're a fighter, and at least to some extent you believe in the same things I do. I hate to put our relationship on a you-scratch-my-back-and-I'll-scratch-yours basis, but if that's the way to get things done, so be it."

"I didn't ask you here to trade favors," Danni said. "I don't want any favors from you, Pat, because you'd attach strings to them."

"Then what do you want?"

"For starters, knock off demands like twenty percent wage increases, sixty-five hours maximum on-duty time, and six weeks' vacation for every woman with three years' seniority or more."

"Why? They're legitimate efforts to correct the inequities—"

"Come off it, Pat. They're ploys to give you bargaining room while you drive Gillespie and Mr. Belnap up the wall."

The union president laughed. "They're somewhat more vulnerable hanging from walls. An angry man doesn't think straight."

"Neither does an unreasonable woman."

Pat flushed—the needle had stung. "What do you mean?"

"You're so busy goading them on short-range issues like money, you make it impossible for them to consider things that are a lot more important."

244

"Such as?"

"Dropping the age and marriage rules. Modernizing training facilities, making improvements in the curriculum. Damnit, Pat, these are items we can agree on—and we'd stand a chance of getting them if you'd quit being so hostile."

"Are you telling me management isn't guilty of hostility? I've only reacted to their anti-unionism. I was perfectly willing to—"

Danni's interruption was an explosion. "For Christ's sake! Did you come in here to discuss working on mutual problems or to go into one of your anti-company tirades? Does it make a damn bit of difference who started the name-calling? Let me tell you something—we've got a very competent, decent vice president of Labor Relations in Larry O'Brien. Gillespie gets into negotiations because you're so belligerent that O'Brien can't do his job without calling on Harmon for help." She paused, knowing anger was futile.

"Let's quit sparring," she said, her voice calm. "I think I can drum up enough support to kill both the marriage and age limit policies, provided you show a little restraint in money demands."

"I don't believe you have that kind of clout," Pat said.

Danni smiled. "Clout, no. Connections, yes. I also happen to have a few facts on hand that'll knock some vice presidents out of their chairs. What the stewardess turnover is doing to Trans-National in terms of unnecessary training expenditures, for example. I can show how that money can be used to better advantage—including a wage increase and some fringe benefits for the union. I'll put my data into the hands of the right people, and you can start taking bows before your members."

"I don't see how," Pat sniffed. "Management'll get the applause, not me."

"You've included elimination of those discrimination clauses in your last three contract proposals. Never mind that you really didn't scrap for 'em because you were too greedy demanding more dough. So this time, try again. Only now you'll win and you'll earn the gratitude of every girl who wants to keep flying after she's married."

"Damned if you don't make a case," the union officer said.

Danni's eyes were bright. "I'll make my move when you make

yours. Lower your sights, and I'll go to bat for you on those other issues."

"That's all?"

"Not quite. Just between the two of us, how about easing off on these grievances? I don't mind a legitimate beef, but you're defending gals who don't deserve defending and you know it. Like Helen Firelli. She's missed more trips and concocted more phony sick reports than any five stewardesses combined."

For the first time since Danni had known her, Pat Martin looked penitent, even a little embarrassed. "Helen's a union member. Please understand, it's my job to stick up for any member, even a congenitally lazy one like her. There are times when I look at a whining, self-pitying, selfish face and I want to spit right in her eye. But they're my girls, too—just as much as they're yours. There's one thing a union and a company should have in common: loyalty that flows in both directions. That's the way you run your shop and that's the way I run mine."

Danni looked at her with newborn sympathy and understanding—this was a side of Patricia Martin she had never seen before. Ray Daley must be wrong about her.

Then again, she thought grimly, *he'd better be.*

"There's only one thing the matter with all this," Daley told her. "It's your baby, and I doubt that Gillespie will accept any baby of yours that's dropped on his doorstep."

"It's no illegitimate baby," Danni argued. "I've got the union's word it'll make concessions in wage demands if the company drops the marriage and age rules. How could Gillespie turn that down, even if I was the one who arranged the deal?"

"Why take a chance? Let me talk to Harold Schumacher. Nobody's more anti-union than our vice president of Finance. If Gillespie thought Harold dreamed up this trade-off, he'd buy it."

"But that's not fair! He'd get all the credit for—" She closed her mouth, for in his eyes she saw disappointment.

"Is that all you want?" he asked softly.

"Of course not."

But even as she voiced the denial, she felt guilt and embarrassment flooding her thoughts. She knew credit was exactly what she did want. Sure it was for the good of the airline and her girls, she told herself with lame defensiveness, but she knew that that was only part of her motive, and it bothered her that Daley now could see through this so easily. Even if their friendship was relatively new, she craved his respect, and for the first time she had given him a glimpse of another Danni Hendricks—the one with consuming ambition. She found herself bracing for criticism.

But he was waiting, too. Waiting for her to admit that ambition. He had always liked Danni for her honesty and intelligence, yet the iconoclast in him was always flashing red signals of cynicism; her blurted remark bothered him, for while it expressed a motivation he could understand, on Danni it was a badly fitting dress of a tasteless design.

He said nothing. He just kept looking at her, disrobing her conscience further with his unspoken disbelief.

"Well," she said, "I'll admit I was trying to look good in front of the brass."

He got to his feet. "Your honesty is refreshing," he said, smiling. "Let's go see Schumacher."

"By God, it's beautiful!" The booming voice of Evan Belnap bounced off the paneled walls of the Board Room and into the unwilling ears of Harmon Gillespie.

"What I'd like to know, Harold," Gillespie inquired, "is why you did this study in the first place."

No TNA officer was better than Harold Schumacher at twisting an intended spear into a boomerang. "I'm surprised you even ask the question," he said easily.

"Surprised?"

"Of course. You must be aware that there are court actions pending on just this subject—legal attempts to overthrow all these discriminatory employment policies. Now, it—"

"*Alleged* discriminatory policies," Gillespie broke in.

"A matter of semantics. At any rate, the possibility, if not the

247

probability, of the courts forcing carriers to retain married or overage stewardesses led me to examine the cost aspects of jumping the gun on the courts. In other words, abandoning our policies before we're forced to. And as the figures I've just presented here demonstrate, the savings would be significant."

"I agree that reduction of stewardess turnover would mean some savings," Gillespie said, "although I consider your projections a bit unrealistic. What I fail to see, however, is why we should take the initiative. The savings would be the same whether we're forced to do it or do it voluntarily."

"Excellent point," Schumacher said. "As a matter of fact, one I thought of myself, and I hied myself off to Legal. Bill, will you tell us what you told me?"

William Carrington, senior vice president, Legal, cleared his throat. He was a lean man with cadaverous features, easy-going and likeable. He had been well briefed by the senior vice president of Finance.

"The survey on which Harold based his cost analysis," he began, "contained one especially pertinent point: if we drop all employment restrictions, approximately ninety-five percent of those stewardesses approaching age thirty-five will elect to remain in the company. There are some three hundred fifty girls in that category.

"The survey also disclosed that more than seventy percent of the stewardesses polled would continue flying after marriage for a period of at least one year. Now, it's true that these figures would apply whether the initiative came from the company or the courts, but consider the *psychological* advantage of the company's taking the lead. You must realize, gentlemen, that the probable court decisions ending all discriminatory practices won't end the controversy. It's my judgment that any carrier subject to an unfavorable court ruling will be open to retroactive lawsuits—by former stewardesses who will want their old jobs back with back pay and full seniority from the day they were forced to resign."

"Which would wipe out your savings," Gillespie interjected.

"Not necessarily. The fact that we voluntarily eliminated discrimination would be a psychological barrier to lawsuits—how high is anybody's guess, but still a barrier. Furthermore, Harold's

248

summary raises a very interesting point: that the stewardess union would become the company's ally in defending such legal action. No union in its right mind would want the seniority rights or even the very employment of their present members threatened by the forced rehiring of ex-stewardesses."

Schumacher saw veins begin to bulge in Gillespie's temples. It was time to throw the knockout punch. "I reiterate: we are offering the union a significantly attractive proposal. There isn't the slightest doubt that our action would strengthen the union, which suffers itself from the high stewardess turnover. And I believe that we can trade off abandonment of discrimination for equally important concessions in their excessive money demands."

To Gillespie, the murmurs of unofficial agreement throughout the room were like the sound of nails scratching on a blackboard.

"Even if everything you say is true," he argued, "I must question the advisability of strengthening the union in any way whatsoever."

Belnap spoke up. "As I see it, it's gonna be strengthened anyway. If we don't climb off discrimination, the courts will make us. So in the long run, the union will win without owing us a thing."

"Right," Daley said. "And I ask you all to consider the public relations aspects—we'll look pretty damned good with a *fait accompli* when the courts are ordering our competitors to reform."

Gillespie's anger and frustration boiled to the surface. "I think it's my right to ask why a survey of this magnitude, directly affecting *my* department, was undertaken without my knowledge."

"Sure," Shumacher said affably. "I figured we might have a chance to save some dough and improve labor relations. I asked Danni Hendricks to help me gather some facts, which she did."

"Which also happened to be an act of disloyalty to me!" Gillespie stormed. "She had no business working for Finance— she's responsible only to Marketing."

Belnap's voice was a snarl. "She's responsible to Trans-National, not to you or any other individual! Marketing isn't a separate airline, Harmon—not yet it isn't."

"She owed me the courtesy of keeping me informed."

"She wanted to but I advised her against it." That was Daley; Gillespie stared at him incredulously.

"You actually told her not to?" he demanded.

"I did, with Harold and Bill's approval. It's no secret she's been urging for years that we drop the marriage and age rules. We all agreed that if you knew Danni did the study, you might be prejudiced against it and try to shoot the whole thing down. Now, Mr. Belnap, I suggest we have Larry, here, get together with Pat Martin and . . ."

Another meeting later that same day involved Gillespie and Frank Ladell. They met for a very private lunch, away from the base.

"All it's done is delay our move for at least a year," Gillespie said. "Even if it's two or three years, considering what's at stake, we can live with it."

"That damned Hendricks," Ladell grated.

"A very smart little girl," Gillespie conceded. "But as we found out today, a very dangerous one."

"You came out of it perfectly," Daley was telling Danni. "No more oppression of elderly stews or anxious-to-marry stews, and you got your full share of credit."

"I wish I could have been there!" Her eyes were shining, but in her joy she missed the slight sarcasm in his voice.

"Kinda wish you had been, too. The old man would have pinned a medal on you. Incidentally, he asked me to give you his thanks—said if there's anything you ever want, all you have to do is tell him."

Danni's happiness deteriorated with a sudden memory. "It's too late to ask for what I really wanted."

"And what was that—his job?"

"I would have liked to have his job ago when Gillespie made me fire my best friend."

"So I heard. Evan wasn't very happy about that."

She stared at him. "He knew all about it."

Daley looked puzzled. "The hell he did. Belnap even chewed out Gillespie for firing your roommate without consulting him first. At a staff meeting not too long ago. What's wrong, Danni? You're as white as a ghost."

She could hardly speak. "That lying, vicious bastard! He told me he cleared Julie's dismissal with Belnap first. I would have gone to Belnap and fought for her but I didn't think I had a chance. I . . . I let it happen when I might have saved her."

Daley put his arm around her. "It wasn't your fault, honey. Not after he lied to you. The old man was in Arizona when Gillespie pulled that little double-cross, and he didn't find out about Granger until he got back. Harmon would probably deny what he told you—he'd claim you misunderstood him."

Danni was crying now. "Julie wanted to resign instead of getting fired. But Gillespie wouldn't let me buy it—and I'll bet Mr. Belnap would have. I didn't even try to see him. I thought it was hopeless."

He patted her shoulder until the sobs dwindled to a few sniffles. "I think you know now," he muttered, "the nature of the enemy."

PART FOUR
(1965–1966)

Chapter 14

Raymond Joseph Daley was an enigma.

For a long time it was assumed he had no social life. He appeared faithfully at company functions but never with a female companion; Harmon Gillespie privately speculated that Daley might be queer but discarded this theory when Harold Schumacher confided one day he had seen the vice president of Public Relations in a Miami restaurant the night before, "with a doll who would have given Belnap a hard-on."

"One of our stewardesses?" Gillespie asked.

"Not this babe—if we ever hired anybody that beautiful, we could charge double for any flight she worked."

Danni wondered about Daley, too. Their association was strictly on a nine-to-five basis, yet it was rumored they were having an affair. Both were aware of the rumor. "Maybe we should have one and the gossip would stop," Danni once joked.

"No thanks," Daley said unsmiling. "My policy can be summed up in one sentence: Never get involved with someone in the company."

Because of those rumors, Daley cut down on the frequency of their lunches together. He was, as far as Danni was concerned, that rare example of a male friend who wanted nothing more than friendship. She invited him to dinner one night and was rather surprised when he turned her down.

"Friend of mine's coming in from L.A.," he explained. "I'll be tied up for the next few days."

"Male or female?" Danni asked. "Not that it's any of my business."

"You're right, it isn't. But if you must know, female."

"Have fun," she said with a cheerfulness she did not feel, and then wondered why. She was too fond of him in a platonic way to be really jealous, and with that kewpie face of his she was never stirred physically.

Her own attitude toward him seemed logical; in the years she had known him she was never quite sure she could explain his attitude toward her. He obviously liked her, but in what way, she could not be sure.

The trouble was, Danni told herself, that she wanted to get involved with someone *like* Ray Daley. She liked his wit, respected his judgment, enjoyed his company, admired his intellect, and cherished his affection. So if not jealousy, there was envy, perhaps, for the unknown woman he preferred to be with.

The years were going by too fast. There were streaks of gray in her soft black hair, and wrinkles had appeared around her deep-set eyes. She accepted these unpleasantries with equanimity; she hated false vanity so refused to do anything about the graying hair. But she kept her weight down and was a lot prouder of her trim body and still-firm breasts than she was worried about a few wrinkles.

"I'm fifteen years older than you, and I could pass that damned weight check today," she would tell those back-sliding girls before whom a set of scales loomed like a guillotine.

The fact that she enjoyed her work and was proud of her accomplishments did not entirely compensate for the occasional emptiness of her personal ife. The scars left by Anthony Buchanan had faded, remembered like the twinges of an old wound that aches in damp weather. Yet the one thing she could never escape was the memory of her sexual commitment to a man she loved, the deliciousness of passion channeled into a relationship of legitimacy and depth.

Eventually the personal void affected her professionally. She became, gradually and steadily, shorter-tempered and less tolerant.

256

She never lost her sense of fairness, but she was tougher, sharper-tongued, forgiving of a first mistake or transgression but not of one repeated. There was an element of fear buried in the affection and respect her stewardesses bestowed upon her; where once she would have been troubled by it, now she accepted her reputation as the price to be paid for command authority.

"I hear the gals are calling you 'The Iron Butterfly,'" Ray Daley told her. "Is that supposed to be a compliment or an insult?"

"Probably a little of both," she answered. "When they act like irresponsible children, they're going to be treated like irresponsible children. How do you think it was meant?"

"Well," Daley said cautiously, "the scuttlebutt on the line is that you're getting to be one tough little cookie."

"Too tough, Ray? Come on, tell me the truth."

He shook his head. "I didn't exactly take a scientific poll. I'd say the better stews think you're great. The below-average ones think you're a goddamned martinet, and the younger girls are scared to death of you."

Danni smiled. "It's one hell of a tightrope. I'm dealing with women who are supposed to be professionals, yet I'm dealing with professionals who happen to be women. If I'm too lenient, they'll walk all over the company. If I'm too tough, I create resentment toward the company. I'm a boss who can't stand sloppiness, indifference, or lack of effort. Yet I'm a woman who understands why one of my sex can be sloppy or indifferent. Remember that old slogan about Boys' Town?"

"Sure. 'There's no such thing as a bad boy.'"

"Apply it to stews. I honestly don't think there's any such thing as a bad stew, not for the first six months, anyway. But once she gets off probation and she has the union to protect her, that's when she can turn sour. That's when her priorities get all mixed up. She changes from 'what can I do for TNA' to 'what can TNA do for me,' and it all winds up on my desk as a disciplinary problem."

"You sound bitter."

"You're damned right I'm bitter. Who the hell wants to be known as The Iron Butterfly?"

*   *   *

The manipulations of Harmon Gillespie had occupied the thoughts of Ray Daley for some time.

He never mentioned to Danni that the gossip about their supposed affair concerned him deeply, for even the rumors hurt his effectiveness as her self-appointed protector. This was a role in which he had reluctantly supplanted Evan Belnap. The old man's influence had been declining steadily with the infirmities of age and the Machiavellian operations of Gillespie and Ladell.

Daley realized that the feuding between the two men had come to an end around the time TNA abolished the age and marriage policies. Outwardly Ladell continued to give the impression that he wanted to be Belnap's crown prince, but he began displaying such cordiality toward Gillespie that Daley speculated there had to be some kind of devious motivation behind the charge.

He was even more worried about Belnap himself. The aging president was abdicating slowly, his authority being peeled away like the layers of an artichoke. He reminded Daley of an obsolete battleship, battered and barely afloat. Outwardly he was his old irascible self, yet Daley could see deterioration under the bombast.

He realized the extent of Belnap's decline the day Harmon Gillespie proposed that Marketing assume "partial" responsibility for route development.

"The intention is to coordinate route expansion with sound marketing research, so we can determine the viability of potential markets," Gillespie told an executive staff meeting.

Andy Arenas, senior vice president of Route Planning, went white with anger. "What the hell are you trying to pull?" he roared. "Never, in the eighteen years I've been with this airline, have I ever made a route proposal without first consulting all departments—Operations, Legal, Finance, Government Affairs—*and* Marketing."

"I never said you didn't," Gillespie smiled.

"Then kindly explain to me why Marketing should have veto power over all route recommendations?"

Gillespie laughed easily. "Come on, Andy, let's not get paranoid about it. All I'm looking for is greater efficiency and imagination in our future route development. This doesn't mean, however, that system expansion shouldn't be based on teamwork. I'm all for that."

Arenas glowered. "Meaning I haven't shown efficiency and imagination? Are you telling me I haven't encouraged a team effort?"

"Quite the contrary. You've always been a team worker. But I'll be honest with you, Andy. A very conservative team worker. Here we've ordered nearly two hundred million dollars' worth of Boeing seven-forty-sevens, with first deliveries less than three years away, and Route Planning has yet to provide us with a feasible new route structure capable of supporting a four-hundred-passenger aircraft."

"The seven-forty-seven order was finalized only three months ago," Arenas snapped. "If you'll recall, I voted against buying ten of those birds when we have only two transcontinental routes. I said I could come up with sustaining routes for five planes, but ten were too damned many."

"And I'd like you to recall, Andy, that Evan himself urged that ten-aircraft contract and—"

"On *your* recommendation," Arenas said.

"Quite true. Because, like Evan, I naturally predicated my support on the expectation that we'd lose no time in developing new major markets."

Daley glanced at Belnap, slouched wearily in his chair at the head of the conference table, and shook his head sorrowfully. He remembered the day the executive staff had voted to recommend that the Board of Directors authorize the purchase of ten jumbo jets. Daley himself, Arenas, and Schumacher had cast the only dissenting votes, and two weeks later the Directors had rubber-stamped the decision. Only it wasn't Evan Belnap who had argued the case for ten 747s before the Board; it was Gillespie. And Daley remembered how he had kept bringing Belnap's name into the presentation . . . "*Mr. Belnap feels . . . Evan is absolutely convinced . . . the president is confident . . .*"

He was setting the old man up, Daley decided. Making sure Belnap would be the fall guy if the 747s failed. And if they didn't, Gillespie would be the hero thanks to the route-development

259

authority he was trying to appropriate. That 747 order had made no sense—it was digging more dirt out of an already deep morass. Trans-National hadn't shown a profit since 1959; accumulated losses for the past five years had amounted to a chilling $193 million, and only two months ago Belnap had caved in and awarded huge wage increases to both the pilots and the mechanics. "We can't afford to take a strike," he insisted. True, Daley conceded, but they couldn't afford those ten big birds, either, and he didn't trust Gillespie with route development, or anything else . . .

". . . And I assure you I'm merely proposing a more orderly, efficient transition into the age of the jumbo jet." Gillespie's unctuous voice assaulted Daley's nerves and he looked at the faces of his fellow officers, trying to glean from expressions how the vote would go. From a few he dredged hope. Arenas was staring at Gillespie with sheer hate, and on Massorelli's swarthy visage was written contempt—Gar even caught Daley's glance and almost imperceptibly winked. Schumacher worried him, however; the senior vice president of Finance was frowning, and Daley could not tell whether it reflected his dislike of Gillespie or something else. Bill Carrington's face was enigmatic, which was typical of the senior vice president of Legal—he could, Daley knew, go either way. Larry O'Brien, vice president of Labor Relations, was a hopeless sycophant when it came to Gillespie—he was scared to death of Harmon, who had gotten him his job at TNA and never let him forget it . . .

". . . And now, Evan," Gillespie crooned, "I'd suggest you call for a vote."

The president grunted unhappily. "Okay, if there's no more discussion—"

"There's been damned little discussion," Daley interrupted angrily. "This whole little scheme smells like a sun-ripened mackerel. It's a hell of a slap in the face at Andy, it's totally unnecessary—except possibly for feeding Harmon's ambitious ego—and it's about time we stopped letting Marketing run the goddamned airline!"

Gillespie flushed, but he kept his own anger out of his voice.

260

"I'll ignore Ray's rather personal and uncalled-for attack on me and let the facts speak for themselves. It is totally illogical to leave Marketing out of route development."

Arenas exploded again. "Marketing's never *been* out of it, damnit! But it has no right to veto power. You might as well eliminate my whole department if you insist on running the show. I'm not going to serve as vice president of drawing route maps that someone else thought up."

"I think," Gillespie said coolly, "that Ray's accusation of ambitious ego might be better directed toward the vice president of Route Planning. Let me speak frankly, Andy. There's no room in this company for empire builders."

"Or overly ambitious vice presidents who'd like to be president," Daley snapped.

Someone in the room gasped, but Daley could not tell who had reacted audibly to his audacity. He could see the reactions on their faces, however—a quick smile from Massorelli, for example; fury from Gillespie; Schumacher's stare of incredulousness. And—Ray Daley would never forget this—pain etched into the craggy features of Evan Belnap, who cleared his throat.

"I think we've had enough of this name-calling," he said quietly. "Let's get the voting over with, and I hope to hell I don't have to cast the deciding vote. There are ten of you guys in this room and I'd hate to have it go five-five."

Which is precisely the way it did go. Massorelli was the only senior vice president to join Daley and three other vice presidents in voting nay; Daley was shocked when Schumacher voted aye. It was up to Belnap, who suddenly looked ten years older.

"Anyone want to reconsider?" he temporized.

Daley looked at Schumacher imploringly, but the latter remained silent.

Once again, Belnap cleared his throat as if paving the way for words that resisted utterance.

"I'll vote aye," he said with a forced firmness. He was deliberately avoiding Daley's eyes and stared instead at Gillespie, whose smile was more of a smirk.

"Thanks," Daley whispered bitterly to Schumacher on the

way out. "You just helped elect the bastard president."

"He's going to be president anyway," Schumacher sighed. "I've got five years to go before retirement, and I'm not risking all I've got invested in my pension."

After adjournment, Daley marched into Belnap's office. "Okay, Evan, why the hell don't you just quit now and hand that sonofabitch the keys to your washroom?"

Belnap's bloodshot eyes flared. "Where did you get the idea I'm quitting?"

"Damnit, you sat there and let him pull off that power play without one word of protest. You even cast the deciding vote. What the hell did you hire me for if you weren't gonna do some scrapping yourself?"

The fire in the eyes flickered and died. "I know," he said wearily. "Maybe we'd better face up to reality. He's damned close to having a majority of the Directors on his side. There doesn't seem to be much we can do about it, is there?"

"There isn't if you persist in surrendering everytime he fires a shot. Most people on this airline hate his bloody guts. They don't want to see him become president. They'll buy the man you choose yourself. But you seem to have chosen Gillespie."

The old man shook his head. "No, that's not true. I have a guy in mind, but I don't think I've got the votes on the Board to get him elected."

"Harmon doesn't have the votes either. Not yet. Which is why we have to keep fighting. Sooner or later, a prick like Gillespie's gonna trip over his own arrogance and he'll lose Board support."

"I dunno, Ray. I want to keep fighting but it looks so damned hopeless. When you come right down to it, outside of the Directors who are loyal to me, you're about the only one."

"No, I'm not. Andy Arenas is with us. So is Massorelli and maybe a few others once they're convinced there's still a chance to stop him. Middle management doesn't want any part of Gillespie—people like Danni Hendricks, for instance."

"Danni?" The old man's chuckle was more of a disdainful snort. "Don't be too sure. I've always had a hunch she had something going with Harmon."

262

Daley's first impulse was to laugh in disbelief, but it was an impulse buried quickly under instinctive suspicion. Evan Belnap's hunches usually were on target. Daley knew the president liked Danni, yet he had made the remark anyway, and that added credence. Ray Daley was no naive idealist about women; he had always wondered whether Danni's hatred of Gillespie had roots involving a personal relationship, a possibility he realized he had discarded because he did not want to believe it. And he was going through the same denying process now—Danni couldn't have had anything to do with the bum. Not Danni. So honest and open. No, Belnap had to be wrong . . .

"Impossible," he declared with more conviction than he felt. "She hates his guts."

Evan Belnap searched the pale face of his vice president of Public Relations and found the truth in eyes that were pained.

"Well, you're probably right," Belnap said with a clumsy heartiness that rang false. "At my cynical age, I think the worst of everybody. Forget I said it."

But Daley did not, could not, forget it. It was typical of him that he asked Danni directly.

"None of your business," she said, and simultaneously wondered how he had found out. Gillespie, probably—no one else knew of their affair. She suddenly felt soiled, cheap, even as she bristled with indignation that Daley had asked.

"Finding out what side you're on is damned well my business," he retorted.

"And who's responsible for that little piece of gossip—Gillespie?"

"If it had been Gillespie, I'd have slugged him. Never mind where I heard it. I just want to know if it's true."

She was trying to peer under his fury for the real source of his question. Did he think she was a traitor or just a slut? Was he angry because he thought she had bedded their mutual enemy, or was he jealous? It had to be the former, she decided—their friendship was almost masculine, based on loyalty rather than attraction between

263

opposite sexes. What right had he to be jealous, anyway? He had never shown the slightest romantic or physical interest in her. He had to be afraid there was an emotional link between her and Gillespie that would make her an unreliable ally. *"Finding out what side you're on,"* he had said. Well, no use lying to him . . .

"It's true," she said. "Or was. I haven't had anything to do with him for a long time."

"Your taste in men stinks."

"I couldn't agree with you more. Is that all you want to know?"

The pain in her eyes diluted his anger. "Okay, I'll agree your sex life is none of my business. But good Christ—Gillespie! Danni, if you think you could go to bed with the bastard again, tell me right now and I'll cross you off Belnap's list of loyal subjects."

"The only reason I'd sleep with him again is to help Mr. Belnap," she said coolly.

"Or maybe yourself."

She flushed but held her poise. "That was the main reason I went to bed with him at all. Par for the course in this man's world, isn't it?"

"Not in my world, it isn't." His look softened momentarily, then hardened into sudden shrewdness. "If there's nothing between you and Harmon anymore, then why can't I shake this persistent feeling that for some reason he's afraid of you?"

"What makes you think that?"

"I wish I knew. But I have this old newspaperman's intuition. It tells me he thinks you've got something on him. Am I right?"

She almost told him but something held her back. And she knew why. Buried deep within her was fear of Harmon Gillespie. Fear that if she brought up that suspicious check and he could explain it away—and the smooth sonofabitch was fully capable of it—he would wreck her own career. If she couldn't make a payola charge stick, and Gillespie wound up being president, he'd exact his revenge. Ambition, she knew, could be a form of fear—the most malignant fear of all . . .

"Maybe," she answered enigmatically. "I'm not quite sure myself."

He knew Danni too well to press her, but she had given him unexpected hope. "I'd wish you'd tell me. It may be the only way to stop him."

"It might. But I'd rather wait. Let's call it a last resort, because if I'm wrong . . ."

"I'd be willing to take a chance. I'm getting scared, Danni. It's Gillespie who's running the staff meetings. Belnap just sits there and sometimes I think the only thing he's fighting is the urge to fall asleep. He's abdicating by default."

Danni frowned. "If it's that bad, why doesn't Harmon make his move?"

"Because Evan Belnap still packs a punch where it counts— on the Board of Directors itself. Gillespie doesn't have a Board majority. There are two, maybe three Directors, who could go either way—for Gillespie or for whoever Belnap nominates as his successor, probably someone from outside the company. Within the company there's nobody with the exception of Harmon, who wants the job so badly he'd climb over his mother's corpse to get it."

"I can't believe anyone could be that ruthless."

"Ruthless," he said quietly, "might also describe you."

She bit her lips to quell a retort to what she knew was deserved. Yes, ruthless. Also cowardly. "I guess I had that coming to me," she said, "but I don't think I'm in Harmon's class."

"Of course you're not. I'm absolutely convinced Gillespie would deliberately force this airline into a financial crisis if he knew the Directors would blame Belnap."

"Are you telling me Harmon would sabotage his own company?"

"You're damned right he would. All he has to do is make the old man the villain and he'll be the U.S. Cavalry riding to the rescue. Hell, he's already got a crisis working for him—we're swimming in red ink and it's gonna get worse. We've dug a hole with the seven-forty-seven order, and that airplane's three times bigger than the seven-oh-sevens we can't even fill. But that's not what worries me. The seven-forty-seven's at least three years away. We've got a crisis parked right on our front doorstep like an abandoned baby."

"Stewardess negotiations," Danni guessed.

"Correct. You getting any vibes?"

She nodded. "Strong ones. I've heard rumors Pat's out for blood."

Daley lit a pipe and watched the smoke curl upward—Danni had the uncomfortable feeling she was watching an Indian war signal. "That's what I was afraid of," he said. "Contract talks start next month. If they follow previous scripts, Larry O'Brien won't get to first base, Gillespie'll step in, and we'll have our crisis. I've seen the preliminary report for the last quarter. Twenty-eight million bucks in the red for just those three months. My God, Danni, a strike would kill us."

"All that goodwill and mutual trust we built up," Danni said sorrowfully. "It's gone down the drain."

Ray Daley was thinking, *That's not all that's gone down the drain. How could she have let that slimy sonofabitch touch her? Shit, I know why—that's the trouble . . .*

She was thinking, *I wonder whether he isn't a little bit jealous? No, he couldn't be—he's always treated me like his sister. But he was really mad. Because it was Harmon, I suppose. He wouldn't have been upset if it had been anyone else. I went to bed with the enemy, that's what bothered him. Maybe I should have told him about the check . . .*

The tightrope she had once described to Daley had become even thinner and more precarious. She was battling Pat Martin and Gillespie simultaneously, getting little or no support from either.

She came in one morning and discovered that Pat had filed a grievance in behalf of a stewardess who had been asked to work a trip on her day off because a flu epidemic had decimated both regulars and reserves. Technically the girl had been within her rights to refuse the flight, but to Danni it was another case of union arrogance—the stewardess had only been asked to work and hadn't been punished for refusing.

The very next piece of correspondence was a memo from Gillespie concerning the below-par performance of a stewardess he

266

had observed on a flight—a woman newly married and thirty-seven years old.

It seems apparent that this woman demonstrates the mistake we made in relaxing our policy. Her indifference, sloppy performance, and general deportment was a perfect demonstration of why married and older women make poor stewardesses. I would appreciate your keeping me advised as to what punitive and/or corrective measures you intend to take.

HG

Danni called the stewardess at home and asked her to come to the office that afternoon. Then she composed a reply to Gillespie.

I will discuss your note with Stewardess Gogarty and assure you that if she cannot offer a legitimate explanation for her conduct, she will be placed on immediate probation. I want to point out, however, that she is not representative of cabin personnel in the categories of married and/or beyond-35.

As I have informed you on previous occasions, I have been monitoring both passenger commendation and passenger complaint correspondence. There still is no evidence to contradict my earlier reports on this subject. The only observable pattern shows a slightly higher ratio of commendations for married and/or beyond-35 stewardesses than for unmarried or under-35 cabin personnel.

The conclusion we can draw from this data, and from your note concerning Stewardess Gogarty, is simple: There are good stewardesses, average stewardesses, and bad stewardesses, and it doesn't seem to matter whether they are married or how old they are.

I will, of course, continue to monitor not only passenger letters but also check-ride reports to see whether a different pattern develops.

DH

The next day she found on her desk an advance copy of the August 1965 copy of *Stud*, a men's magazine. Clipped to the issue was a note.

Danni—turn to page twenty-eight. HG is raising hell and wants the girls fired. Call me as soon as you've digested the contents.

Ray

She turned to page twenty-eight and groaned. It was the first of an eight-page feature captioned: "The Bare Facts About Those Flygirls!" The unclothed stewardesses included three from Trans-National—one of them, Alexis Jennings, occupied an entire page. She was identified in the cut line as "the holder of a Master's Degree in Applied Psychology whose hobbies include knitting, square dancing, and working with underprivileged children."

Danni shook her head; she knew Alexis slightly, was positive that she hadn't gone beyond high school, and suspected that she couldn't have knitted anything capable of keeping a hamster warm. Scattered throughout the article accompanying the pictures were "eyewitness accounts" of cockpit orgies, cabin orgies, Blue Room orgies, and galley orgies. The concluding line made Danni wince:

"It is easy to see that the so-called 'Mile High Club' (airborne intercourse about 5,000 feet) is fact, not fiction—so join the Club, boys!"

Danni was reaching for the phone to call Daley when it jingled. She knew who was calling even before she answered.

"This is Harmon." His voice was modulated but from long experience she recognized it as a softly sputtering fuse attached to a keg of dynamite. "I told Ray Daley to send you the August issue of *Stud*—have you seen it?"

"I just this minute glanced through it. Pretty bad stuff."

The dynamite went off. "Pretty bad? It's absolutely disgraceful! I want all three girls fired and I want it done within the next two hours! That Jennings lives here—the other two are New York-based. You can fire Jennings yourself and I suggest you call Millie Halper in New York and tell her to terminate the others. Is that clear?"

She privately thought he was overreacting, but she phrased her response diplomatically. "I don't blame you for being upset, but firing them may give the magazine that much more publicity."

"That's just what that goddamned Daley told me, and he's

wrong. You're both wrong. They've disgraced their profession and degraded the company. Fire 'em!"

"On what grounds?" she asked innocently.

"For starters, try immoral conduct."

"Posing nude might not be construed as immoral conduct if they take us to court," Danni warned. "Short of prostitution, which is illegal in itself, what a stewardess does when she's off duty is pretty much her own business."

There was silence at the other end, but Danni was unable to tell whether he was furious at her opposition or thinking about what she had said. She decided the best course was to let him cool off. "Look, I'm inclined to agree with you—they should all be canned. But just in case the cure might be worse than the disease, let's sit on it for a day or so. I'll contact my counterparts at some other carriers and see what they're doing about it—that layout includes girls from other airlines."

Gillespie seemed mollified. "How long will it take you to check?"

"I'll get right on it. I can meet with you at four today and give you a rundown."

"Well," he said with rare uncertainty, "I don't want to be totally unreasonable and hasty. I'll see you at four."

Thanks to Daley, however, the meeting was held in Evan Belnap's office instead of Gillespie's. "It's better psychologically to keep it away from Harmon's home ground," he explained to her.

Belnap came into the meeting with Daley's arguments firmly embedded in his mind. In fact, the president casually dismissed the whole affair as "just one of those things."

"I think the reputation of our entire stewardess force is at stake here," Gillespie declared.

"I don't disagree," Danni said, "but of all the airlines I contacted, only Delta is firing the girl who posed. American and United gave theirs two weeks' suspension and the others haven't decided anything yet—which means they probably won't take any action. My own feeling is that we should do likewise. That crummy magazine would like nothing better than a little free publicity."

"They don't have to get any publicity," Gillespie argued. "Not if we fire them and say nothing about it."

Daley shook his head. "No soap, Harmon. *Stud* must have sent advance copies to every city desk in the country—I've been answering queries all day, and every damned one of them asks if we're gonna fire the girls."

Danni had an inspiration. "If there's any disciplining to be done," she suggested, "maybe we should let the union do it."

Belnap glared at her in surprise. "The union? What the hell could they do?"

"Issue a statement denouncing the girls. Something to the effect that they've damaged their professional image and contributed to sexist prejudices."

"How about expelling them?" Belnap asked eagerly. "That sure as hell would take us off the hook."

"I doubt whether Pat would do anything that drastic. As a matter of fact, if we lower the boom she'll probably take the opposite tack and file a grievance."

There was silence, broken by Belnap. "She wouldn't listen to top management, Danni. Maybe you could talk her into issuing a statement."

"I'll try. I can't promise anything."

"I guess it's decided, then," Daley said. "We do nothing."

Gillespie sighed. "Not quite. Let's follow United and American's example—suspension."

"I'm against that, too," Daley said. "Any kind of punitive action will be reported by the press and that's exactly what we don't want. Evan, how do you feel about it?"

The old man looked up from the full-page spread on Alexis Jennings. "Let's see what the union does." He looked again at the nude photo. "Actually, when you come right down to it, she's got lousy ankles."

Danni went into her meeting with Pat Martin armed with last-minute ammunition. A stewardess had brought her a copy of a mimeographed communication addressed to "All TNA Stewardesses" and signed by the union president.

270

Effective immediately, it is recommended that in your cabin PA's the following be included as part of your opening remarks: *We are on this airplane primarily for your safety.* This is designed to counter the sex symbolism management persists in foisting on us, and to impress the public with the true nature of our professional responsibilities. I request that all loyal and concerned union members report to me the names of stewardesses failing to adhere to this new practice.

"I saw your letter about cabin PA's," Danni began.

"Oh? What did you think of it?"

"Technically, you're right. Federal Air Regulations require a minimum number of cabin attendants for safety reasons, and the FARs say nothing about service. From a practical standpoint, it's stupid. It's an excuse for providing poor service simply by declaring it's not their main job, and as such it smacks of pure union propaganda. But if you think I'm going to raise a fuss about it, you're wrong."

"That's a surprise. I figured you'd blow your stack. I know damned well Gillespie will."

"No, Pat, I agree with you about sexism. It's wrong and we should do something about it. That's why I wish you'd issue a statement criticizing that *Stud* layout."

"I'll do nothing of the sort. It's a typical management ploy."

"What are you talking about?"

"Obviously management wants the union to do all the public relations work and make me come out of the mess with three of my girls mad at me."

"You're *not* mad at them?"

"Disappointed, not mad. After all, if the company would pay decent salaries, maybe stewardesses wouldn't be tempted by offers from magazines like *Stud*. I regret what they did, but I'm not going to castigate them publicly. It's over and done with, and frankly I have more important goals to reach than to punish three dumb dames who made a little mistake."

Danni's smile was disdainful. "So much for all that talk about sexism. Pat, I despise your anti-management bias, but this is the

271

first time I've ever realized you're a hypocrite. If we fired that trio, you'd be rushing to their defense with three grievances."

Pat Martin nodded placidly. "A certain amount of hypocrisy goes with the job. I'm not proud of it any more than I'm proud of what those damned fools did for a few lousy bucks. But I'm a realist, too. With contract talks coming up, I need every bit of membership support I can get."

Once again, Danni found herself repelled by Pat yet admiring her for a purposefulness that was no less strong than her own.

"I told Gillespie you wouldn't issue any statement," she said. "So I'm not too disappointed. I think the whole thing will be forgotten quickly, too." She hesitated, then blurted out what was on her mind. "Take some advice, Pat. Don't get too greedy in those negotiations. We're swimming in red ink and I can tell you a strike might sink the airline."

"Fuck the airline," Pat Martin said.

It was a relatively new stewardess named Sandy Heller who tipped Danni off to the forthcoming union demands.

Danni liked Sandy. She was self-assured and brilliant, and there had been rumors that a small clique of stewardesses was talking about running her against Martin in the next union election.

"I guess you know about the cabin P.A. Pat wants us to make?" she asked Danni.

"I do."

"Well, I don't want the union telling me what to put in any P.A. And I don't like Pat's turning us into a bunch of Gestapo agents, squealing on everyone who doesn't agree with her tactics. Can she make trouble for us if we ignore that P.A. order?"

"Theoretically, yes. We have a closed shop, which means every stew must belong to the union, so I suppose she could put pressure on the company to fire an expelled member. My guess is that she wouldn't go that far—she's threatened expulsion before but she backed away from it every time."

"Don't be too sure," Sandy said with such dark bitterness that Danni's eyes narrowed.

"Has she threatened you?"

"No." The girl hesitated. "I think you might as well know what she'll be demanding in the next contract. There was an executive council committee session two nights ago. I wasn't there—I'm not on the council—but Val Jackson was and she told me."

"Even Pat has to have her token black on her executive council," Danni remarked. "Go on."

"One of the demands will be the assignment of two extra stewardesses on every flight. Their only responsibility would be to handle whatever emergency came up. They'd do the safety briefings and the mask-lifejacket demos. They wouldn't be allowed to help with service. Pat would call them safety directors, and they'd be picked by the union, not the company."

"She must be nuts! We'd need thirty percent more stewardesses! Of all the feather-bedding brainstorms, that one takes first prize. What else does she want—dupes of Belnap's private john key issued to every stew?"

"Don't laugh. She'll demand that one lavatory on all seven-oh-sevens be set aside for exclusive crew use. The pilots would be allowed to use it but only with the senior stew's permission. And she wants to eliminate all IFS."

Danni smiled despite herself. "I can just hear Penny Cockrell when he has to pee and some senior tries to stop him. I'm not surprised about the IFS—she's never liked them. Anything else?"

"She wants to take seniority rights away from supervisors—that old demand she didn't get the first time she proposed it. Remember?"

Danni nodded. "I remember. Gillespie would have given in, but Belnap raised so much hell it never got off the ground. I hope that's all."

"Not by a long shot. A thirty percent wage increase, overtime after the first fifty on-duty hours per month, and double time for flying weekends and all holidays except Christmas, Thanksgiving, and New Year's—they'd draw triple pay. Also eight weeks' vacation with pay and a fifteen percent premium for working any trip operating between seven P.M. and seven A.M. This last one will curl your hair. There'd be a hundred-dollar penalty payment to any stew whose grievance has been upheld. I guess that about covers it."

And that, Danni mused, *just about tears it. Even if half the demands were met, Trans-National couldn't afford it. If Ray is right about Gillespie looking for a major crisis, Pat is playing right into his hands.*

"Sandy," she said, "a combination of any two of those demands would sink the airline. We're in deep trouble if the company gives in, and we're in just as deep trouble if there's a strike. Pat's got to be out of her mind."

"Maybe," Sandy said, "but she's serious."

"That I can believe. Sandy, don't go yet. I want to sound you out on an idea of mine . . ."

As a matter of protocol, she took her information right to Gillespie. To her surprise, he seemed unconcerned.

"Bargaining points," he said cheerfully. "Just bargaining points. Inflated demands that can be deflated without loss of face. Typical union strategy. I don't anticipate any real problem."

"I wish I could be that sure. She may give in a little, but I have this sinking feeling that she won't give as much as you'd like."

Gillespie pressed his hands together in the manner of an obsequious undertaker about to ooze condolences. "And on what do you base your sinking feeling?"

"Her increasing belligerence. I think she's afraid she might be losing her grip on too many members. It's my guess Pat needs a contract so far ahead of the rest of the industry that it would make her a permanent heroine."

"Well," Gillespie said with a peaceful smile, "we aren't about to give her one. So you go back to work and forget about it."

She didn't go back to her office immediately. She stopped in to see Ray Daley and briefed him, drawing fresh concern from his response.

274

"I don't like it," he told her. "I don't like it one bit. I agree with you that Martin's going to be unreasonable, which adds up to what we need like an epidemic of social disease."

"A strike?"

"Correct. Which, in turn, leads me to speculate on another possibility. Want to guess?"

Danni said, puzzled, "This time I don't follow you."

"You'd better." He looked at her with troubled eyes. "The only person in this goddamned company who wants a strike worse than Pat Martin is Harmon Gillespie."

Chapter 15

Gillespie began to worry Danni; he was suddenly nice to her.

It all started with his acquiescence in the case of Alexis Jennings and her two erring colleagues; without protest, he let the matter drop. Then came unexpected approval of a pet project—Danni had suggested that Trans-National sponsor an interline flight supervisors' seminar on "Motivation after Probation." He not only let her pay for the seminar out of Marketing's budget but also agreed to deliver the opening remarks.

"It was a damned good speech," she marveled to Daley during what had become a weekly lunch. "I didn't think he had it in him."

"He didn't," Daley told her. "I wrote the speech, and you're right—it was damned good."

"I should have known," she said. "But he's been Mr. Nice Guy lately."

"Don't be a sucker," he said with unusual harshness. "He's buttering up everyone in sight. When the time comes to name Belnap's successor, he'll want every Director to feel that he has management support. Hell, he's even buttering me up—he told me yesterday that as soon as the budget permits, he'll back my idea for establishing an aviation news-reporting awards program for the media. The first time I suggested it, he told the old man it was nothing but legalized bribery."

He glanced at the menu, his face sullen. Danni inspected her own menu and saw nothing but that unhappy expression, as if it had been superimposed over the print.

"My making love with him a long time ago—it still bothers you, doesn't it?"

He was as honest as she. "Yes."

"Why?"

"That's a stupid question."

"No question is stupid when the answer's important."

"It's stupid when you should know the answer. You can go to bed with anyone you please and for any reason you want. I just happen not to like this particular reason. And you know bloody well what I'm talking about. You already told me why you did it."

"Don't be sanctimonious. I'd still be flying the line if I hadn't."

"No, you wouldn't," he said, and there was sadness in his tone. "Anyone with your intelligence and imagination would have been promoted into management eventually. Maybe it wouldn't have happened as fast, but it would have happened. Without . . ."

She finished it for him. "Without prostituting myself."

He didn't reply; their eyes met in a silent collision.

It was Danni who broke the uncomfortable silence. "I'm sorry, Ray. I . . . I badly need friends, and I'd hate to lose your friendship over something that happened a long time ago."

"You haven't lost it. I need your friendship, too." He grinned. "What the hell, we're going into World War Three together."

"Right. Let's order—I'm starved."

But she was thinking, *I guess I lost something. Along with my self-respect . . .*

Negotiations on the new stewardess contract opened November 12, 1965.

The advance information Sandy Heller had given Danni proved to be accurate—except that Pat Martin had added one demand. Henceforth, stewardesses were to be called "flight attendants," a nomenclature she argued was more in keeping with the dignity and importance of their profession.

277

After three weeks of haggling, there emerged two concessions: the company agreed to accept the "flight attendant" designation, and the union dropped its demand for separate toilet facilities on 707s.

Two more weeks of fruitless negotiating went by. Pat called for a strike vote, setting February 15, 1966 as the deadline for a walkout. That would be thirty days after the start of the cooling-off period required under Taft-Hartley. The vote was narrower than Pat wanted. Of the 3,000 stewardesses casting ballots, nearly 1,000 voted against striking; Pat talked loudly about "overwhelming support," but the two-to-one ratio was relatively slim for a strike vote—slim enough to convince Ray Daley a strike could be averted if the company made a few concessions.

He imparted this belief to Harmon Gillespie at an executive staff meeting. The Marketing vice president's response was a firm rejection.

"We can't afford to budge," he declared. "Any concession by the company at this stage would be a confession of weakness."

"We might as well confess something that's already apparent to the union," Daley said. "We're in one hell of a financial bind and we can't take a strike."

"And you want us to make concessions? I'd rather take the strike than spend ourselves bankrupt by caving in to highway robbery."

"Harmon, almost a thousand stews voted against striking. There are probably at least another thousand who don't want to go out but went along with the union just to demonstrate solidarity. Even the girls know Martin's demands are unrealistic. If we give just a little, they'll take us off the hook."

Evan Belnap broke in, his voice reflecting a kind of desperation. "We could afford to compromise on a few items, Harmon. For example, how about sweetening the pot a little on money? I'd be willing to go for extra holiday pay and a modest wage increase— say five percent."

Daley caught nods of approval from Harold Schumacher, Andy Arenas, and Garland Massorelli. He cut in quickly. "From the standpoint of public relations, we're at a disadvantage if we're as

278

stubborn and unyielding as the union itself."

Harmon Gillespie half-rose out of his chair. "I can't believe what I'm hearing! How any responsible officer of this company could be fully aware of its precarious financial position and still suggest giving three thousand employees a wage increase is absolutely beyond my comprehension! I mean no disrespect toward you, Evan—I know you regard all employees as members of a family and that you're trying to be fair. But do any of you think that Pat Martin would accept a little extra holiday pay and a five percent wage increase as justification for calling off a strike? To her those are ounces, gentlemen. Nothing but ounces to a greedy little tyrant who's demanding tons!

"Now, I'm not denying that somewhere along the line we can make a counteroffer of sorts, if only to show we're bargaining in good faith. But I give you my word that we will destroy ourselves if we show the tiniest sign of weakness. Until Martin demonstrates that the union itself is bargaining in good faith, we must stand firm—not to invite a strike but to prevent one!"

There was an uneasy silence around the table, broken finally by Daley. He toyed idly with the empty water glass in front of him, staring at it as if words were written on the bottom like crib notes.

"Seems to me," he said slowly, "that what you're describing is the irresistible force meeting the immovable object. I'm sorry, Harmon, but for my dough that ain't collective bargaining. If both sides are going to sit around waiting for the other to make the first offer, all we're gonna have moving around here come February fifteenth are the picket lines."

Gar Massorelli squirmed uncomfortably in a chair. "Sounds to me like we're damned if we do and damned if we don't. Ray thinks we should compromise to prevent a strike and Harmon tells us that'll invite one. I don't know whom to believe."

Harmon Gillespie recognized the open door and marched in. "You don't have to believe either of us," he said. "I'm perfectly willing to let another senior officer take over these negotiations if you consider my position intractable. Evan, for example—I remember quite a few years ago he prevented a pilot strike by the simple process of threatening to resign as president if they walked out. Perhaps an, uh, emotional approach of that kind might break the impasse."

Beautiful, Daley thought with reluctant admiration. *He knows damned well the one man in this company who hates Pat Martin even worse than he does is Belnap. One session and they'd be at each other's throats. Gillespie would wind up with a strike and clean skirts. In fact, he couldn't lose even if the old man got her to agree on a contract—he'd have to give way so much the Board would murder him. Sure, Harmon would probably love to let Belnap take over . . .*

But the president refused to take the bait. "That emotional approach, as you phrased it, worked on pilots, not stewardesses," he pointed out. "Most of those guys were personal friends. We really were a family in those days . . ."

Yet in his refusal, Daley knew, lay vindication for Gillespie, not defeat. Not one senior officer in that room wanted any part of labor negotiations and Gillespie knew it—the only alternative to the senior vice president of Marketing was the president himself, and by making the offer Gillespie had won a kind of support. It mattered little that junior executives like Daley opposed him—he had skillfully overcome all objections by the process of daring anyone, including Belnap, to do better. And once the old man had backed off, Daley knew Gillespie remained in command.

In fact, Harmon was smiling now. "I assure you I'll make every effort to prevent a shutdown," he declared. "But I also assure you I don't intend to give away the company. I will not make any concession other than what this airline honestly can afford. Do I have the support of my fellow officers?"

He glanced around the room, his eyes challenging. No one spoke, although Massorelli opened his mouth briefly, then closed it with an almost imperceptible sigh. Schumacher, the only other senior vice president who might oppose Gillespie, shot Daley a look of helplessness.

Gillespie's eyes rested on Belnap. He waited.

"I'm sure you have our support, Harmon," Belnap said wearily. "I just want to make sure you act as fairly as you do firmly—it's a damned narrow bridge we're crossing."

Ray Daley swallowed hard—and remained silent. As he explained to Danni later, "The old man didn't want a Pier Six brawl—I think he knew in his heart I was going to accuse Gillespie of fomenting a strike."

"I wish you had," Danni said. "It would have been like lancing a boil."

"Maybe. Maybe not. The two senior VP's I trust—Schumacher and Massorelli—don't agree with me. I've hinted to both of them that Gillespie's motives are suspect, and they simply refuse to believe that a responsible officer would sabotage the company. I don't know what the hell to do. Pray that I'm wrong about Gillespie, I suppose."

"For many reasons," Danni said with deliberate ambiguity, "I know Harmon a hell of a lot better than you do. I wouldn't trust him as far as I could throw a Pratt and Whitney engine."

"Agreed. But I could say the same thing about Pat. The ironic part of this whole mess is that they're both hell-bent on crippling this company, yet for different reasons."

"You've missed the common denominator," Danni corrected. "Desire for power. In Gillespie, it's ambition. In Pat, it's a desire for revenge."

"Revenge?"

"Exactly. Getting even with the corporate ogre for all the injustices perpetrated on her members for so long."

"Then what's the answer?" Daley asked. "What do *we* do?"

"We get both of them off the battlefield," she said. "Away from the negotiations. Provided negotiations collapse first, which is almost certain."

Daley could only stare at her. "How? You're giving me a goal without the means."

"The means add up to a couple of long shots. So long that I don't want even to discuss them with you until I lay some groundwork. If everything works out, we get rid of one first and then we go after the other."

He brightened. "I know you've got something on Gillespie—something you wouldn't tell me. So he's the first . . ."

"No. We have to stop the strike to get some breathing room.

Gillespie won't negotiate with anybody. So the first target is Pat Martin."

The first target was doing her best to be obnoxious to the second.

Her adversary, in turn, treated her either with silence or sarcasm—whatever he calculated would upset her to the highest degree. In their meetings, they might as well have been facing each other alone, although both were flanked by other negotiators. Larry O'Brien and Bill Carrington from Legal assisted Gillespie, while Pat's team consisted of three line stewardesses whom she had hand-picked as mirroring her own attitude toward the company.

Belnap insisted that Ray Daley sit in on all negotiating sessons—"But you don't have any vote," he added warningly. "You're there to observe and report back to me how things are going. Just keep that Irish trap of yours shut."

Daley didn't object to the gag, and he was glad that his presence gave him a chance to keep Danni posted on progress—or lack of same. And there was far more of the latter than of the former. A glimmer of hope rose when Gillespie surprised everyone by offering a three percent general wage boost and a handful of fringe benefits dealing mostly with scheduling. Pat Martin called the offer "absolutely inadequate."

"Jesus," Daley recounted morosely to Danni, "she said no without even consulting with the rest of her committee. Then Gillespie withdrew the offer, and everything hit the fan. Larry O'Brien suggested they call in an outside mediator—it must have been something he thought up on the spur of the moment and hadn't discussed with Gillespie. Harmon gave him a dirty look, but damned if Martin didn't take Gillespie right off the spot—she said the union wouldn't accept mediation under any circumstances because no outside person could judge the situation fairly. So they went back to square one."

The next development was Pat's unexpected counteroffer—a twenty percent wage boost and overtime starting after fifty-five on-duty hours instead of fifty.

"Gillespie laughed in her face," Ray told Danni. "He said the only thing the company would agree to was renewal of the old contract with no changes whatsoever. Carrington and O'Brien just sat there."

"Did Pat blow her stack?" Danni asked.

"No. She just reached under the table and brought out a picketing sign—you know, the usual 'ON STRIKE AGAINST LOW WAGES AND POOR WORKING CONDITIONS' bit. Harmon said she was trying to pull off 'immature psychological warfare' and told her it wouldn't work."

The next day Daley informed Danni that negotiations had collapsed, with no further sessions scheduled.

"And that's the way things stand," he told her. "It's the fourth quarter, we're on our own five-yard line, and the two-minute warning has just sounded. Just tell me what the hell you've got up your sleeve to budge Martin."

"Only a handful of girls really want a strike. That's her Achilles' heel."

"Big deal," he scoffed. "Their negotiating team wants one. Since when have the rank-and-file dictated bargaining terms?"

"They might if they were given an alternative to a strike."

"What alternative?"

She didn't answer him directly. "Buried deep in Pat Martin's list of impossible demands are some legitimate gripes. They've been obscured by her grandstanding ultimatums. Mostly what the stews want involves dignity and a sense of importance, things they'll never achieve as long as they're under Marketing's jurisdiction. I want to take them out from under Gillespie and give 'em some independence."

Daley's face reflected disappointment. "Into Operations? What makes you think Frank Ladell would be an improvement over Gillespie?"

"Nothing whatsoever. I'm proposing that In-Flight Service be made into an independent, separate department headed by its own vice president."

He stared at her. "All you'd be doing is changing bosses. Granted Harmon's an oily bastard and Ladell thinks In-Flight could be run by three freshmen from the Harvard Business School. But that doesn't mean you wouldn't get another Gillespie or another Ladell as In-Flight vice president."

"I'd put a woman into the job," Danni said. "Someone who's been a stewardess herself. Someone they can relate to and trust. Someone who'll listen to them and welcome their input."

"And you think you can stop a strike with that? All you've done is revise the demands. You haven't changed the negotiating teams—and nobody can tell me either Gillespie or Martin would go for this. Why the hell should they? Gillespie would obviously hate anything that reduces his power and Pat would consider it pure pablum, nothing compared to what she's demanding—less work for more dough. That's a mighty attractive goal compared to your intangibles."

"True," Danni admitted, "but you're omitting a couple of mitigating factors."

"Such as?"

"People want and need dignity. I'll concede that an independent In-Flight department doesn't guarantee dignity, but damnit, Ray, it's a step in the right direction, especially if a woman heads it with the rank of a full-fledged vice president. And don't forget these kids will form a very reluctant picket line. They're looking for an out. All they need is an excuse *not* to strike. I'm giving them one. And incidentally, I'm buying time for the company."

"How?"

"In exchange for the new department, a six-month extension of the present contract—a temporary wage freeze if you will, during which time the company will have a chance to take some positive steps toward financial improvement while the new vice president of In-Flight will work jointly with a union committee to draw up guidelines for a new contract. A damned good contract, by the way. One that gives the stewardesses some voice in department policy-making, without costing TNA its shirt."

"Danni, you're operating on pure theory, plus some wishful thinking. All you have is a paper plan with no idea of whether the stews would want it. They can be just as short-sighted and greedy as pilots or mechanics."

Danni smiled triumphantly, as if Daley had just walked into a well-set trap. "They'll go for it, I promise you. I've already talked to quite a few and it's all they need to pull the rug out from under Pat."

"A few? You've got a couple of thousand to persuade."

"I don't need a couple of thousand. All that's necessary is a handful of nonmilitants with some persuasive abilities of their own. A cadre of natural leaders—the majority will follow them just as they've been following Pat and reluctantly at that. You see what I mean about offering an alternative?"

Daley chuckled. "Your job description sounds autobiographical," he observed.

"Damned right it does," Danni said. "Which will be Pat Martin's chief objection when I drop the bomb."

February 14.

The bar where they met was across the street from the Training Center—"Fifty-five-ten's watering hole," Julie Granger had called it.

Danni picked it for its convenience and privacy and hoped that for Pat the nostalgia of the place might override her hostility. The Hangar Bar had been their oasis during training.

But five weeks of comradeship couldn't compensate for a decade of enmity; Danni knew it was hopeless before she finished outlining her plan. Pat Martin's disgusted expression gave her the verdict.

"If I brought that proposition up to the members," Pat said, "they'd be justified in impeaching me."

"Tell me what you don't like about it."

"I don't like anything about it. It's nothing but an uncollectible promissory note, a mortgage nobody can pay off. It's a management fraud; I can't even believe you thought it up—it's Belnap's idea, isn't it? Sounds like something the old dinosaur would try."

Her tone as much as her words set Danni off. "You're the dinosaur, Pat. The kind of union leader so full of venom you'd take the whole airline down the drain, including your own members. This isn't a fight between the stewardesses and the company. It's a personal feud between you and the company. God knows, I hold no brief for Harmon Gillespie, and while I love old Belnap, he's as full of blind prejudice as you. All I care about is preventing a strike that nobody wants, and preventing it in such a way that nobody loses face."

Martin's face contorted. "You once called me a hypocrite. I can call you the same thing in spades. You'll be sitting pretty if we're stupid enough to buy that meaningless bribe of yours. A separate, independent In-Flight department! Headed by Danni Hendricks, I'll bet my last dollar. Well, I won't let you get away with it."

Danni's eyes clouded. "Then a strike is inevitable?"

"At twelve-oh-one A.M. tomorrow, there'll be pickets covering every base on the system."

Danni leaned across the table as if to make sure the union president could see the contempt in her eyes.

"By one minute after that witching hour of yours," she said, "there will be enough names on a recall petition to dissolve the present union negotiating committee. Sandy Heller, Val Jackson, and many other girls are already gathering names—they started an hour ago. According to union bylaws, all they need is a simple majority."

It would be to Danni's everlasting wonderment that Pat Martin didn't explode. She turned white, and she seemed to shrink as if Danni's words had pounded her deeper into the chair. But she did not lose her composure.

She lit a cigarette and only her trembling hands gave evidence of turmoil. "I have to hand it to you, Danni. You're the smartest hypocrite I ever met. Tell me, do Belnap and Gillespie know about this?"

"Belnap knows enough to call a special executive staff meeting tomorrow morning. The company will go for this, Pat."

"You've been a busy girl, haven't you?" Pat said quietly.

Danni's eyes probed the pale face, trying to judge whether Pat's calm was a sign of capitulation or a kind of deadly stillness.

"It's not too late to call off the strike. The recall petition can be stopped. Tomorrow you could go before the executive staff meeting yourself and tell—"

"No!" Into that one word came all the union leader's fury. "I've still got some clout and you're going to find out just how much. I'll take that recall petition of yours, and by midnight tomorrow I'll have it stuffed up your ambitious little ass!"

When she left, Danni went to the bar's phone and notified Ray Daley of what had happened.

There was a second phone call a few minutes later.

From Pat Martin to Harmon Gillespie.

Chapter 16

Ray Daley reached Danni around eleven that night, the panic in his voice so apparent that she turned cold.

"We're in trouble. Gillespie knows the whole story and he's already talked Belnap into blocking your plan."

"He can't block the recall petition—it's already in motion. And if it goes through, there won't be any strike. Why would he want to block it?"

"That separate In-Flight department. All the promises you've made for a good contract six months from now. That's what he's trying to prevent. So he convinced the old man you're trying to give away the company for your personal gain."

Danni's heart sank. All her carefully planned strategy was threatened with total disaster, all her dreams of new stature and authority about to go up in smoke. All she had done, so willingly and with such brutal calculation, to climb a ladder that now led nowhere except to oblivion. And she could blame herself for what had happened—by tipping her hand to Pat, she had ignored Ray's warning: both Gillespie and Martin wanted the strike.

"It's my fault," she muttered. "I told Pat Belnap had been briefed but not Gillespie. She must have contacted him."

"Never mind how it leaked. What we're facing now is one big double-cross of every kid who votes for recall. And when the troops find out the company is reneging, they won't wait six months to strike."

288

"Pat's probably already spreading the word," Danni said miserably.

"Undoubtedly. I think it's about time to play that second long shot. Tell me what you've got on Gillespie."

She hesitated, her mind a cauldron. Suppose that check had been for legitimate consultant work? If Gillespie could explain it away, she would have shot her last ammunition and left herself open for whatever revenge he wanted to extract. And he would be cruelly vindictive—of that she was sure. If she kept quiet, there still was a chance to salvage something of her career. She might hate him, but she had the confidence of an attractive, desirable woman that he did not really hate her, that she could still exert influence on him. Why was she sticking her neck out, anyway? To save an antediluvian like Belnap? Out of loyalty to Daley? He'd go down the drain with her if Gillespie won in the end . . .

. . . If Gillespie wins. He'll become president, that hypocritical bastard, provided the airline can even survive a strike. He'll crucify anyone who fought him—good people like Ray. What kind of a whore have I become that I can think only of saving my own skin? What would happen to my girls under a mean, arrogant little dictator like Gillespie? What would happen to me? To get anywhere, I'd have to crawl and eat dirt and maybe even sleep with him again . . .

Decision came with that last imagery.

"What time is the executive staff meeting?"

"Eight A.M."

"Can you call Gillespie and have him meet us at seven-thirty—either in his office or in yours?"

"I can call him, but suppose he tells me to go fly a kite?"

"If he does, you can give him a choice—he sees us, or we see Belnap first and the senior officers next."

"What the hell good will that do? I still—"

"Shut up," Danni said coldly, "and listen . . ."

If Harmon Gillespie was nervous, his poise was an effective mask.

"I want you both to know in advance," he said, "that nothing you can say will alter my opinion that this plan of Danni's is unacceptable. I very much regret this recall petition because, in effect, you're promising the girls something you can't deliver. So if you're here to argue about it, you're wasting your time."

"That's not why we're here," Daley said affably, "but inasmuch as you brought up the subject, what's wrong with the plan? It'll stop the strike."

"Delay, not stop. Provided the recall goes through. But I'll be happy to give you my specific objections." He paused. "First, a separate In-Flight department is not only unnecessary but extravagant. Its alleged advantages are mostly emotional. Its very independence will create problems of enormous magnitude, for what Danni is proposing is a tiny little empire of stewardesses protected from all the other departments and headed by a vice president whose loyalties would put the girls' interests ahead of the company's. Second, the plan is obviously self-serving, what with Danni, here, running for office on a platform she had no right to build."

"What if I withdraw from any consideration?" Danni blurted. "I'm perfectly willing to stay on as chief supervisor and have someone else head the new department."

Daley shot her a glance of surprise—this was something she hadn't discussed with him.

Gillespie shook his head. "Sorry. A noble gesture but a futile one. The department you've proposed would be a disaster regardless of who ran it. I've already discussed this with Evan and he agrees with me. Now, do you have anything else on your minds before we adjourn?"

"Yeah," Daley drawled. "Tell me about Gillespie Aviation Consultants, Incorporated."

Gillespie's face could have belonged to a chameleon. He went white, then slowly turned crimson. "What are you talking about?"

Daley turned to Danni, and nodded. "Your turn."

"That corporation you set up as a receptacle for supplier kickbacks," Danni said. "That's what we're talking about."

"That's a lie! My consultant work is completely above board. You have no right to accuse me—"

"Hold it, Harmon," Daley snapped. "You know damned well Belnap has forbidden any officer of this airline to operate any outside ventures. I'm quite sure Evan would be interested in hearing all about Gillespie Aviation Consultants. He'd even be more interested in hearing about the kind of clients who make out checks to Gillespie Aviation Consultants."

"Perfectly legitimate clients," Gillespie said—but in his voice Danni sensed a wary fear.

"Such as Eaton Uniform Creations?" she asked. "Such as a ten-thousand-dollar check for services rendered—two weeks before they got a quarter-million-dollar contract for our stewardess uniforms? What did they consult you about, Harmon? How to pay you off without anyone finding out about it? How many suppliers are bribing you?"

Gillespie looked at her; she could feel his hatred. It was almost like heat enveloping her. *He knows*, she thought. *If Ray weren't here, he'd kill me. Like Tony almost did, a million years ago . . .*

But she was wrong. He didn't really know, and he was both bluffing and blustering. In his anger, he had forgotten the Plaza Hotel. "I don't recall any such check," he declared, "nor any such specific amount. Eaton has been one of my clients, but—"

Danni said, "I saw the check, Harmon. It was in your coat pocket the night"—she stopped, conscious of Daley's eyes on her—"the night I was with you in New York."

Self-control fled. "You dirty little sneak!" Gillespie raged. "You had no right to go around like a cheap spy! Why don't you tell the so-very-righteous Mr. Daley, here, what the hell you were doing in my room in the first place?"

"He already knows," Danni said calmly. "But I don't mind telling you that for the first time, I'm glad I went to bed with you that night. Otherwise I wouldn't have stumbled on that check when I went looking for a cigarette. I'm not defending my morals, Harmon. But it's about time someone started questioning yours."

"I'll tell Belnap about you!" Gillespie shouted. He was out of his chair and moving toward Danni when Daley stepped between them and shoved him back into the chair.

"You'll tell Belnap, chum, but it won't be about Danni. There were two people in that bed so you'd be incriminating yourself. No, you'll talk to Evan and it'll be all about your sudden change of heart."

"Change?" Gillespie said hoarsely. "What change?"

"That you've decided to accept Danni's plan for a new In-Flight department."

"I'll be goddamned if I will! You don't have anything on me. Not one bit of evidence. That check . . . it was for a favor I did . . . I mean, some work I did . . ."

Daley grinned. "You think I'm bluffing," he purred, "so maybe I'd better tell you there are three telephone numbers sitting on my desk. One belongs to the regional office of the Internal Revenue Service. The second is that of the U.S. District Attorney. And the third is that of a Mr. Jerome Eaton, who, when he hears about the mess you're in, will wish he had never met you."

He looked at Gillespie's crimson face and it was as if he could read the man's mind. "And don't bother calling Eaton so you two can fix up some kind of covering story. There are laws against payola, not to mention its being a large no-no in this company. Plus the possibility of tax evasion, of course. And, like Danni suggested, we can ask a few other suppliers about your little racket."

"You're still bluffing," Gillespie breathed uncertainly.

"No, he's not," Danni said. "I'm perfectly willing to testify under oath that I saw that check. You're the one who'll have to explain it."

Gillespie swallowed hard, clenching his fists into white-knuckled balls. "Okay, Daley, what do you want?"

Daley glanced at his watch. "It's almost time for the staff meeting," he said. "I wish I could ghost-write another speech for you but I don't really think I have to. You can ad-lib a few remarks. Something to the effect that in spite of your initial opposition, you've reconsidered your position after talking to a number of people including line stewardesses. You now feel that Danni's plan for an independent In-Flight Service department has considerable merit and deserves a chance to be tried out, particularly in view of the fact that it gives us a pretty good chance of avoiding a walkout. That sound reasonable?"

"Is that all?" Gillespie muttered.

292

"Not quite. You will also tell your fellow officers that if the recall petition succeeds, you feel it's in the best interest of both management and employees that you step out of all future negotiations—to achieve a fresh approach, unfettered by past recriminations and mutual ill-will. Nice phrase, by the way—it'll make you sound very statesmanlike. Oh yes, one more thing."

Gillespie just glared.

"If you forget any of these lines, don't worry. Danni and I can prompt you."

The painful capitulation made, some of Gillespie's old show of authority flared. "She has no right to be present at an executive staff meeting."

"She does this one," Daley said. "She's the author of the only way out of a strike."

But Danni was thinking, *Suppose the recall petition fails . . .*

"How," Danni asked Ray after the staff meeting, "did you get all that dope on him between eleven last night and seven this morning?"

"What dope?" His voice was innocent.

"I.R.S., a U.S. district attorney, Eaton . . ."

"Oh, that. Bluffing comes easy to an old poker player. Make 'em think you've got more than you really have. Works almost every time—he just wasn't sure what cards we were holding and he didn't dare take a chance on calling. Actually, it wasn't so risky. Nobody would go to the trouble of setting up a dummy corporation unless there were some kind of tax evasion shenanigans. I was guessing but he wasn't sure. When he exploded, he was admitting guilt. So we're in business again, Danni—let's go count votes."

Command headquarters had been set up in Danni's office, manned chiefly by Sandy Heller, who was in charge of tabulating the petition head count. By 3 P.M. some of the early euphoria had given way first to mild concern and then to outright pessimism; it was apparent that while the stewardesses from the big Miami base had seemed to swing against Martin in the first returns, the momentum had slackened, and reports from other bases indicated strong support for the union president.

"I can't understand it," Sandy wailed. "We're running neck-and-neck in Miami but we're having trouble almost everywhere else."

"Simple," Danni remarked. "The girls in the outlying suburbs don't know Pat as well as we do here."

Ray Daley had been present since the staff meeting ended. "I'll bet the union's phone bill for the last eight hours could keep me in tobacco until the year two thousand," he commented.

Danni tossed him a slight smile but she was worried. Defeat of the recall position would make a strike inevitable, and their power play against Gillespie would mean little if Pat Martin won. It could even give Gillespie's ambitions a new lease, while killing her own . . .

. . . Here I go again . . . thinking only of myself. But I can't help it. It's my plan, my future . . .

Her concern deepened with a call from a stewardess based at Kennedy International.

"It doesn't look good, Danni," she reported. "We're getting a lot of resistance—Pat's spreading the word that the whole plan is a self-promotion scheme for you, and a lot of girls seem to believe her."

"I can't very well blame them," Danni said. "How many names have you gotten?"

"A little over two hundred, but I was hoping for at least three hundred at this stage. If we could break even here, we'd be in good shape—JFK's the most militant base on the system."

"Well, keep trying."

"I will. How are the other bases doing?"

"Not much better than yours. We're still short of a majority everywhere. Miami started out like a house afire—three hundred in the first two hours. But it's slowed down and I'm scared. Pat's reaching a lot of people."

She filled Daley in on the JFK report and he nodded glumly. "It's too late now, but I wish we had spread the word that you didn't want that goddamned job. It would have pulled the rug right out from under Pat."

Worry and fatigue had drawn her nerves and self-control taut. "Damnit, I do want it! I deserve it!"

"Then why did you tell Gillespie you'd withdraw?"

She was close to tears. "I meant it when I said it. I was desperate. Maybe I should have said it sooner. What the hell am I supposed to do—wear sackcloth and ashes? God, I wish I had never thought up the damned plan."

"No, you don't wish that," he said with a softness that somehow was more cutting than anger. "You wouldn't be Danni Hendricks if you wished that."

"My name isn't on the plan," she said bitterly. "I didn't advertise for the job."

"You didn't have to advertise," he reminded. "Pat's doing that for you."

At 7:00 P.M., five hours before the strike deadline, Danni and her cohorts looked at the makeshift scoreboard she had hung on one wall.

	FLIGHT ATTENDANTS	
BASES	TOTAL	SIGNATURES
MIA	1,005	420
JFK	699	223
ATL	740	302
CHI	248	212
DCA	654	283
	3,346	1,440

There was silence, broken by a gurgling sound from Daley's clogged pipe—it might as well have come from his constricted throat.

"Jesus," he said softly, "Chicago's in the bag, but overall we're two hundred thirty-four names short of a majority. Does anyone know where the hell we can get two hundred thirty-four signatures in the next five hours?"

"Everyone's still working hard," Danni reminded him. "We have girls meeting every incoming flight at every base."

"So has Pat," Sandy Heller said gloomily.

At 9:05 A.M., after canvassing on all bases, the number remaining was down to 227.

At 10:00 P.M., not a single additional name had been added. Pat Martin picked that moment to walk into the office, carrying a picket sign. She marched over to Sandy and thrust it toward her. "Might as well get used to carrying it," she said. "You're scheduled to start walking in front of the terminal at midnight—and you'd better be there or I'll boot you out of the union."

"Go to hell," Sandy said with more bravado than defiance, making no move to take the sign.

Pat leaned it against the wall and turned toward Danni, a contemptuous smile on her lips. "I hear you're not doing so good."

"The night's not over," Danni said. She had an almost irresistible urge to break the picket sign over Pat's head. When the union president left, Danni looked at the sign, then at the tally board, and finally at the wall clock behind her desk.

10:02 P.M.

The phone rang seventeen minutes later. Danni picked it up.

"This is Val Jackson. How's it going?"

"I feel like Davy Crockett at the Alamo," Danni said. "Does that answer your question?"

"Relax. I've got a hundred twenty-five more signatures!"

"A hundred twenty-five?" Danni yelped. "Hang on, Val—Ray, add that to the Miami total."

"Five-forty-five—a majority of the base with room to spare!"

Danni said into the phone, "Val, that's great—we're over the top here."

"I would have called sooner, but my crews have been driving all over town and they just got back to my apartment. How many more to go?"

Danni did some fast mental arithmetic. "A hundred nine."

"I'll go over the list again and see if we've missed anybody—

but don't count on it. We've hit just about every stew in this base."

"Thanks, Val." Danni hung up. "A hundred nine," she repeated. "Can we do it?"

"Let us pray," Daley breathed. "Come on, phone—ring again!"

It did. At 10:43.

It was JFK reporting, with eleven new signatures.

The number was down to ninety-eight.

At 11:05, Atlanta reported in with another thirty-six.

They were sixty-two short.

At 11:43, Carol Veskos called from Washington.

"Danni, you got your majority yet?"

"We need sixty-two more names."

"Well, you'd better break out the booze. I've got seventy-one new signatures in my hip pocket!"

Danni shrieked and threw the phone receiver into the air.

"Washington's over the top!" she shouted. "We won! We won!"

She ran to Daley and hugged him as whoops and cheers sounded through the room. Sandy Heller picked up the picket sign Pat Martin had left behind her and broke it into two.

"We won't be needing this damned thing anymore!" she announced amid loud applause.

"I gotta go meet the press," Daley suddenly remembered. "But first things first." He opened a drawer in Danni's desk and pulled out something she hadn't seen him deposit—a bottle of Chivas Regal. "Go get some cups," he ordered. "A victory toast is in order . . ."

Shortly after midnight, Daley called in the news media and announced that a majority of TNA's flight attendants had voted to dissolve the union's negotiating committee.

"There will be no strike," he said.

And not one of the usually observant reporters caught the glance of affection and gratitude he tossed in the direction of Diane Victoria Hendricks, who was standing off in a corner watching him, tears of triumph glistening in her brown eyes.

*   *   *

With the victory came the doubts, the gnawing knowledge that Pat Martin's attacks on her were too close to the truth. The strategy Danni had forged had, indeed, been based on the personal reward inherent in its success—she had written a script in which only she could play the heroine.

Or so she thought. Until Ray Daley told her opposition had developed against her. Up to that point, she had been telling herself virtuously that she could swallow such disappointment—her offer to withdraw before the recall vote had been sincere; defeating Gillespie and preventing the strike were more important than her own advancement; promotion to vice president would smack of a payoff; etc. . . . .

But when Daley informed her the appointment was by no means certain, she knew she had been lying to herself. She had fantasized that if she ever received such news, she would take it philosophically. She didn't.

"Who's the other candidate—Trudy Simon?" she asked. "Or should I say candidates?"

"Right now, there aren't any. Including yourself."

"What the hell's that supposed to mean?"

Without answering, he handed her a piece of paper. "Look this over. Then we'll talk about it."

She took it suspiciously, as if he had offered her a dead fish. "Go ahead and read it, Danni," he instructed. "It's the draft of a letter Belnap is sending all stewardesses."

She began reading, her jaw tightening as the typewritten words marched before her eyes.

To All Flight Attendants:

I wish to thank and congratulate you for your decision to continue the present contract for another six months. This mature and much-appreciated action will enable your company to make plans for a more secure financial position involving all employees.

Inherent in the agreement to postpone the strike was a promise on the part of the company to establish an independent In-Flight Service department. We have already begun to implement this promise by means of gradual stages, culminating eventually in the selection of a qualified person to head the department as a staff vice president.

The first stage, which I am ordering to be effective immediately, is to remove all flight attendants from the jurisdiction of Marketing and Sales. They will report directly to Miss Diane Hendricks, whom I am appointing Acting Director, In-Flight Services.

I also am naming Miss Hendricks to serve as a member of a special management committee which will work jointly with a similar group selected by your union to arrive at an equitable, mutually satisfactory new contract. As a former line stewardess, she will provide valuable insight into your needs and problems.

Evan Belnap
President

Wordlessly, she handed the letter back to Daley. He smiled uncertainly.

"Well, how does it strike you?"

"Like an unwanted pregnancy," she said sullenly. "Whose idea was this . . . this double-cross?"

He stopped smiling. "Frankly, it was mine. Incidentally, there's a pretty good raise that goes with it."

"I don't give a damn about the money. You know it's not what I wanted. What I've been dreaming about."

"Sure I know. And I'm sorry. But you might as well know which way the wind is blowing. And when I felt that breeze, I figured I'd at least make a pitch for some kind of promotion and a raise."

"The only wind I feel," she said tautly, "is the hot air from that letter. Look, I hate to sound like a disappointed prima donna, but that job warrants a vice presidency. I'm getting screwed without benefit of intercourse."

"You shouldn't look at it that way," he scolded mildly. "At least you'll get the department started, you'll have all the authority of a vice president, and—"

"All the authority without the title. Which means I'm banned from executive staff meetings unless invited. Isn't that the case?

You bastards just don't want a woman sitting in on those sanctified sessions."

He nodded unhappily. "Danni, I argued for you. No one was opposed to you personally—they're all damned grateful for what you did. But they just won't buy a woman vice president, and right or wrong that's the way it has to be—for now, anyway. Later, they might reconsider."

"When the sun rises in the west, they'll reconsider," Danni said scornfully. "I'll give you ten-to-one odds right now they'll wind up with a man in that job. One hundred dollars to a thousand, Ray. Is it a bet?"

"No bet," he said wryly. "On the other hand, who knows? Well, will you take the job, Miss Acting Director?"

"Do you think I should?"

"I do. Damnit, you've got what you wanted—an independent department and you're on the new management negotiating committee. Everything but a title."

"Everything but a title," she repeated. She fought back tears— *Vice presidents*, she thought bitterly, *don't cry.*

PART
FIVE

(1966–1970)

Chapter 17

The new Acting Director of In-Flight Service discovered she hadn't changed jobs—she had merely increased her workload.

When Belnap called her in to discuss her new duties, she was told no one would replace her as system chief stewardess supervisor.

"I don't understand, Mr. Belnap. Somebody should take over or things will be in a shambles."

"They'll be fine. Your old job overlaps into your new one. For the time being, you'll have to wear two hats." She looked surprised as well as disappointed, and he held up a hand. "Don't worry. We'll get around to replacing you as soon as possible."

"About as soon as you get around to naming a vice president of In-Flight," she said, incapable of preventing the bitterness from showing.

He had the grace to appear embarrassed. "The trouble is," Belnap explained, "we haven't decided In-Flight's jurisdiction. For example, we aren't sure whether food and beverage service should be retained in Marketing or transferred to In-Flight."

"It belongs in my department," Danni said.

"That may well be, so let's keep it on the back burner for just a little while. When things shake down a bit, we'll take another look at your workload. That sound fair?"

"I guess so," she said doubtfully—she had the urge to continue the argument but she was too fond of the old man. "I promise you I'll do the best I can."

He beamed. "I know you will. Incidentally, your fellow members on the management negotiating committee will be Larry O'Brien and Bill Carrington. I'm counting on all of you to be fair but tough—don't give away what we can't afford."

If she didn't change jobs, she did change offices, and she acquired the luxury of a secretary, a divorcée named Grace Denham. Danni's new quarters were larger, though not as large as a vice president's, she couldn't resist thinking, and she plunged into her work with a kind of grim enthusiasm.

She had once fantasized a flood of congratulatory letters upon her appointment as vice president of In-Flight Service; she received exactly one upon her appointment as Acting Director, and this was from Penny Cockrell.

Dear Danni:
    I was extremely disappointed to hear about your promotion. After the training I gave you, I expected you to have Belnap's job by now.
                                                              Love,
                                                              Penny

She laughed. Good old Penny. He had caused her so much grief, yet he had also saved her job the day she missed that trip. Funny how the future depends so much on the past.

For the first time in weeks, she thought of Tony Buchanan. Part of her, she knew, would always wonder about marriage and children and the security of love channeled toward one chosen man. She had become, she philosophized, the classic career woman, subordinating virtually everything to her job. And the job itself made this easier than ever before—the demands on her time were immense, and her infrequent twinges of loneliness were brushed aside, ignored like a mild case of the sniffles.

It was generally conceded, though with some reluctance on the part of Gillespie and Ladell, that she performed well in her first major task—helping to negotiate a new stewardess contract. Torn between her resolve to treat the girls fairly yet conscious that she was representing a money-tight management, she performed a skillful balancing act that earned her the respect of her colleagues.

The fact that Sandy Heller was on the union negotiating team

304

helped immeasurably—she had Pat's toughness but not her bellig-erence. Danni sold Carrington and O'Brien on a strategy of remaining firm on wage demands but being extremely flexible on less obvious fringe benefits—improved meal allowances, a slightly higher company share of pension plan payments, establishment of a joint company/union grievance committee, and a fee schedule for off-duty work such as uniformed appearances at public functions. The wage increase was held to five percent, and for this concession Carrington and O'Brien accepted Danni's suggestion to toss in an extra week's paid vacation.

She had not forgotten her pledge to make the flight attendants feel they were participating in as well as working for the airline. It was her idea to include on the uniform selection committee one representative from each base. She sneaked this in as a contract provision after Carrington tipped her off that Gillespie had denounced the rumored proposal as "abdication of management jurisdiction." Once it became a contractual obligation, there was nothing he could do about it.

Actually, her dealings with her old foe weren't as traumatic as she had feared. It was no secret around the airline that he was trolling for another job, and to Danni he acted more indifferent than hostile.

The man he wanted to succeed informed the Directors he intended to retire as soon as he found an able replacement. Trans-National seemed to be righting itself, the prevention of the strike providing the impetus needed for recovery. As Danni began her fifth month as Acting In-Flight Director, the Civil Aeronautics Board granted TNA two prime new routes—Miami–Seattle via Las Vegas, and Miami–Anchorage via Houston.

"We've finally got somewhere to put those seven-forty-sevens," Daley told Danni, "and Boeing's agreed to cancel four of those birds we ordered in exchange for our buying another six seven-twenty-sevens—I think we've turned the corner."

"That's great," she said, with a lack of enthusiasm.

"You got problems?"

"Not really. It's just that I'm probably the last so-called officer to hear about the new Boeing deal—and if you hadn't told me, I suppose I would have had to read about it in the newspapers."

He sighed. "Nobody's keeping secrets from you. I just found out about the Boeing deal myself—Belnap told me to get a press release ready by Friday, after staff meeting. What the hell's eating you?"

"I guess I'm still hung up on the vice presidency," she admitted. "That business about Boeing was symptomatic—I think my department's important enough to warrant my being at staff meetings. And I would be if I had the title I deserve."

"That title's not nearly as important as the job itself, and how you're doing it. You might as well resign yourself to never being a vice president—just because you're a woman. It's stupid and unfair but that's the way this world is run. If things change, you might get a crack at it. Bill Carrington's a great admirer of yours—he says that without you there wouldn't have been a contract so satisfactory to both sides. And incidentally, he's also grateful for that memo you sent him."

"About the passenger who suffered the heart attack? I figured he put it in a file-and-forget drawer."

"If he did," Daley said, "he just resurrected it. The passenger's family is suing us for negligence."

"Suing? On what grounds?"

"For not ascertaining that there was a qualified physician on board who might have helped the victim."

"Damnit, but there was!" Danni said. "I put that into my report."

"I know you did. You also said that when the senior flight attendant asked him to help, he refused. Obviously he was afraid of a malpractice suit if the passenger died. So later he denied that the flight attendant had ever approached him—and that's the basis of the suit. It's the flight attendant's word against the doctor's. Carrington wants to settle out of court as quietly as possible—he doesn't want the publicity of a trial because if we lost, there'd be an epidemic of litigation. In-flight heart attacks happen all the time and . . . what's that look on your face? One of your brainstorms?"

Danni's eyes were shining. "I'd like to attend the next staff meeting," she said. "I've got a couple of ideas on the subject."

"Try 'em out on me first."

"Assuming we can't depend on a doctor to volunteer medical aid, our only recourse is to supply our own."

"We already do," Daley said. "As far as basic first aid training can—"

"I think we should improve our training."

"But it's as good as there is in the industry."

"As good, yes. But it could be better. I'd recommend adding a course in emergency cardiac resuscitation to our initial flight attendant curriculum, and also teaching it during recurrent training. The Red Cross would be glad to cooperate."

Daley shook his head. "We'd still get sued if a passenger died."

"No, we wouldn't. We'd get sued if a smart lawyer claimed our training was inadequate. This way, no such accusation could be made. In effect, we'd be teaching flight attendants to do as much as any doctor could. It'll work, Ray—I'll bet anything in the world it'll work."

He gave her a look of pride. "Seems logical. What's your other idea?"

"Put top management personnel through a simplified form of emergency training—first aid, evacuation, et cetera."

The look of pride was replaced by one of alarm. "What the hell for? I, for one, am too damned old to be jumping into chutes, and I'm too damned busy to learn how."

"You wouldn't be too old if the plane were on fire," Danni reminded him. "You and those cohorts of yours should be acquainted with the basis of E.P.s. If there's an accident and one or more flight attendants are incapacitated, you might well have to take over. You're the people on this airline who fly the most. You're the ones who'd benefit the most from this training. And it'll improve relationships between management and the flight attendants. You'll get an idea of what they go through, and they'll know they've got someone to help out in an emergency."

He shook his head. "I don't know. It sounds good, but I don't think they'd buy it."

"Why not?"

"Too much time away from their jobs. Maybe an element of

fear—be a pretty big comedown for a vice president if he couldn't pass the course. You'd end up giving a few of 'em inferiority complexes."

"Which'll do them good," she said. "Ray, I know I can sell them. How about arranging it—my going to the next staff meeting, I mean?"

"I'll try," he promised, "but don't be too disappointed if I can't."

He called her the next day to report that he couldn't get her suggestions on the agenda. "Maybe next week," he added.

"Or next year," she said.

The following Friday, he emerged from the staff meeting and went to her office.

"They bought your idea for beefing up training, provided it doesn't cost too much," he told her.

"That's nice," she said, barely glancing at him.

"I thought you'd be pleased," he said sharply. "What the hell more do you want?"

"I wanted to be there myself, not have a surrogate lawyer presenting my case. What about executive training?"

"As I expected, they didn't go for it. The feeling was that they couldn't spare the time for something they might not have to use for the next fifteen years."

Danni glared. "It's what I expected, too. You had no right to try selling something you didn't even believe in yourself. All I asked you to do was arrange for me to be present when my ideas were discussed, and *that* you didn't do. So the result is a lukewarm "maybe" on one suggestion and a flat "no" on the other. Thanks a lot, Ray."

"You're welcome!" he snapped. "But for your information, I made the pitch only after they turned me down on inviting you." His voice turned strangely formal. "I've been instructed to tell you to put your recommendation for emergency resuscitation training into a written memo along with all cost estimates. If you want to add a paragraph urging your appointment as a vice president, go right ahead."

He stalked out of her office before she had a chance to answer. His hostility frightened her. *Of all people the one I don't want to alienate,* she thought, *is Ray. I'm taking all my frustrations out on the one man who's on my side. Sometimes I wonder why he bothers to put up with me. He sure doesn't show any romantic interest . . .*

She sent him a simple note of apology and added her thanks for what he had done. *"I seem to be doing more grousing than grinning lately,"* she added. The next day, he sat next to her at lunch and greeted her with a friendly "Hi."

"Get my note?"

"Yep. I liked it."

"Well, I meant every word. *Am* I losing my sense of humor?"

"Nope. Strain of command."

"Baloney. I'm used to command."

"Not quite at this level. You're a department head."

"*Acting* department head."

He stopped chewing his sandwich. "Still got that vice presidency crap eating at you?" he asked, but he did not wait for her to answer. "Stop it! It's a goddamned cancer, that ambition of yours. It's taken over your personality, even your judgment."

He had stabbed her yet she smothered the instinct to retort. "I'll concede my personality," she said softly, "but why do you think my judgment's gone sour?"

"Not sour. It's more like an endangered species. You flew right off the handle because I couldn't wangle that personal appearance you wanted so badly. You made up for it with your note—showed me you were still capable of a little humility, which in this case was a form of good judgment. All I'm saying is that potentially your obsession with being a vice president is nothing but a time bomb. Am I right?"

She smiled. "I suppose you're right. But ambition's no crime."

He looked directly into her eyes. "Your sleeping with Gillespie was a crime. It was motivated by ambition."

She was trembling now, but she kept her voice cold. "How do you know I didn't go to bed with him just because I wanted sex?"

"Because you told me before why you did it. And because I know you, Danni. At least, I think I do. Sometimes I wonder. Finish your soup—it's getting cold."

She was energetic, eager, and efficient in her work; she was also impulsive and mercurial, a by-product of her confidence in her ability. She came up with a plan to base seniority partially on merit instead of solely on tenure. A passenger commendation letter, accumulated unused sick leave, and extra flights would earn points to be applied to seniority.

Her intentions were good and her foresight admirable—she was looking ahead to the time when Trans-National, forced to furlough for economic reasons, might be able to protect a few superior flight attendants who happened to have low seniority.

But her proposal, as she gave it to the executive committee in the form of a memo, was woefully complicated; it got nowhere. To her surprise, the union rejected it flatly as a contractual violation and informed Danni it would not even discuss such a plan if she resubmitted it in future contract talks.

"There is absolutely no way we'd buy anything like that," Sandy Heller told her. "Your theory looks logical but only on paper, because theory is all it is. We'd have every junior girl on the system soliciting commendatory letters just to get more seniority. You know that as well as anybody. You used to tell us in class that the practice was nothing more than pandering."

When Danni complained to Daley that the union was being arbitrary, he showed little sympathy. "Good idea but impractical. Seniority is sacred on this and every other airline. I told you that when you sent the plan to the executive committee."

"You also told me Belnap liked it," she said.

"He liked it because it smacked of anti-unionism. So, by the way, did Gillespie and a few others who think unions are a form of social disease. Just remember what questionable allies that proposal drew out of the woodwork and you'll feel better about losing."

"I never feel better about losing," she said. "Anyway, one reason I lost is that I wasn't . . . "

She stopped, flushing.

"You weren't there to fight for it in person," Daley finished for her. "Horse shit. You lost because the majority on the committee

310

knew the union wouldn't go for it. And I mean majority—Belnap, Gillespie, and Ladell were the only supporters you had."

She could not hide her surprise. "You voted against me?"

"Damn right I did. You put Sandy Heller into orbit with that plan and things are going too well with the union to ruffle her feathers."

"Sandy's as narrow-minded as you damned brass hats," Danni stormed—and then wished she hadn't, seeing Daley's face cloud. "I'm sorry," she said. "That's being unfair. I guess I just hate to lose, especially over an idea I think has merit."

"Some merit and too many holes," he said. "Let's go to lunch."

"Okay." But she was thinking, *That was the first time Ray wasn't on my side. And I'll bet it isn't the last . . .*

A coolness began between them, a chill that he generated and she reciprocated. Her work was tension-inducing in itself; the feud with Daley made it worse. She missed his counsel, his wit, and most of all the knowledge of his presence—the comforting assumption that he was there if she needed to talk to someone. And, as usual, she sought sublimation in her work for what she had lost with Ray.

Gradually the "Iron Butterfly" sobriquet acquired a connotation of almost reluctant affection. Only the new flight attendants called her "Miss Hendricks"—she was "Danni" to everyone else, from cleaners to vice presidents. She gained a reputation that spread beyond her own airline; requests for speaking engagements were frequent, invitations to conferences more constant than she wanted. On more than one occasion, listening to the post-speech applause, she thought of that desperate, last-ditch discourse on Eleanor Roosevelt.

Sheer fatigue eventually caught up with her. Her boiling point lowered, her patience deteriorated, and her tongue grew barbs.

Daley came to her office one Monday morning, requesting the daily assignment of four flight attendants to the Aviation/Space Writers convention in Miami.

311

"For Christ's sake!" she said. "That's fifteen bucks per girl in extra pay and you want four girls each night over a three-day period. Damnit, I've got flights to staff and a budget to operate under."

"That fifteen dollars comes out of my budget, not yours," he reminded her. "And don't tell me you can't furnish a total of twelve flight attendants out of a base with over a thousand girls. What the hell's wrong with you?"

She started to say that Ray Daley and his turncoat attitude were what's wrong, but the words were never uttered. He unexpectedly grinned in a way that had always been an application of cool water on a fever.

"Getting to be quite the little bitch, aren't I?" she said, with a smile of her own.

"Well, let's say it shows. And I don't like it. You've been working too hard. I hear mine isn't the only head you've bitten off lately. Ease off a bit. Relax—go out and get . . . drunk."

His hesitation hadn't escaped her. "What did you start to say—laid?"

His face darkened. "I said drunk. Your getting laid is out of my bailiwick." As if by magic, though, his black look dissolved and the grin was back. "I've been acting like a shit toward you," he said. "It's not *all* your fault. I'm sorry."

"You're forgiven," she said eagerly. "Not that there's anything to forgive." She hesitated. "How about coming over for dinner tonight? I'll cook us a couple of T-bones."

He shook his head. "Sorry."

"Okay. Maybe some other time." She knew from his tone there would be no other time. She couldn't figure him out. Anger had passed fleetingly over his face like a thundercloud when she had teased him about getting laid. It was as if one part of him wanted her and the other part was repelled—almost like Tony, she thought miserably. She felt a sense of failure again, a sense of guilt. Well, at least she and Ray were friends again. But why did she feel so empty and disappointed?

* * *

312

Danni's truce with Daley failed to halt her increasing irritability toward everyone else. She was caught in a vicious circle—determined to look good, she drove herself unmercifully and took her fatigue and frustrations out on subordinates and superiors alike. Every mistake by a subordinate was a menace to her own success; every rebuff by a superior was an insult to her intelligence. That she was enormously capable saved her from serious recriminations. "She's a female George Patton," Evan Belnap sighed, "but like Patton, she gets things done."

It was Belnap who finally called her in and lectured her on the evils of overwork.

"Fine," she said when he had finished. "How about giving me some help—like appointing a system chief supervisor?"

"Sure," he agreed, so readily that she stared at him.

"It didn't take long for you to make up your mind," she said. "Why didn't you do something about it before?"

"You didn't ask me, and I wasn't about to bring it up—look at all the dough we've been saving."

She wanted to hit him and hug him. "Can I hire anyone I please?"

"It's your ball game, Danni. Got someone in mind? From within the company, I hope."

"In a way, yes. Julie Granger."

He leaned back reflectively. "Isn't she the stew you fired a long time ago?"

"I fired her, but it was under duress. Anyway, she'd be great. Lately I've kept in touch with her. She's flying for World Airways but I think she'd be willing to come back. Do I have your permission to call her?"

"Sure. I said you can hire anyone you please." He paused. "As long as the salary's in line."

Thank God, Danni thought. *Now, at last, I can make it up to Julie. She said she was cured, and I believe her . . .*

"Bless you, Mr. Belnap," she said. "I'll call her right now."

When Danni had left, Belnap picked up his phone and dialed an interoffice number. "Ray? Evan here. I talked to her like you suggested and you were right—she's gonna contact that old roommate of hers. I think Danni'll calm down a bit now . . . "

Julie arrived in Miami two weeks later and moved into Danni's apartment temporarily—they agreed it would be better to eventually live apart. Their reunion was a tonic for Danni. Her relationship with Julie was far easier than it had been when Danni was chief supervisor. Now both were management and there was little gap between them.

They were more of team than a boss and a subordinate—a slick, efficient tandem in which they complemented each other's strengths and compensated for weaknesses. Danni could override Julie's initial reluctance to discipline, while Julie provided a buffer zone for Danni's impulsiveness.

Yet while Danni's tension diminished, it did not disappear. Julie could absorb part of her workload, but she could do nothing about Danni's persistent restlessness, her yearning. Danni began dating an editor with a Miami newspaper she had met at some function. He had called the next day and invited her to dinner. But after going out with him several times, she called off the relationship.

"Here we go again," Julie complained. "He's good-looking, intelligent, and reasonably well off. Now you tell me you don't want to go out with him again. Didn't you have anything in common?"

"Airlines," Danni said.

"That's a pretty good start. What's wrong with that?"

"He hates the airlines, that's what's wrong. Every time I've been out with him, he's denounced the industry in general and TNA in particular. If I went out with him again, he'd tell me *Coffee, Tea or Me* was a true picture of flight attendants."

Julie looked at her thoughtfully. "If you ever do get married, it'll have to be someone in this nutty business."

"Probably," Danni agreed. And she knew Julie was right. It was not just having common interests. It also meant common beliefs, sentiments, and even problems. In her emotional blood-stream were airline people, airline humor, airline courage, airline dedication. That was the cornerstone of her friendship with Daley. Someone *like* Ray, that's what she needed . . .

". . . now, take Ray Daley," Julie was saying as if she had been in telepathic communication. "There's the kind of guy who'd be just right for you. Never could figure you two out—all that obvious affection wasted on pure friendship."

"That's why we're friends—our relationship is pure. How about answering the phone—it's probably Ralph and you can tell him I'm out."

Julie went into the bedroom to pick up the phone. She emerged a minute later. "It's for you—someone named Betty Markel."

"That's my aunt," Danni said. "Wonder what she wants?" She disappeared into the bedroom; when she came out Julie bolted to her feet. Danni's face was sheet-white and her mouth was quivering.

"Danni, what's wrong?"

"My father. He's . . . he's dead."

When she boarded a TNA flight back to Miami two days after the funeral, she was numb with grief and guilt.

Her father's death, from a massive coronary, was hard enough to bear. But her mother was unable to cope with the crisis. Danni had made all the burial arrangements and then came face to face with Bea Hendricks' tearful pleas that she be allowed to come live with Danni in Miami.

"You're all I've got now," she sobbed. "I can't bear to be alone."

Danni tried hard to say no without hurting her. "Stay with me a couple of months, Mom, then we'll talk about it again."

"No. I want your solemn promise I can stay with you. You'll see, honey, it'll be just mother and daughter again. Like when your father went to Europe on that research trip. We had fun, didn't we? The two of us?"

Danni knew they would be at each other's throats. Her mother wasn't seeking a daughter's companionship—she wanted Danni to

315

substitute for her husband; she was grasping in desperation.

"I was ten years old when Dad took that trip," Danni pointed out as gently as possible. "I'm thirty-five now and we live in two different worlds. You don't know anyone in Miami; you'd be lonely. I work long hours, and I'm often away on business trips."

"Is your job more important than your mother?" Mrs. Hendricks sobbed. "Your father would have wanted me to live with you."

What *would* her father have really wanted, Danni wondered. Bea had never balanced a checkbook, paid a bill, or assumed any other financial responsibility; John Hendricks had pampered and coddled her to the point of helplessness. For a fleeting moment, Danni felt resentment toward her father—his legacy was an almost unbearable burden. Then she remembered his pride in her. The trembling of his hands when he had pinned on her wings. Their long and deep relationship, not just father and daughter but friends who confided in one another. The way he blended discipline with compassion, solemnly listening to her side of a dispute before making a parental decision. And the last letter he had written to her . . .

> . . . I know you're disappointed about not being named a vice president. But you were always impatient even as a little girl, and while impatience can be synonymous with determination, it also can be synonymous with hasty judgment and a lack of perspective. All I can tell you is to do the best job you can, and if events don't meet your expectations and dreams, you will at least know you've done your best. My pride in you for what you have accomplished is boundless regardless of what happens. I truly relish the title "my daughter" more than I do the title "vice president."

In her heart she uttered the cry of every survivor . . . *Why did he have to die?* And when she turned back to her mother, torn between filial duty and what she knew was the right course, she temporized. "Let me think about it a little more, Mom," she said.

* * *

In the end it was her aunt, Betty Markel, who came to her rescue. When Danni confided the dilemma to her, she went into a huddle with Mrs. Hendricks and emerged with a solution.

"Your mother's going to come live with us, Danni. I convinced her it was best, that you had your own life to lead with a responsible job demanding all your priorities."

"What did Mom say?"

"Well, to be truthful, she's not happy. But she'll get over it when the shock's worn off. She's just not thinking clearly. Someday she'll realize that, and in the meanwhile take my advice and in a few weeks invite her to visit you—yesterday we buried the only security she's known since her childhood. All you can give her is assurance you still love her. She doesn't believe that right now, but she will."

"Thanks, Aunt Betty. You've saved my own sanity."

But sitting in the plane, sipping a martini she could hardly taste, she could hear her mother's accusing voice . . . *You're heartless, Danni . . . selfish . . . .*

"Danni?"

She looked up. Harmon Gillespie was standing over her seat—she hadn't noticed he was aboard, for she was in the first row of first class and he had been sitting in the last.

"I was sorry to hear about your father," he said. "Nobody's sitting next to me—come on back. Maybe the company will do you some good." When she hesitated, he added with a wry smile, "Even my company."

She managed a smile in return and sat with him for the rest of the flight, their conversation devoted mostly to minor business matters. Before they landed, he suggested that they have a final drink in an airport cocktail lounge.

She accepted, mainly because she dreaded the thought of going back to her apartment and drinking alone—Julie had moved into her own place. But while they were waiting to be served, she saw Ray Daley. He was with a woman, a blonde, and it was obvious he had already spotted Danni—as their eyes intersected, his were full of disbelief. Or was it hate, she wondered?

She had one drink with Gillespie and left, refusing his offer to drive her home. She noticed that Daley and his date had already gone. What she hadn't noticed was that Gillespie, too, had seen them.

Chapter Eighteen

It had been the look in Ray Daley's eyes that disturbed her. A look that bordered on accusation. And what was she being accused of? A friendly drink after a chance meeting? Of course, Ray didn't know about their meeting on the plane. All she had to do was explain how it happened and everything would be fine. It irked her that she should have to explain anything—she was being judged guilty until proven innocent. But after all, Ray did hate Harmon's guts, and evidently he had gotten the wrong idea. As if her affair with Gillespie had started up all over again. Ray deserved an explanation, even if she had to swallow a little pride to give him one.

The next morning she made a point of dropping into Daley's office.

"About your seeing me with Harmon last night," she began. "I guess it . . . it looked a little funny to you. I want you to know how it happened."

"No explanation necessary," he said, with a terseness that invited explanation.

"He was on my flight home, Ray. We were just having a drink before I went home."

"Okay. No big deal. I was just surprised, that's all."

The strain of the past few days had made her testy. "Why surprised? He's still an officer of this company. You act as if I were consorting with the enemy."

319

"I said no big deal. Let's drop the subject."

"Fine with me. Sometimes I wish you'd grow up." She marched out, and not until she reached her office did she regret the show of temper. But it was the start of a series of bad days—work had piled up on her desk and not all of it was the result of her being away for a week. The workload, Julie notwithstanding, was beginning to be intolerable again. Belnap had decided that food and beverage service should be transferred from Marketing to In-Flight. Danni did not complain—the move was a compliment to her, and it was accompanied by rumors that it had presaged Gillespie's departure from Trans-National. But the demands on her were horrendous, for now she was involved in menu planning, dealing with suppliers, and a new kind of passenger complaints. "I'm now in charge of cold soup and overdone steak," she told Julie.

When passenger steak grievances hit what she considered epidemic proportions, she took the matter up with the director of Food Service, a happy butterball of a German named Manfred Klauss whose Kaiser Wilhelm mustache belied his easy-going disposition.

"I know most of the complaints are petty," she told him half-apologetically, "but I have to answer these damned letters and maybe you can tell me what to say."

"I can tell you what you *should* say," he replied, "but you'll never be able to say it. Let me tell you the facts of life about airline steaks. We buy nothing but U.S. Choice tenderloins, the same quality that goes to the best restaurants. The meat company packs the tenderloins and ships them frozen to the caterer. The caterer thaws, trims, and then freezes them into loglike molds which are cut to ensure even portions. Next the steaks are wrapped, packed, frozen again, and rethawed. The caterer then puts on those grill marks so they look as if they've been cooked outdoors. Then they're chilled to thirty-eight degrees, carried out to the airplane in a cold-food box, and finally cooked by a flight attendant in an oven you can only pray is calibrated properly. That poor damned steak has been through so much by the time a passenger gets it, he's lucky if it's edible. That's the sad but true story, and if you want to put all of it into your letters of apology, be my guest."

"No thanks, Manny. I'll give 'em stock answer number three: We've instituted corrective measures with the caterer and we're sorry it happened."

On Danni's desk when she arrived at work the next morning was an interoffice memo from Belnap.

To All Department Heads:

Mr. Harmon Gillespie has resigned as senior vice president of Marketing and Sales to become president of In-Flight Menu, Inc., the airline catering firm. His resignation, which I have accepted with regret, is effective immediately. At the next Board of Directors meeting, I will ask that Mr. Paul Bekins, vice president of Promotion and Advertising, be elected to succeed Mr. Gillespie with the rank of senior vice president. A successor to Mr. Bekins will be named shortly.

Evan Belnap

Danni's first reaction was one of triumph, yet she was surprised to also feel a tinge of regret. The minute she read Belnap's notice, her memory banks whirled and clicked in a montage of the past—Harmon's devious scheming to get the old man's job; his arrogance, dishonesty, and hypocrisy. The little things and the big things he had done to hurt her, from his unholy alliance with Pat Martin to the way he had forced her to fire Julie. But she could not help also recalling how he had championed her, given her opportunities to advance. The kindness he had shown when her two classmates were killed. The almost wistful tone in his voice on the flight back from her father's funeral—*"Even my company,"* he had said, with a humility she had not known he possessed. She could not blame him for having been her lover—that, she knew, had been a premeditated affair on her own part. She decided she was glad he was leaving but also glad that he was not heading for oblivion in disgrace. That In-Flight job was no comedown— although she couldn't help wondering what strings he had pulled to

321

get it. The very thought made her chuckle to herself—it was just like Harmon to wangle a corporation presidency after suffering a career defeat that might have crushed a less resilient man. *Well, she mused, so ends a part of my life—one I'm not particularly proud of but one I don't think I could have changed. Now whom do I fight with? Ladell, probably—certainly not Bekins. He's a decent, capable guy* . . .

On impulse, she went to Daley's office to discuss the news. Maybe he'd be willing to have dinner with her that night to celebrate their final victory.

"He's gone upstairs to see Mr. Gillespie," his secretary said. "Belnap wants some kind of press release on the resignation."

"Just tell him I dropped in. He can call me when he gets a chance."

But he never did call. She had been in her office for an hour when Ed Perkins phoned, his voice excited.

"Did you hear about the fight between Ray Daley and Gillespie?"

"Fight? They're always fighting."

"Fighting with a capital F, as in fisticuffs. Ray knocked him on his butt. Schumacher told me they had to pull him off Harmon or he would have killed him."

Stunned, Danni asked, "Does Harold know what started it?"

"Nobody knows. Apparently Daley went into Gillespie's office to show him some press release. Next thing anyone knew, Gillespie's secretary was running down the hall screaming for help. Harmon has a busted nose, three teeth missing, and a black eye."

When Danni ran down to Daley's office, he was gone.

"He said he thought he may have broken a bone in his hand," his secretary informed her breathlessly. "It was all swollen—he said he was going to the Medical Department. Did you ever hear of—"

Danni left before the sentence was finished. She raced to Medical and found Daley had never been there, nor did he return to his office that day. She called his apartment when she got home, but there was no answer. The next day she walked into his office, staring first at his bloodshot eyes and then at the cast on his right hand.

"That must have been some right hook," she commented. "Mind telling me what it was all about?"

"Yeah, I would mind."

"Come on, Ray. There must have been some reason you slugged him."

His jaw tightened. "There was, but I'll be goddamned if I want to talk about it."

She didn't like the defiance in his voice. Suspicion infiltrated her mind. "Was it anything involving me?"

"No, it wasn't. He said something I resented so I popped him. Look, I'm in a lousy mood, my hand feels like it's busted all the way up to my collarbone, so be a nice lady and get the hell out of here."

The coldness between, once thawed, was back. There were no more lunches together, no more visits to one another's office, and, on Danni's part, no more seeking of his counsel. Her concern over the fight, her fears that she had caused it, turned into resentment—she suspected her drink with Gillespie was at the bottom of the flare-up, and in her conviction of innocence she considered Daley's reaction childish and unfair. She couldn't understand Ray's anger. It couldn't be jealousy—why should a man who had never even asked her for a date have a right to be jealous? Ray bore grudges, she decided; Gillespie had been a sworn enemy and even that innocent drink at the airport had been interpreted as disloyalty. She was curious about what Gillespie could have said to ignite the violence. Certainly not the fact that he had slept with Danni—Ray already knew that. Finally she decided that her supposed disloyalty had caused the fight—a reason she judged to be ridiculous. If Ray Daley were that immature, she was better off without him . . . their friendship hadn't been as deep as she thought.

There were times when she was moved to make peace and then resisted the temptation. Her pride was one factor; his obstinacy was another. She was too fiercely independent to buck this stone wall, yet she had to fight frequent urges to run to him as she always had in the past.

Inevitably, the coolness between them heated into outright conflict, and it was one of her own decisions that lit the match. Belnap had asked her to prepare new hiring standards for male flight attendants in the wake of a court ruling that the airlines were discriminating against men.

"While you're at it," the president continued, "better take a good look at the training curriculum in case we have to change anything for the men. Better set up a meeting with all our interviewers so they'll be briefed on the standards, and—why the unhappy look?"

Danni frowned. "You promised me I could go out to Boeing and see how the seven-forty-seven's are coming. Remember—I asked whether I could make the trip and you said yes. I've already made the arrangements."

"Christ, I guess I did," Belnap said. "Well, go ahead and get to work on the other matter as soon as you get back. When do you leave?"

"Next Sunday night. I've already got my passes."

She was conscientious enough to feel a little guilty, knowing perfectly well that the task of integrating male flight attendants was more important than going to Seattle. But she had thought up the Boeing trip on the spur of the moment, relishing the idea of mixing work with pleasure. *Damnit, I deserve the trip,* she told herself.

The subject of male flight attendants came up at a staff meeting just before Danni was scheduled to leave. The next item on the agenda was the formation of an industry anti-hijacking committee.

"We've been asked to send a representative," Belnap said. "Any suggestions?"

"Send Danni," Ray Daley said. "Virtually every hijacking starts with coercion of the cabin attendants."

"The other carriers will be represented by high-level security personnel," Frank Ladell said.

"All the more reason to send Danni," Daley replied. "The committee needs some flight attendant representation—she'd be perfect."

Belnap interrupted. "Well, she can't go anyway. The committee meets in Washington next week and she's going to Seattle Sunday night—to see the seven-forty-sevens."

"Whose idea was that?" Daley asked.

"Hers. She asked some time ago if she could go and I had to keep my promise."

Daley's face darkened. "Seems to me hijacking's more important."

Belnap nodded. "You're right, but she had her heart set on Boeing. Matter of fact, I told her we also needed her input on male hiring qualifications, but she promised to work on 'em when she gets back. Frankly, she probably needs the trip—she's been a holy terror lately. Fired three girls last week and the union's grieving all three cases. Don't look so glum, Ray. We can make do."

But Daley was hardly listening. After the meeting, he went to Danni's office—the first time he had been there for weeks. She looked up, surprised but pleased.

"Hi, stranger."

"I hear you're going out to Boeing," he said without preamble.

"That's right."

"I think you should stay here. Belnap says he asked you to work on male hiring qualifications but you held him to his promise."

She bristled. "So what? There's plenty of time to establish those standards. I'll do it when I get back from Seattle."

"By the time you get back from Seattle, we'll be buried under applications. Or don't you have any sense of priority?"

"As much sense as you!" she retorted. "The seven-forty-seven's important, too."

"Don't kid me. That Seattle trip is just a junket, isn't it? A chance to be wined and dined by Boeing. Reliving that seven-oh-seven mission you're so fond of recalling? Be honest—Julie Granger could handle it. Your job is here or wherever you could do the most good. Seattle ain't it."

Her eyes filled with tears. "It's none of your damned business where I go!"

"Unfortunately, I seem to have made it my business. I recommended that you represent us on the airline hijacking

325

committee—it meets in Washington next week. Only that's when you'll be at Boeing. A prime assignment and you've blown it, not to mention your dereliction of duty on those hiring standards."

She was flustered. "I . . . I didn't know anything about the committee. Is it too late . . . ?"

"If you wanna go tell Belnap you've had a change of heart, be my guest. I'll be damned if I'll go back to him and plead your case."

"Well, neither will I!" she exploded. "I'll go to Seattle as planned and you can go straight to hell!"

On his face was a look she had never seen before, a mixture of anger and sadness, or regret.

"Danni," he said quietly, "I'm already there."

After he left, she sat staring at the phone as if it were a crystal ball. What bothered her most was that she knew he was right. She *had* held Belnap to his promise, even though she knew the problems the hiring of male flight attendants would produce. And that committee assignment—vital, challenging . . . vice presidential stuff, she thought wryly. Too late now—Belnap must have picked someone else. That Daley. After all this animosity, he had recommended her anyway. What was with the man? That cryptic last remark of his—what was he trying to tell her? . . .

She sighed, picked up the phone, and dialed Julie's office. "Julie? How would you like to go to Seattle . . . ?"

Grace Denham, her secretary, brought in the afternoon mail, and Danni followed her usual habit of picking out the most interesting envelope first. She had no difficulty making a choice from this particular batch—she spotted the "United Air Lines Executive Offices" in the upper-left corner and tore it open.

Dear Miss Hendricks:
Your name has been mentioned favorably in connection with a position that has recently opened up here at United—namely, Director of Cabin Services.

326

We are fully acquainted with the fine work you have been doing at Trans-National, and with your splendid reputation throughout the industry. It is our sincere belief that you would find this post at United both challenging and rewarding, and I have been authorized by President George Keck to offer said post, effective as soon as you can make the necessary arrangements to leave your present airline.

We would like to hold a specific salary decision in abeyance pending a personal discussion, but I can tell you we are prepared to meet any reasonable demands.

I will look forward to hearing from you.

Sincerely,
Oscar Remington
Vice President—Personnel

Her first impulse was to run straight to Ray Daley. She decided instead to confide in Julie and showed her the letter.

"Have you told Ray?" Julie asked.

"No," Danni said. "Why should I?"

"Well, you've always gone to him for advice and—"

"Damnit, I don't need his advice, even if he were willing to give it. Anyway, I know what he'd tell me— 'Take the job and get out of my hair.' That's what he'd say. I haven't asked for his opinion for a long time and I'm not going to crawl to him now."

Julie smiled. "I think you should tell him," she said.

"Why?"

"Because he wouldn't want you to make a mistake."

"What mistake?" She waved the letter. "This damned thing's a blank check. All I have to do is fill out the amount. They'll meet any reasonable demand, they said. That gives me some bargaining power. God, Julie, I'd take less dough than I'm making here if they'd promise me a vice presidency."

"You sound like you've already made up your mind."

"I'd be crazy not to accept. United's a great airline. What have I got here? One large, fat promissory note they'll never pay."

327

"I'll drink to that," Julie said with an enigmatic smile. "Maybe they'll give me your job when you leave."

It was much later, when Julie returned home, that she paced her apartment for several minutes and then dialed a number.

Ray Daley's home phone.

"I'm absolutely opposed to electing her a vice president," Frank Ladell said firmly. "I have no quarrel with her capabilities, but a woman has no business being an executive officer."

Paul Bekins, Gillespie's replacement, sighed. "We promised the flight attendants that In-Flight Service would be a full-fledged, independent department headed by a vice president, and a woman at that. It's been a year since we made the promise."

"There was nothing in writing to commit us to the selection of a woman for the job."

"The promise was verbal," Ray said. "But it *was* a promise."

Bill Carrington shook his head. "As Sam Goldwyn once said, a verbal promise isn't worth the paper it's written on. However, isn't this whole question moot? We've had no demands from the flight attendants to name a woman vice president, so why not stay with the status quo? Ray's asking us to take action that doesn't seem necessary."

"It's bloody well necessary!" Daley said angrily. "I just got through telling you Danni will go to United—for a hell of a lot better shake than she's getting from this company."

"So let her go," Ladell said. "With our blessings."

Daley glared at him. "You'd say that after all she's done for Trans-National? Why you ungrateful—"

"Hold it," Belnap interrupted. "I think I have the ideal solution. Let's match United's money offer and make Danni Director instead of Acting Director. Maybe a vice presidency later."

"When later?" Daley demanded. "You know damn well you'll never do it!"

"Come on, Ray," Harold Schumacher said. "Evan's compromise is very fair."

"Not quite." This from Gar Massorelli. "Hell, I can't say I'd be overjoyed to have a woman sitting in on these meetings, but we owe that kid something. She's good. She's damned good. She deserves more from us than dropping the word 'acting' from her title."

"Semantics," Ladell declared. "As a matter of fact, Ray, I'd like to remind you that it was your idea to name her Acting Director. The whole original compromise was your suggestion, and—"

"Only because at the time I knew damned well I couldn't get more than two votes to make her a vice president. I was temporizing but now I've changed my mind. We stand to lose one of the most capable young executives it's ever been my privilege to work with—an *executive*, mind you. Not a male executive or a female executive, but an *executive!* Let me ask you something, Bill—were you just giving me a bunch of crap when you told me you couldn't have negotiated that contract without Danni's help?"

"That's what I said," Carrington admitted. "But that doesn't mean she's qualified to be a vice president."

Schumacher broke in. "I have a suggestion. Why not name her an assistant vice president? That way she wouldn't be eligible for executive staff meetings unless the agenda required her presence."

"Now, *there's* an idea," Belnap rumbled.

Ray Daley was on his feet and his fist slammed down on the table. "The idea stinks!" he shouted. He stared around the table, his eyes bright. "All of you, listen to me. What do we expect of any vice president—man or woman? Initiative, guts, independent thinking, imagination, loyalty to the airline, competence. This girl has all those qualities in greater measure than most of us in this room. The fact that she's female hasn't one goddamned thing to do with what's at stake. And what *is* at stake? Our own responsibility to her. Our own duty to fulfill promises that were made to three thousand employees."

"The promise," Belnap said, "was to be fulfilled in stages."

"We've reached the final stage now," Daley said grimly. "I move we elect Diane Hendricks vice president of In-Flight Service."

Belnap hesitated, surprised that Daley had laid down the gauntlet so quickly; he would have preferred putting his own suggestion or Schumacher's into a motion first. He glanced helplessly at Ladell, who caught the signal.

"In no way are we legally bound to make her vice president," Ladell said. "As a matter—"

Daley slammed his fist down again, so hard that the water glass in front of the president jumped. "Screw your legal crap! We're *morally* bound. My motion is on the floor and I'd like to know if there's a second."

"Second," said Massorelli.

"I have to question Ray's motives in this whole matter," Ladell said. "It's common gossip you have a . . . a deep relationship with Hendricks. Before voting, I believe it's only fair to ask whether it has influenced your support."

Belnap, afraid that Daley was going to throw a punch at the senior vice president of Operations, started to rise but sat down again quickly. Daley was smiling.

"An appropriate question," he said. "I've heard that gossip, so let's get it all out in the open. Yes, I've had a deep relationship with Danni. A deep *professional* relationship. God knows it's been neither social nor romantic. My support is based on my tremendous respect for her ability, her courage, and"—he looked straight into the somber eyes of Evan Belnap—"her integrity."

"That's good enough for me," Massorelli growled.

"It isn't for me," Ladell insisted. "I don't care why you're so gung-ho for the goddamned dame—it's just a lousy idea."

"Not lousy," Carrington said. "Merely premature—and unnecessary."

This time it was Belnap's fist that hit the table. "Motion's been made and seconded. All those in favor?"

Five hands went up—Daley, Massorelli, Bekins, Arenas, and O'Brien.

"Nays?"

Five more hands.

"History repeats itself," Massorelli whispered to Daley. He glanced at Belnap. "Here it comes."

330

The old man was looking in the direction of Frank Ladell, a flicker of a smile on his lips. It was not Ladell's face he saw, however.

It was Harmon Gillespie's.

"I'll vote aye," said Evan Belnap.

Danni only suspected Daley's role from what Julie had told her—"I had to let him know about the United offer," she said. "It wouldn't have been fair to the company to let you leave without someone putting up a fight."

"Was it Ray?"

"Damned if I know. Ask him yourself."

She did and got one of his noncommittal grins as an answer. Even that pleased her—she hadn't seen him smile for a long time.

"Well," she said, "I figure you must have had something to do with it so I'll say thanks and let it go at that."

"Maybe your gratitude is unwarranted. I might have voted against you."

"Did you? I wouldn't be angry if you had. You voted against me once before—remember?"

He nodded and the smile dissolved. "I remember. Maybe it's better if you think I did it again."

She ignored the remark because she did not understand it. "I don't care, Ray. I finally got what I've dreamed about for a long, long time. And I'm still grateful to you. I've . . . I've missed our being friends. Depending on you to pull on my reins when I got too fractious."

His eyes narrowed; she could swear they were full of pain.

"Better get used to pulling on your own reins," he said. "You're a vice president now—for which, incidentally, my congratulations."

"Somehow," Danni said, "I have the feeling your congratulations lack sincerity."

He smiled again. "You'll never know."

She was thinking, *I wonder how he did vote. Well, no matter. I got what I wanted. Vice President Diane Victoria Hendricks! I wish*

Dad were alive—boy, he'd be proud. Prouder than that bastard Daley . . .

The next day she heard the news. Ray Daley was leaving Trans-National.

The official announcement said he had been named senior vice president of Advertising and Promotion at Eastern Airlines. Unofficially, the word was that Eastern had almost doubled his TNA salary. Only Evan Belnap knew more was involved than money and title, but Evan Belnap said nothing to anyone.

Daley refused the usual farewell party for departing executives. "If you throw one, I won't show up," he told Belnap. He was gone a week after the announcement was made.

In that period he had failed to be at the first staff meeting Danni attended as vice president. She resented his absence, not realizing that she was upset because subconsciously she had relied on his presence to offset her nervousness.

Her fellow officers were pleasant enough—somewhat wary and ill-at-ease, though, and she knew it would take time for them to accept her naturally. She was far more bothered by Daley's failure to say good-bye to her. Their only contact that last week had been a brief meeting in the cafeteria. She was just finishing her lunch when he sat down next to her unexpectedly—just like old times.

"How are things going?" he asked.

"Fine. I just moved into my new office—three doors down from yours. Drop in one of these days."

"Well, I'll try. Pretty busy cleaning up all the loose ends." He hesitated, then put his hand on her shoulder. "If I don't get around, I do wish you luck. And I am glad your dream came true."

"Thanks, Ray. I appreciate that."

"Mind one final word of advice?"

"Of course not."

"Give the guys time. They might resent you at first, but that's because they're just not used to a woman at their level. You've got a reputation for being a scrapper, and that's what they not only expect but will resist. Walk gently, speak softly, and sooner or later they'll start taking you for granted."

She chuckled. "Taking a woman for granted is something of an insult."

"That's not what I mean. Taking your presence for granted—when that happens, you'll really be a vice president." He looked at her hard and long, and for a second she thought he was going to lean down and kiss her. But he didn't. His lips tightened as if he were trying to prevent more words from emerging. "See you around," he said finally, and he was gone.

She felt an instant emptiness, a sense of loss greater than when they had been feuding. Without the slightest physical intimacy, he had come to know her better even than Julie. More than ever she was aware of how he had provided the deep companionship she had sought and never found outside the airline. She had looked forward to their occasional lunches more than she did to a date with an attractive man, yet curiously—perhaps because their relationship had been so natural and comfortable—she never could analyze why. The fact that they had been professional equals had blurred her own attitude toward him; she assumed that this explained his persistent rejection of any association beyond friendship.

Except that once he left, he never called her.

In her moment of professional triumph, she was puzzled and hurt. She realized that at the very pinnacle of her career, the three most important men in her life were no longer part of her life. She could accept the absence of father and lover—death was unalterable. It was far harder to accept Daley's deliberate severance of a bond she had once thought unbreakable. Eastern's headquarters were less than a mile from Trans-National's, but Ray Daley might as well be three thousand miles away.

As far away as my father, she found herself thinking.

So her success had a sour taste—maybe Ray Daley had assumed a kind of father image. In some ways, they had been alike, John Hendricks and Ray. Both blessed with a serene yet steely calm to which she clung in times of stress. Maybe she had been wrong about her feelings toward Ray. Maybe it wasn't just friendship but instead a relationship nurtured by the fact that too much distance had separated her from her actual father. That last letter from John Hendricks. She could remember it by heart . . .

. . . while impatience can be synonymous with determination, it also can be synonymous with hasty judgment and a lack of perspective. All I can tell you is to do the best job you can . . .

Wasn't that exactly what Ray had always told her? He *was* like her father. *Well,* she mourned, *it's one hell of a time to reach that conclusion. Now they're both gone. Dad's dead and Ray—he must still hate me because of Harmon. I just wish I didn't miss him so much . . .*

Daley's replacement only served to remind her how much she missed him. He was an ambitious type who viewed Danni's vice presidential status in much the same fashion he would regard the purchase of a new aircraft or a particularly newsworthy annual report. Danni, he decided instantly, was News.

She went along with his early efforts to publicize her status as a woman vice president of a major airline. She appeared on talk shows, subjected herself to countless interviews, but finally drew the line when he announced she had to go to New York to tape an appearance on *To Tell The Truth.*

"There's an executive staff meeting tomorrow morning," she told him. "You'll have to cancel."

"They won't miss you at the meeting," he made the mistake of saying. "The show's more important—you can't buy publicity like this."

She took a step toward him and for a minute he was afraid she was going to hit him. "That's it," she raged. "I've done everything for you and this airline, but no more. I've left work undone, missed meetings, and ignored major projects just so you could exhibit me as some kind of freak. You can take all your interviews and stuff them—and don't you *ever* have the gall to tell me one of your silly assignments is more important than a staff meeting!"

Once she had set her own ground rules, she got along fine

with the new vice president of Public Relations. But he was not Ray. He wasn't at all like Ray.

Another chapter closed, too. Shortly after Daley's departure, Pat Martin dropped into her office.

"Came in to say good-bye," she announced, and Danni thought she had never seen her look so relaxed, even happy.

"I heard you were going with the Flight Attendants Association in Washington. As safety director, isn't it? Sounds marvelous, Pat. I wish you luck and I mean it. Maybe we'll be working together on some project one of these days."

Pat smiled. "Or working against one another. No, I don't think that's fair. We usually did see eye to eye when it came to safety. And a few other things, too."

Danni studied her curiously. "Never could quite figure you out. A hell of a lot of good ideas, plenty of brains, an oversupply of bitterness. If you could have controlled the bitterness, you'd still be president."

Pat shrugged. "It's a little late for self-analysis, I'm afraid. Maybe I was jealous of you—who knows? Anyway, there have been times when I wished we could have been friends instead of enemies."

For a long time after Pat had left, Danni thought of the past. Of Marlene Compton . . . of Penny and Tony and that wedding gift to Mary Beth . . . of her affair with Harmon . . . of Rose and Betty Jo . . . of Ray Daley.

She sighed and went back to work.

Daley had once irreverently called the 747 "Evan's last erection." It definitely was his swan song. When the first delivery came, he announced his retirement, effective after the March 28, 1970 inaugural flight from Miami to Las Vegas and Seattle. Danni was aboard at his invitation.

The old man was in his personal heaven, so proud of the great new bird that his enthusiasm was infectious. The 747 was not just a new airplane but a technological milestone, and Danni looked on amused as he prowled through the cabin, chatting and joking with passengers—he didn't stay in his seat for more than twenty minutes all the way to Las Vegas.

When he saw Danni smiling at him, he sat down next to her, patting her hand. "I must be acting like a goddamned schoolboy, but I can't help it," he said. "This beautiful, magnificent creation—my God, only forty years ago I was flying Ford trimotors and thinking there'd probably never be a bigger airplane built." He grinned. "Lord, how far and how fast we've come in only four decades."

There were tears in his eyes; impulsively, Danni kissed his leathery, heavily veined cheek. "I don't blame you for being proud. And I'm proud of you, too. You made all this possible."

"Good way to bow out," he murmured. "Got one hell of a successor lined up. Can't tell you his name yet, but he's a senior vice president with another airline. Great track record. Young, progressive, personable—you'll love him."

"Like, I hope, but not love. That's reserved for you."

He grinned mischievously. "Platonic love. Grandfatherly love." He chuckled. "By God, if I had been ten years younger, you never would have made vice president."

"No? Your mistress, maybe?"

"My wife, damnit. Haven't had a wife since Emma died seventeen years ago. I figured nobody could take her place and I was too old to go looking for an inadequate substitute. Then I met you—ten years was all I needed, by God! Just ten fewer years and I would have courted you."

Danni squeezed his hand. "Mr. Belnap, if it had been five years, you'd have had a deal."

She had been summoned to Belnap's office and she was shocked at the sight of the packing cases littering the thick green carpet. They reminded her of wooden tombstones on a manicured lawn. She shook off a feeling of sadness.

"You said you wanted to see me," she said.

"Yeah. End of the line, girl. The Directors meet tomorrow to announce my successor—same guy I told you about. The old airline'll be in good hands, I made sure of that."

"What are you going to do? Besides taking a well-deserved rest."

"Rest? I'd die if I rested. That's for tired old men ready for their funerals. Hell, no—I've got me a beautiful little ranch just outside Tucson. I'm gonna breed Arabians, ride horseback every morning, and play golf every goddamned afternoon. Know a lot of people out there already, so I won't be lonesome. I want you to promise me you'll come visit."

"That's a promise," she said, her eyes sparkling. "Provided you let me ride one of those Arabians—I didn't know you were a horse lover, too."

"I might have guessed it," he said with a trace of sadness. "Horses, airplanes, and old sailing ships. We have everything in common except the most important thing. Age." He cleared his throat. "But that's not why I called you in. Remember the first time you were in this room?"

"I sure do. We talked about Horatio Hornblower."

"And you took a likin' to that model of the *Victory*."

She walked over to the miniature ship, once again fondling the tiny sails and running her finger along the line of gunports. Her back was to the old man.

"While I'm cleaning out this goddamned office, I figured you might like to have that ship. I want you to take it home. Let's say it's an expression of gratitude—for being a friend."

She wheeled around, startled. Belnap's back was to her, his chair facing the big window that overlooked the courtyard of the General Offices building. She started to protest, then decided not to. The gesture had come from the old man's heart and she had no intention of spoiling it with coyness. "I'll always treasure it," she said.

The president spun around. "Take it with you now. Before some stupid sonofabitch packs it away by mistake. But before you go, I have to ask you something. Personal. Sit down."

She sat, hands folded primly across her lap, staring at a weatherbeaten face that could have been a topographical map of the Arizona land to which he was going. There was a surprising

337

grimness to that face, too. As if for some reason he was angry with her.

"I assume you heard all about Ray Daley's little donnybrook with Gillespie," he said.

She nodded.

"Do you have any idea why Ray decked the bastard?"

"No, I don't." Why had her heart started to pound?

"Well, I'm gonna tell you. Nobody else will. *Daley* wouldn't if they held his feet in a fire for three hours. It seems he went into Harmon's office that day to say good-bye and made some joking remark about Gillespie's taking you with him so he'd have someone to fight with at Flight Menu. Harmon said he wished he could but not to fight with—that you were about the best piece of tail he had ever had. Including the night you came from your father's funeral. And that's when Ray slugged him."

Danni turned white. Only by effort could she force words out of her stricken throat. "I'd like to know where *you* heard this. From Harmon?"

"Nope. From Daley. Day after it happened. I took him out to a bar. He wouldn't tell me what the hell happened in Gillespie's office so I figured a little booze would improve his communicative abilities. It took about five straight bourbons but he finally started rambling on about what a great girl you were and how the hell could you get mixed up with a prick like Harmon. And then he told me what Gillespie said. For my own personal edification, was it true?"

The paleness blossomed into deep red. "We were intimate, but that was a long time ago. It was over before Ray ever came to this airline. He . . . he lied about that other time, that no-good, dirty bastard!" She burst into tears of frustrated rage.

Belnap reached out to pat her shoulder. "I figured as much," he said softly. "I told Ray that Gillespie was probably lying, but the damned fool wouldn't listen to me. He said you told him you and Harmon had an affair once and I guess he was ready to believe anything."

"He should have asked me himself!" Danni sobbed.

"He couldn't. You had him all torn up inside. For all his

wisecracking, he's the most sensitive, insecure guy I've ever known. Out of all his mumbling at that bar, I gathered he decided you weren't the marrying kind. Strictly a career girl willing to do a little bed-hopping now and then. Do you know why he left us for Eastern?"

She dried her eyes with a handkerchief, fished from her purse. "More money, I suppose. That's what he told me."

"Money my Aunt Tillie! He just couldn't stand being around you anymore. Seeing you everyday, all you went through together—it was tearing him apart."

"Did . . . did he tell you all this?"

"Hell, he didn't have to. I came so damned close to matching Eastern's offer, it made no sense for him to leave. There had to be a different reason, and you were it. He got you that vice presidency, Danni. He rammed it down our throats. And not just the vote itself. He's always pushed you, praised you. If there was any kind of a tough assignment around, he'd bring up your name."

She nodded with sudden understanding. "Like recommending me for that hijacking committee?"

"Right. What you never got through that thick if beautiful skull of yours was how he really felt about you. He decided the only thing in the world you wanted was to be a vice president. So that became his goal, too. And once he succeeded, he figured it was time to get out of your life, because you didn't need him anymore."

Evan Belnap rose out of his chair. She had never seen him look so tall, so youthful, so commanding.

"Young lady, I love you like a daughter. So as a father to a daughter, I'll give you a little advice. The sun will set in the east before that silver-haired ninny gets up the courage to tell you he loves you. You're a vice president now and I think you'll make a damned good one. But I have this persistent feeling that down deep, it wasn't all you really wanted. So if you ever need a husband who's good enough himself never to be known as 'Mr. Hendricks,' you could do a hell of a lot worse! Now get your butt out of here—I've got more of this goddamned packing to do."

* * *

339

She didn't trust herself to drive her own car. She called a taxi to take her to Eastern's General Offices, showed her TNA I.D. to the receptionist, and got directions to Daley's office.

He was alone when she burst in, but it would have made no difference if there had been a dozen people in that room. He looked up, startled.

"Danni! What the hell—"

"You sonofabitch! You forgot to kiss me good-bye!"

She fell into his arms.